"A masterful storyteller, Turnquist takes you on a magical journey of discovery in this poignant tale of innocence and growing up. *The God of Sno Cone Blue* is a delightful read."
D.K. LUBARSKY, AWARD-WINNING ARTIST AND AUTHOR

"Marcia has created a compelling character in Grace, one whose great personal loss is redeemed by a great personal discovery."
ROD GRAMER, AUTHOR, THE GOOD ASSASSIN

"Grace is a modern match for Tom Sawyer, with a grand spirit and enough spunk to weather the heartache of losing her mother at a tender age. Along the way, she gains the wisdom to recognize the breadth of her mother's love through a series of posthumous, sometimes shocking letters delivered in the years that follow. With a driving style and a colorful cast of eccentric characters, author Marcia Coffey Turnquist fiercely delivers equal parts laughter, sorrow and the kind of joy that will stay with you long after you've finished the book."
LINDA NEEDHAM, USA TODAY BESTSELLING AUTHOR OF EVER HIS BRIDE

"A very thoughtful novel full of heart and compelling characters."
ELISA KLEIN, EDITOR, PORTLAND SOCIETY PAGE

The God of Sno Cone Blue

Marcia Coffey Turnquist

Marcia Coffey Turnquist

This book came to fruition in the hours my children were in school though never far from my mind. I dedicate it to them, Macklin and Amelia.

Prologue

I saw the face of God once, in the summer clouds over my backyard fence. One minute it was water vapor and the next: *My God, it's God!* That's what I thought, anyway. I was a kid all those years ago and the preacher's daughter, so naturally impressionable. And who hasn't seen shapes in the clouds? Elephant, crocodile, Alfred Hitchcock's puffy profile. Why not throw God in there too? But it didn't seem like that, like some childish fantasy.

The minute before I was running home over the grass, hopscotching dandelions that flashed under my feet. Halfway there, I changed my mind about going inside. It was the sky, the way it invited me to take a running leap and soar up past the power lines. I did the next best thing and flopped to the grass instead, sniffing a chest full of its weedy perfume. The sky was blue as a carnival sno cone, with choppy clouds like shaved ice, except for one that poured all silvery and strange, like the jar of mercury my teacher once brought to school. I fell into a trance watching it, and then features took shape, two eyes, a nose and a mouth, swirling like mercury into endless combinations, all different and unexpectedly alive. The connection I felt was profound, like strings to my heart and a thousand other points. I lay there with my arms wide, paralyzed and mesmerized, and thought: *This must be God.*

Then the swirling stopped at features I knew in an instant. They were the same eyes I see in the mirror every day, my mismatched irises, one dark and one light, but something was wrong. The feelings vibrating along the strings became electric, primeval and scared. The face was mine and not mine, suddenly warped with the mouth protruding. I had to get away from it, but I couldn't. The strings had me paralyzed. They kept me there and made me look. Just when I was sure I couldn't stand it any longer, they fell away, into the endless canopy of the sky, and the face that was mine and not mine dissolved. When the only thing left was sno cone blue, I sat up and sobbed.

It may seem strange, especially for a preacher's daughter, but until now—almost 50 years later—I haven't told a single soul about that vision. Especially not my father. I was a kid in the grass. In our church, you didn't mix the sacred and profane. But, more than anything, because it didn't make sense to me, not before my mother's death or the letters she sent later.

The letters. Once held so close, then tucked away. I might have left them under my bed forever if my own children hadn't found them and come at me with a flood of questions. Looking into their faces, I had to wonder, why hadn't I told them the story long ago? But I knew why, for the same reason my mother kept it from me all those years. It was no fairytale.

Was I ready now?

Unfolding my mother's pages, I became the wide-eyed girl who first got them and read her words: *I wasn't always a Preacher's Wife… I made mistakes along the way.* I remember how it felt, reading each letter and aching for the next, how they gave meaning to my vision and sent me chasing the God of sno cone blue.

Chapter One

I never knew anybody quite like my mother: uneducated but smart, brassy but sweet and hardly what you'd expect in a minister's wife. "A California wild hair," she said when I was young, one of the few hints I ever got of her upbringing. If Momma talked about her past you learned to listen quick.

One story I remember turned out to be a lie, and one of plenty. She said right after my birth my name came to her out of thin air: Mercy Grace. I figured she was either overcome by the Holy Spirit or delirious. Neither was true, I found out much later, and neither explained the absence of a birth certificate, which I never bothered to ask about, enthralled as I was by the story of my own birth. My last name, Carsten, was The Reverend Thad Carsten's, of course, the man I always pictured pacing outside the delivery room, and why wouldn't I? He was the only father I ever knew.

"I stopped calling you Mercy after a while," Momma explained, "'cause people twitched when I said it."

"What do you mean twitched?"

She laughed. "Like it meant something. Like: Mercy how the birth mashed her head!"

The delivery wasn't an easy one, on her body or my skull. "It took several months to round out," she admitted. By then she'd resorted to using my middle name. And that's why I'm called Grace—by default you could say.

I always knew my real birth date at least: July 27, 1958. It was a simpler age in America's history: the calm before the cultural storm. The decade that followed—the years of my innocence— brought a generation gap, a sexual revolution and Vietnam. I hardly noticed. They were two-dimensional images on the convex eye of our old Motorola TV, or what Dad liked to call *The Cyclops,* as in, "Better turn off The Cyclops before it rots your brain." Despite that, life was promising, like a stack of sealed envelopes in the church offering plate. And how could it be any different, with a father and mother in good standing with Jesus? When I was the preacher's daughter and the path ahead of me abundantly clear?

We came to the Portland parsonage in 1966 when I was eight. At the time, I didn't want to move from our small Willamette Valley town since it meant leaving friends and starting the third grade somewhere else. Plus, I knew almost zilch about Portland. Though "big city" in my eyes and the largest metropolitan area in Oregon, it was more accurately mid-sized as cities go, big enough to offer some culture but small enough to escape with a few bucks' gas in your car—which would have been perfectly fine by me.

The parsonage, at the eastern edge of the city limits, had been home to a series of preachers' families and would end up as the setting for my own two childhoods: the one before our lives changed and the one after. It was years before I noticed some of the walls in that house were warped and wavy.

"I get the big bedroom!" I hollered after checking upstairs.

My little brother Jimmy was too young to care, barely old enough at a year and a half to climb to the second floor. It wasn't really the size of the bedroom I liked but a curious midget door through the floral wallpaper. It had a wing-nut latch that Jimmy couldn't reach and behind it an attic big enough for a busload of friends. I was thrilled, until my father poked his head in.

"Watch your bacon," he said, adjusting his sturdy, dark-rimmed glasses. He showed me how the flooring inside stopped at three feet with only bare two-by-fours beyond that. "Step off the brink, you'll end up in the kitchen sink."

The rhyme was nothing unusual. My father plucked them from his brain like a monkey plucks fleas. "Go the distance with God's assistance!" was the sort of thing he would say. I tolerated it by rolling my eyes behind his back, or, on that day, performing pirouettes across the beams the minute he left. Preacher's kid or not, I was no saint traipsing around on stubbed toes. What I imagined, most of the time, was a string of X's trailing my name, one for each sin I'd committed; there were flocks of them by then, crazy ravens cackling at me. But what did I care if God was watching my back?

The limited attic flooring was wide enough for my personal possessions of the day: a small, key-lock diary, a deliberately-naked Ken and Barbie, and an always-changing stack of books. I remember walking around most of the time with my face in one, figuring it was the one trait I'd inherited from Dad. I didn't have his stature or coloring, like Jimmy, or his tendency to rhyme and proselytize, but his love of books, absolutely. When I wasn't playing outside or doing pirouettes over the ceiling, I was reading: at home, in the car, or even during his Sunday sermons, long as I could hide a book behind my church bulletin.

My parents liked Portland from the start, no doubt because we moved there in the summer. Portland summers are unbeatable: cool clear nights and warm days with the snowcapped Mt. Hood shining on the eastern horizon. The rest of the year—from Halloween to the Rose Festival in June—is the rainy season. To pass the time, kids in our neighborhood jumped mud puddles down our block. It was the 1960s, what else was there to do?

It's very rare in Portland when the rain turns to snow. The thing to watch out for is freezing rain. It comes like the plagues to Egypt and coats everything: a silver thaw over the landscape, but on the roads, the invisible and deadly black ice. Except when the black ice falls white, which it did one December day. I remember that morning well—and not just for the strange weather. It was the first time in my young life I saw my parents as lovers.

Dad's whistle came first that day of the storm, a three-note trill that jarred me awake but never seemed to budge Jimmy.

"Rise and shi-ine!"

I groaned. It was still dark outside. Did he have to be so excited so early?

"I don't think you'll have school today," he called up.

I was down the stairs the next minute, my nightgown splayed over the heat vent. I put my face to the dining room window as Dad came up beside me in his winter boots. At six foot four, he was hard to miss.

"It's deep!" I wiped away the condensation.

Under the streetlight our front yard was like the cover of a Christmas card. Snowdrifts piled high as my shoulders—high as Dad's in some places—with a sea of white obliterating the street. Where our driveway should have been, a submarine rose, pushing what looked like a periscope into the twilight.

"The Buick!" I yelled.

"It's completely buried."

Momma called from the kitchen, "Leftovers tonight. I'm not getting to the store through that." It was odd to see her up so early, and, like Dad, fully dressed since she always had a hard time shaking the night. It wasn't just sleep, but a strange gloom she wouldn't talk about. Her hands cupped a mug of coffee, the bribe Dad must have used to get her up.

"Can I go out now and build a snowman?"

"Not on your life," Dad said, zapping me with his Preacher Eye.

Was I in trouble? I tried to remember. "*After* I get dressed?"

"You won't build a snowman today," he said mysteriously. "I'm afraid there's something you two are missing. Head on out, you'll see."

When I pulled open the front door, cold flakes swirled at my bare feet. I stepped out, expecting to sink into a powdery cushion, but fell hard on my butt instead.

"You all right?" Momma called, trotting over in her rain boots. When she saw I was, she broke out laughing, we all did. The spot I'd hit had shattered. Everything was covered in ice, a thick coat of it: the drifted snow, the shrubs, the trees.

"Looks like it warmed up overnight," Dad said, "enough for rain."

"Warmed up?" I shot back through chattering teeth. "It's freezing!"

My bare feet slipped when I tried to stand, so he hoisted me piggy back and stomped down the porch steps. In the east, the sky shed navy for bright blue.

"They predicted the snow," he said. "But not the freezing rain on top. What the good Lord has in mind, you never know."

Momma's rain boots crunched behind us. "Look at *that*." It was the dawn she meant, coming in streaks now over the eastern horizon. In a flash, every mud puddle, broken fence and bad paint job down our street was a crystal paradise. Chandeliers of ice dangled around us, completely captivating, like a Sunday sermon that sucks you in despite your best intentions. I broke off a spear and flung it, and it skidded clear across the yard to the big tree, spinning out under the wooden swing.

"Know what I heard about that tree?" Dad said.

"Nope."

"It's a Tree of Heaven, the kind that shoots up so fast you think it'll take you clear to The Kingdom."

I imagined climbing the icy branches, rising all the way to the pearly gates.

"Know what else?" The pastor was fired up and pitched me higher on his back. "That tree is old. See how thick the trunk is?"

"It's like twin trunks stuck together." I liked stuff in pairs. "Double your pleasure double your fun with Doublemint Gum."

"*Anyway*," Momma said.

"Anyway," my father continued, "Mrs. Crookshank, across the street, says it's older than she is. She used to wander here when she was a girl."

"That must have been *eons* ago." I felt the Preacher Eye again even through the back of his head.

"The point is, that Tree of Heaven was here before our house, the church, all the houses down the block. Then some folks came along to build a church and parsonage on this very spot. A coincidence?" He breathed. "Maybe not."

"Look dad," I told him, anxious to point out something myself. I had my finger over the church next door, the wrought-iron cross on its roof. Usually stark and gray, it was draped in white and twinkling in the morning sun.

"That's really somethin'," Momma said.

We watched it a while in the still cold of the morning until my bare toes started to tingle.

"Can I get down?"

Dad must have expressed something to Momma, because her

mouth curled with the slyest smile. I wouldn't realize until much later what an unlikely pair they were: my father, homely as an ex-boxer and graying besides, and my mother, a young beauty with a schoolgirl's blush. I could *feel* him looking at her.

"You know what?" he said to me. "I'll bet you're light enough to stand on this ice." He bent forward to set me down, and he was right. The hard sheet held under my feet. I took a step, listening for cracks, then made a run for it, diving to my belly and sliding headlong over a surface slick as egg whites. It was crazy fun. I didn't lose speed until I crashed through a crusted snowdrift.

"Ahh!" I screamed. Powder coated my nightgown, my hair and face too. It fell in my mouth as I panted and laughed. But my feet, deep in the snow, were on fire. I bolted for the porch, shattering the ice with each step, and so did Dad, though I didn't guess why before I saw Momma's face. The whites of her eyes made full circles around the blue.

She tried to escape, but he scooped her up, her coffee flying, as I high-stepped into the house using our foot holes. I didn't shut the door, though, there was too much to see. My father was running like a linebacker clutching a football. He pounded over the ice as she squealed, "No, no, no!" and "Put me down!"

But he didn't put her down. He stormed the yard, gripping her legs while she squirmed and laughed with her mouth wide. He was headed for the snowdrift I'd torn up. He swung her down and knelt by her side, flinging fistfuls of powder in the air. When she was dusted over, like a snow queen on her winter bed, when she stopped laughing and the rhythm of her breathing slowed, he leaned in, ever closer to her frosted lips, and kissed her.

I giggled, loving every minute of it.

In the next breath, he drew back and she jumped in those old rain boots to straddle his hips and pin him down. It wasn't much of a struggle; he even helped her some before he rose up to her mouth again. This time, the kiss lasted forever. Momma had her back to me, so I couldn't see her expression when he pulled away, but I caught his. It was a good thing he hadn't pointed those eyes at the ice, he would have ruined everything melting it.

Chapter Two

That day in the snow—and a thousand others—are memories I later held close, for barely two years after our move to Portland, my mother, my beautiful mother, was gone like the ice in our yard.

I can't remember much of her memorial, not the things people said or failed to say, but I remember sitting in the church pew with my bony knees, clutching a rosebud I stole from one of the flower sprays at the altar. I cupped its petals and when I got home, put it in water to watch it open. But it never did. Three days later, it was slumped over dead, still a bud on its stem.

On Sunday of that same week, a letter arrived that shocked me stiff. It didn't come the usual way, by U.S. Post, but simply appeared in the metal mailbox on our front porch. Until that moment, I'd hardly noticed that box, even with the lid that squealed every time you opened it. Black against the white siding, it was just another detail in the landscape of my childhood, like the living room furniture or the shrubs in our yard. But after the letter, it grew bigger than its measurements. It called my name and taunted me: *Come here now Grace to lift this lid and peer inside, and if you find nothing, absolutely nothing, I dare you to gaze into the deep void instead.* And who could resist? Like a locked door sprung open, that mailbox beckoned me.

The morning it all started, my father called me to the front porch. He must have spotted the letter when he went out for the Sunday paper. Had he stood there a while, dazed? His faith never wavered after Momma died, but his moods did. He crossed through rooms like a passing shadow, big enough to put out the lights.

As I went by he mumbled "...special for you," and I thought, since when does a ten-year-old girl who doesn't bother with cereal box offers get special mail? It didn't even occur to me that Sunday wasn't a postal delivery day, nor were Saturdays back then, so it had been two full days since our mailman had passed by.

A random tune played as I stepped out, the wind chimes Momma had hung with no way of knowing the flimsy thing would outlast her. Always small for my age, I rose up on tiptoe to the open mailbox. Where the front panel dipped away sat a white envelope with a strangely familiar air about it—and *my name*, front and center.

I froze.

My heart stuttered.

It looked like it was hovering, floating like litter over a vent. If the mailbox hadn't been bolted to the siding, I would have guessed it was floating too—and the house and porch with it. I grabbed hold of the envelope. There was no stamp or postmark and where the return address should have been, only a scrape of dull pencil. Except for the ink at center, the rest was blank.

Grace, it said.

It wasn't so much my name but the handwriting that shook me: my mother's. The stark G, the loop of the e. No question. She wrote with her left hand, a trait I'd inherited, and the back slant, the details were hers. I spun around to the tinkling chimes, expecting her there, laughing and spitting out an alibi: *All that dying was a hoax, Grace, didn't you guess? One of those Candid Camera moments. I've been at Camp Magruder all this time on a retreat for ministers' wives—hah!*

But the porch steps were bare. No camera, no Momma, only a weed, shriveled up from the summer heat. And what did I expect, since I had seen my mother dead? Since we'd all been warned it was coming?

The night it did I wasn't ready. How could I be? My mother's friend Georgia had gone home, and Jimmy and I were playing a game of Candy Land on the living room carpet. Jimmy marched past Gum Drop Mountain, bouncing the board as usual, when a noise came from the back hall: a curious, high-pitched sound like a mewling kitten. We didn't have a kitten. Had one slipped into the house? I got up. Sunlight streamed through the side window, low and yellow, but disappeared in the darkness that clotted the hall. As I made my way toward my parents' bedroom, a hand slipped into mine. It wasn't like Jimmy. Normally, he'd yank me back to the game.

Soon as we stepped into the room, I knew. Her head on the pillow, her skin ashen. She was empty as an overturned flower vase. The source of the noise was no kitten. My father sat on the edge of the bed, his broad shoulders hunched forward, weeping.

In that moment, every crack in my psyche crumbled. I couldn't stop the anguish, the pain and grief from boiling up. She was gone. *Gone!* I ached to say goodbye or see her smile one last time, but that was impossible. She wouldn't rise up for me like Lazarus for Jesus. She'd never open her eyes again. I must have whimpered, because my father turned, fighting the contortions that ripped through his face.

"Oh Daddy!" I hadn't called him that in years. He pulled me forward—and Jimmy too—and wrapped his arms around us. *Oh, Daddy.* The thing we prayed would never come, came anyway. She was the preacher's wife. She was *my mother*, God, how could you?

It was a little more than a week later that I stood on the porch with her letter, there in my hands, as if from the grave. Two small dents, top and bottom, marred the envelope. From a rubber band? I turned it over, my fingers trembling, tore it open and pulled out two pages. It was her handwriting, sure enough, like mine though far more graceful. I recognized the paper too, the same eggshell stationery she'd kept on her bed stand—next to the Bible, the water glass, all those sick pills.

On the first page, near the top, she'd sketched a picture: a figure outside a window. It didn't surprise me. Momma did that a lot, doodling and sketching, mostly silly, enchanted places like castles on mountains and horses racing the wind. She had a talent for it, but we'd only teased her for her hokey scenes.

"If I can't be a great artist," she once said, "I might as well be a hokey one. Besides, it eases my mind about things."

I never thought to ask her *what* things. Or whether they existed still.

That letter opened a new dimension for me, one between life and death. I read it and read it again, until there came a day when I knew it by heart. But I don't mean the words on paper: *My Dear Grace.* I hear her voice as she speaks to me and I'm a girl again, suddenly and completely.

My dear Grace,

I'm here, Momma.

I've been propped in this bed way too long now, wondering how to start this. But what words can a mother say at a time like this? I love you? Yes, I love you. I don't want to die? No, I don't want to die.

Of course not, Momma.

But whatever I write sounds desperate, or worse, hollow. Not at all the way I feel. So I gave up trying to get it right. The best I can do is keep moving this pen, till this page is as full as my heart.

It's only been the past couple of weeks I felt the cancer taking over. I've come to think of him as a war general worthy of five stars. General Hodgkins, I call him, for Hodgkin's Disease. Picturing it like that, like an old codger, makes it easier, see? Then it's not just me in this battle alone.

I want you to know I fought hard to survive this, would've kept fighting if there was the slightest chance of winning. But you know what the encyclopedia calls Hodgkin's? Fatal. I had to stare at that word a long time before it sank in. A real long time.

The Cobalt treatments gave us hope for a while. We thought maybe, just maybe, we could prove the encyclopedia wrong. But then it was back, ol' Hodgkins had been biding his time. As we say in the Lord's Prayer, Thy will be done.

I'm tired out by almost anything now, just glad I can still get to the bathroom and kitchen on my own. Seems like I'm barely up, then back to bed, so it probably won't be much longer. Your father, he sees it too, yearning and praying for me every minute. He wanted to get me to the church this morning on the notion that being right there in God's House would save me. But we'd already tried that. I grabbed the headboard and said he'd have to break my wrists first. It took a while, then he fell over me like a little child... I hate to do it, Grace, I really do, but it's time Thad made his peace with what is.

The hardest part of dying is leaving you and James without a mother. Think of it, honey. All your childhood I've been there for you, when you skinned your knees, when you rushed in from playing, starved to death, when it was time to say prayers and go to sleep. Now I can't even climb the stairs to tuck you in. I tell you dear daughter, that brings me more pain than this ol' General ever could.

Jimmy's so little, he might not remember me at all. But let's face it, he's a boy through and through, and he'll have what he needs most in his dad. It's you I worry... worry about Grace. Not only because you're a girl... but because you'll remember. It won't be easy... not easy, no... even for an Ace like you.

My mother's voice had grown weak. I could feel her fatigue.

These covers are heavy... Thad? So heavy. Did I forget them in the dryer?
Oh, lord I think I left a while. But I'm back now, sweetheart. It's so hard to clear your thoughts when you're this tired.

I saw her sitting up now, running a hand through her pillow-mashed hair.

I've been thinking lately, Grace, about this lake trip we took once when you were small, when you still had baby fat and ruddy apples in your cheeks. You couldn't swim yet, not by a long shot, but you splashed around and stared at the tiny fish at your feet, trying to catch them. You were so smart, and so determined my heart swelled till it almost burst. I can still picture you trying to catch those fish, dipping your hands and coming up empty, all that water rushing down.

Your Dad said something about getting a net to catch them in, and you should've seen your face, lit up like he'd promised Disneyland. When the two of you went off to the lake store, hand in hand, I sat there hoping with all my heart they'd have a net. And when you came back, waving two, one in each chubby fist, I laughed with the joy only a mother can know. And that's the heart of it, sweet child. The simple moments hurt so much to give up.

You know what's odd? Sometimes I see you years from now on your wedding day, all grown up, waiting in a room as the church fills. In my mind it's clear as a bell. You're standing there at the mirror in your white dress with a tender smile, just standing there, waiting, so beautiful and hopeful. Then my heart breaks for the way the room feels because I'm not there. Your own mother, Grace, not there! Oh, how I ache to be there, sweet bride, on that glorious day. I ache to be there right down to my bones.

But I realize, in some ways, it could be worse. I have some time, at least, before I'm gone. Just yesterday, it dawned on me what to do with it. I'll write to you—this letter and more—about my childhood and growing up. I'll tell you my story. I don't expect it'll be easy, weak as I am, but it'll be worth it, no question, the closest I can get to being here.

And, Grace, there's something else—things I want to confess that few people know about. I wasn't always a Preacher's Wife. I was a girl once too, and I made mistakes along the way. Odd as it seems, I get a feeling sometimes that you sense it, but how could you? Either way, you'll know the whole story soon enough. In due time, dear, in due time.

It might feel strange when you read this, Grace, but I'm watching you this minute out my bedroom window. You're in the backyard, behind the house, with that measuring tape—remember? The soft, white one from my sewing basket? You're stretching it with your arms like a little bird checking *its wings. Did you see my sketch of you at the top of this letter? Some day, little bird, you will fly. Heck, you'll soar— even if I'm not there to see it.*

I'm afraid my hands are shot now and I'm awful drowsy. But don't worry. I'll write again soon. Ol' Hodgkins'll have to cripple these hands before I quit.

My love always... always and forever,
Momma

Always and forever. I still hear her saying those words the way I did when I was a child, that same voice, crossing the years to the woman I am today.

And the letter: it's old and brittle now, though I remember the first time I read it, when I held it in my hands and the pages went limp with my tears. Even that very first time, I knew the day she meant, the day I had the measuring tape. I saw myself, goofing around in the backyard, a regular Tomboy measuring a garter snake I'd found in the grass. And all the while, she lay in her bed, slowly dying. Oh, that memory stung! I wanted to go back there so I could run to her bed and crawl in next to her, the way I should have and never did.

That letter was a gift I didn't deserve...

And an obsession. It made me frantic for another and deeply curious: What mistakes had she made? What did she think I might sense? I racked my brain, but not the foggiest idea came. She'd promised to write again soon, but what did that mean? There was no date on the letter, only the number 1 on the first page, and she was *dead* for Pete's sake. My father insisted he didn't know what was in the letters or where they were kept, that my mother had only told him they would come. I burned with curiosity: how would she have them delivered? How did she deliver this?

In due time, is all she'd said, in due time.

Chapter Three

We transferred to Portland—in the years before my mother's death—because of some strange habits practiced by Methodists. In this case, shifting pastors from church to church every handful of years. It's a curse or a Godsend, depending on your point of view. Has the old pastor gone musty? Here's somebody fresh! At our new assignment, that was Dad, that was *us*.

For my parents, the transfer meant moving up: bigger town, bigger church. The committee on pastoral relations managed a pay raise for Dad, though it was still a modest subsistence. Keep in mind, in those days, my mother came with the package. She would work just as hard as The Reverend, without pay. She would fit the traditional mold of preacher's wife. This was the expectation, anyway, and we all know what can happen to expectations.

Take the size of our new congregation. In the mid-1960s, before freedom was the new religion, most churches continued on a crest of growth. But not this one. We noticed it the first Sunday we were there. Several pews stayed empty for the early service, and the second service was filled with blueberry bonnets, what I called the old ladies for the way their hair dye turned out. Blueberry bonnets and their misters are always the pillars of any church, but they're hardly known for having babies and spurring growth.

Tons of young families lived in our neighborhood—and lots more past the school—plus Dad could deliver a fine enough sermon, the trick was getting them there to begin with. I learned firsthand it would be a challenge from a kid on his bike.

"Church is stupid," he said, popping a wheelie on the dirt road.

"Oh yeah?" I shifted the box I carried from our U-Haul.

"Didn't you hear? There's a smart guy by the name of Knee-jump who already figured out God is dead."

"That so?" I watched him charge through the biggest mud puddle on Pardee Street. "Well my Dad's the preacher. If God up'n croaked, wouldn't he be first to know?"

The kid didn't answer, just popped another wheelie and rode off.

We'd landed in one of the saltier veins of the Pacific Northwest, already the poorest region for church going in the nation. Most of the people who lived near us were white and on the lower end of middle class, not much more than a pot of spaghetti away from poor. They saved S&H Green Stamps. Their children wore hand-me-downs and never gave it a second thought. And most of them—like the wheelie-popping kid—didn't attend *any* church. My Grandma Carsten had a theory for this. "We're a long way from the Bible belt and right next door to the devil's home state," she chirped, meaning California, of course, land of Hollywood and unspeakable sins. But, I wondered, was it really that simple? After all, Oregonians despised Californians. Heck, our governor once told them to "Come visit, but don't stay."

I thought the theory of the Oregon Trail made better sense. The people who braved it crossed the country in covered wagons. Covered wagons! Along the way, they fought Indians, starvation and death. They practically *had* to be jaded. By the time they got to Oregon, were they too far gone to bow down to God? Were their descendants now all tough-skinned wheelie-popping kids? *Yes*, I decided, it's what my father was up against.

The church he was appointed to lead was called Good Shepherd Methodist, which, as it turns out, wasn't typical. Most Methodist churches are named for their location or historical significance: First Methodist Church, for example, or Fremont Street Methodist. But this church's founders had been in a pinch: the location was the corner of Southeast 105th and Pardee Street—in the Pardee Neighborhood near Pardee Park. They'd heard "Let's all party at Pardee Park" enough to steer clear of Pardee Methodist. So they made a list of names and Good Shepherd it became.

Built in the 1940s, the architecture of the church was straightforward enough: a wood and brick A-frame with an adjoining office wing. The cross in its steeple stood high over neighboring houses, which would come in handy when I needed to find my way home.

The first time I climbed the church steps and went inside the double doors, I was disappointed. The flooring was worn and the walls dingy with age. Another set of doors landed me in the sanctuary, not just dim, but dark as a closet. Soon as my eyes adjusted though, I saw it wasn't a total loss. There at the back of the chancel was the prettiest stained glass I'd ever seen: Jesus the Shepherd in better than Technicolor. Olive branches framed the Shepherd's head and a pearly lamb lay in his arms. So elaborate, it was practically Catholic. When I moved in close, it dyed my bobby socks a dozen shades. Later, as I wandered outside, I realized you couldn't see the stained glass from the street. The best feature of the church and it was tucked away.

But everybody knew the parsonage next door. It was an easy bet for borrowing an egg or a cup of sugar, a place where anybody could stop in for help. Plus, the congregation figured they owned the house since it happened to be church property. At least they avoided using the spare keys floating around. Estimates for the number of copies ran into the dozens. For important reasons, we were told: *Remember when the pipes froze and the preacher wasn't home? Remember when we surprised his wife and painted the living room safari gold?* The way I saw it, that parsonage might as well have been made of glass.

My mother learned this lesson the hard way when she exposed herself to a church committee—and I mean *exposed*. It was an accident, of course, but no less demoralizing. I wanted to blame the church secretary, Honey Martin, except Dad swore it was his fault, that Honey was only doing her job. You see, she'd been scheduling meetings at the parsonage for years, whenever the pastor was needed. The old preacher liked it that way and Dad agreed to give it a try then immediately forgot to tell Momma. The night of the meeting he was called out to an emergency just as Momma hopped into the shower. It wasn't very often I got such chances, so I snuck in to watch TV, which is why I'd tuned out the bathroom noise. It was a steady ringing that pulled me from my TV trance. Men and women from the church were mashing our doorbell.

I opened the door, triggering the events that happened next: the group filed in about the same time Momma grabbed a towel; they headed for the dining room as she zipped down the hall. At the table they froze, for here came Sharon Carsten, still in her early 20s and fresh as Eve in a fig leaf. I tried to warn her, but it was too late. She slipped to the floor like a seal on wet rock. *Slap!* Worse still, the towel flew: There were her breasts and all the rest, without even a square of bikini for cover.

Oh Momma.

The men in the group tried to look away, without success. And who could blame them? The new preacher's wife, like a pin-up girl, was bared to the world. The whole table watched as she performed her next act: hopping to her feet and singing "ta da!" before disappearing into the hall, her bare butt churning.

There was no meeting that night. The group was long gone when Dad got home and Momma explained to him what had happened.

There wasn't a whole lot to tell.

"I'm more embarrassed that I made a joke of it, you know, Preacher Man?" She usually called him that in playful moments though this wasn't one. "Half of them were men and the looks on their faces—you should've *seen* them." She drank from her coffee mug then, which I was pretty sure held liquor, a definite no-no in those days for the wife of a Methodist minister.

"I doubt it's as bad as you think," Dad said, ignoring the mug. "My guess, come Sunday, they'll forget the whole thing."

She shook her head and so did I. She'd gone out singing "ta da!" I couldn't imagine any of the other women singing "ta da!"

"Look at it this way," Dad said, wrapping his arm around her. "They're Christians, aren't they?"

The men of the church had trouble remembering this. Come Sunday, you could almost see them disrobing my mother with their eyes—in the sanctuary, no less! I overheard a couple of women having trouble too, wondering how she wound up buck naked before "a whole committee."

"It's hard to shower in your clothes," I said, since they hadn't seen me standing there.

In the end, Dad was right. My mother wasn't defined by that scene in the kitchen. There'd be plenty to choose from along the way.

Chapter Four

From the moment I knew about my mother's letters, they were on my mind: When would I get another? How many would I get? Before long, I started stalking the mailbox. I could hardly ignore it, the way it gaped at me when I passed, trying to pull me in. Every morning, like a secret agent, I came down to inch close to it while my father was in the bathroom shaving. Not that he would've thrown a fit. He knew about the letters. He'd explained, "They're for you." Still, the look in his eyes when he said it—the misery and envy—didn't fire me up to paint the town. So I got good at playing an agent. I was no longer a preacher's kid, but a high-stakes player in an international game of espionage. I learned my father's habits, which floorboards didn't creak, ways to ease open the front door so he wouldn't hear the suction. Since burglars rarely struck in those days, we didn't have deadbolts or fancy locks and sometimes even neglected to lock our doors at night. Besides, it hardly seemed to matter with all those parsonage keys floating around. So my mission was easy enough: slip down the stairs, twist the knob, and ease my way out to the mailbox. The squeaky lid always threatened to give me away, so I raised it in the breathless way you'd lift a gun from a double agent—and still it squealed. I'd always rotate to check on Dad, then dip my hand in the mailbox, which came up empty, every time. What the blazes did I expect anyway when our mailman came in the afternoons?

Still, a letter *had* been delivered. It had been summer, when her grave was still fresh. If only I knew who'd brought it: a delivery service, a secret friend, or some shaggy-haired wild-eyed psychopath?

Every night when I lay in bed, I tried to will Momma to send another, like it was within her power. She took the shape of an angel then with fairy wings, swooping down from the heavens with a letter in her—what, teeth? Somehow I couldn't give my mother both arms and wings. I thought of her grave next and the headstone with her name: Sharon Louise Carsten. Underground, did she look the same, or was her face melting away? It gave me shivers. I imagined her as a ghost then, floating like mist over our walk. In her hand she carried an envelope, the same bloodless color of her skin. And when she touched the mailbox, it screamed, just like it did when I lifted the lid.

Picturing another delivery didn't make it happen. More weeks passed and, eventually, months. Once or twice my father spotted me on the porch, and though he didn't throw a fit—or even react—I gave up my little game of international espionage. So much time had passed, I started to think there wouldn't *be* another letter. Until he found one, again on a Sunday. It was much later, almost Christmas, I remember, because of the tree we'd barely decorated with a handful of balls and the plastic Rudolph Jimmy liked. I was reading a book next to it when my father called me to the entryway, holding the door against a cold wind.

Chang-a-lang! sang Momma's chimes in a driving rain. And there it was in the open mailbox: another envelope with my name. The paper was dry under the roof overhang and floating again, just like the Rudolph Jimmy had hung on our tree. I reached out and felt a thrill, something Christmas—our first without Momma—had failed to stir in me that year.

No postmark on this one either, just those small ghostly dents and her hand at center. But there was one difference. In the left corner, instead of a return address, was the number 2, carved with a dull pencil in a heavy hand. *The second letter with a number 2?* Some spy I was, Miss Brilliance at work. The pencil mark on the first envelope wasn't a scrape but the digit 1—because the envelopes were numbered! Whose writing it was I couldn't be sure, a style, squat and squared, I didn't recognize. But if someone had numbered the envelopes, there had to be *many*, didn't there? Why else bother? My heart thundered. How many had she written? A handful? Dozens, held together by a rubber band?

When I came back in, Dad was there at his desk beside the stairs.

"Be ready for church in an hour," he said.

I nodded then sprinted past him up the stairs and into the attic. Jesus said when you pray, go in your room and close the door. My mother's letters felt like a prayer, solemn and personal, and I figured the attic was a few steps better than my room.

I opened the midget door and pawed around on the plywood floor. The space had never been wired for electricity, so I'd stashed a flashlight inside. I turned it on now, closed the door and opened the envelope. She'd written plenty in the second letter, several pages, front and back. By the time I'd smoothed them over my knee and adjusted the beam, I could hear her voice.

Dear Grace,

I've been thinking about you...

You too, Momma.

...where you are in life, almost the age I was when we arrived in Napa Valley. You might find it hard to believe since you're in it, but childhood goes by fast, much faster than it ought to I'm afraid. It was on that ranch, down in California, that I saw the end of mine.

I haven't said much about it. Those times. They weren't easy. Not under the iron fist of my mother Astrid and her nasty mean-streaks... or Pops with his drinking. He could get lost in a bottle and not come home for days.

Her father a drunk? Her mother mean? She'd never told me any of that.

But I see now, Grace. There are lessons to be learned, and maybe that's the best I can leave you.

It's a good thing I have the energy today, because there's so much I want to say. First, not all of my childhood was awful. Some parts were even beautiful in that valley east of the Mayacamas Mountains and Pacific Ocean. In fact, when I picture myself the way I was then, I think of you, running around barefoot, turning your face to the sun. Such passion I had, I wanted to scream it to the world!

As for the shoes, I had some of those too for school and town. But I wasn't happy until I kicked them off and got a good layer of dirt between my toes. These are the memories that make me laugh and want to tell you everything. Since ol' Hodgkins is resting today, I'll do my best.

I leaned back, resting against an attic two-by-four.

When we arrived on the property in 1954, the first thing I wondered was why they called it a ranch. It didn't much look like one. Most of it was on the fancy side of things, groomed and gorgeous but a touch eerie too. The strange feel started early, when you left the little two-lane road north of St. Helena. First thing ahead were redwoods and undergrowth so thick you could hardly see. There was a stone bridge Pops practically drove off, singing "Happy Trails to you..." behind the wheel of our '49 Chevy. Astrid hollered and he whipped the wheel just in time before we ended up in a creek.

It stayed dark in those woods, and cool, until we came out on the other side. Then we saw it in the blinding sun, a gen-u-wine castle, as Pops called it, jutting pretty-as-you-please from a low-slung hill. I rolled down the window and my dog Chipper hopped up next to me. Maybe it was the sunlight or maybe the view, but my eyes watered like the dickens as I took it in, the gray stone walls and twin towers. I knew we wouldn't be living there, we were the caretakers is all, but it was something just to see it. I mean, here we were from the flatlands of Bakersfield, used to rundown rentals and motel rooms!

At the foot of the castle, was a garden of flowers I could smell on the breeze and all around this stair-stepped grounds and groomed lawns that made it all look like a fairytale. It wasn't, of course. Every inch, Pops said, was the sweat and toil of Chinese coolies who once worked the valley. He told us the whole story as we drove in that first day... what I realize now he probably learned at the local bar. It went something like this: a French wine master built the place in the late 1800s during Napa Valley's first wine boom, when wine flowed like water, which was something Pops could appreciate.

The place was called Chateau Genevieve after the young woman the wine master loved. He designed the lower level as a winery and the upper level for her, which made Astrid grunt, the way she grunted at anything sentimental. "But the poor sap made a fatal mistake," Pops said. "He assumed the girl loved him back. Two times he went to France and two times he came home alone. When he finally paid attention to his vineyard, it was choked with disease."

"What happened?" My brother Doug wanted to know. And Pops answered, "He went bankrupt," which made Astrid laugh so hard I thought she'd hack up a tonsil. "Serves him right," she barked, "tryin' to live in a damn castle!" I wouldn't have admitted it to Astrid, then or ever, but I felt sorry for the young wine master. He'd had a dream, for a life and livelihood, and lost them both.

Still, a part of his dream survived because we were looking at it: the castle and grounds returned to life by an army of caretakers before us. It was brown as the tree-studded hills where the vineyards once grew, but a Garden of Eden around that castle. And oh, how I itched to wander it! So lush and green, with pea-gravel walking paths going anywhere you pleased.

Olive trees with knots like an old woman's knuckles lined the gravel drive as the Chevy's tires crunched by, and every so often we passed a giant eucalyptus in a cloud of perfume. A small orchard of fruit trees stood off the drive too: apple and apricot, pear and prune. "And you can eat as much as you want," Pops said, "so who needs that musty old castle?" Our home was to be a cottage, so cramped and small Doug and I would share a room, tacking a sheet from the ceiling for privacy. But what the heck did we care? We had all the rest to look at!

The drive took us past a rose garden with blooms red as a dust-blown sun, then over another bridge to the castle, where huge doors leaned out over us. I asked Pops if we could open them but he said, "Naw, it's the old winery. Been locked up for years." Which reminded me he hadn't finished his story. You didn't have to tell Pops twice.

He explained how the disease that pestered the wine master wrecked vineyard after vineyard across the valley. A kind of plant lice at the roots. As time marched on there was prohibition and the Depression, then more years when wine didn't sell well. To the day we came to the valley, hardly anybody would touch grapes. "Eye-talians mostly," according to Pops, "the only smart ones of the bunch."

It was an Italian who ended up owning the ranch, though not for grapes. Dr. Rossano was his name. He was a surgeon from San Francisco with a wife and son. He took to the old property and decided to make it a vacation spot. "The Rossanos are rich," Pops said, like we hadn't figured that out already. "So rich they only show up when they feel like it." Then he gunned the Chevy and we climbed the drive, up and around to the back of the castle and a sparkling pool. "Wow!" is all I said, but Astrid was on me. "Don't get any ideas. The only way you touch that pool is to clean it."

I knew the entrance to the living quarters was somewhere close because Astrid had talked about it. So while she looked for the keys, I got restless. I'd never been in a castle before. But the minute the car stopped, Astrid laid out the rules. "Yer not steppin' foot inside," she told Doug and me. "I don't want anything broke." And that was that.

The next week we enrolled in school and quickly fell into a routine. Chores in the morning, off to school, then back to the ranch for more chores. Besides the yard and garden work, there were animals to feed, the cow Doug milked, and for me the patio grounds and swimming pool. "Don't fall in and hit yer head," Astrid warned. "Might be nobody here to fish you out." But that pool was so tempting, Grace. Sometimes when she wasn't around, I slipped in anyway, and skinny dipped right *there under a California sky.*

Most days, though, when I was done with my chores, I headed for the barn and the part of the ranch that actually looked like a ranch. There was a roaming goat, a cow and chickens, plus two horses of "the finest pedigree," which meant don't even think about riding them.

Even still, we had to get the horses used to us, so we could saddle them up when the Rossanos wanted to ride. That was a challenge, Grace. One of the horses was a huge stallion with moods dark as his black-coffee coat. We couldn't let him anywhere near the mare. I was 12 then, not even big enough to hoist a saddle. The first time I tried to lead him, he spooked and I got dragged across the barn. It was Doug who tended the stallion after that.

The care of the mare, then, fell to me. But I wasn't complaining. She was the most beautiful creature I'd ever seen, not quite white or gray, but more like silver, with a shining mane like polished steel. She was almost as tall as the stallion but sweeter by a mile, following where I led and holding still for me to brush her. Her coat shined in the sun like the colorless agates on the castle drive. I loved to turn her into the corral and then sit on the fence to dream of riding her, my yellow hair flying with her silver mane in the wind.

I called her Lady Agate and, before long, started to pretend she was mine. I'd hurry to the barn to run my fingers down her nose or feed her and that crazy stallion a treat from the garden. I started sketching her on paper too, teaching myself to draw, the way her head came up when she saw me, the way her hooves tucked when she pranced.

The next summer when the owners came, I groomed her as usual and watched Doug get the saddles on. But I was jealous as a jilted lover when they rode away. Dr. Rossano and his son kept the horses out for hours!

By the end of that summer, Grace, it wasn't enough to feed and groom her, or even draw her on paper. I had to ride that beautiful mare, I just had to! But I knew the risk. Astrid would kill me if she found out, not to mention the Rossanos. The scrubby caretaker's girl riding their horse?

The whole thing made me edgy with nerves. But I couldn't think of anything else till I came up with a plan. Believe it or not, Grace, the rest of my life traces back to that time. If I had an ounce of energy left, I'd tell you more, but the fact is, my strength is sapped. How I dared to ride Lady and the trouble it brought me, will have to wait.

Till next time, sweet child,
Momma

The first time I finished that letter, I brought it to my face and breathed it in. My mother had lived a life and dreamt of things I never knew, and now I would have that part of her in her letters! I'd given up on her childhood years before since she wouldn't talk about it, but now her memories would be mine. I jumped to my feet, picturing letter after letter in our mailbox. Where would I keep them all? Where would I—I sucked in a breath and choked on my own spit. What if letter after letter was only her intention? What if she got too weak to write?

I tried to remember. How often had I seen her in bed with her pen and stationery? Once or twice? I had two letters already. Could this one be her last? I braced myself against the attic door. Had General Hodgkins taken that from me too? The thought made my stomach pitch, like I was standing in loose sand at the edge of a cliff.

I lifted the letter, held the flashlight closer to it. But her handwriting looked all right, didn't it? It didn't look like the handwriting of a woman on her last breath. *Maybe I didn't see her writing because I was gallivanting through the backyard with that stupid measuring tape. I should have wrapped it around my skinny neck and yanked.*

I folded the letter and slid it back into its envelope. The truth was, there was no way to guess the number of letters my mother had written. Two or four or four dozen. All I could do was wait—and who knew how long?

I sighed. I'd kept her first letter in my underwear drawer, away from the preacher's eyes, but I needed a better place. I shined the light around the attic, scanned the pile of books I had there: The Chronicles of Narnia, The Secret Garden. I pulled out Misty of Chincoteague, a pony story, and slipped it between the pages. Momma would have liked that.

For the first time I knew why she drew her hokey pictures: castles and horses, their feet off the ground and nostrils flared. Suddenly an old pencil sketch over her bedroom bureau meant something to me. I shut off the flashlight and left the attic.

Dad was in the kitchen with Jimmy, cooking breakfast, so I snuck past them, down the hall to his bedroom. Over the bureau in its flimsy wood frame was the drawing, the one I'd assumed was only fantasy. There they were, no doubt about it: Lady Agate with her shimmering coat and, on her back, the girl that was my mother, all this time, the wind in her hair and in that mane, and I never knew. It blew goose bumps over my arms.

Chapter Five

My mother didn't talk about riding horses. The closest she got was a comment about the old barn behind the parsonage. We were in our back yard at the time, all those years ago, digging up sod to plant roses. Or at least Momma was digging. Jimmy and I were preoccupied, getting each other filthy. She stomped on the shovel and hit a rock, stomped again, then took a break to look out past the yard.

"Isn't it strange, there's a barn right there, smack dab in the neighborhood?"

I dropped the dirt clod I was crumbling over Jimmy's head and turned around. Behind the parsonage and church on the far side of the back fence, stood a rotting barn, property of the ramshackle farmhouse near it. An old homestead, we'd been told, from around the turn of the century. The only reason it survived was proof of our location—just outside the boundaries of Portland's city limits.

The truth was I'd done my best to ignore the place. I'd overheard kids on the block discussing its inhabitants: they kept voodoo dolls of people they hated, they ate spiders off the walls, they used newspaper in the bathroom instead of toilet tissue—I mean *newspaper!* I didn't know if it was true, but I didn't care to find out. I could see plenty from a distance and the place was creepy, a throwback to a time before crisscrossing streets. The property knifed, dully, behind the newer houses on the block. The end farthest east, behind the church, was a mess of overgrown woods that, behind the parsonage, morphed to a blackberry jungle that spread to the barn. Not that I have anything against blackberries—they're great when August comes and you can stuff fistfuls into your mouth. But those vines were never-ending. They choked everything behind our fence all the way to the barn, with fingers that gripped its wide-spaced, postage-stamp windows.

My mother saw something different. "It's picturesque, don't you think?"

"Um," I squinted. "Looks to me like it's been there about a million years." And it did. The walls sagged so heavily, one more vine and the whole thing might implode. Then again, maybe it was the vines holding it up.

"I love barns," she went on. "Old and new. They remind me of horses. Wouldn't it be fun to sneak over there and take a peek? There wouldn't be horses, but still…"

It made me wonder if she'd lost her mind. There were enough thorns between the fence and barn to shred us raw. I pictured a newspaper-stained hand in some moldy bathroom and decided the last thing I wanted was to step foot over there.

Three days later I would, thanks to Dad and his bright ideas. His plan to grow the church was to canvass every house in walking distance. Since I never considered the old farm "a house" it didn't cross my mind. Still, there were other houses we approached that seemed shady, and I don't mean in the sense of being tree-lined. Shouldn't a preacher be more choosy? I thought.

"The thing is," I piped up, taking three steps for each one of Dad's, "the people we invite to church should be the *right* people, right? I mean we can't just invite *everybody*."

"I see, Grace, and who are the right people?"

"You know, Dad, the Godly kind, people who are clean and stuff, nice and everything."

"Ah, as in 'Cleanliness is next to Godliness'?"

"Exactly."

"Grace?"

"Yeah?"

"When's the last time you had a bath?"

"Well, that doesn't count 'cause—"

"When, Grace?"

"I don't know, Wednesday or maybe Tuesday, I—"

"Well since this is Saturday, you can't be too clean yourself. Maybe there's a little more to this than soap and water."

I sighed. Smart as he was, Dad still had his blind spots. It was well after breakfast and we carried two stacks of invitations between us. Dad had dictated the text to Honey, who'd cranked out dozens on the church's mimeograph machine: *Come share in the Joy of our Lord at Sunday services. Times listed below.* The pastor wore standard attire for the mid-1960s, a white shirt and narrow tie, and I wore my Sunday best, including patent leather shoes about a half-size too small since we couldn't afford new ones yet. I decided to do the talking since I'd had years of practice around church.

"Good morning," I started as the first door swung open, "we're inviting you to Good Shepherd." My father had the urge to step in then, but I pivoted on my patent leathers to hold the floor.

"I'm Grace and this is Pastor Thaddaeus James Carsten, named after two disciples in the Bible. You can call him Pastor Carsten or by his first name if you like. It's 'th' like think and 'ad' like bad: Th-ad."

Oftentimes, my little speech was followed by a moment of silence—or a suppressed laugh—which I figured was because of my eyes, the left vacant blue, and the right mud brown, to no fault of my own. I'd even taken to calling myself "lop-eyed," just to prove I wasn't touchy. I knew the question people wanted to ask: which one is your real color? But I was glad when they refrained since I didn't have a clue.

We continued like this, house to house, in the rising heat until blisters rose on the backs of my heels and my throat shrank like a salted slug. We'd come full circle to the farmhouse, though I was slow to notice and for good reason. Our block was oversize, twice the width of most and a full three blocks in length, which hid the old place square in the middle. Besides, I'd remembered the popsicles at home in our freezer, which put the hurry back in my step. I had Pardee Street in my sights when Dad stopped on 102nd and looked right. There was the farmhouse swimming in a heat mirage. A fence surrounded it and some kind of field, cut in spikes like a bed of nails.

"Can we skip it?" I asked. Pardee was *so* close. But the look on his face was answer enough.

My father pushed the gate and it quivered open, chasing two stray cats from the dry grass. I held back—a little cagey myself—to look the house over. At two stories high, it was deep into the property and leaning first to the left and then to the right depending on which way I tipped my head. Behind it a fair ways was the faded barn, and then the flip side of Good Shepherd. Tired old fencing circled it all, the same that snaked past my own backyard. It wasn't keeping much out—so the cats—but I wondered what it was keeping in. The windows weren't just closed, but shuttered tight.

"Looks like nobody lives here," I said, taking the pressure off my blisters. "Besides, I heard they marry their own cousins and stuff."

Here came the Preacher Eye. "Which one is it, Grace? Nobody lives here or they marry their own cousins? Because I don't see how it can be both."

I kicked the gravel and gave him my *Who knows?* shrug.

"This grass here looks like cut hay. And there's a pickup at the top of the drive—must be somebody who drives it." He flexed his jaw, and I knew something was coming. "What is it, Grace, that a charitable heart does?" I sighed. It was a Pastor Carsten original.

"A charitable heart doesn't berate or discriminate."

"Al-most."

I peered past my sticky bangs. He let Momma get away with her less-than-perfect English, but not me. "A charitable heart doesn't berate *nor* discriminate?"

"That's it! Onward and upward."

Such joy in being the preacher's kid. At least my blisters had gone numb. I followed as my father scraped up the packed-earth drive, past the ancient pickup to the steps of a wooden porch. It felt like trespassing. There was a small sign at the front door that he read under his breath. "No solicitors."

"What's a solicitor?" I whispered.

"Not folks with an invitation to church, Grace. Ring the doorbell."

I couldn't find one, so I rapped on the wood instead. When nothing happened, I raised my fist to knock again and the door came open. A woman's face squeezed into the gap, jumpy and mean—like she might have a taste for spiders after all. I almost turned to Dad and mouthed, "Told you so," until I remembered my manners.

"Good morning, we're the new preacher's—"

"We don't take no solicitors," she said. Her eyes went from mine, which obviously hadn't impressed her, to my patent leather shoes.

I clicked them together. "Sunday shoes," I said for no good reason.

"Damn it." A voice came from inside. "Can't they read?" I was about to say damn right I could read, I was damn good at it, in fact, since I always had to shut off The Damn Cyclops, when the damn pastor stepped in.

"Sorry for the intrusion, ma'am. We're not solicitors. I'm Pastor Carsten, new to Good Shepherd, and this is my daughter, Grace."

In a flash at the woman's side was a boy, about my age, with a crew cut at the top of a long, chalky face. He stared at my eyes, then screwed up his lips like he'd bit something rotten. Probably a spider he kept in his cheek.

"Grace and I have been walking the immediate area with invitations to our church service," Dad said. "We also have Sunday school if the boy is interested—"

Just then the woman fell back and a man took her place. He was almost as tall as my father, but thin and wiry. I stared at his mouth where a cigarette on his bottom lip defied gravity. Under it, the cleft in his chin flared his whiskers like the spokes on my bicycle tires.

"New preacher, huh?" The cigarette bobbed.

"Yes sir, Thaddaeus Carsten. I grew up in farm country around Gresham as a matter of—"

"Think I give a shit?" I stepped back and covered a knothole with my shoe. It's not like I'd never heard swearing before. Momma even cussed, but the thing was, never on purpose.

"…'cause I seen damn well how it works—" he was saying, "ever' damn preacher that comes along. You're sellin' religion is what. The more I buy the better chance I got at heaven. Well you ain't gettin' any of my money off that con." The man didn't act drunk or anything, just ornery.

"I didn't catch your name, Mr.—"

He sucked his cigarette red. "Any of your damn business?"

I wanted to run to my father, say "Okay, time to go!" but my feet were swollen and my shoe stuck to the knothole, a glob of pitch or something had me frozen up my spine.

"McEgan," the boy said with a grin. No sooner was it out of his mouth than the man clapped him on the back of his head. A pat or a smack, I couldn't tell which.

"Same McEgans as the ones used to own all this land," the man said, thrusting his cigarette like a pointer. "Ever'thin' you see and most of what you don't, includin' that church and cozy little abode you're livin' in."

"Mr. McEgan, I—"

The man tossed his cigarette and stepped forward to crush it. He was so close now he could shave his whiskers in Dad's glasses. "I don't consort with a church that *steals property*."

The boy grinned at this turn of events and practically did a two-step.

"Heaven sakes, Mr. McEgan, the church didn't—" Dad sounded tired. "The parishioners paid off that mortgage years ago."

"My grandfather cleared that land, every acre, so don't tell me what some damn parishers did!"

"That's right!" the boy said, hands on hips.

"Now git the hell off my property before I throw you off!"

"As you wish." Dad turned and descended the steps, in no particular hurry. "You know," he said, coming around again, "it might come as a surprise, but I'm more interested in your salvation than what you might put in an offering plate."

It was then that McEgan snorted—and spit. A long, straight shot that zipped past the porch rail, just missing Dad. The boy laughed and I stared. Spittle hung from McEgan's chin, suspended over the bicycle spokes.

Finally, Dad turned to me and said, "Come along now, Grace." And I broke from the porch and flew down the steps, never once looking back. By the time I reached the gate and Dad joined me, the house appeared as it had before, uninhabited. I caught my breath and checked the bottom of my shoe, but it wasn't a bit sticky.

"Evangelism," Dad said, "sure can be trying." He lifted the latch and pulled open the gate.

"I tried to warn you," I told him. "Some people aren't cut out for God."

Dad said "We'll see" or "You'll see," but I'd stopped listening. I was picturing Momma, at home fixing our lunch. By the time I'd cleared the gate, I had popsicles on the brain again and took off skipping.

Chapter Six

My mother came to me often after she died. I remember running around, jumping rope or playing in the yard, and she'd be there, alive in my memory: laughing with her head back and mouth wide, or back in that infamous moment singing "ta da!" on the kitchen floor. I'd stop and hold my breath, try to keep her from going fuzzy.

It happened in the evenings too, the time she would have been in the kitchen. As I looked over a recipe and tried to remember how she made it, her form would appear beside me, rubbing garlic over a roast or tossing vegetables into a pot. Only when Jimmy frog-hopped through, crashing his Matchbox cars into the baseboards did I notice she was gone again. Jimmy was a constant reminder of our reality, as much in need of a scrub down as the floor.

It wasn't long before I started imagining I *was* my mother in the kitchen, wearing her apron, cooking from scratch and botching it all because I never bothered to pay attention. I drank from her coffee mug too and even tried a sip from what was left in her bourbon bottle. It seared my throat the whole way down. Sometimes I saw my old self there at the counter, chatting away with her while she fixed dinner, both of us oblivious to the disaster racing toward us. She'd been so alive at the stove. So real and so near. Now I stood in her place, a sorry substitute.

My father lost interest in food. He sat in his recliner with his Bible open like before, except now he kept The Cyclops on. "For company," he said. It gobbled up entire evenings in our home with the likes of Gunsmoke, Mayberry RFD and Carol Burnett, a show my mother had loved. When the canned laughter drifted into the kitchen, it made me about as giddy as it did my dad.

But I had one thing in those days that he didn't: my mother's letters. Whether she'd intended it or not, they gave me a reason to press on, to try another recipe from The Good Housekeeping Cookbook stained with her food-spill fingerprints. I wondered often about her letters, waltzing past the mailbox when I thought about them. But what could I do? Dad claimed to know nothing and I knew even less. I figured when another arrived, it would simply appear, like my memories.

It was springtime before another did. I found it myself after I got up on a Sunday morning and came down the stairs by way of scooting on my butt. Through the living room window, I spotted a flock of starlings and hopped up, thrusting the door wide to see them scatter. Amid their panic and fluttering wings, I heard the chimes sing and when I turned for the mailbox, there it was. Before the birds had disappeared, I was in flight with them, up the stairs and to the attic, the envelope flapping at my side.

My dear Ace-face Grace,

I'd forgotten she called me that, *Ace-face* or just *Ace*. But now it rolled off her tongue again.

There's so much I want to tell you, Ace. So much to lay out. Are you ready for the story of how I rode Lady Agate? If you're anything like me, the way I love horses, I'll guess yes.

You guessed right, Momma.

The fact is, Grace, it took me weeks to work up the guts. I distracted myself by picking prunes on nearby farms for a little cash. We all did in those days. I was caring for both horses then for a simple reason: the stallion had bit Doug on the head. Since he'd never been too keen on horses, that was the last straw.

I'd learned to manage the stallion—to a degree—but

there was no question it was Lady I'd ride when I was ready. Tired of worrying about the saddle, I decided I'd hop on bareback like they did in the movies. All I needed to make it happen was a day when Astrid was busy.

Lucky for me, it came soon enough. On a foggy Saturday morning the phone rang and when Astrid hung up she was in a mood. "Mrs. Rossano wants the light fixtures cleaned in the castle," she said. It was the sort of thing Mrs. Rossano did, call up out of the blue with some odd job. Astrid usually dumped the work on Doug and me, but this time it was inside the castle.

"There's enough fixtures in those rooms to light up Bakersfield!" she barked. I pretended to feel sorry for her as I folded laundry. But soon as she left, I shot out the door. Hay and water for the horses and potato peels to keep the stallion happy, then I let myself in with the mare. I gave her some peels too, then climbed the half-wall to jump on, my only witness the calico cat we kept as a mouser.

It was an adventure, Grace, to slide onto Lady. I'd never been on a horse before. But the first time I tried it I couldn't stop sliding and ended up on the concrete floor. I brushed the straw off and climbed up again, more careful this time—and what do you know, I was on horseback! It was wonderful, Grace, a thrill to sit up so high on that silver mare.

After a minute, I pushed my heels into her flanks a little too hard and she lurched. Then I tried it more gently and she went forward, step by step, out the door of the stall. So much power ran through her, Grace, I was no more than a flea on her back. We heard the stallion as we came out, but to my relief Lady went the other way.

Staying steady wasn't easy. That beautiful coat was slippery, so I tried to relax when she took a step to keep from tipping the wrong way. I didn't know a thing about steering a horse, especially without a bridle, and it froze me up. When she stopped we just sat there for the longest time. Then finally an odd thing happened. I got an itch or something, down my leg, and when I moved, she moved. I tried it again on the other side, an ounce of pressure from my thigh and she stepped the *other way. It was amazing!*

Within minutes, I was turning her this way or that by a simple nudge or a squeeze. I even got her to step backwards with a tug on her mane. Who needed a bridle? I'd heard that mare was smart, but it seemed like more, like she could read my mind.

Something came over me then, Grace, and I decided to go for it. I nudged Lady to the back corral and her usual running space. Part of it was hidden from the cottage, but only part, so I knew I was taking a chance, even Chipper figured that, the way he crept alongside us with his tail tucked. If Astrid spotted me, she'd beat me senseless.

But it was foggy, and I was banking on that to hide us. Right away, Lady surprised me and went for the gate, trotting and jarring me so hard I almost fell. When we got there, I could see the cottage, scrubbed white in the fog. But the air wasn't as thick as an hour before. If Astrid was looking, she'd see me for sure.

On the other hand, I was at the gate, wasn't I? I put my bare toes out and lifted the rope tie. Can you imagine? In a blink, we were out, my fingers tangled in that polished mane, my heart thumping with her powerful hooves, faster and faster. No gentle nudging now—only hanging on for dear life! Would I fall off and hit my head, wake to Astrid's face over me? Or not wake at all?

And then it happened, Grace. Lady Agate's trot melted to something different, something smooth. The ground below us was a blur and there was Chipper, sprinting alongside. We were in a full gallop, chasing the wind and busting free! Free from the ranch, free from Astrid and my endless chores. I never felt so good in all my life! I was no longer the hired help, the poor caretaker's daughter, but a princess on the back of that horse.

I leaned forward into Lady's withers, gripped her mane, and laughed. "Go Lady, go girl!" Oh I laughed and laughed on the back of that horse. We were flying over that hillside trail, and what a ride!

Sometime later Lady slowed and I realized even in fog there was plenty to see. I stroked her neck as I took it in, the rolling slopes and overlooks, scattered vineyard posts from days gone by. I breathed deep to fill my lungs and swore I could smell the ocean, heck, the farthest reaches of the earth!

We rode a long ways that day until I started to wonder if we were lost. But a minute later, I spotted the neighbor's drive and realized we'd gone east. Yep, there was the road across the creek and the old concrete reservoir past it. We'd ended up on the town side of the castle. Lady walked through a stand of trees where old, strangled vines hung. When I got closer I saw they were grapes and popped a few in my mouth. And you know what? Strangled or not, they were the sweetest I ever tasted.

After that day, Grace, I was hooked. I snuck Lady out every chance I could get. I still worried about getting caught. I still pictured Astrid beating me. But more than anything I wanted to ride that horse.

It so happens I kept my secret a long time... clear through winter and into spring. Then in one fell swoop, it was out. I'll try to finish that part of the story in this letter, sweetheart, but I'm so tired. When I can see straight again, okay?

I pictured her in her bed then, easing back and closing her eyes. I'd seen her like that many times when she was sick, terrified she was already dead. I would inch forward, toward the bed, until her eyes opened. The memory of that feeling, the way I could breathe again when she smiled, pulled me back to her letter.

It's late afternoon now and I'm rested. Georgia's fortified me with a cup of tea while she fixes dinner. She says ten minutes is what I've got to finish this letter so I can talk to her. "Yes ma'am," I tell her. You learn to do what Georgia says if you know what's good for you.

I heard Momma's laugh. She adored Georgia. They got along great despite obvious differences: Georgia black, my mother white, Georgia older by five or six years. None of it mattered.

Where was I now? That's right, on that day I got caught with Lady. Well, let's see, I'd been sneaking around for months by then, watching for Astrid, listening everywhere for that sharp-gravel voice. I never even considered somebody else might learn my secret. But when I rode back into the barn, there he was, Salvatore Jr., the owner's son.

Plenty of times the summer before I'd brought the mare to him, but we'd hardly said two words to each other. I was the caretaker's daughter and he was the rich city kid. He must have come up from San Francisco for spring break. Soon as I saw him, I tried to pull Lady back, but it was no good. The expression on his face is something I'll never forget.

"You've got some nerve," he said. Imagine how I looked, Grace, sitting bareback with bare feet on that beautiful mare, his mare. Sal was three years older and not only rich, but cocky. I felt small, like a naughty child. Another teenager was there too, and my brother Doug, who got so riled up he sent Chipper into a barking frenzy. "What the hell you think you're doing?" He hollered.

Sal picked up Lady's hoof, ran his palm down her foreleg. She was shining with sweat and still breathing hard. "No saddle?" he said. I sat like a wooden soldier with a wooden face. "No bridle?" I still sat. He walked around the horse, his jaw tight.

Finally, he ran his hand down her nose. "Stella, you're all right." I wasn't sure what I'd heard. "Stella?" He thrust his chin out. "It's her name, fool, and the stallion's Cesare." His eyes were on me, so I answered with a stare of my own, thinking, What an ugly name. I'd heard Pops do the Marlon Brando thing screaming Stella!

Sal smiled then, so slow and mischievous it made me squirm. I didn't know much about him besides what I could see: average height, like Doug, but darker, his eyes black as Lady's. The other kid came forward then, saying, "Who is she, anyway?"

But Sal ignored him and looked from my tangled hair all

the way to my filthy feet. "What makes you think you can ride my horse? I want you down." For some reason, Grace, I couldn't budge. I was 13 that summer and small for my age, and Sal was 16. "Right now!" When I still didn't move, he grabbed me and pulled, and I fought back, kicking, until I remembered he was the owner's son. It's not so good to kick the owner's son.

He yanked me down and locked eyes with me, and then suddenly his grip softened. His hands were still at my waist and still charged, but different now, and it made me shiver. "What's your name?" he said. My name? I thought. He didn't even know my name? He'd just called me a fool for not knowing the horses' names. "Sharon," I said. "My name is Sharon."

"Sharon, huh?" The way he looked at me made my cheeks burn. "So Sharon, how would you like to add riding to your chores?" I didn't understand at first. "Stella needs the exercise when we're not here," he explained, "Cesare gets enough tearing it up in the yard." Was he really saying what I thought he was saying? "I'll tell your mother to make it part of your job," he added, "but could you do me a favor and use a saddle?"

Excited as I was, Grace, my face must've fell. I didn't know the first thing about saddles and Lady's was heavy. When I told him as much, he said he could show me, maybe even give me riding lessons, but before I could answer, his friend was there. "Come on, Sal, look at her. You really want that using your stuff? What she needs more than anything is a bath."

I didn't mind it when the friend laughed, or Doug either, but for some reason when Sal did, it stung. When he turned to me again, he was back to his old self. "On second thought, why don't you stick to bareback?" I raised my chin and said, "I'd rather learn the saddle." He started to smile but then turned with his friend and left the barn.

And now, Ace, that's where I'll finish up for today.

Do you have to?

Georgia's back and says the clock's run out on my ten

minutes. But I'll be back, sweetheart, with more later.

My love until then,
Momma

It was always so hard to arrive at the end. I could have read forever about her life on that ranch, the cocky rich kid and that wonderful horse. But here I was again. I'd waited *months* for this letter, for its three pages, front and back. To my mother it must have seemed like a lot, it probably exhausted her to write so much. But it was never enough. Reading her letters was like riding Lady, feeling the wind in my face, leaving my life in a blur behind me.

It was a long time before I leaned back and unfolded my legs. Long enough to put my right foot to sleep. I was late for breakfast, that's for sure. I stretched out my ankles and drew circles with my toes, feeling the sting of new blood. If I didn't leave the attic soon, I'd be late for church, a habit I seemed to be developing. I went back to the letter and ran my fingers over my mother's words. On second thought, what did I care? I flipped onto my stomach and began again, full out running for the Napa hills.

Chapter Seven

It was easy to recognize my mother in her letters: the free spirit, the defiant child. But as time went on I realized something was missing: her dark episodes, even a mention of them. Had they always been with her or did they creep in slowly as the years passed? Even now, I can't forget them. I never will. They were as much a part of her as the sound of her voice or scent of her skin.

To be fair, the life of a preacher's wife isn't easy, and the glass walls of the parsonage were enough to make anybody anxious. After her nude show before the church committee, she bought a terrycloth bathrobe to wear out of the shower—never again just a towel. She didn't drink often, but if she needed a splash to "calm her nerves," she'd sip it in the kitchen where she could dump it down the drain if somebody happened to drop by. Not that alcohol was forbidden for a minister's wife, but close enough. Methodist ministers were sworn teetotalers in those days, and their wives were expected to follow suit. Since my father never cared for the stuff, abstaining wasn't a problem. Momma, on the other hand, called it a rule to be broken.

The truth is, my mother had a number of traits you wouldn't expect in a minister's wife. She'd say "shit" when she dropped something, and then "shoo-oot" to cover it up, which didn't fool anybody. At church my father played deaf, but at home he'd say "Shaaaron," and she'd respond, "Sorry, Preacher Man," and plant a kiss on his cheek. You knew, by the way he looked at her, she was forgiven every time.

My mother also had a flare for style that wasn't typical for a minister's wife. She wore clothes she sewed herself that bordered on daring—or as daring as you can get and still stand by a preacher's side. She sewed her own clothes and mine to save money, she said, but I knew better. She loved every minute on that old Singer, jamming the foot pedal to the floor as the console shimmied across the Linoleum. She could take pattern pieces from one dress and pair them with another or sketch an altogether original design as I watched her over the spines of my books. There was always a hitch. Seams were sewn and ripped out, curse words launched and bitten off, and then just when you thought the whole thing was a bust, it came together like a dream.

My favorite was a dress Momma made for special occasions: weddings, graduations—her own memorial, as it turned out. It was simple enough: a black-velvet shift with a flaring cover in sheer white, but the lines and the flow of it, the blend of textures: it was pure Sharon Carsten, bright and dark, opaque and translucent, modest with a shot of moxie. In the end, when it came time for her burial, my father naturally reached for that chiffon-draped velvet dress.

My mother lived a life of contrasts. Happy most of the time, but with bouts of melancholy that downright scared me. They reminded me of her watchful spells, the times she tracked me with her eyes, except they were more intense and more disturbing.

The first I remember happened long before Portland, on a day the two of us went to Dairy Queen. She was pregnant with Jimmy then, but not yet full term. I can see her rounded belly in a roomy dress and me in my sandals with the rubber daisies at my toes. It was an ordinary day, except for what happened at the counter, which I wouldn't understand for years: she ordered three vanilla cones with only two of us there to eat them.

"That for Daddy?" I asked.

The question made her fumble, and she dropped one on the floor. We stood staring at it, the flattened ice cream, the inverted cone, until her hands started to shake. She doubled over and started sobbing, which convinced everybody in the room she was having that baby.

Somehow I knew she wasn't.

"It's okay, Momma." I stood patting her back and trying not to worry, but she wouldn't tell me what was wrong. Ice cream trickled down my wrists before she straightened up and took me home.

They were rare at first, her dark episodes, or at least that's how I remember them. But soon enough they took on a schedule: bad mornings followed by watchful spells that dissolved with the brighter parts of her day. Afternoons and evenings were her happiest, when she was the mother I loved.

Either to spare us or to hide, I don't know which, she stayed in her bed most mornings and suffered alone. She called it her "blue hour" and shrugged it off like every mother had one. Sometimes, when I went down the hall, I could hear her crying through her bedroom door. I'd stand there and think about going in, to pet her hair or blot her tears, until something better—my hula hoop or twirling baton—came to mind. Away from that door, at least, it was easier to forget.

Before long I started to think of her bedroom as a damp, dark cave. Inside, she was held hostage by the beasts and demons in Revelation, the one book my father rarely preached from. And why should he? There's plenty of good in The Bible to go around, why focus on the nightmare at the end?

I didn't know why Revelation had a hold on my mother, just that snarling things haunted her bedroom, with the heads of dragons and the tails of snakes. All night long they sucked up her joy until the morning light made them slither away, back to the pages beside her bed. The only day they gave her a break was Sunday, when they didn't dare pick a fight with God.

The rest of the week, Monday through Saturday, my father filled the gaps by cooking breakfast. "Thad's diner couldn't be finer!" He'd say, flipping a pancake up over his head. It was the perfect distraction for Jimmy and me. He jabbed that spatula around the kitchen like a knight in shining armor slaying our dragons.

For a while at the new parsonage, when we were still unpacking boxes, my mother was up early, and I caught myself hoping we'd ditched her beasts in the move. Portland was a two-hour drive from our old home and possessed not only a big art museum, which she loved, but multiple department stores. From the start, she got up with the rest of us, ironing fabric to sew into curtains, and I caught myself hoping we'd made a clean getaway.

But somehow, about the third week, her beasts found her again. I was in the kitchen that morning, dumping pickles in the garbage for the jar. They were packed in tight, so I flipped the jar over and pounded the bottom. Just as I gave it another whack my father appeared, looking sour as the pickle vinegar. Preacher or not, he wasn't above spanking and here I was, dumping perfectly fine pickles into the trash.

"Your mother's not feeling well, Grace. Why don't you stop in, try cheering her up?" Not a word about the pickles. I considered arguing, but he was my father, the pastor, and oh-so-big. I watched the last of the pickles splat onto coffee grounds and screwed on the lid.

"Okay," I said, slinking past him.

There wasn't much light in my mother's room. There never is in a cave. I peered past the door—for dragons or snakes—but didn't see any. Momma was on the bed, not crying at least. She looked like a doll with its eyelids stuck open.

"Momma?"

It was too quiet.

"Don't you feel good?" My ankles twitched as I crossed the carpet. The breath of a slithering beast? Her Bible was on the bed stand with its zipper open: the route back to Revelation, I was sure of it. I set my jar on the carpet and took a step, careful to stay back from the bed skirt.

"It's sunny outside. Can't you come out with me and Jimmy?"

The white line gluing her lips cracked open but no words came out. I checked the carpet and went for it: down on my knees to rest my head on her nightgown. She smelled good: like clean laundry and Noxzema skin cream.

"We're going to catch ladybugs and stuff—" My voice vibrated through her chest "—and I found a pickle jar to put them in. But don't worry, it was empty." Another X to join my flock. When she spoke, her words floated over me like a puff of feathers.

"How would I have made it without you, Grace?"

"Huh, Momma?" My voice vibrated through her chest.

Limp fingers stroked my hair. "Never mind, sweetheart... sometimes its better not to know."

At my knees, I felt a tickle, so I got up to rescue my jar. "If you come with us, you can have this one for yourself," I said, thrusting it out. But she didn't budge. A minute later I was in the hall, moving fast, *Sometimes it's better not to know* whispering behind me.

My father was the dependable one, back on duty as breakfast cook as I zipped into the kitchen—and we had bacon! By mid-morning, my mother was "up n' at 'em" as Dad would say, as if the beasts in her bedroom were only something we imagined.

Chapter Eight

It took me years to learn the truth about my mother's demons. The clues came in her letters, one by one, until doors swung open to places that startled me. It was a long time coming. Seasons vanished between her letters. The whole earth shifted on its axis and came back again.

Somehow I missed it, the first anniversary of her death. It was late August of '69 and I was gazing out the bay window, not thinking about the date on the calendar or how much of my summer had evaporated. The Vietnam War raged through the hippie era. Man had walked, more like bounced, over the surface of the moon and we'd watched it all on the TV.

A light breeze came through the house and Dad was on the lawn, on his way back from the church. It was Friday night, a weird time for him to go over. His eyes were puffy behind his glasses, and it hit me: the light outside was just like it had been *that* night, one year earlier.

An ice age passed before he filled the entry. We were like strangers in those days. He didn't say much and I hardly listened. But he came to me the next minute, wrapped his arms around me and wept.

Two days later, when I shuffled downstairs, Dad nodded toward the front door. It was Sunday morning, a long time since the last letter. With a rush of energy, I yanked open the door and, sure enough, there it was. The chimes were still. I jumped up to smack them before I snatched it from the mailbox. The same ghostly dents, the same *Grace* at center. Would it tell me more about the silver mare, the one I rode now through my daydreams? On my way up the stairs I opened it and started reading, immediately hearing something else.

Dearest daughter,

Lately, I'm struggling, and not only with this body. Troubled thoughts eat away at me too. You want to know the questions I plan to ask God?

What Momma?

Why courage fails, my own in particular. Why sin and tragedy have to hurt the innocent. When I think about the pain in this world, the grief that's ahead for you too, I want to curl up under my covers and hide forever.

But where would that leave me?

I don't know, where?

Alone in the dark, that's where. You'll find good in this world too, Grace, and forgiveness, and when you do, hold tight, and you'll stay sweet, like those strangled grapes I found near a castle not so many years ago.

I eased down to the attic floor.

Some folks let life turn them bitter—and my mother was one of them. I never knew for sure why, though Pops had a pretty good guess. "She didn't want kids, plain and simple," he said, "but I found out too late." He told me all about it once, when he was sloppy drunk. "I met her after my firz wife ran off, when I zecided what I needed was some babies." He said Astrid went along right away. It was the first proposal she'd ever gotten.

But she hated being a mother, Pops explained, and grew

bitter. He didn't really know why, though in the end, it doesn't matter. What mattered was it made her angry and she let the anger turn her mean.

Why do I tell you about this now, Grace, when ol' Hodgkins has me practically beat?

I don't know, Momma.

Because I want you to know, while I still have time, why I never talked about my own mother. Astrid Peterson was a hard woman. She had no use for me or Doug, except to work us like dogs. You want to know her favorite saying when we were kids? "You get done with that job, you can spit-shine the floors." If she saw us idle, even after we'd worked all day, she'd put me to churning butter—a job so slow she knew I hated it—and send Doug down to mow the grounds.

Don't get me wrong, Grace. It's not that we minded work. We knew our station in life. We couldn't afford fancy clothes or new bicycles, much less a TV, which everybody seemed to be getting in those days. We understood all that. It's just that Astrid was such a bear. She made us rake pea gravel that had hardly been touched since the last time we raked it. After a while, Doug and I got the idea to jump over all that pea gravel so there wouldn't be footprints to fix. But Astrid would snarl, "Rake 'em anyway!"

I don't know if my mother was always cruel. I have a memory from a long time back on a night I was sick with fever. She came in to sit with me and put a cold rag on my forehead. I remember having awful dreams and calling out "Mommy!" through the night as she blotted my forehead. To this day, Grace, it's the only fond memory I have of her.

I didn't call her mommy for long. Around the time I turned five, she told Doug and me to address her as Astrid like everybody else. Very soon, after enough reminders from a tree switch, the word mommy disappeared from our language.

I decided the only reason she'd nursed me to health was to work me to death. But the odd thing is, I still craved her attention. I thought I'd done something awful wrong to make her hate me so much. I did everything faster and better, and so did Doug. But what we craved never came. In all the years I lived with Astrid, she never once told me good job or anything half as tender.

But, Lord Almighty, was she good at insults. "You call that pan clean?" she'd say, "The billy goat can lick it cleaner'n that." If Pops was nice and called me perty, she'd say, "Perty don't count when you got cauliflower for brains." Then she'd thump me upside the head. I got to hearing cauliflower more than I heard my own name. To this day, Grace, I can't stand that vegetable, maggot-white as it is.

I suddenly realized she'd never cooked it, not once, my whole childhood.

It was just before my 14th birthday that I gave up hope things would ever change. I remember it well. A perfect fall day with bright sunshine on coloring leaves. I met Doug after school and we kicked a can around, waiting for Pops to pick us up. There wasn't any school bus in St. Helena in those days, and we got tired of walking the two miles home. Pops was working a road crew and promised to pick us up when he was done. It was Friday and payday, but we were optimistic. Half an hour went by, and then another. When Doug remembered Jersey, that it was past her milking time, we hit the road.

We hadn't walked far when a car pulled up, a big Bel Air. It was Hazel Clayton who lived on the ranch south of us. I don't know why, but when we hopped in, Doug told her Pops was on a job interview. I shot him a look. We all knew the truth, even Mrs. Clayton. He was in the tavern by now. But she didn't even blink. She told us, "Call me Hazel," and said it was no problem to give us a lift. She drove all the way up the ranch drive, past the castle, to the cottage door.

"Hello Mrs. Peterson!" she called when Astrid came out on the porch, "I found two strays in town." Astrid answered by mumbling something about "not wantin' us spoilt." I knew what my mother thought of Hazel, that she was too cheerful, but I also knew she tolerated her and even took favors from her. I remember Hazel pulling away that day and wishing so hard I could go with her, wishing it until my chest hurt. It seemed to me that cheerful wasn't so bad.

Soon as the Bel Air dipped out of view, Astrid tore into us, chewing Doug out over Jersey and sending me to the orchard to pick apples. By dinnertime, when Pops still hadn't showed, we ate in silence at the kitchen table.

It was after dark when he finally drove up. I was putting away dishes and Doug, always smarter that way, had made himself scarce. As I closed a kitchen cupboard, I heard the Chevy coming real slow up the gravel drive. I stole a glance at Astrid, listening to the console radio, and watched her eyes shift at the sound of the tires. I remembered then it was payday. Astrid never forgot. What we earned as caretakers only covered the basics besides our rent: groceries and gasoline, enough clothes to keep us decent. The little extra Pops brought home was spent on the rest: medicine, car repairs, whatever came up.

But Pops had a habit of spending his paychecks at the local tavern. Astrid had warned him the next time would be his last. She'd even threatened him with a butcher knife. As the Chevy picked its way over the drive, she got up, so I shoved all our knives in a kitchen drawer. When she went for the porch, I followed behind.

Something was off about the Chevy that night, but it was hard to tell. Not enough light from the screened-in porch. Then Astrid opened the screen and we saw it: a huge dent in the driver's side with ugly streaks along the powder-blue paint. Pops leaned his graying head to the window and the door came open with an awful screech. He tossed his cigarette out and practically fell on the gravel beside it.

"Hullo Astrid," he said, "I'm afraid the Chevy's been in a lil' scrape." He was talking in his whiskey-drenched way, the way he sounded after he'd spent considerable cash: just wait'll you hear the story and all that. Pops was a storyteller all right, especially when he was three sheets to the wind. I could almost hear it already: the car was drivable, he'd say, and lucky *thing...*

But the next words out of his mouth were "I'm lousy hungry, whaz for supper?" Pops wasn't afraid of Astrid, but he wasn't a fool either. He staggered around the spot where she stood, rigid as a tree stump. When he saw me, he pushed some loose change in my hand with a "Here yeh go, Sis." Always the generous drunk. It was probably what was left of his paycheck.

I came up next to my mother, trying to think of something to say. She kicked the warped door shut and the window flashed past. "At least the window didn't break," I said. Astrid turned, and fast as a rattler, smacked me so hard I went down, hitting gravel.

I was stunned. Not that she'd never hit me before, but she usually laid off when Pops was around. I looked up suddenly as he came at her, grabbing hold and throwing her against the Chevy as she grunted her surprise. He had her wrists and he leaned in close, cussing like a sailor until she promised to lay off. Then he flung her arms out and stumbled away up the cottage steps. When the screen door slammed, Astrid stepped over me. "Get up, Cauliflower," was all she said.

I got an ugly black eye that night, and had to stay out of school a whole week before it healed. I was ashamed of my face but more than anything that it was my mother who'd done it.

It just so happens it was the same week of my birthday. When it came, Astrid sliced up some orchard apples and baked a pie, but I didn't feel like eating it. She still hadn't said a word about what she'd done. After dinner, Pops cut a piece and stuck a wooden match in it. He told us a story then about a brawl he was in once and the double-shiner he got from it. "A heckuva lot worse than yours," he said laughing. When the story was done, he touched his cigarette to the match and said, "Make a wish, Sis," and they all sang Happy Birthday.

I was only a girl then, Grace, but I vowed never to hurt my own kids like that. I made that promise over and over in the mirror as my eye went from purple to green to yellow that week. I thought I'd never been so sure about a thing in my life.

But as time went on, I started to doubt myself. I got mad at stupid things. I picked fights with Doug and kicked the billy goat for eating the roses. I found out later it was deer at the roses when Pops shot one for venison. Then I felt sick about kicking poor Billy. What the devil was wrong with me? Would I end up like Astrid?

Of course not, Momma.

Years later, Grace, when you were born, that same fear got big again. When you cried and I reached for you, I saw Astrid's hands, not mine, and I heard Pops laugh. I picked you up anyway and held you close, waiting for the shaking to leave.

As time went on and I watched you grow, an idea came over me. Whatever my faults, whatever I'd done, I didn't have to be like Astrid, I could be different and learn to love. I'm here to tell you, Grace: it was you who taught me that, taught me how to be a mother. Not Astrid, but you. If I only got it half right, is it still worth something?

Everything, Momma, everything.

We'll see, sweetheart, we'll see. My love to you always, Momma

I grabbed hold of an attic two-by-four and pulled myself up. My throat ached, but I couldn't cry. I'd been cried out for a whole year. I never guessed what my mother had gone through. Not once, in all our years together, had she been cruel to me. Not once had I questioned her love. Like the floor under my bed, it was there every day when I swung my feet out. The more I thought about it, the more her absence opened under me like a yawning hole. You can fall into a place like that, you can disappear.

I slammed my eyes shut, trying to think happy thoughts: a cherry Slurpee, my Schwinn bike, a never-ending stream of letters in our mailbox. Finally I took a breath and opened my eyes. Under the flashlight, on the attic floor, my toes were splayed out, knobby and white. I stared at them until I felt the plywood pushing back. Such odd little body parts, toes, so stubby and short. Her image came to me then, with me in the bathroom. I was sitting on the counter as she held my feet over the sink, clipping my toenails. How many times in my life had she done that? How many?

I wasn't sure what I felt for Pops, but, preacher's kid or not, I hated Astrid. She was vicious and cruel. I'd never seen a picture of the woman and I wondered what she looked like. Then a chill came over me: with my strange lop eyes and mop of dark hair did I look like her?

I thought of the anger building inside me since my mother's death and my skin went clammy. Were her letters some kind of warning? Was the poison of Astrid in me?

Chapter Nine

Glass houses are as handy for looking out as for looking in. I learned that from our dining room bay window the week I found my best friend. Momma was still with us then. I remember watching her from the window seat as she cooked at the stove. I loved that rounded, jutting window. On the church side of the house, it was my spyglass on the neighborhood. From behind my mother's curtains, I could see out past the Tree of Heaven to our neighbors on Pardee, or check out what was happening at Good Shepherd. On weekends when there was a wedding at the church, I'd swing into action to stalk the bridal party—all the way to their dressing space.

"The Preacher's Kid always brings ice water and crackers before holy matrimony," I'd say with a tray in my hand. "It's in the church Book of Discipline." Which it wasn't, of course. But how else could I get close enough to run my hands down their hangered gowns? From the bay window, I had a good view of the church basement too, through a bank of windows along an outdoor stairwell. It's where the wedding receptions took place with the mysterious guest of a lop-eyed girl.

Sometimes I got a little street schooling from my view of the stairwell: teenagers smoking cigarettes or making out like tangled octopi in rough surf. I knew better than to snitch and be considered a tattletale, so I played stupid instead.

"You know that redhead from the church youth group?" was

the sort of thing I'd say at dinner. "A necklace must've broke down her blouse today 'cause this boy was trying *real* hard to find it."

Not long after Dad and I canvassed the neighborhood that first summer, I was alone in the bay window, trying to think up something to do. Dad was at Good Shepherd and Momma had escaped her blue hour to give Jimmy a bath. My eyes were misty because Travis had just shot Old Yeller. I rested my chin on the spine of the book and thought: if I stare outside hard enough, *something* might come along—a stray yeller dog of my own or maybe even a new friend. As a PK, I already had strikes against me. Worst of all, kids assumed I was a Goody Two-shoes, too prim to be any fun. Despite lots of introductions at church, I hadn't found a friend and the start of school was weeks away.

"God bring me a friend, God bring me a friend," I prayed every night.

The view outside didn't look promising, the empty lawn to the church and the Tree of Heaven in its summer green. I started to get up, to wander to the fridge, when something moved near the back of the church. The fence? It was the barely-standing McEgan fence, where the woods grew thick. A second later it swayed again. Was it McEgan? No, I realized, he was taller than the fence. Then suddenly over the top a head popped up with two hands. They fired at the church, I didn't know what, but something fast. The stained glass was so close, I imagined it shattering to a million bits.

"Momma!" I called, but she didn't answer.

I leaned to the window for a better look—the boy with the crew cut? McEgan's son? He was small enough that I could take him, scale the fence and pounce on his chest. "Check out *them* Goody Two-shoes!" The hands rose again, so I jumped up and raced out the back in time to hear *whap!* Whatever it was hit the stained glass.

"Hey you, knock it off!" I ran fast as I could, over the grass, up the slope. *Whap.* I looked to the church, hoping for Dad, but his office was at the front of Good Shepherd.

The hands kept going, and now the ping-a-ling of *breaking* glass. In the next step I was close enough to see it: a slingshot. I whipped around to the window and froze. Red splotches covered the panes like splats of blood, dozens of them, and a hole, way up high, glared back. Fighting the urge to run to my father, I turned instead to the horrible boy—and stopped. The face glaring at me had the same chalky appearance, but was framed by long, stringy hair. A *girl,* tall and skinny, a little older than I was. She hid the slingshot and lifted her nose. Suddenly the boy was with her, propped by his arms on the teetering fence. They had to be brother and sister, they looked so much alike.

"I saw what you did," I said.

"Oh yeah? Looks to me like you can't see nothin'. One of your eyes dead or what?"

I couldn't stand her already. The answer was no, of course, though I'd used that angle in school more than once. *I didn't see assignment, Mrs. Moses, my blind side, you know.* Even better was inventing special powers, like seeing through walls or detecting lies, but I wasn't sure it would work on a McEgan. I almost went for broke and blurted out the official name: *heterochromia iridis,* which you can be born with like I was, or develop after an injury, until I had second thoughts. Any mention of an "injury" might give these two ideas.

"I see fine in both eyes," I said. And I did—fine enough to see the scum line on the girl's teeth.

"Then maybe you saw who chucked the crab apples at the church," she said.

So that's what they were: *crab apples.* Loads lay on the ground, and zillions more in the tree over their heads. Little red cannon balls. The girl was matter-of-fact. "We heard a noise, but we never saw who done it, did we Butte?"

"Whatever you say, Appoline." The boy grinned. Butte and Appoline, oddball names for oddball kids.

The girl looked like she knew good and well how to fight, but I couldn't help myself. "If you didn't see anything, then how come you know it was crab apples that hit the window? It's so obvious you did it it's stupid."

Appoline climbed the fence, ready to eat me alive. But just as she got a knee up, she stopped, staring at the church parking lot and a blonde on a bicycle. The three of us watched her pedaling from the asphalt onto the grass. She looked nice enough, which made me wonder why this McEgan girl was backing down.

"Oh great, it's Snaggletooth," Appoline jeered. "I don't go

anywhere near a Shelby."

"Why bother?" Butte laughed. "Watch this!" He snorted and sent a hawker flying, just like his dear old dad. I tried to dodge but it hit me square in the chest, jarring the McEgans into a laughing fit. By the time the blonde pedaled up and dropped her bike, the spot on my shirt was soaked through.

"What the hell happened?" she said.

Despite the hawker, I smiled. "They wrecked our Jesus window."

"Couple of jackasses."

I laughed out loud.

"Who's gonna believe what some blind, freak-eye saw?" This was Appoline now, still giggling at the fence.

"Freak?" The blonde said. "Look who's callin' somebody a freak! What grade are you in *now*, Apple? Second?"

Apple stopped laughing. "Bitch!" she yelled and added a gesture I'd never seen with her middle finger in a kind of salute. The blonde rushed the fence and the McEgans backed away, disappearing into their woods.

"Same to ya!" the blonde said, raising a finger the same way. Then she collapsed to the grass.

"Thanks," I said, plopping next to her. "Thanks a lot."

When she smiled I caught a glimpse of the snaggletooth—one of her canines was too high—but it was a good smile all the same. "Can you believe she flipped us the bird?" she said.

"Flipped us the what?"

"Ca!" She re-cocked her finger.

"Oh, *that*. Heck no." It's a mandatory skill for a Preacher's Kid: pretending to know stuff when you really don't. As for "the bird," which I practiced that second, I'd ask my father later what it meant.

The blonde said her name was Sandy Shelby, and she didn't mind my eyes at all. She had lived up the street all her life and never once heard of a girl in the parsonage.

"Butte's a jerk. I'm always stuck with him in my class." She brushed back sweaty hair and looped a lock of it under her snaggletooth. But when she caught me looking, she closed her lips.

"He doesn't scare me," I offered.

"Me neither," she mumbled. "But watch out for Appoline. She flunked two grades already, that's how come she's so tall." As Sandy talked, I tore up grass to wipe the hawker from my shirt.

"She don't mess with us Shelbys. Not since my sister gave her a fat lip."

That explained it, I thought. Sandy frowned at my shirt, turning green from the grass, then looked to the church.

"Hey—a window's broke!" She jumped up and ran as I followed close behind. "Hot damn! They could go to JDH for this!"

"Jaydee what?" It was out of my mouth before I could think.

"H—don't know that either? Well I guess since you're the preacher's kid. It's where all the jackasses end up." She drew her finger across the glass. "This crap's sticky."

"They had a slingshot." I reached down, collecting spent ammo from the grass. They were small as gumballs, bruised and split. "See? Crab apples."

"That's so funny!" On her nose, the freckles shifted. "That's what we call her, you know: Crab-Appoline. She's such a bitch, isn't she?"

Since I wasn't allowed to gossip—or cuss—I focused on the window, pretending to study it. The hole was somewhere over the Shepherd's head. "I sure hope somebody can fix that."

"Where's your folks? Let's get 'em."

"My Dad's in the church, I guess."

"Great! Wait till he calls the police, Old Man McEgan will shoot up the neighborhood like before."

"He shot up the neighborhood?"

"Not exactly. But he hauled out his shotgun and everything, pissed off about some tax accessivements thing. He hates preachers' guts, you know." Sandy smiled, pleased to give me such news.

"Why?"

"Oh, don't take it personal. He hates everybody. His wife and kids too. It's an old story, my dad says, lost his land, then his senses. But he loves that shotgun, pulls it out whenever he gets the itch."

Having met "Old Man" McEgan, I didn't doubt it. I could see part of the farmhouse and I pictured him there, raising the barrel. The church and parsonage were easy targets.

"I'm not telling my parents," I said.

"But they'll see the hole and this mess, du-uh."

"Yeah, except nobody has to know who did it but us."

Sandy glared at me for about a century. "Maybe you're right," she finally said. "Even if we did tell, those jackasses never get punished. Plus this way we can get back at 'em when they least expect."

The name Sandy fit her well. She was gritty as a sucker dropped in a sandbox, but an answer to a prayer all the same. I'd asked God for a friend, I just hadn't been specific. As I stood there, grinning, she spit out the lock of hair and slipped in a dry one, not bothering, this time, to close her lips.

Chapter 10

As seasons passed, I started to notice things about my mother's letters: not only were they delivered on Sundays, but they seemed to come at regular intervals. If there was a pattern, couldn't I figure it out? Slip into spy mode and wait for the messenger? The thought made my heart jump. If I caught him in the act, if I figured out who he was, maybe I could track down *all* the letters.

The problem was, I didn't have a pattern yet, just Sundays, ages apart. I could hardly stay in spy mode for a month of Sundays. I tried to think: when exactly had the letters arrived? Miss Brilliance hadn't bothered to record the dates. The first came on the Sunday after her memorial, but the others, when? Sunday mornings in different seasons, but not exactly following the seasons. I remembered waiting all through the fall and nothing came. Then the second letter arrived in December. After that, it was sometime in spring, and finally the fourth letter, late summer again. Was it even a pattern? To find out for sure I'd have to record the dates. I'd have to wait for another letter.

It felt like waiting for the second coming.

Weeks passed, then all of fall, the tug of the letters eventually easing up. I no longer thought of them every second. One morning as I came home in my soggy shoes, Pardee mud hitching a ride, I spotted something from a distance in our mailbox. The lid was open and white showed where the front panel dipped away. It was a

Sunday, about four months since the last letter. *Could it be?* I'd played hooky from church that morning and slipped out the back door so I wouldn't be seen. In a light drizzle I'd wandered the neighborhood until I could no longer hear the church organ. Now the music rose again as I came up our driveway opposite the church. The benediction. The second service was just ending. *Had I been out that long?* I made a beeline for the mailbox. It was an envelope, sure enough, and the right eggshell shade of white.

As the organ music swelled, I leapt up the porch. I'd waited so long for this, and now it came at me like a shout: *Grace!* A letter, a letter, a *letter!* I snatched it up and dashed to the attic, anxious to hear her voice.

Dearest Grace,

I get a little panicky sometimes, desperate to do what I can for you before I leave this earth. I'd like to protect you all your days, if that was possible. But all I can do is record my thoughts, the things I've learned in this short life. I don't exactly feel worthy, but that's beside the point. This is for you, sweet daughter. So here goes, my best advice:

*Above all else, follow your dreams. Chase them down and capture them. They're a gift from God, pure and simple. And if life throws you trouble, never give up. Dreams only get away from you if you let them.

Okay Momma.

*Stay strong and always keep learning, because the world is cruel to the weak and ignorant and only the strong can stick up for them. Do stick up for them, Grace, even when it scares you. You'll live a better life than I have.

*This one's simple, Grace: Pray. When you're happy, when you're sad. You'll be amazed how it changes things, especially you.

Now you're sounding like Dad.

*But listen to your instincts too, honey, because they're

often right and they'll protect you.

*And finally... get advice from older role models like your Father. Don't assume they're out of touch because they're older. They're the ones with experience. They've already made mistakes.

Okay, all right, but can you please *get back to your story?*

Since I don't want to pile on too much, I'll stop here with the advice.

Yes!

Except for this: Be careful choosing your role models. I didn't have one in Astrid or Pops, that's for sure. About the only thing I did have back in those days is plenty of spunk. Despite Astrid, despite all the ranch work, I was full of energy and life.

I leaned back against the two-by-four to take it in.

Since that spring day when Sal caught me on his horse, I was obsessed with what he'd said, the part about riding lessons. I kept wondering if it was something to hope for.

The truth is I thought a lot about Sal and that smile Pops called his coyote grin. He'd told Astrid just like he promised that I'd ride the mare, and I was grateful. I spent the next two months out on the trails. But I knew the privilege was only temporary. And, just as he said, when they came back for the summer, I had to give up riding. Instead, I climbed to the barn loft to watch them go out, way up high where nobody noticed me.

Sometimes Dr. Rossano rode when he was up from the city, but most times it was Sal and his friend. I learned a few things watching them from up in my perch. First, that Sal was a solid horseman, whether he was on Lady or that crazy stallion. And second, that they all rode better in the saddle than I did bareback.

Sal was busy that summer, so we barely talked until, out of the blue, he came to me. It was late August and I was at the chicken coop. I didn't hear him coming and his voice made me jump. "How's your summer been?" he said.

It was a funny question, Grace, since I'd worked most of it. "All right," I told him, "My summer's been all right." He said his family was packing up, leaving that very day back to the city. "Oh," I answered. What else was there to say? He smiled then, that sly smile, and leaned on the chicken coop. "But aren't you glad? I thought you'd be glad." I collected another egg and looked him over. "Because you're leaving?" The fact was, Grace, we all worked harder when the Rossanos were there. He laughed. "No, no, no, because you can go back to riding Stella."

Stella. I still didn't like the name. "Sure," I said, "I guess so." Then I turned to poke through nests for more eggs. "I saw you, you know," he told me, "more than once out on rides. Up in the loft watching us." I think my face must have turned red. "I was curious about the tack is all, what it's like to ride in the saddle." He grinned. "So do it."

He made it sound so simple, Grace, like I should've hoisted one of those huge saddles a long time ago. It was easy for Sal to be cocky. He was older. He was rich and confident. I faced him square on and told him, plain and simple, "I can't," which I thought was already clear. It made me feel like such a girl though, and when he laughed, I almost spit.

"It's not funny," I told him. He shuffled his feet and tried to wipe off his smile. "Your brother can saddle a horse, right?" "Sure," I said, "but he doesn't like horses, so I don't bother him. Besides I can get hold of her mane and swing a leg up, so I don't need a saddle." I was mad, Grace. What did this boy know about me?

When he spoke again, I was surprised. He actually sounded sincere. "I could show you, maybe give you those riding lessons." I turned to face him, I couldn't help it. "You mean it this time?" He looked away, toward the castle, and cleared his throat. "The thing is," he said, "if we go, one of these days, we'll have to be careful... My parents, you know?"

I did know. The owners' son and the hired help? "It won't be for a while," he said, "maybe a long while since I don't know when we'll be back." I didn't hesitate, Grace, but said it straight out, "I can wait," because the fact is, what else did I have to do?

A strange sensation overwhelmed me and I quit reading. For the first time I knew what my mother felt, surrounded by wealth but not a dime to her name, under the thumb of the Rossanos and Astrid to boot. Anything to look forward to was better than nothing.

The attic walls were closing in. I dropped the letter and escaped through the midget door to my bedroom window. Outside, the bare branches of the Tree of Heaven dripped with rain. I slid open the window and stood there, just breathing, for the longest time.

Chapter 11

It was afternoon before I went back to the attic, after lunch and a walk to Sandy's. Some good it did me. Sandy wasn't home. When I opened the midget door, I found the flashlight on. The beam was so weak it was useless. I wandered downstairs to look for batteries, found none, then jumped on my bike for the corner store, pedaling like a fiend to burn off steam.

Half an hour later, after I'd loaded the flashlight, I went back to the letter.

A wet winter rolled in from the Pacific the year I waited on Sal Rossano. We sprayed the castle roses to keep the rust away and stopped worrying about watering the grass. It was after the birthday I told you about, when my gift was a black eye. I was in the eighth grade by then, with a lot going on. My first period, for one thing, when I got no help from Astrid.

Like that's a surprise.

The thing is, Grace, she never said a word about becoming a woman. One morning at school I found blood on my underwear and the more I thought about it, the more worried I got. I decided I must've hurt myself riding Lady, some kind of punishment for the thing I loved most. When the bleeding stopped, I was relieved.

But the next month it came back worse than ever. This time It was Saturday and I was home in my work jeans. When I saw the stain, the bright new blood, I thought I'd reopened something and now I was dying. It looked bad enough to bleed me to death. I couldn't go to Astrid, I knew she'd tell me it served me right for riding that horse. And I was too modest to tell Pops or Doug, so I curled up on my bed with Chipper and a dishtowel to wait for the end. The ache in my belly convinced me it was near.

Then Astrid walked in. I couldn't see her at first because of the sheet Doug and I had tacked up, but I heard the murmur of her shoes. Chipper did too and jumped from the bed. He was a smart dog. When she came around the sheet, she had my jeans in her hand, the ones I'd stuffed in the dirty clothes.

"I see yeh started," she said, holding them out so the stain showed. I thought she meant started to die and I stared at her, the scowl on her mouth, shocked at how casual she was. A second later I got a feeling I was missing something, but all the while she just stood there, waggling the jeans.

"We'll have to soak these," she growled. She had something else too, bulky and white. "It happens to every girl sooner or later, though you're on the later side." She took one look at me and let loose a cackle. "Jesus, Cauliflower, it's yer period. You don't know a thing about it, do you? Don't the girls down at school tell yeh anything?" I shook my head. My ranch life made it hard to keep friends.

"God awmighty," she went on, "don't be so dense. It means yer fertile." Fertile was how Astrid described the vermin that pestered us: rabbits and pack rats, raccoons and squirrels, and a multitude of mice the calico cat batted around. All of them fertile and filthy as far as she was concerned.

"Use this for now," she said, and the white bulk hit the spot where Chipper had been. I sat up and she laughed again. "You put it between yer legs girl," she told me. "Oh, and yeh might want to clean up. Mrs. Clayton's on her way. She'll run yeh to town for supplies since I don't have the time." And that was that, as far as Astrid was concerned. She went out to wash the jeans

and her hands of the whole bloody mess.

I'll never forget Mrs. Clayton and her kindness. She insisted again as I said hello, "Call me Hazel." Then she drove me into St. Helena just like Astrid said. At first I was embarrassed, but Hazel was so sweet, I started to relax. "I let Astrid know we'd be a while," she said, "since girls ought not to hurry when they go shopping." I smiled, but didn't tell her that I never went shopping.

Hazel had a handful of coins from my mother, and we spent most of them at Vasconi's drug store. Then she took me to Fashion Land to pick out a brassiere—my first, can you believe that, at 14? I remember the bra had a little pink rose in the front. When she saw me in the dressing room and the sorry condition of my underpants, she picked out a few of those too and a belted dress of a quality I'd never dreamed of wearing. I knew Astrid's coins wouldn't cover it, not the bra or panties either, so I stood there in the fitting room, trying to refuse that dress. But Hazel wouldn't let me. "I have to see that color on you," she said. "I just love periwinkle blue."

When I put it on, saw how pretty it looked, I had to fight to keep from crying. Not once, in my whole life, had anybody treated me so kind. "There, now, see?" She said, smoothing my hair back from my brow. "You'll wear that dress out of here with no arguments." I have to admit, Grace, I sure liked the sound of that.

I found it easy to talk to Hazel. She was sturdy like Astrid but with eyes that were always smiling. She dressed for ranch life but painted her nails and kept her hair in a modern bob. She was older than Astrid and her children grown, but young at heart, especially for a recent widow. She laughed often and never cackled, not once.

"Here I go again, talking too much," she said, as we strolled through St. Helena with me feeling like a real lady in that periwinkle dress. "Talking is fine with me," I said, skipping around to face her. "There's not a whole lot of talking on the ranch."

I took a chance and opened up to Hazel that day, described my life and my pencil drawings. I told her about Lady too and how I dared to ride her when I wasn't supposed to. And guess what, instead of scolding me, she called me brave! Can you believe that? Brave!

It turns out Hazel had horses of her own that she loved like I loved Lady. She had birds too and said she thought it a wonder I could draw because she couldn't sketch a bird beak to save her life. I got a real kick out of that, couldn't sketch a bird beak! Hazel really knew how to make me smile.

Before the day was out, she took me to The Sweet Shop and bought us malted milkshakes. And here's the best part: long after the shakes were gone we sat and talked, about school and life and anything we pleased. It ended up a fine day, in spite of Astrid, one of the best I can remember.

The reason I tell you this story Grace? Your own path to becoming a woman will start one day too, and maybe when you least expect. We both know I won't be there to help, but I've made sure somebody will. I want you to have that much. Georgia Johnson is your Hazel Clayton, sweetheart. She's on board, ready to be there the minute you need her.

I lowered the letter. Georgia? Of course. Who else would she ask?

She's here again today, trying to get food into this white wisp of a friend. Can't you just see her with that heavy tray? Can't you just hear her haranguing me?

I could.

"You need a rest and some sustenance, girl!" she tells me. Ah, Georgia. Without her, I'd shrivel to nothing. And she's right about me needing a rest. I've gone and worn myself out again. I'll sign off now, Grace...

Already, Momma?

Just remember, call Georgia when your time comes. She'll be there whether you like it or not.

My love always,
Momma

Good old Georgia. My mother had pegged her right. She was a spitfire who never let anybody get in her way. Soon as she finished her work at the church, she would powerwalk across the lawn to get to Momma, then stand at her bedside threatening bodily harm to get her to eat. She spent hours at our house, talking to Momma and making her laugh. When the pain got worse, she stayed longer.

I sat up straight. *Could Georgia be my mother's messenger?* Momma had trusted her, no doubt about that, and she'd been to the house after Momma had passed—a number of times. Was she the one? I started to get up, then stopped and slumped back. There were problems with the theory. First, Georgia lived clear across town. Wouldn't it be odd for her to drive all that way in the middle of the night?

There was something else too. Georgia was the curious kind. If she had something to do with the letters, wouldn't she ask about them, wouldn't she snoop around? But her visits had trailed off after Momma died. In fact, now that I thought about it, she hadn't been to the house in more than a year. Then I remembered why. Her own mother had had a stroke, and she was taking care of her.

I sighed. It didn't seem like Georgia could be the messenger.

A gust of wind crackled the roof and brought me back to the letter. It was hard to picture my mother the way she was then: growing up, coming of age. But even harder to imagine it happening to me. Would I stay petite like her or end up tall like my dad? Would the embarrassing bumps under my shirt become breasts? The whole idea seemed foreign, like it would happen in another dimension—or never at all. Then again, what did I have to lose? I was only 11. I could hardly remember being a girl.

Chapter 12

Each new year meant another trip through the church calendar: Advent to Christmas, Lent to Easter and back to Ordinary Time. With Momma gone, we were sleepwalking through it. A new decade arrived. *This is the dawning of the Age of Aquarius!* Hair grew longer and tempers shorter. Nixon was president and Southeast Asia was still a mess. It was 1970, the year I would turn 12.

Easter came early that spring, I remember, in late March. I decided to wear an old dress because my mother had made it. It was short on me, but not quite short enough to be a mini-skirt, just plain outgrown. The cuffs of Jimmy's slacks were high water too when he rambled down, so I decided it wouldn't kill me to walk him to Sunday school. Too bad playing hooky from church wasn't an option at Easter.

No letter had come since that wet December day. The Tree of Heaven wore bud-tipped stalks, and the tulips were up in the front yard at Mrs. Crookshank's. With Jesus out of the tomb once again, I set my sights on another resurrection—my mother's—through the strange portal of our mailbox. When would she come again? All I could do was guess, based on the timing of the other letters: about every four months. Until I recorded more dates, it was the best I could do.

Using that measure, it put my next target at two weeks past Easter.

The plan I came up with for that Sunday was simple: get up early to watch, with the lights out, from the dining room window. I wasn't even sure what to watch for: a person or a ghost? On the night before that Sunday, I sat on my bed and chewed a hangnail, wishing my wind-up alarm clock would move faster. But the longer I sat there, the slower the hands moved. Jimmy was asleep and Dad was downstairs as The Cyclops chattered through a Saturday night movie. I twirled the alarm hand and wondered where to position it: 5 a.m. or 5:30? Would that be early enough? And that's when I realized: I didn't know when my mother's letters had arrived, not exactly. We'd only *found* them on Sunday mornings. For all I knew, they could have come the night before! Miss Brilliance had struck again. The clock tumbled from my lap as I ran to the window. Had my mother's ghost come and gone? The front yard was dark, except for a soft glow from the streetlight. I sailed down the stairs, past Dad in his recliner and to the mailbox, flipping it so hard it only yipped. Inside: one dead moth, her powdery wings stiff in that bottomless pit.

It meant I still had my chance.

I closed the lid and, like a moccasin-footed scout, padded back in the house. Dad's head, against the back of his chair, hadn't moved, so he was probably asleep. I snuck opposite him to the dark dining room and, quick as the wind, scooted a chair to the big window. I could have traveled with Chief Joseph and the Nez Perce tribe.

I sat Indian-style and trained my eyes on the walk. It wasn't easy. I could hardly keep still. When I caught my knees bouncing, I forced them down with both hands. The TV went to commercials— Alka-Seltzer, Shake N Bake—then back again several times, but out on our walk, nobody came. I closed my eyes, just a minute, to rest my head on the back of the chair when almost instantly it was cold, and in the chill…

…I hear footsteps, small footsteps, falling away. I have a feeling now, the same I've had many times, that I'm right handed, not left—that I have been all along because I can make letters with this pencil. Big letters. Until I'm all of a sudden too tired even to hold the pencil and—

"Grace?" My eyes flew open. Dad stood over me in the darkness. "What in Sam Hill?" This was the closest my father ever came to swearing. "Why aren't you in bed?"

"I don't know." And I didn't, steeped as I was in the dream. He flipped on the overhead, zapping me with the light and then his Preacher Eye. I flexed my right hand and stared. The pencil was gone. Then I knew again—with every ounce of me—that my left hand was dominant, like it always had been. So strange was that feeling.

"A watched pot never boils, you know."

What did he mean? I sat up, looked out the window and remembered. "Oh—I guess not." But how did he know? My view of the walk was a pretty good clue.

"Up to bed, young lady."

"But Dad—"

"But nothing—"

"Do you know when—"

"No I don't. But I do know you can't make it happen sitting here. Up to bed."

On my way up the stairs, the dream closed in again like a strange, parallel world. It felt so real... but it didn't make sense. Then my thoughts went to the mailbox and I turned around—to Dad, aiming his Preacher Eye. I couldn't have missed something, could I? I would have heard that lid squeal.

Up in my room, I whipped the alarm hand to 5 a.m. and cracked my windows to the spring night. I had memorized the pitch of that mailbox—I could sing it out loud if you asked me—and I played it in my head as I crawled under my covers. The room was dark except for the street light through the bare branches of the Tree of Heaven. After a while, the vibrations of my father's snoring rumbled up from downstairs...

...until it's a softer sound, a whoosh-whoosh, like a small heartbeat. Suddenly there's a basket here with a lid latched tight, and I'm drawn to it, to the whoosh-whoosh under that lid. I go closer... and closer, ready to unlatch it, when it strikes me that I already know what's in that basket, because it's me. I can feel it. But how can I be there when I'm here? I move closer and closer still, desperate to open it, but the basket gets smaller and farther away and when I

reach for it, before I get my hand on it, I hear it cry—

I sat up and gasped. Was it only a cry in a dream… or was it the mailbox? It was still dark outside. I held my breath, listening for footsteps or the hum of a car on Pardee. There was nothing but the rumble of Dad's snoring from downstairs. The room was chilly, all the windows still cracked open. I left my bed and went to the front window, touching my nose to the screen. It didn't look like anyone was there, but I couldn't see the porch.

I crossed the room and braved the landing, forcing my legs down the stairs one at a time. At my sides the darkness formed ominous shapes that just as quickly liquefied. In the entry, I felt for the door, twisted the knob and pulled it open. The porch light glowed and slices of light from the street made the grass crawl. At the Tree of Heaven, the rope swing rocked slowly, back and forth. Was it the night breeze or had somebody bumped it? I couldn't see anybody. Then again, those twin trunks were wide enough to hide a grizzly. Two grizzlies. *Double your pleasure, double your fun.* I thought about calling out or hotfooting over to take a look, but I was too jittery, too afraid of what I'd find. I watched instead, through the steam of my breath. When no ghosts or grizzlies emerged, I eased open the mailbox and flinched at the squeal. Inside: the same moth, dead and broken, all alone. How had she gotten there, anyway?

Overhead, the porch light was an insect graveyard: wings and bodies, legs and antennas. Ashes to ashes, dust to dust. I pictured the moth flying into the light, hitting it over and over until she tumbled down, dead like the rest. What was she after? What were any of them after? I closed the lid and ran back up to bed.

Chapter 13

I wish I could say I woke up early the next morning and nabbed my mother's messenger. But the truth is, I was so exhausted from the night before, I slept straight through that clattering alarm. The sun was up when I finally rushed down—to the moth and nothing else.

It was one week later that my father brought in a letter and I nearly fell over. I was off by one week? One lousy week? For a minute neither of us moved, and then I snatched it from his hand and thundered up the stairs.

Hello Ace,

One thing I've learned as I tell this story is to write while I'm rested, so I can stay awake longer and have some chance of getting it out. Don't be surprised then, sweetheart, that I go right back to the ranch.

Fine with me, Momma.

It was late that year, already the start of summer vacation before Sal Rossano showed up again, when the blossoms are off the trees but their fruits only tiny versions of themselves. I was 14, more like a woman, and curious to see him. Would he notice? Would he be surprised? The way it happened, the first surprise was mine.

I was in the barn that afternoon, feeding vegetable peels to the horses. I'd finished with Cesare at one end of the stables and moved to Lady at the other. As the mare reached over the half wall, I heard a rustle and there he was, Sal in the flesh. I almost dropped that bucket on his city shoes. "You scared me!" I said. When he smiled, I had a keen sense of how I looked, in my pedal pushers and stained blouse. Sal was rumpled some from the car ride, but clean. He always looked clean.

"You cut your hair," he said. Well Grace, it was the one thing I forgot. The hair that hung to my waist was chopped to my chin, probably the biggest change of all. I pushed a handful behind my ear. "I couldn't keep it in a pony tail so Astrid cut it. Where's your friend?" "He's not coming this summer," he said. "My folks have some people up, and they're already by the pool with their martinis."

Sal was 17 that year and broader through the shoulders than the last time I saw him. He looked like Dr. Rossano, except wilder, always wilder, like the coyote behind the grin. He reached out and pulled the hair from behind my ear. It was butchered more than cut, and when he saw it, his mouth twitched. Nobody would ever butcher his hair like that. We heard Jersey then, crying like a baby to be let in, and the silence between us settled heavy as her milk.

Finally, he said, "I was wondering if you're still interested in going out—riding I mean." I blinked. "With saddles and all?" "That's how it's usually done," he said, grinning. I was instantly excited. "You bet I'm interested! Right now?" He laughed. "I'll have to change my clothes first, but why not?" He eyed my feet. "And you might want to get some shoes."

I ran back to the cottage and—wouldn't you know?—got shanghaied by Astrid into hanging laundry. I couldn't think of a good excuse, so I went ahead fast as I could and got the clothes up on the line. By the time I returned to the barn, Sal was there in his riding boots. "About time you showed up," he said. But he didn't look angry. He was smiling, and he had Lady by the tack wall. "You'd better take my horse, since she's used to you already." He handed me the blanket and I got it over her just fine. Then he hoisted the saddle, saying I could do it myself if I centered my weight right. "Use the milking stool if you need to step up." I was happy and relieved I didn't have to try it in front of him.

As he pulled the cinch, he talked me through every step. "Wait for the exhale to get it tight, then pull again. Stella is easy enough, but Cesare likes to hold his breath." It didn't surprise me. Nothing about that stallion surprised me.

Next came the bridle, which is awkward as heck the first time you try it. Sal held it out to me, reins and all, and I hesitated, no idea where to start. "Madame?" he said, bowing with his arms outstretched. I had a clear view of his dark hair as he held the pose, the way it rolled in shiny waves. Near as we were to San Francisco I'd only been to San Pablo Bay once, but he reminded me of that water, the way he smelled of the fog and sea. I took the reins and curtseyed, and when he stood and winked, caught myself thinking of him, for the very first time, as a friend.

"Go ahead," he said, "try it." I turned and put the bit to Lady's mouth, but her nose came down. It didn't help that Sal was right-handed and I'm left. "No, no, no," he laughed, lifting my hand. "Get the reins around her neck first and stand this way." He turned me around so I was positioned next to Lady, the same direction she was looking, my head at her neck. Then he moved in beside me, took my hand with the crown under her neck and my other with the bit to her mouth. "Be firm, but gentle, like this," he said, guiding my fingers, and before I knew it, she took the bit. I'd done it and it felt good!

A little maneuvering with the crown piece and it was over her ears. "See?" he told me, "You're an expert!" If he hadn't been three years older and the owner's son, I might've kissed him that very minute. Instead I just stood there, grinning like a schoolgirl. "You're welcome," he said.

When Sal brought the stallion out, I went ahead and put my foot in the stirrup and stepped into Lady's saddle. It sure beat jumping on. Two shakes later, when he finished with

Cesare, he saw me there. "I guess you're ready," he said with a chuckle.

We took the horses out on the trail after that, with Chipper as usual trotting behind. It felt different with all that leather, harder to sense Lady's movements. But there was plenty to like about it too, the creak of the leather, the control and stability. Plus, I finally felt, as Pops would say, like a gen-u-wine rider. Sal was quieter on the trail than I expected, checking the castle until we were out in the hills. But I watched how he handled the reins and that helped.

We got together like that a few times, and he was right about the saddle. I could lift it just fine when I put my back into it. It was such a feeling, Grace, I could finally do it myself! Each time we went, we slipped out of the barn, quiet and slow, but the minute we reached the hills, tore out thundering over the trails.

One afternoon, after we'd been riding a couple of weeks, Sal turned up a narrow run to a rocky overlook. It surprised me that he knew the place. I went there on foot sometimes to escape Astrid when I needed space. And who wouldn't? The view was so big it stole your breath. Copper-rimmed mountains rose in the distance and the sky whispered colors of the ocean. It got us talking, for the first time, about something other than the horses.

"Don't you wish you could paint it?" he said, pulling the stallion up short. I shot him a look. Grace, I'd sketched that scene not a week before and thought how much better it would look in color. But how could Sal know? "What?" he said. I shook my head and told him "Nothing," but I wasn't much of a liar except where Astrid was concerned, and he got it out of me right away.

I explained how I'd taken to drawing, and not just the hills. I said it was his horse I sketched most, the way she moved, the curves of her back and legs, things like that. "Stella?" he asked. "I call her Lady Agate," I said, and right off I was sorry. It sounded like something a child would choose. He didn't laugh, though. He said, "She shines like an Agate, doesn't she?" And I nodded in complete agreement.

Sal's eyes flicked to the horse and back to me. "Stella is Italian for star," he said, which made me feel somewhat better about the name. He had such a beautiful smile, I couldn't help but smile back.

"I'd like to see your drawings sometime," he said, "Would you let me?" Well, I have to tell you, Grace, nobody had ever asked me that before. Astrid called drawing a waste of time, Doug thought it was something lonely girls did, and Pops? I don't think he ever noticed. I told him I wasn't good or anything and that the only art I ever saw was in schoolbooks. I blushed then, realizing Sal had probably seen museums all over California, heck, all over the world.

"We'll have to fix that," he said. He told me there were paintings at the chateau he could show me, plus his mother's art history volume with all the Impressionists in it. He started naming names I didn't know: Renoir, I think, Pissarro, and Monet. "I don't think it has van Gogh," he went on, "Wasn't he a Post-Impressionist?" Which, of course, really threw me. "Anyway, we'll go soon," he promised, "when the time is right." I knew he meant when his parents were gone. "I'd like that," I told him.

So that's what I was thinking about, Grace, when I walked home from the barn that day, going with Sal inside Chateau Genevieve. I was curious about everything, anything and everything, and the inside of that castle was the one place on the ranch I'd never been. My mind shot to Astrid, she'd have a fit if she knew, so I decided not to tell her.

There's a certain thrill in reliving these stories, Grace, so young and impressionable I was then. But I'm afraid it's also draining. Georgia's due here before too long, and I'd hate to be too tired to appreciate her. She's so good to me. Maybe if I close my eyes now, I can rest a while before she comes.

Be good, Grace. Be happy.
Momma

I took that letter to bed with me that night. I read it over and over until the lines blurred, until they rearranged into the image of her. Suddenly she was a girl, standing in the window of a castle tower so high it pierced the clouds—inside the castle! A ribbon of starlings rose up around her as she caught my eye and smiled...

In the morning, the letter was crumpled between my shoulder and the sheet. I pulled it out: my mother's life before she knew her destiny. She'd said her childhood ended on that ranch. But what of it? Nobody stays a child forever, just look at old Mrs. Crookshank and her shepherd-staff spine. A dozen childhoods could disappear in the time it took those bones to bend.

I refolded my mother's letter and carried it to the attic. It belonged with the others in my latest hiding place, between the pages of Little Women—early on, of course, before Jo leaves or Beth dies. It was a school day, Monday morning, and Dad was stirring downstairs.

Chapter 14

I'll always remember the summer of '66 as our summer of innocence. Momma was still healthy and our troubles few. In fact, the vandalism at the church was as bad as it got.

Just one day after it happened, Sandy and I were half out of our skin because no one had discovered it. Our part-time janitor apparently missed the mess on his usual rounds, and Honey and my parents hadn't been in the sanctuary. But Sandy and I, we couldn't stop thinking about that window. We kept itching for somebody to find it. So, with no better idea in mind, we climbed the Tree of Heaven and threw our voices to passers by. Sandy had seen a ventriloquist do it once and swore it was easy. All you do, she said, is firm up your lips and throw your voice through the crack. "Over he-ere, behind the church!" we called to our targets on Pardee. But they only looked up and said, "Huh?" Even Mrs. Crookshank waved from her porch across the street. What else could we do but wave back?

Another day disappeared before the most unlikely person of all found the mess: our church music director. He was the type who could walk through toilet overflow and not notice until it soaked his shoes. Mankiewicz was his name, Bob Mankiewicz, but we all called him Manny for short. And everybody liked him, despite his many quirks, including a strange distrust for bookmarks. To avoid using them, he lined up multiple hymnals on the organ rack instead, each one opened to a song he would play. Sometimes there were so many hymnals on that rack, they teetered at either end. And that was the limit. For any one service, Manny would play only as much music as would fit on that rack.

Most people thought he was simple, but Momma swore he had flashes of genius, the way he could hear a tune once and play it forever. He knew the numbers of every hymn too and the dates they were composed. The trouble was getting the words from his brain to his lips. When the telephone rang at the parsonage that afternoon, I picked it up.

"Carsten residence, may I ask—"

"It's Manny on the, on the phone," he said, "Come qwa-quick." and then *click*. It wasn't even clear that he meant *to the church*. But when I repeated what he said to my parents, they dropped what they were doing. It was Thursday, after all, choir practice Thursday. I grabbed Jimmy and followed behind, singing, "Jesus wants me for a sunbeam..." to preempt any suspicion. Once in the church, my parents headed for the office, since that's where Manny would have used the phone. But soon enough, they saw me standing at the sanctuary doors.

"I thought I heard somebody," I lied as they hurried past.

You couldn't miss it. The stained glass was cloudy and the hole a punch of daylight. And there was Manny, pacing the chancel with that hitch in his step. "Not good, good at all," he kept saying. In his hand was a hunk of glass, a piece of Christ's hair by the look of it. Dad took it from him and stood in silhouette before the window.

"There's a rock here, Manny." He squatted to pick it up. "Did you see it come through?"

A rock? I thought. Didn't he mean a crab apple? I went closer as he held it up. It was a rock all right.

"Did this just happen, Manny?"

Manny looked around like he wasn't sure. "I was going for hymnals and the glass pa-popped under my shoe." He indicated the choir loft where his shoe had had the encounter. "Somebody could get cut."

"But this rock, Manny, did you see anything?"

"No sir. Just pa-pop under my shoe."

Momma came forward then and took his arm. She had a way

with Manny that calmed his stutter. "Since nobody's here for choir yet," she said, "how about some iced tea at the house?"

"Iced tea, yes," he said nodding.

When I turned around again, Dad was out the door at the back of the chancel. I thought about following, but didn't trust my acting abilities. If he knew who busted that window, he'd go straight to Mr. Shotgun himself. I sat in a pew instead and jiggled my knees.

From the far side of the window, Dad's outline appeared, hazy at first, then clearer, as the tips of his fingers became dots on the glass. The whole scene made my blood boil, especially the hole, high up over his shadow. A minute later the door swung open and Dad stepped in. He was talking to his hand—or something in it— and bouncing his palm.

"…what in Sam Hill these are…" he mumbled. "Whoever did this must've mixed the rock in on accident."

On accident? But Appoline broke that window on purpose! I thought. And yet, what Dad said made sense: there was only one rock and one broken pane. Either way, the McEgans were guilty. *Guilty, guilty, guilty.* When my father glanced up, he caught the look on my face.

"Grace? Do you know something about this?" I shook my head—or tried to—as he came down the steps and lifted my chin.

"You don't know a thing about these little fruits, are you sure?"

I knew *Yes sir* was the answer he wanted, as in: *Yes sir, I'm sure.* But he'd also asked *You don't know?* I had it made in the shade.

"No sir," I said and held his gaze.

Chapter 15

I don't know how my father was so clueless about crab apples. He could find Katmandu or Caracas on the globe or explain salmon migration like the Encyclopedia Britannica. Plus, he was the *preacher* for criminy's sake, one step removed from God himself. I pranced around the neighborhood at times full of this, what I considered one of the few perks of being the preacher's kid.

He'd read the Bible so many times he had most of the Gospels memorized, and I quizzed him from the Revised Standard Version he kept by his recliner. I'd crack it open, slide the thinner-than-candy-wrapper pages to the New Testament and challenge him to recite any old verse. If I stumped him, I got a quarter to blow on candy at the corner store. If he won, I had to memorize the verse myself.

"Luke 16, verse 13," I remember asking him.

And he answered, "Oh, let's see... 'No servant can serve two masters, for either he will hate the one and love the other, or he will be devoted to the one and despise the other. You cannot serve'—"

"God and money," I said, snapping the book shut with a sigh. No quarter for me.

Most evenings I'd find him reading, if not the Bible, then histories, biographies or Methodist publications, which he would summarize for me. A teacher at heart, he gave me lessons from the time I was small about the founder of Methodism, John Wesley. He was a brave thinker, Dad said, who declared it no sin to ask the big, important questions. Take the ones I came up with: What does God do all day? Do they eat in heaven? And is there also a pearly key?

"That's not precisely what Wesley intended," Dad said, "but just for now, it'll do."

Discussions of a higher order were common in our household, more common than board games or cards, especially gambling games which he strictly forbid. And the only TV shows we were allowed to watch were the educational ones. Once, when he caught me sneaking an episode of Gilligan's Island, he lingered until Gilligan took a coconut to the head. Then he whistled and said, "You must have a book somewhere," which he knew was an easy bet, since he brought me mountains every month from the library.

But somehow, from my father's vast tree of knowledge, no crab apples grew. Maybe he'd never seen one or they didn't grow out in the boonies of Gresham where he was raised. Whatever the reason, it was the first time in my entire life I knew something he didn't. I'd been too nervous that day in the church to say it, too scared of McEgan's shotgun. Now I itched like a poison-oak rash to inform him. Until Sandy beat me to it.

"They're crab apples," she said, tempting me to ram one up her nose. It was Saturday morning—the clock ticking to Sunday services—and we were outside at the stained glass, Dad and Manny opposite Sandy and me.

"There's a crab apple in our yard that's real pretty in the spring," Sandy said, dropping one of the split fruits to his palm. "But you can't eat 'em unless you make this jelly that only retards have a taste for." Her eyes shot to Manny "Oops, sorry" but he didn't seem to notice.

Dad ignored the comment. He already knew Sandy as the girl who'd taught me the bird. "Crab apples, huh?" he said. "Must be immature."

"Yep," I told him, snatching it up. "But they're different from real apples, not even a bit sweet." I took a bite and spit it out, feeling the sour pangs invade my jaw. "See?"

"Ah," Dad said.

The church janitor was AWOL again, so Dad and Manny had swung into action, dragging out ladders and supplies as Sandy and I donned our bathing suits to help out. In no time at all, we'd sprayed the stained glass—and everything else in sight. When we doused Manny in his shirtsleeves, Dad took pity and sent him home.

The crab apple stains came off easier than we expected after we'd given them—and each other—a few good soakings. It was nice work for an August morning. Now and then I felt eyes on me, but when I spun around to the McEgan fence no one was there. As we finished up, Momma came over.

"Not bad," she said, cutting Jimmy loose. "I bet it hasn't shined like that in years. Is there still glass in that busted pane?"

"No," Dad said, descending the ladder. "I pulled it out."

"Can we be done now?" I tried. I was muddy to the knees.

"I think you've done plenty," Dad said. "Tell you what: why don't you and Sandy go inside—see how it looks." He turned the hose on us then for a cold rinse as we squealed around the corner, all the way to the front steps and into the sanctuary.

"I win!" Sandy panted.

"No you didn't, you weren't even—" The glare hit me at an angle and I turned. Just over the Shepherd's head, where the pane was cleared, a starburst flared, spinning and pulsing, and below it, in front of the glass, arched a rainbow of color.

How in the world—? My knees buckled to the carpet like a push puppet's as I reached for Sandy, who was still going on about the race. "...my door is swinging harder, which proves I—hey, why are you on the ground?"

"Don't you *see* it?" I said. The colors were phenomenal; I would see them in my dreams for weeks to come.

"See what?"

"At the window—don't you see it?"

"I see a hole, so?"

It was starting to fade, and by the time I was on my feet again it was gone.

"Well?" Sandy said, "Spit it out."

I couldn't fathom how she'd missed it. "I saw something, a flash of light and—You didn't see it? Where the hole is?"

"No-o."

"But—" I headed down the aisle, Sandy following, until my bare feet were on the vent under the window. It was strange for the two of us to be in church in our swimsuits, our *wet* swimsuits, but this was stranger.

"When we first came through the doors, I saw... I think... you know, the thing in pictures over Jesus' head? A *halo*. It was really bright, like a star, with all these rainbows shooting from it."

"Right. You're doing that X-ray vision thing where I'm s'pposed to think oooh, I wish I had lop-eyes just like Grace."

"No I mean it! I really saw something. It was spinning and everything!" The carpet had a bubble in it and I jammed my toe in it, squishing it flat. "I *mean* it."

She turned her eyes on me without moving her head.

"You don't believe me," I said.

"Well..."

I marched back to the pews and sat down.

"Well *I* didn't see anything," she said. "Here's the thing, maybe when you ran up the stairs you got dizzy. Or since it's so dark in here, there was a flash, you know, from outside." She sat next to me. "I mean, this isn't the *Twilight Zone*."

The elastic on my suit irritated me, so I lifted my butt to adjust it. "No," I said, "I guess not."

"Well don't feel bad. Lots of kids think they see stuff. I thought I saw the tooth fairy once, with ballet slippers and everything. The tooth fairy, Santa Claus. I believed it all, till I found out it was all a crock."

I lifted my elbow and popped her in the ribs. At the oddest times she could make me smile.

"I guess you're right." I sighed. "It was probably just the sun." We sat there, staring forward. Except for the broken pane, the window looked normal. Clean and shiny and normal.

"Grace?"

"Yeah?"

"I know you're the preacher's kid and all, but, sometimes, don't you wonder if..."

"What?"

"You know, if the whole thing with God is like that, like Santa Claus and the tooth fairy."

"You mean a crock?"

Now she popped me. "I wasn't going to say it, but yeah."

"Why? Do you?"

"Mostly. I mean, why would God let things happen—bad things? Like when my cousin got in a car crash. Why would he?"

I turned just enough to catch her expression. I'd had those thoughts plenty of times, the kind Methodists were allowed to have, but I'd never come up with a good answer and it bothered me, sometimes more than I wanted to admit. Leave it to Sandy to drive the point home.

"What happened to your cousin?"

"Killed by some jackass. Head on." She pursed her lips. "She had the best dimples you ever saw."

I heard the ladder fold outside and my parents talking.

"Don't worry," Sandy said, "I won't tell your dad. I just want to know what you think."

I adjusted my suit again. "My dad says we live in a fallen world. We're not *supposed* to understand everything. When bad things happen, maybe God has a reason we don't know."

"That's bull. What reason could there be for breaking my cousin's neck?"

"I don't know. How should I know?"

"It's bull," she said, standing. "Besides, it's what your Dad says, not you."

The window hadn't changed.

"Sandy?"

"Yeah?"

"If you don't believe, then why come to church?"

She draped a lock of hair under the tooth. "I don't know. We're friends, aren't we? And I figure it can't hurt. I mean, the first year I knew about Santa I faked it and got presents. If it turns out there's a heaven, maybe I'll get in." She smiled her Sandy smile, the one punctuated by a lock of hair. "Besides, my mom says since I started coming to church I don't cuss so damn much."

I snorted a laugh. There was a knock on the back door and we hustled up the chancel to open it. Dad was on the other side with the bucket of rags.

"How's it look?" The halo crossed my mind, and I almost told him about it, until I remembered Sandy.

"Great." I said, rising on my toes and bouncing down. "Clean and shiny like you wouldn't believe."

Chapter 16

After my mother's death, it wasn't God I obsessed about, but her letters. My mother struggled through a terminal illness to write them. She spent hour after hour on those pages. But why? To tell me her life story? To teach me about boys—or horses? The purpose remained elusive, like sunlight off the moon off the walls of my bedroom. I remember lying on my pillow at night, thinking the answer was in her letters—if only I could find them. But how? Her messenger was a thief in the night, a shadow on the breeze. I might as well capture a ghost.

I was 12 years old then and pretty much on my own when it came to the letters. Sandy listened to me, but she didn't really care, not the way I did. And Dad was no help. In almost two years since my mother's death, he hadn't come up with a single clue. He said my mother told him about the letters, but he never knew what they were about. Either that or he was lying. But since he'd counseled me against lying more times than I could count, I couldn't imagine he'd go that far.

Nobody around me showed the signs I craved: a guilty voice, shifty eyes or a telltale nervous twitch. Since the letters came on Sundays, I kept wondering if the messenger was right under my nose, somebody on staff at Good Shepherd. I went over and searched the church, every nook and cranny, and came up with nothing. It didn't surprise me. Manny was too absentminded, the janitor was AWOL half the time, and Honey couldn't keep a secret if you paid her.

I decided the only surefire answer was to catch the messenger red-handed. But how? Since school was out for the summer, I had plenty of time to come up with a plan. When Dad headed to the church one morning, I put Jimmy in front of The Cyclops and hurried to his desk beside the stairs. I shuffled through my father's papers—his marriage license, diplomas—until finally, in a bottom drawer, I found them: his old calendars. Luckily for me he kept them around as an informal record of church affairs. I grabbed the two I needed, plus the current for 1970, and sprinted to the attic.

On my stomach on the plywood floor, I flipped on the flashlight. Then, starting with the oldest calendar, I paged past the Devil's Punch Bowl, Silver Falls, and Crater Lake, returning to the day my mother died. And just like that, there it was, under the image of Multnomah Falls. A memory flashed. We'd gone hiking to the top once, when Jimmy could still ride on Dad's shoulders. I saw the bridge partway up, the way the mist coated Momma's hair and made us laugh. If the cancer was growing then, we didn't know.

The page before me was riddled with notes, for church meetings and appointments, except for the day my mother died, one of the few squares left blank. Another memory flashed. The smell of death. A rolling contraption. Men who took her and held me back when I couldn't stop screaming.

I shook it off. Six letters had come to me since then: two in the year she died, three in the next and one so far this year. The time between them was somewhere around four months, but I couldn't be sure. I hadn't started tracking the dates until the last few letters. I pulled out the middle calendar and flipped it open, then ran my finger over the pages, counting from the first date I recorded with letter number four. I had to trace several pages before I knew: the number of weeks between the fourth letter and the fifth was 17. Not 16—or four months—but 17. I double and triple-checked and got 17 every time. Then I counted from the fifth to the sixth, spilling over to the current calendar and the latest letter. 18 weeks. That was weird. I was positive an early letter had come at 16 weeks. I sat up, thumped my forehead with the flashlight. Way to go, Miss Brilliance, spot any pattern now? 16 weeks, 17 and 18. The next had to be 19! But why? Why one more week with each letter?

My forehead stung where I'd bopped it with the flashlight. Maybe the answer was simple. Maybe she figured I'd grow up over the years, grow more patient. It made sense, didn't it? That I could wait longer as I got older? Then another thought: one more week would add up over the years, stretching the letters out. Was that part of her plan? To make them last? She'd wanted them to be a presence in my life. *The closest I can get to being here*, she'd said.

The longer I sat there, the more convinced I became that 19 weeks was my answer. I slid my finger over the current calendar, counting from the latest letter forward. Two... four... six... all the way to 19. It put the arrival of the next letter in early September, as good a time as any. I even convinced Sandy, who was hardly ever convinced of anything. Then, more carefree than I'd felt in ages, I dove into summer.

In August, Grandma Carsten took Jimmy and me to her new place out in Troutdale, a vacation for Dad more than anything. We cooled off in the Sandy River (which I imagined was named for my friend) while Grandma groused about a rock concert at McIver State Park. "It's to keep the longhairs from the Legionnaires," she said, smacking her lips around a horehound candy. "And guess who's throwing it? Just go ahead and guess, just guess, any old guess—the *governor*!"

The events of that week didn't affect us much, but they sure were a sign of the times. Civil unrest, President Nixon and the Vietnam War. I remember watching it on the news: the veterans arriving downtown and the Woodstock-like scene that drew hippies the other way. The funny thing is, the plan worked, which really messed with Grandma's head. "Filthy longhairs," she said to the TV, "let the veterans at 'em I say!" For me, the whole thing was a welcome distraction. I didn't think of my mother's letters that entire week... or have a clue that the next had already arrived.

It was September before I found out, the Saturday night before the 19th Sunday. I'd become the sleuth again, scooting down the stairs to sneak past Dad as he watched the TV. I kept my eyes on the half-wall, just in case he got up, so when his head popped into the stairwell I almost peed.

"Grace," he said. "Why are you up?"

"I don't know—" I *had* peed. "...tomorrow's Sunday."

"Yes it is." He knitted his brow. I knew the look. He was trying to remember if his sermon was ready. Always the church and congregation, always God to the end of days.

"Oh," he said, "oh my word."

"What?" I stood up, a trickle of pee sluicing my leg.

"I'm sorry, Grace." He cleared his throat. "When you were at Grandma's a while back a letter came. I completely forgot." He *forgot*? How was that possible? And what was this: was he turning red?

"A letter?" I croaked.

"From your mother. I'm ashamed to admit it, but I—" he didn't finish the thought, and, sure enough, he *was* turning red. He adjusted his glasses, the rims dark against his flushed cheeks. "I don't suppose you can wait until morning? It's pretty late."

While I was at Grandma's? But that wasn't 19 weeks! A sudden notion that he'd done it on purpose set me on fire. "How could you!" I screamed. "The only thing I care about and you *forgot*?" It was the first time I yelled at my father and I went for broke. "I hate you. You hear me? I hate you!"

Half expecting him to come after me and spank my butt, I stood there shaking, my breath ragged. But he didn't come after me. Instead, he shuffled to his desk, papers rustled and a drawer closed. He was climbing the stairs now, my mother's envelope a white flag in his hand. Soon as he was close enough, I grabbed it with a savage swipe.

"I mean it," I yelled, "I hate your guts!" Then I ran to my room and slammed the door. I'd wet my pants and I didn't even care. It wasn't until I had the flashlight on that I saw the worst: the flap on the envelope was tucked inside. My father, the so-called "man of God" had read my letter—how dare him! Even *he'd* said they were for me.

My thoughts raced from him at the mailbox to where I'd been when the letter came: Grandma's house. Suddenly I despised her too. The only thing she'd said about Momma the whole time I was there was "Poor child, she was so young..." as if she'd never even grown up to be my mother. I pictured her crystal dish, the one filled with horehound candies, and me smashing it to the floor. What person in her right mind ate horehounds anyway? They smelled worse than my pee-soaked underwear.

Chapter 17

I was mad at Dad, mad at Grandma, mad at myself for missing the date. I'd have to wait for the dead of winter for the messenger again. Oh sure God, I could handle it, why not ask me to hold my breath? But what was I thinking, talking to God, when all of it was a crock, like Sandy said? When he was a farce, like dear old Dad?

I peeled off my wet underwear, tucked my nightgown around me and sat down. I started the letter and started again until, finally, I could hear her voice and, strange as it seemed, that she was happy.

Dearest Grace,

I write these letters hoping you'll look forward to them.

Oh Momma, if only you knew.

I'd like to think they make you smile.

Not at the moment, but keep trying.

You know I wish I could do more, I really do, but at least you'll hear my story and—with any luck—learn from it. That's the plan, anyway. So let me get back to it...

Fast as you can, Momma, fast as you can.

From the minute Sal mentioned the castle, I was excited about going inside, flying high just thinking about it and our conversation on the ridge. It was the first time I'd discussed art with anybody, that's for sure! When we rode into the barn and put up the tack, I wasn't ready to go home. But Sal realized the hour and said he had to get back. He acted like Dr. Rossano had a temper to match Astrid's. The two of us parted ways where the road split, one path to a cottage, the other, a castle.

We had a dinner bell on the porch that Astrid rang for meals and chores, and since I hadn't heard it, I took my jolly ol' time getting back. Chipper and I stopped by the chicken coop, and I gave the billy goat a good scratch between his horns.

Along the way I thought of the castle, imagining Sal and me riding the horses there. It wasn't like we would do such a thing, but I pictured it anyway just for fun, riding through that Garden of Eden and dismounting at the old winery, which I knew full well had been locked up for years. Still, I kept picturing it as I wandered to the cottage that day, Sal and me, as the harvest doors opened wide.

A funny feeling made me snap out of it. The kitchen door was ajar and Astrid was there, acting like she was hiding something. Since she hadn't seen me and she hated being startled, I eased the door wide and, quiet as a cottontail, slipped inside. What was she doing? It didn't look like cooking. Then I remembered. She'd spent the day up at that nursing home in Calistoga, a cleaning job she sometimes worked for extra pay. I was betting she just got home.

I tiptoed sideways until I saw what she had... the money tin! Astrid kept that old canister hidden from all of us, especially Pops, who' was likely to drink it up. He wasn't around to keep Astrid in check, and neither was Doug, so I knew I was taking a risk. If she caught me spying, there'd be hell to pay.

But I was more curious than scared, so I stayed put. Astrid's short, brown hair was ratted, but I could see the side of her face and the backs of her arms as they bounced. Was she counting money? When she lifted her hand, I caught a glimpse of something in it. It wasn't bills but something shiny. She examined it close, then wrapped it in a handkerchief and stuffed it inside. I heard the lid clank before she bent over and shoved the whole thing behind the flour sack.

That's where she kept it? I thought. Behind the flour sack? Doug and I had looked high and low for that tin but never suspected such an easy place. She shut the cabinet door and stood up. Uh-oh, I realized, now I was in for it. But instead of turning, she stepped to the refrigerator. I waited a minute, then made my move, grabbing the door and calling "Howdy!" which practically blasted her out of her shoes. But in the next second I knew I'd fooled her because her lips weren't pinched. She only cursed me for startling her while I sang "Sorry-sorry-sorry" and ran off down the hall.

In my room, I plopped on the bed. What was she hiding? I knew her orders well enough. Don't touch that tin. Not ever. But I was curious as our calico cat to peek inside. It wasn't the money. I knew we needed it for expenses. I just wanted to see what was in there.

I got my chance that same night after dinner. While I filled the kitchen sink to do dishes, my parents went out to the porch. Doug was in town, spending the money he'd earned raising a beef calf. I figured if I moved fast enough, I could get a look in that tin before anybody was the wiser. When the soap bubbles rose over the sink and I could smell Pops' cigarette, I pushed my wrist past the flour sack and, sure enough, found the tin.

Then my nerves got the best of me. Astrid was so close. The last thing I needed was to get caught. I stepped into the living room and listened at the open door. They were still on the porch so I took a breath and tiptoed back to the kitchen. I tried the lid, but it was tight as a bottle cap. I yanked and it barely budged. When I yanked again, it flew, crashing like a cymbal across the floor.

"What the hell, Sharon," Astrid hollered from the porch, "you tearin' up the damn kitchen?" Pardon the language,

Grace, but this was how Astrid talked, how I learned it myself. I scrambled for the lid and hollered back, "No-o!" while I listened for the murmur of her shoes. I'll never forget the sound of those shoes, Grace, it was enough to make your hair stand.

I grabbed the lid and called out, "It's okay, nothing broke!" But I was shaking, afraid she'd recognize the sound any minute and come barreling. "Well, it god-damn-well better not have," she said. She wasn't in hot pursuit, at least not yet.

I went back to the counter, planning to shove the lid on and forget the whole thing, but I peeked in, only a second and couldn't resist. Shaking like I was already caught, I fished inside. There were a few bills, 5's and 1's, and beneath them a bed of coins. I felt my way, trying to keep the coins quiet until I found what I was looking for: the handkerchief, wrapped in a ball and tied in a knot.

I picked at it until the knot came loose. There was a monogram on the hanky, an A and something else. It could've been Astrid's, but I was too nervous to look for long. The cloth opened and there it was, blinking at me: a ring with a huge splash of diamonds, so beautiful and so out of place in our tiny kitchen. One big stone, almost as big as Mrs. Rossano's, sparkled from the center with smaller diamonds at its sides.

Was it some kind of inheritance? Astrid said when folks died their relatives got their stuff. Had that happened to us? Then I realized we didn't have relatives who could own a ring like that. Astrid's side was ham-hock poor, Grapes of Wrath Okies who came out of the Dust Bowl. She talked about it often enough, as if practically starving to death was something to brag about. And Pops' folks weren't too much better off.

Oh but that ring was pretty. I slipped it on. It was loose, but not by much, so it had to be too small for Astrid. I held my hand under the sink light for a better look. The band was old, but solid, and the diamonds made rainbows on the kitchen wall. I turned it this way and that to make the rainbows do a dance.

Just then I heard a chair scrape and remembered where I was. I whipped the ring off and rolled it in the hanky. Unable to remember if there'd been one knot or two, I tied one and slipped it in the tin. The front door creaked and footsteps murmured as I shoved the lid on. Astrid's footsteps, sure enough. I knew I couldn't get the tin behind the floor sack quick enough, so I stuffed the whole thing in the quickest place, the refrigerator.

"What the hell was all that noise?" she said at my back. I forced myself to slow down. "Nothing," I told her, "I dropped a pan is all." In my hand was the pitcher of milk and I clicked the fridge door closed. Don't look inside, I said to myself, whatever you do, Astrid, don't look in the fridge. I thought of the custard then and my blood went cold. Astrid was big on custard, from Jersey's cream and fresh eggs. Is that what she was after?

I felt heat at my back now—and Pops was way out on the porch. "You just had milk with dinner, Cauliflower," she said, "You a bottomless pit?" I reached for a glass, saying "I guess so." The shoes murmured again until her voice was at my neck. "You guess so?" She stood there, breathing at my neck, while I poured, watching my aim, or aiming at me, I wasn't sure which. It was all I could do to keep from spilling that milk. "You gotta dirty up a whole 'nother glass?" She didn't really want an answer, so I waited, convinced she would head for the fridge next and I'd be toast.

"You better get on those dishes," she said, "slow as you are." And sure enough, here came the murmur. But I was in luck, she was headed down the hall! The second I heard the bathroom door, I jumped like lightning and had the tin back in its place lickety-split. It took ten times longer for my heart to calm down.

Later that night, when I crawled in bed, Doug was still out, and I was glad for the solitude. I had so much to think about. I could see the castle towers outside my window, and I thought about going inside. I thought about the sketches I'd show Sal and the artwork he'd show me. And I thought of that strange and beautiful ring tucked away in our kitchen. I figured it would stick around, that I could rifle through the money tin any old time to try it on. Hah! That's what I figured, anyway.

But it must be odd, Grace, to hear me go on like this. I get wrapped up in the details, I'm afraid. If Georgia was here, she'd *say I'm running myself ragged with all this writing. And here's what I'd say back: just how can I tell my story without the details? I wouldn't know, sweetheart, I wouldn't know.*

My love till next time,
Momma

It *was* odd, I thought, lowering the pages to my lap. What did any of it have to do with me? I relaxed my grip on the flashlight and leaned back. The ring, for example. I'd never seen it, and the way she talked, I never would.

I thought of my mother's wedding band then with its small dot for a diamond, and it struck me, what had happened to *it?* Was it something *I* should inherit? I considered asking my father, leaving the attic to head downstairs, until I remembered that he'd read the letter and how much I hated him and all. Didn't it figure? Just when I needed him?

I shined the flashlight on the ceiling and drew circles over the two-by-fours. On the other hand, I'd already bawled him out, what was the difference? I pushed open the midget door and stuck my head through. The TV was on in the living room: the whoop-whoop of helicopters.

I went down and there he was, same as usual. It was Vietnam he was watching this time, on the news. Tattered camouflage, blood and bandages. I was sick to death of looking at it. Even the church had been wounded by it, the umbrella now ironically known as *United* Methodist. The General Conference had called for withdrawal from the war two years earlier, and congregations had divided over it. Some even split for good. But not ours. Strange as it seems, my father's grief had held us together. He watched Vietnam with the same eyes that watched the TV, and it made my blood boil.

"Dad?" I moved closer and crossed my arms, but he only sat there with his Bible.

"Dad!" He didn't jump; he hardly heard me anymore.

"Hmm?" Injured soldiers filled the screen, some on stretchers, one riding piggyback to a waiting helicopter. My father's eyes traveled to me, so tired behind his lenses, I almost felt sorry for him. Until I remembered how I hated him.

"The ring in Momma's letter," I said, "Do you know what it's about?"

He took a breath. "'Fraid not." He didn't deny he'd read it. Didn't even try. His eyes returned to the TV, where a band of hippies taunted police, and suddenly I wished Grandma were there so I could watch her girdle twist up in a knot.

"But didn't Momma ever talk about it? She must have talked about it."

"I'm afraid not."

"And you don't know whose it was or *anything?*"

"Sorry to say, I don't."

"But why would she bring it up? Why would she even—"

"My guess, Grace? It's really more about her mother."

"What *about* her mother?"

"I don't know. And what's the point of guessing? Best you can do, in my opinion, is wait for another letter."

Yeah, and you better not touch it, I thought. The TV had returned to Nam, where the helicopter, with its bloody cargo, lifted off.

"Oh and Dad."

"Hmm?"

"What about Momma's ring, *her* wedding band? What happened to it, you know—after?"

He sighed. "It's still with her, Grace." In the ground, he meant. "I didn't have the heart to take it off."

Great. I stared at his profile, the crooked nose, the smudged lenses. What had my mother seen in him? What?

Without another word, I left his side and went upstairs, throwing myself on the bed. From that night on, when I pictured my mother's ghost at our mailbox, her wedding ring—the one my father didn't have the heart to take off—was there on her finger.

Chapter 18

The summer of '66 was as endless as summers get. Part of it I spent in the sanctuary, bursting through the doors like I had with Sandy, or tiptoeing at a new angle toward the stained glass. But I never did see another halo, or whatever it was that had buckled my knees. With our first good rain, Momma convinced Dad to patch the hole with plastic, and that ended that.

Two things happened that fall worth repeating: My mother's beloved Georgia first came to us, and I entered the third grade in my new school, the same school Sandy had known all her life. The building was a maze of hallways, but not completely awful, except that I'd landed in the same third grade class as Butte McEgan. His alias at school was no surprise: *The Hawker*. I sat two rows ahead of him and, when he cleared his throat, tried not to flinch. Sandy was in the classroom across the hall and couldn't decide whether her luck was good or rotten. She had a Butte-free class, but the two of us were split up. Plus her teacher was an old goat, while I got the new recruit, Mrs. Potts. "Does she *have* to be so pretty and nice?" Sandy whined.

I learned three things about Butte that fall: one, he considered my home-sewn clothes "prissy threads;" two, he had no problem eating from our discarded lunch trays; and three, foul as he was, he would never outdo his sister, because at Pardee Elementary, Apple McEgan was the reigning bully. Word was she'd steal your lunch money if you so much as looked at her. I never saw her do it myself, but that was beside the point. She was sickly-looking and reeked of mildew. When Apple came near me on the playground, I struck up a conversation with Mrs. Potts: what she thought of the new math or when she and her husband would make a baby. Apple was a low-life; what was the point in talking to her?

Luckily for me, my school days zipped by.

It was sometime in early fall, about the time we got our third-grade Bibles, that Georgia came on the scene. She was looking for the church, I remember, though it wasn't a Sunday. It was after school and Sandy and I were in the yard, taking turns on the rope swing. I saw her green Ford first, an older Fairlane, as it rolled under the Tree of Heaven. Sandy didn't notice a thing. She was upside-down on the swing, her dress flipped and her butt to the sky, her panties as orange as Orange Crush. I gave her a spin and she twirled, the Orange Crush going round and round.

"Psst!" I said when the car door opened, but Sandy stayed under the dress.

A woman got out, a Negro woman, and I quit pushing the swing. I hadn't seen that in the neighborhood before. What the good Lord has in mind, as Dad would say.

"Psst," I tried again.

"Good afternoon ladies," she said. She had a southern accent, which made afternoon sound like aftahnoon. "Maybe you can help me." I slapped Sandy's butt and she somersaulted to the grass, her blood-filled head as bright as the underpants.

"Huh!" Sandy said.

The woman was square-shouldered and tall, and wore her hair in an Afro the size of a kickball. In her hand she had a newspaper, neatly folded.

"Ah'm wonderin'—" she consulted the print "—if Ah found the right place."

Suddenly I knew why she'd come: the job! Good Shepherd's janitor had quit the month before, to the relief of the church, and Honey had put an ad in the classifieds. It was hard to forget with her running around all the time yapping about it. "A quality custodian is reliable and on-time," she'd said, "hard-working and ship-shape!" She hadn't mentioned black or female. While Honey never dared anything blatantly bigoted, she talked about Negroes and their neighborhoods like there was no need to say more. Plus she'd vowed to find the best *man* for the janitor's job, which had always been held by a man. At the moment, she was inside the church, unaware of this Negro woman with the kickball Afro.

"You looking for the janitor's job?" I asked.

"Matter of fact, Ah am. The paper only had an address."

"Well you found it, all right. It's here at the church."

"So you say."

"She's the preacher's kid, so she should know," Sandy added in her best little-brat tone.

"Ah grew up with a preacher's kid and it ain't easy to live up to."

I smiled, figuring her for smart right away.

"Ah'm Miss Johnson. Georgia Johnson," she said, showing beautiful white teeth with a sliver of a gap in the front. "But call me Georgia if you don't mind." "Georgia" came out like "Joe-ja" and "Mind" like "mine," but the sound was pleasant. She put out her hand and I shook it, the first black hand I'd ever touched.

"I don't mind," I said. "I'm Grace, and this is my friend Sandy."

"Oh yes, Sandy with the colorful bloomers." She laughed while Sandy curled her lip. "Would you mind showing me inside?" She said to me.

"Not at all," I told her, feeling quite proper.

When Georgia entered the office, my stomach went tight. It was the way Honey looked up, like she couldn't decide whether to grab the valuables or bolt for the door. "C-can I h-help you?" she said, sounding more like Manny than herself.

"Ah hope so." Georgia said, stepping to the desk. She explained why she was there and extended a hand over Honey's desk. I had to give the woman credit. She waited a long time for Honey to shake it.

"I just don't know," Honey said, running her fingers over her dress. "You see, the pastor isn't in right now. In fact, he's out, and I—"

"Is there an application for the position?" Her voice was gentle but firm. "Ah could fill it out now and come back later to meet The Reverend." When Honey didn't answer, she withdrew an envelope from the folds of the newspaper. "These here are letters of reference. Ah'm part-time at a commercial laundry and Ah have plenty of experience with janitorial—"

"Yes, ma'am, but the pastor isn't in at present and—"

"I got it!" I jumped forward. "I'll get Momma!" And I ran out fast, before Honey could object.

The truth is, I couldn't be sure of my mother's reaction to Georgia, though I sure hoped it would beat Honey's. There were plenty of things about this woman to like: the kickball Afro, the southern drawl, but best of all, she wasn't the least bit intimidated by Honey. When I came back with Momma in tow, Honey was in a lather; we could hear her clear from the entry.

"...not a PIECE OF CAKE," she was saying as we hurried down the hall. "It's a LARGE CHURCH with bathrooms upstairs AND down."

"Ah understand." Georgia was saying, "but Ah guarantee you Mrs. Martin that Ah'm perfectly capable—"

"Hello there," Momma broke in, prompting a look from Honey of pure relief like I'd never seen. Momma set Jimmy on his feet, and without hesitation held her hands out to Georgia. "Thank you for coming."

"Don't pay this no never mind," Georgia said, taking her hands, "but you look more like the preacher's daughter than the preacher's wife."

Momma laughed. "I consider that a compliment. Have you seen the church yet?"

"Just the entry to here."

"Good. I'll show you around." She glanced at Honey whose lips had gone white with anger. "Then Honey can get back to her work."

Outside the office, with the door closed, Georgia whispered. "Ah owe you my life!" And the two women shared a quiet laugh. They were near opposite in appearance, tall and dark, petite and blonde, but clearly at ease in each other's presence. By the time they reached the sanctuary, they were trading childhood stories, Momma's from California, and Georgia's from the state she was named for. Sandy and I listened with fascination: Momma was sprayed by a skunk once. 'Possum ain't bad if you're hungry enough.

"You ate 'possum?" Momma asked, her eyes wide.

"Only when we had to!" Momma gave Georgia a small slap to the arm. I hadn't seen her so relaxed in weeks. The two of them kept talking as they continued down the hall, Georgia explaining how she left the South when she was 20.

"Ah was chasing a man, of all things. It's hard to believe that was eight years ago."

"Did you catch him?"

"Pard'n me?"

"Are you married?"

"Oh," she laughed. "Yes. Ah mean Ah was, till he learned Ah couldn't have kids. Soon as money got tight, he ran like his feet were on fire and his butt catchin'."

Momma squealed, then threw a hand over her mouth. "Oh I'm sorry, that's not funny."

"Honey child, don't be! That was ages ago." She flicked her wrist. "Besides, my mother and sister moved up here, and Ah'm an aunt five times over." Her feet slowed, "Ah do miss the South though. Ah miss the country."

"I know exactly what you mean," Momma said.

They went into the sanctuary next, as Sandy and Jimmy and I following behind.

"How long you been hurtin' for a janitor?" Georgia asked, running a hand over the back of a pew.

"If you count the time the last one was here, *years*." They laughed again, then stopped in the center aisle and leaned on opposite pews.

"If you ask me, God's house deserves better." Georgia brushed the dust off her hands.

"You a Christian, Miss Johnson?"

"Please—" her eyes flicked to Sandy "—call me Georgia. And, yes. Ah'm Christian as they come, down at New Hope Baptist every Sunday. Lord Almighty, isn't that beautiful?" It was the stained glass she meant, and I started, wondering if she'd seen something. But the glass only shined in its usual way.

"It hasn't been too long since *it* was cleaned," Momma said.

From the sanctuary our little troupe traveled back down the

hall to the women's restroom. When we stepped inside, a foul odor coiled around us.

"Seems to me," Georgia said, fanning the air, "this here needs help right quick." The smell itself wasn't a surprise, but until that moment I hadn't noticed the sinks and countertops, nowhere near "Godly" when you got down to it.

"Honey and I trade off," Momma said, "but we haven't kept up. She's got the office work and I... well, I've got Jimmy."

At the moment, he was crawling under the cabinets. "Hallelujah to that," Georgia said. Momma grabbed the seat of his pants and pulled him out, but he fussed, so Georgia put him to work, daring him to duck under a stall door. There were two in the bathroom and this one had a sign that read "Out of Order."

"Now give that door a pull," Georgia said after he'd gone under. The door swung open and Jimmy stood there with his baby-toothed grin.

"So, what's the problem?" Georgia said, patting Jimmy as she made her way back to the toilet.

"Not sure. Out janitor couldn't get the right part. It's been on the fritz for weeks."

Georgia jiggled the handle. "It don't look plugged."

"You should see the line in here on Sundays. Honey's about pulled her hair out."

"God knows we wouldn't want that." She lifted the back off the toilet and looked around. "Grace?" she called and I hopped forward, impressed she'd remembered my name.

"Be a peach and run out by the coat rack for that wire hanger on the floor." Sandy and I hurried out and, just as she'd said, a hanger had fallen from the coat rack. I snatched it up before Sandy could.

"This it?" I said, hurrying back.

"Sho 'nuff." Georgia was quick, twisting the hanger till it came open, then bending a piece back and forth. "You start worrying this wire enough, you can feel it." She let us touch it where it was hot before she proceeded to break it in two. With the shorter end she made some sort of contraption, looped and angled. I wondered what hole she would poke it in until the whole thing disappeared inside the tank. A minute later she pushed the handle and the water roared down.

    "Easy as pie," she said.

    "Sho 'nuff," Momma said, and they laughed like old friends.

    Before the month was up, Momma had fixed Georgia's position as part-time janitor at Good Shepherd, though it didn't happen without a fight. Word went around that a Negro woman wanted the job, and questions started flying about her background. Was she trustworthy? How did we know? And why should we hire from her neighborhood when there were applicants in our own? All of this riled my mother until she came up with a plan. It was a brilliant move: she hijacked all the applications from Honey's desk and presented them to our lily-white hiring committee with the names and addresses covered in white out. There was no way to tell who was who.

    "This, I believe, is how Jesus would do it," she said, passing the pages out.

    Based solely on work experience, Georgia Johnson was a shoe-in. Half the committee cheerfully proceeded, while the other half bristled over Momma's sleight of hand. Chalk up another for the preacher's wife.

    In the end, there was nothing to do but hire Georgia. Most who backed the decision considered it a good deed done for a local Negro. But Momma knew better and so did I. We were lucky to have her. As for Honey, against her own better judgment, she held her tongue. After weeks of frustration with the women's bathroom, she couldn't argue with a working toilet.

Chapter 19

I still remember the way it felt, wanting to get inside the messenger's head. Days, weeks, *months* passed with me trying to guess the next delivery. I was determined to figure it out, but more than anything, I wouldn't be fooled again, not the older, wiser me. Next time I'd be ready. I'd aim my flashlight at the messenger's face if that's what it took. I had studied the envelopes plenty of times, staring at those heavy pencil marks: so far, the numbers one through seven. It sure didn't look like a ghost's writing. What ghost could push a pencil that hard? Everywhere I went I peeked over shoulders for writing styles. But people don't run around writing numerals very much.

I considered my mother's friends. Georgia Johnson was top of the list, but she'd been overwhelmed with the care of her own mother, which is why I hadn't seen her in so long. Several members of Good Shepherd came to mind next: Mack Glenn from the church council who'd repaired her sewing machine more than once; Tracy Beck, the Trustee, who considered her profanity endearing; and Eloise Krantz, who shared her Sunday school duties. Except... hadn't Eloise and my mother argued—a few times? I sighed. Eloise didn't seem right. In fact, none of them seemed right. There wasn't a shifty eye or nervous twitch in the bunch.

I thought about candidates outside the church. Sandy's parents, for one, down the street. But Sandy swore there were no letters in her house: she'd searched high and low and only come up with her father's Playboy magazines, the ones we paged through with gumball eyes. I would have bet my piggy bank my mother hadn't chosen the Shelbys.

Then who? I stood at the window and scanned Pardee Street, from the farthest house, coming nearer, finally ending at Mrs. Crookshank's. Momma and I sometimes took the old woman grocery shopping. Come to think of it, Mrs. Crookshank's little bungalow was the perfect location for the letters, wasn't it, right across the street? I almost ran over there that second until I remembered her severe hunchback, how she hobbled around like Quasimodo. In the dark, Pardee Street would be a moonscape. Mrs. Crookshank would fall on her face.

I hated to admit it, but I was stumped. Without some other clue, I'd have to wait for the next stakeout—clear to Christmas! I no longer believed in Santa, but somebody was coming, and I vowed to put a face on him if it killed me. This time I'd cover all possible drops: 16 weeks, 17, 18, whatever it took.

I won't bother recounting the first attempt, since nothing happened. And the following weekend, the last before Christmas, started the same way: Saturday night was a bust. But the next morning, on the 17th Sunday, things got interesting. When my alarm clattered in the dark I sat up, a rash of goose bumps down both arms. The room wasn't cold, had I sensed something? I grabbed the flashlight and crept to the landing. The stairwell was oily dark, like a tunnel through a black hole. I flipped on the flashlight, pointed it low and started slowly down the steps. My plan was to check the mailbox, then head to the kitchen to fix cinnamon toast. A sugary slice would keep me occupied in the dark. Partway down the stairs, I shined the flashlight to my left, where the wall ended. No one at Dad's desk or in the living room. The recliner looked lonesome and so did the Christmas tree. I kept going to the bottom, finally swinging the beam to the dining room. The Formica tabletop shined back. Three steps later I had the door open and my hand on the mailbox. A quick yelp showed an empty box, nothing more. Something moved in the yard, and I spun around. Shadows lurked, the grass crawled, but no eyes looked back. Down the street, Christmas lights twinkled through the trees.

I went inside and soft-stepped to the back of the house where I could hear Dad's breathing, steady and even. When I circled around, toward the kitchen, a dull thump stopped me cold. *Thump* it sounded again. It was coming from outside. On windy days, an arborvitae sometimes blew against the gutter, but it didn't sound quite like that. When the silence continued, I inched forward until my toes hit the cold Linoleum and everything went abuzz! I shot to the wall light—ready to scream—but it was only the refrigerator humming to life. *Okay, Miss Brilliance, cool your jets.* I decided to leave the light on, just for a bit, to calm my nerves and make my toast. Not a minute later, as I sunk a slice of bread in the toaster, I heard it: that squeal-like-no-other from our mailbox.

Someone had lifted the lid.

Everything in me urged *run and look*. But I couldn't. In the moment it counted, my muscles had petrified. *Go!* I screamed inside. But I could no more make a move to the door than the slice of bread sweating in the toaster. Was that the chimes I heard now? *Hurry go!* And still I stood, stiff as a mannequin, picturing wafting forms and paper-thin ghosts at our door.

Suddenly the thought of the back door lifted the hair on my neck. It was only a few feet behind me, in the alcove adjoining the kitchen. I eased around—was it locked?—and made a run for it, shoving the lock in when I got there. Then I saw it through the alcove window, a figure on the back lawn!

I jumped away to whip off the light, then slipped back, close to the glass. There it was—the figure again—between the parsonage and church. Was it coming toward me or going away? My heart pounded against my nightgown as I tried to decide. I caught the angle of a leg then and knew it was leaving, the knees pumping in jerking rhythm in the shadows behind the church. My mother's messenger was no ghost. It moved with the weight of the living and ran like a man. I tracked him a few seconds longer as he crossed the churchyard toward the street. Was something familiar about him? But he disappeared too fast. Oh, why couldn't I have gone to the porch when I had the chance? I shoved my fingers into my hair and pulled.

In the next breath, I was flying, flipping on lights as I went. When I got to the front door, I yanked it open. The chimes sang softly on a night with no wind, an eerie lullaby. There was nothing on the walkway, not even the Sunday paper, but the mailbox was open and there it was, sure as the figure in the yard, another letter. I grabbed it and shut the door, locking it as I did in one swift motion. The envelope was Momma's, sure enough, with the same writing front and center: *Grace*. Had it been in the man's coat, or did I imagine it felt warm?

Chapter 20

Still shaking—and mad at myself for being scared—I wedged the flashlight under my arm and opened the envelope. As I hurried up the stairs, a small pop came from the kitchen: my toast. Had it all happened that fast? More anxious now than hungry, I continued up the stairs, trying to focus on my mother's voice.

Hello Grace,

If only I had your energy, the way you jiggle the mattress when you come sit with me.

I remembered sitting at the edge of her bed, and it helped.

I can barely keep this pen moving, let alone jiggle something. One day I'm fighting the good fight and the next I'm down again. But I won't trouble you with that. Today's a good day, so I'm hunkered down to write again. At the moment, I hardly remember where I left off. It's these pills, I think, they affect my head. Were we still in that summer I was 14?

I skipped the attic and crawled in my bed. *Yes, I think so, Momma.*

Sure, I remember... the promise of the castle and the ring in the money tin. Not long after Sal Rossano talked about it, he did take me inside Chateau Genevieve.

I knew it...

It was dark and cool in there, compared to the sun off the swimming pool. For a minute, I couldn't see, and then the room took shape. "We call it the Great Room," he said, and I could see why, it was big enough to swallow three whole cottages the size we lived in. Fancy fixtures dotted the walls and there was a flickering fire at the big hearth to our right, but most of the light came from the arched windows at front, the ones you could see from the grounds outside.

I waited, not sure what to do, until Sal motioned me in. He said his mother was in town, and his father on call in the city, so we had the place to ourselves. When I took a few steps there was a dull echo, reminding me of the shoes on my feet. I'd worn the periwinkle dress from Hazel Clayton and my old saddle shoes were a sorry match for it.

The bulk of the room was open space, with sitting areas here and there. But the most eye-catching feature was the fireplace, almost as tall as I was. "Do you always have a fire in there?" I asked, and he said, "Hardly ever. I built it because you were coming." I won't pretend that didn't make me feel special, Grace.

Sal nodded toward the hearth and the painting over the mantle. It was a magical scene of a valley and snowy mountains. "It's the best piece of art in the chateau," he said, "a Thomas Cole." He explained how his mother found it for practically nothing, that she'd studied Art History. Of course I'd never heard of Thomas Cole, Grace. Heck, I'd hardly heard of any artists back then.

"Go ahead," he said, "see what you think." I went closer and decided it was dreamy and sweet, what I know now as the romantic style. Cole's skill was amazing, from the spires of the mountains to the tiniest lines on every leaf.

"Not bad, huh?" Sal asked. "Not bad?" I answered, "It's like a dream!" I thought of my own pencil drawings then and heard

Astrid call them a waste of time. "I could never paint something like that," I told Sal. But he flashed his coyote grin. "Never say never, and besides from what I've seen, you could do better." I studied his face. Did he mean it? The day before, I'd showed him some sketches, but I wasn't sure what he'd seen in them.

"You have a great eye for composition, Sharon," he said, like he'd heard my thoughts. I didn't exactly know what composition meant, Grace, but it sounded good. At the hearth, Sal reached up and brushed a finger over the painting. "It's oil," he told me, "my mother's favorite." "You can touch it?" I asked. He looked like a scoundrel then, like the coyote behind the grin. He said his mother wouldn't approve, but he did anyway. I giggled at his naughty streak and placed a finger where his had been. The surface was smooth and cool.

"Wait until you get a look at the impressionists,' he told me while he stoked the fire. "You'll think you stepped into another world." Sal gestured to a nearby couch where the book sat and said he'd get us Cokes from the kitchen. Cokes, Grace! It was a rare treat for a girl raised on raw milk.

When he came back, he shook his head that I hadn't touched the book, then sat next to me and flipped it open. I was surprised, right away, at the very first print, like nothing I'd seen. Up close, it was a mess of brush strokes, but held back, completely stunning, a dark lake under a ruby sun. Fat strokes of red kicked up waves on the water.

Sal handed me a Coke and I took a sip, savoring the sweet burn. More lake scenes came next, with bright fishing boats and old bridges, the strokes thick and quick. I soaked it all in, wishing I had paints to try it myself. There was so much freedom in the style, they made the painting over the mantle look like a photograph.

Sal turned some pages of text, then more art when I stopped him, struck by a girl in a sea of flowers, so charming. "It's a Monet," Sal said. "Monet," I repeated. Even the name sounded beautiful. Sal said he'd done the water lilies on the cover too.

August Renoir came next, a garden party, then Cezanne

and Manet. "There's a woman artist in here too," Sal said, finding the page, "Mary Cassatt. Some of them painted together at Montmartre." "Montmartre?" I asked, and he explained it was a place in Paris where he'd been once. I looked at this boy sitting next to me, who'd traveled to cities I could only dream of: Paris, France! "You'll go one day," he told me. But I didn't think so, Grace, not even then.

The longer we paged through the prints, a restaurant scene, a bleak cityscape, the closer I came to understanding them. The style, I mean. It was a Degas that did it, the view on stage at the ballet. "It's like you can feel it," I told Sal, "the way it was to be there." His dark eyes lit up. "Exactly! It's why they're called Impressionists, and aren't you clever to figure it out?" Well, I'd never been called clever, Grace, and it overwhelmed me. I'm almost embarrassed to admit it, but with the intensity of the paintings and the castle and Sal's words, I started to cry.

"I didn't mean to upset you," he said. I shook my head and explained I wasn't upset, but overwhelmed. It was a minute before he spoke. "I want to ask you something, Sharon, since you're an artist." His face was close to mine. "If you painted this scene, of the two of us here, how would it feel?" I pictured it then, just for a minute before blurting it out, "Wonderful!" and Sal's laugh echoed off the castle walls.

We'd been talking and sipping our Cokes for an hour or so when the front door opened and Mrs. Rossano's heals clicked into the room. Sal stood and so did I. "Oh, hello Sharon," she said, clearly surprised to see me there.

"Howdy-do and hello," I said, always sounding like an idiot around her. Mrs. Rossano was refined and beautiful, a Northern Italian with light eyes, not to mention college educated, a rare creature in my world. All at once I felt ridiculous, periwinkle dress or not, like I ought to be on my knees washing the floor. Sal told her he brought me by to see her Art History book, that I was very good at drawing. "You should see."

"Oh?" Mrs. Rossano pulled off the gloves she'd worn into town. "That's a lovely dress, Sharon," she said. I could tell she wondered where I got it, but she didn't ask and I didn't offer. She wanted to know how my mother was since she hadn't seen her all day. Then her eyes went to the coke in my hand and I nearly set it on the table until I caught myself and found a coaster. "Thanks," I told her—about the dress—then folded my hands.

"The last I saw Astrid," I added, "she was up checking the water table at the springhouse since the sprinklers were on all morning." While I waited for her to answer, I studied my shoes, so warped and scuffed, I wanted them to disappear. She never did answer, so I said, "I guess I ought to get back." Her lips smiled when I walked past her, but not her eyes. She said, "It's lovely to see you" as I passed out of those stony walls.

The next day Astrid found out I'd been at the castle and hit the roof. She was on me like a badger when I came in from chores, would've chewed me to a pulp if Doug hadn't gotten between us. "I don't believe it!" She bellowed, coming at me. "Cavorting around Chateau Genevieve like yer somethin' else. Know yer place girl!" She was livid, out for blood. I ran to the bedroom as Doug held her off.

"Havin' Co-colas with the owner's boy?" she fumed. "Next, you'll be lounging by the goddamn pool instead of cleaning it!" Her fists were clenched as we pushed the door shut and got the dresser against it. Her fury wasn't for me alone. She was mad at Doug too. "If we lose this place 'cause of that idiot sister of yours," she screamed, "You'll both be on your own, yeh hear?"

When she finally gave up pounding, Doug whispered to me what I'd missed. That same morning after I left the house for the chicken coop, a police officer came. "Police officer?" I asked. Doug kept his voice down. "It was something about that rest home in Calistoga. Some jewelry gone missing." My mind shot to the ring. "Did he come inside?"

"Yeah," Doug said, "he asked about some dates while Astrid practically begged him not to trouble the Rossanos." The whole time Doug filled me in, I kept picturing that money tin behind the flour sack. When he finished, I started to tell him about it but he cut me off. "What's the money tin got to do with it?" I *explained how I'd stumbled on Astrid putting a diamond ring in that tin. "It'd knock your eyes out." It only took him a second before he insisted on seeing it. I agreed, but made him promise first not to take anything from that tin, not one red cent. "I'm not nuts!" he said. "She's probably memorized every date on every penny."*

Then the two of us hopped out the bedroom window. "By the way," he said when we hit the ground, "if I were you, Sharon, I'd keep my distance from Sal Rossano—or leastwise, don't get caught." I looked him over and nodded. Doug could be a pest sometimes, but against Astrid we were allies.

Later that night, we did as planned and got the money tin out, but the ring was gone. In its place was a stack of bills, hundred-dollar bills. It had only been about a week since I'd seen the ring. "She must've pawned it for the cash," Doug said. "I bet she stole it off some ol' lady." "You really think Astrid would do that?" I wondered. But the minute I said it, I knew he was right. "It probably wasn't the first time either," he added.

Hard as it was to take, Grace, that Astrid was a thief, it all made sense with what came later, her obsession with money, no matter what it cost the rest of us.

What do you mean, Momma?

Now, sweetheart, I'm so drained out I'll have to finish here for today...

Not yet!

I'll be lucky, at this point, if I can sign my name.

My love,
Momma

I dropped the letter. Too soon. Always too soon.

At least I knew this: the ring *was* about Astrid like Dad guessed. She was a thief—on top of being mean. Great, I thought, since her blood dirtied my veins. But why was my mother telling me now, and what was the cost to "the rest of us"?

I went back to the first page, her trip to the castle and the art. Then a memory crowded my mind. It was from the parsonage, around the time my mother first got sick. I went looking for her one afternoon and found her sitting on her bed. Beside her on the bedcover was a leather case I'd never seen, expensive-looking, about the size of a briefcase. She was trailing her fingers over it, absentmindedly, when I came in.

"Hi Momma." I had the weirdest feeling we weren't alone in the room. But I looked around, and nobody else was there.

"Oh—Grace," she said. "I didn't hear you." She slid the case to her lap, and I got a whiff of the leather, earthy and nice. She'd enrolled in a watercolor class, she said, something she'd been wanting to do for a long time. I didn't understand until she opened the clasps. Elegant brushes and tubes of paint were lined up in that case.

"A paint set! Where'd you get it?" It was beautiful, sleek and expensive, but I could tell it wasn't new. The charcoal pencils were well worn and several of the tubes had dried paint on their caps.

"Oh this? I've had it since I was a girl." She coughed, what we all assumed was only a cold.

I reached in and picked up a tube of bright yellow. "Can I paint something? Can I? Can I?"

"Maybe later, sweetheart. I should get going. My class starts in a little while." She took the paint tube, a little too quickly I thought, and closed the case. Fancy letters were stamped in the leather, the letters SLP.

"What does that mean?" I asked, touching them.

She pulled the case away and went to the closet. "Just my maiden name, silly: Sharon Louise Peterson. Monograms were popular in those days."

"Oh."

She looked tired, a bit pale, and coughed again.

"Where'd you get it?"

"It was a gift, Grace, a long time ago."

"From who?"

"Nobody really, just a friend."

I didn't press her and it was all she said.

As I folded the letter and tucked it back in its envelope, I pictured that case and the smell of the leather drifted back. Why had my mother been so secretive about it? Then I realized, shouldn't that case still be somewhere in the house?

Chapter 21

I always knew my mother liked art, the way she sketched the world around her. Sometimes she'd take Jimmy and me to the Portland Art Museum and stand for long stretches with her lips parted as we put scuff marks on the floor at her feet. What I didn't realize then was her talent for it.

The first I recognized this was an unlikely place: the lawn between Good Shepherd and the parsonage. We'd been in Portland about a year by then. It was 1967, a late-June morning and we had two rows of tables set up in the yard. Dad and Manny had lugged them and some chairs from the church basement because my mother had asked. Those two would have emptied the church if she'd asked. The tables were covered in Good Shepherd's art supplies—paper and pencils, brushes and paints—and surrounded by children there for Vacation Bible School, our summer day camp.

The theme that year was Momma's idea, from the book of Romans: "so we, though many, are one body in Christ…" We would demonstrate the concept of "many," my mother explained, by painting portraits of each other. There to help her were Eloise, our Sunday school teacher, plus Honey and Georgia, who naturally drifted to opposite tables.

My mother stood at the head of one row, near Sandy and me, with a dozen small bottles lined up at her hips. She had paints to match everybody's hair. "Your skin too—or as close as I could get."

Georgia stiffened when she heard this, and came over to stand beside her. "You got somethin' in there to match me?"

"You mean black?" The way Momma fidgeted made my insides squirm. "Sure, there's black in here somewhere. Ri-ight... here." And she held it up.

Georgia blew a raspberry. "Let's just see." Then she screwed off the top and swiped the paint across her forearm. It was asphalt goo against milk chocolate.

"Does *that*," she said, "look right to you?"

"I guess you're not exactly *black*," Momma said. "How about this?" Next to the asphalt went a smear that virtually glowed.

"Well, kiss my griddle!" Georgia said and the children squealed.

"Not white either?" Momma asked. "Then how about this?" She held out a bottle of green and the table shrieked. What we witnessed in the next two minutes made Honey fume: Georgia flinging colors as the whole lawn came to life. Her arm was a mess of paints, with nothing close to the tone of her skin. Finally, just one bottle remained. Georgia sniffed it and sneezed, slapping the big gloppy mess over Momma's apron. There was no doubt now it was a stunt. Georgia smeared the apron—mixing colors here and there—while Momma stood in mock horror and the children howled. When one glop muddied to a tawny brown, a near-match to her skin, Georgia popped some to her nose and the crowd cheered.

"How's that, y'all?" She said cross-eyed.

"Can we get on with Bible school now?" Honey said.

It was a few minutes before that happened, when Momma—still smiling—instructed us to divide up in twos.

"Now, it's your turn," she said, raising her finger to the air. "But don't touch the paints yet. You have to sketch your partner first."

Naturally Sandy and I buddied up, and we were quite a pair, one of us snaggletoothed and the other lop-eyed. Luckily for us, Momma started with the bigger picture.

"For the head, first draw an egg-like shape," she explained, skidding her pencil over the paper. "Then put the eyes near the middle, not way up in the forehead—see?"

She held up a sketch that didn't look like much: two lima

beans on a goose egg. I was glad when nobody laughed. The next minute she began to fill in the rest. Some of the kids had started their own drawings, but I kept watching. The face on Momma's paper was beginning to look like somebody. I glanced around—not one of the kids—and there was Georgia, still cleaning paint from her arm. By the time she saw my mother's drawing, we both knew. The lima bean eyes, the bonbon nose: it was her.

"How do you *do* that?" I said, standing up.

"I don't know, Grace, it comes with practice."

"Not to me," I protested.

Many others left their seats, including Honey, and before our eyes on that piece of paper, another Georgia appeared: the sliver between her teeth, her temples and high cheekbones, other traits I hadn't even noticed. This couldn't be described as doodling. My mother was a goddess! We all stared as she finished the portrait with a billowing Afro.

"Wow!" one of the boys said. "It looks just like her!"

"Does it ever." This was Georgia, coming closer. "May Ah?" Momma nodded as Georgia studied it, then flipped it around so the rest of us could see. "Who'd have guessed, Grace, your own sweet Momma?" She was impressed. We all were. I couldn't help giggling, for my chest swelled in that moment, all the way to my throat. Whatever people whispered about my mother—good or bad—they couldn't deny this. Not Honey, not Eloise, not anybody.

My mother's talent wasn't the only revelation we experienced that day. Around lunchtime there was another, one I'd just as soon forget.

"Hey look, they're pink!" a girl named Emmy said. She meant the Dixie cup drinks Honey balanced on a tray. "Is it Kool-Aid?"

"No, it's lemonade," Honey corrected.

"*Pink* Lemonade!" Emmy squealed. "My favorite!"

And that's when it happened, when the voice came out of nowhere. "There's no such thing as *pink lemons,*" it said.

We looked around. No one on the lawn had spoken. Where had the voice come from? The Tree of Heaven, the rope swing?

"I *said,* stupid-heads, there's *no such thing as pink lemons!*"

The shade under the tree was black as lava rock in the noon sun.

"There's a song I know about it," the voice went on. "I bet you *idiot-heads* don't." Then came laughing, a strange, disembodied chortle.

"Who's there?" Momma called, shading her eyes.

"Come on over," Georgia added.

I tried shading my eyes too, until I could see the rope swing, but it was empty.

"Why don't you *make* me?"

"Well Ah'll be." Georgia chuckled.

"Why on earth would we do that?" Momma said, "This is a church don't you know?"

No answer.

"Here's an idea, why don't you join us. We're having lunch and there's plenty to share."

"To tell you the truth," Georgia added, "Ah wouldn't mind hearing that song of yours."

"Then sing it your *own* stupid self."

"Just *who* you callin' stupid?" Georgia said. When nobody answered, she cleared her throat. "On second thought, maybe you can't sing. Maybe *that's* why you won't try."

We heard rustling then and a dim shape dropped to the grass, took several steps and burst into sunshine. Apple McEgan, joy of joys. I looked at Sandy and she at me. Apple's mildew germs were all over our tree. Had she been watching us all morning?

"Hello, young lady," Momma said.

"That's no lady," I whispered, "that's the girl who flips the bird."

"Oh heavens," Honey said.

Apple stood there, and to our amazement, launched into song:

"Six-teen tons of greasy, grimy go-pher guts, mu-ti-lated monkey's meat, sa-tu-rated birdies feet, one pint jar of all-pur-pose por-poise puss, sit-ting in your pink lemon-ay-ay-ade."

We were stunned. Not by the lyrics; she was a McEgan after all. But because Apple could sing. Despite her personality, the skin-and-bones frame, her voice was lovely, clear and bright and captivating.

"Oh!" Momma said. "That was wonderful!"

"Proved *me* wrong," Georgia agreed.

"*That's* what's in pink lemonade," Apple said. She stood there reveling in the attention, swinging the pouch she wore over her shoulder. Plenty of times I'd seen that pouch, made from some kind of animal fur—sewer rat I would have guessed if it weren't so blinding white.

"How 'bout joining us?" Momma tried.

Nooo! I thought.

But Apple came to my rescue. "I don't *go* to school," she said. "I don't have to ever again." She batted the pouch now, back and forth, between her palms.

"Well this is Bible school and you can come if you like," Momma replied. "But every child goes to *school.*"

"Not if they set it on fire."

Momma was speechless, like everyone else. Apple started to leave, then hesitated when she saw her advantage. She came forward instead, sauntering in her bare feet over the grass to Eloise and her tray of sandwiches. As she passed, I caught a whiff of mildew. There were holes in her shirt and dirt marks where her butt bones pounded her shorts. She piled sandwiches into the crook of her elbow and flipped her long, stringy hair. "I'll skip the lemonade," she said.

No one spoke as she left, cutting over the lawn toward Pardee. She'd finished one of the sandwiches by the time her feet hit the dirt.

"*Did* she set the school on fire?" Momma asked.

"Naw, she's only bragging," I explained. "She got sent home for a fight and when they let her back, she set fire to some garbage that burned a wall. After that, they kicked her out for good."

"Oh Lord, she *burned a wall?* Are they sure it was Appoline?"

"A bunch of kids saw her do it, and they found the matches in her pouch."

She'd stopped swinging it as she walked, focused on the sandwiches.

"Horrible child," Honey said.

"I don't know." Momma came back. "I mean, look at her." Appoline hopped a mud puddle and disappeared down Pardee. "She's just a wisp of a thing."

"And so alone," Georgia said. I could forgive Georgia for

that, since she was a downtrodden Negro and all. But *Momma?* Since when did she feel sorry for a low-life like Appoline? For the first time in my entire existence, I agreed with Honey.

Chapter 22

It should have been easy to find my mother's paint case. I could have done it myself if I'd bothered to think. Instead I asked Dad, who suggested the bedroom closet—right where Momma had left it.

Upstairs on my bed, I breathed in the leather and popped the clasps, opening it ever so slowly, like it held eternal secrets, the cure for cancer or the Holy Grail. Inside, I found the same paint tubes from years before. She hadn't used them much since then and I wondered, had she given up on her classes? Yes, that was right. The chest congestion and fatigue. "Dog tired," she'd said. I shook off the memory before the old dog could claw in.

The case was in good shape, despite being old, the lining only frayed along an upper edge. Could I claim it as my own? I didn't think my father would care. The only thing he cared about anymore was whether I skipped church, which, by the way, I was getting pretty good at.

Drumming my fingers down a row of paints, I singled out a tube, the same I'd held years before. Cadmium Yellow, Finest Artists' Watercolor, it said. I screwed off the top and squeezed out a yellow ball. What could I paint with it? A field of flowers, a fiery sun... or maybe a happy face, flat and plastered? The thought reminded me of Grandma Carsten, how she'd slipped another 5-spot in my hand the week before, trying to bribe me to perpetual happiness. Instead of feeling happy, I felt put out, obligated to feel grateful. I'd mumbled a weak "Thanks" then considered stealing more from her wallet—until I remembered Astrid and how her blood poisoned my veins. What a chill *that* gave me.

With the paint case in my lap, I thought about Grandma's money. I could buy art paper with it, couldn't I, try my luck with Cadmium Yellow? Maybe it would ward off insanity since, thanks to my mother's messenger, I sure felt headed there. He must have seen me in the alcove window that dark, early morning, because he'd stopped following any pattern. The next delivery skipped Sunday and arrived mid-week, and what could I do about it? I'd searched everywhere for that jerking gait, keeping one eye on the usual suspects and the other hunting more. But neither eye—left or right, blue or brown—had spotted anything.

Sometimes I dreamed about staging an ambush, crouching in the bushes night after night until he came back. But I never could picture what happened next. Would I spot him first or would he spot me? And what then? It was hard to believe he'd just hand over the remaining letters: "Never mind what your mom wanted, kid. Here you go." It was even possible that I'd scare him away—for good. No, I had to identify the messenger secretly, so I could sniff out the letters behind his back.

But how?

Another envelope had arrived—on a *Thursday*. Was I ever going to pin him down? The folds were now loose and the paper softening since I'd already read it several times. Sunday morning I was back in the attic, reading it again.

My dear Grace,

I'd give anything to see you now, how much you've grown, how much you've changed. Anything to do more than picture it.

I wish I looked more like you, Momma.

You're self-conscious about your eyes, I know that. Too young to realize imperfections are a part of beauty.

Right.

But it's true! Ask yourself this: Where would art be without them? Variation is what's interesting, Grace. The way you are is what's interesting. Even Thad swears by this, and he's a good man, darling...

I don't know about that.

...the kind my own father could never be. Pops, Pops. I have to admit there were times when he tried. He'd swear off booze and return to the ranch, keeping Astrid off my back. He liked working the orchard best, picking fruit or pruning branches, and all the while he'd tell stories that sprang to his mind. "Did you ever hear...?" he'd start, and if I had, I wouldn't admit it, because I'd rather hear a repeat than nothing at all.

But it never lasted long. A day or two and he'd be gone, drowning those same memories. It's not that I hated being alone. Most of the time it offered room to think and to ride Lady through the hills. It's just that I got too much room. So when Sal showed an interest in being friends, I wasn't about to let anybody get in my way.

I understood the danger, or at least thought I did. What was it Doug had said? Keep your distance. Don't get caught. I took that to heart, skimming leaves from the castle pool before the Rossanos were up, staying clear of the grounds. But most of all, I made sure Astrid knew. "I'm done at the castle," I'd tell her, then I was out the door again to feed the chickens.

I did this only a few days, until what I hoped would happen actually did. Sal came to me. He showed up one afternoon when I was in the barn, the one spot Astrid avoided like the plague. "How's my favorite artist?" he said, strolling in with that coyote grin. "How many artists you know clean horse stalls?" I said, tossing a pitchfork of straw his way.

From that day on, he was coming to the barn almost every day, and more often than not after he'd been in the pool. It wasn't just the swim trunks and casual shirt that tipped me off. He smelled like the chemicals I poured in. I teased him about it once, and the very next day, he carried a rose the size of a pomegranate from the castle garden. "For you," he said with a nod, "a lot better than the smell of chlorine." I played along with a "Thank you, sir," and then tucked the rose away. I knew better than to bring it to the cottage. There was no sense taking a risk that Astrid would see it.

Mostly, I was never sure when I'd see Sal again. Even in summer, the family left sometimes without a word. Back to San Francisco or away on some exotic trip. Other times, they brought guests, which meant Sal was too busy for me. Even on days when he did stop by, his time was limited, especially when his father was around. He'd sit a while, then check his watch and be gone.

Lucky for me, Dr. Rossano was in the city a lot, on call at the hospital. That's when Sal loosened up and wanted to go for rides. Those were the best times, Grace. I had Lady and my freedom plus a friend to share it with. My riding improved by leaps and bounds during those days. Sal was excellent in the saddle and wild as a jockey straight out of the gates. He pushed me to speeds I never dared on my own. We'd start out fast, laughing and racing into the hills, then switch to a quieter pace so we could talk.

Before too long, Sal opened up. "My father wants me to be a surgeon," he said one day, "but I can't see myself chained to the hospital night and day." It wasn't easy for him to admit, I could see, but I wasn't sure how to respond. I thought of his personality, his love of riding and his wild streak. "You have to do what's right for you," I finally told him.

"You think you'll end up an artist?" he asked. The truth is, Grace, I'd never really thought about it. Silly as it seems, the only place I'd ever pictured myself was on that ranch. "I like to draw," I told him, which made him laugh. "Oh come on, Sharon, you have to do better than that. What do you like about it?" In that moment I realized suddenly how important my art had become. But the answer to his question What did I like about it? wasn't easy. I had to stop and give it some thought.

"When you find something of your own," I tried, "that you can put on paper, it's..." I held up, stuck on finding the right words. Cesare nickered and the rest came. "It's like riding. You know? Going full-out on the trails and wishing it would last forever? It's like that only there's something that does last forever... something almost sacred about it." I felt my face flush. "It's hard to explain." But he smiled and told me I'd explained it very well.

Our friendship developed quickly after that. We talked about the Impressionists Sal had showed me at the castle, and how art captures truths about life. We talked about the ranch and how we both loved being there. We got along so well, it seemed, that Sal sometimes forgot who I was. "You're lucky," he told me once, "that you get to stay here all year 'round." I searched his face for the joke, since I cleaned his pool and groomed his horses, but I didn't find one. "What's so funny?" he demanded. "You are," I told him, "you are."

Sal was 17 that summer, headed for his last year of high school, and when I told him I was three years younger and only bound for the ninth grade, his jaw dropped. "You sure?" I laughed. "I think I know how old I am!" He pulled Cesare up next to me and compared our hands, but I yanked mine back and told him I'd been in high school for years already, which was a fib, of course. Seventh grade put me in the same complex as St. Helena High, but it didn't mean I was in high school. "So I suppose you'll graduate early?" he teased, and I practically pushed him from Cesare.

In a very short time, we learned a lot about each other and about the horses too, since we saw so much of them. We figured out what wild plants they liked, what startled them, and, as it happened, how they reproduce. It came as a complete shock to me, Grace. I'd seen smaller animals mate, of course, Chipper was a frisky one, but I'd never even considered the process with horses. Even when I saw it, I didn't understand.

It was still June when it happened, but unusually warm, so we'd decided to skip riding. Cesare was in his stall and we'd put Lady out in the corral alone. We always kept the horses separate, but the funny thing is, I never guessed the true reason, only assumed it was because of the stallion's temper.

Anyhow, we had just climbed the fence to sit when we heard

it, a banging from inside the barn. We'd closed the barn door, so the noise was hard to pinpoint. Was Astrid there, ready to catch us talking together? I looked up then and here he came, thundering around the side of the barn. Cesare had busted from his stall! I barely registered what I was seeing before he was over the rail. He made it look easy, flying over that fence like it was nothing. When he hit the dirt, Lady took off and he ran after her. I almost laughed until I looked at Sal. His face had turned to stone. Was Lady in danger?

Cesare tore through the corral, rearing up on his hind legs. While there'd always been a barrier between them, a wall, a fence, a rider, now there was nothing. Then Lady did the oddest thing and backed toward him, flicking her tail. When he reared again, landing his weight on her, I screamed. Had he gone mad? I jumped into the corral, trying to get to her, but Sal grabbed hold of me.

"You'll get hurt!" he said. I spun around. "But Cesare's gone crazy! He's hurting her!" Sal's hand was on my arm, his face red as the castle roses. "Sharon," he said, "it's natural." I didn't understand what he meant and it must've shown. "Cesare's a stallion, fully loaded, and Stella, your Lady, she must be in heat."

I glanced back, saw the thrusting and then I knew. I felt so stupid then, and embarrassed. "She'll be all right," Sal said. But I couldn't look at him. I ran from the corral, all the way to my rocky overlook to be alone. Good thing in the weeks ahead there were other things to talk about, because Sal and I, we never spoke of it again.

As time went by I grew used to his company, to hearing his thoughts and telling him mine. Where else could I report news about the ranch, the water table at the springhouse or the billy goat's shenanigans? I'd even started to open up about Astrid. So it's no surprise that every so often that summer, when the Rossanos went back to the city, I was lonelier than ever, counting on the horses and my pencil drawings to get by. I never stopped listening for that jeep on the castle drive. If I heard the gravel spit, I knew it was Sal. Nobody else drove like that. I'd drop everything and run to the rise to look for him, *always careful not to let Astrid see me.*

I knew the Rossanos would leave for good when September rolled around. Only once in a blue moon did they show up during the school year. So as summer came to a close, I had to steel myself. I knew, very soon, I wouldn't have Sal for months on end. If anything happened that I longed to tell him, it would have to wait.

Sal must've felt the same, because the day they left, he came and found me at the springhouse. He didn't say goodbye, but touched my cheek and studied my face a long while. When he left, I couldn't watch but ran for my pencils and whatever paper I could find.

You want to know what's funny? Something did happen that winter that I longed to tell Sal. Something exciting. But it's a long story, Grace, one to fill several pages. And wouldn't you know, Georgia's here and I'm exhausted. At least I got a lot on paper today. It took hours, and more breaks than I can count, but I'm tired now, sweet child, down to my bones.

I love you dearly, never forget that.
Momma

I sighed and lowered the letter. My mother's experience felt oddly familiar: she'd found a friend and lost him again. Immediately, I realized why. It was the way I experienced *her*. She was with me, there in the letters, then gone again. It was why I read them over and over. But I was powerless to get what I really wanted: the rest of her story. What had she said? Something exciting was about to happen. But what?

Suddenly Dad whistled from downstairs. Perfect. I fidgeted with a hangnail. I'd completely forgotten it was Sunday morning. I caught the hangnail between my teeth and pulled. Some good that did me. If only a bleeding hangnail was an excuse to skip church.

I went straight to my father and claimed a stomachache instead. The odd thing is, he bought it. When he and Jimmy left the house, I turned on The Cyclops to its latest prank: nothing but church on Sunday mornings *ha ha ha*! I tried a book then, but my thoughts wandered, back to the ranch and my mother's art. She'd turned to drawing in her frustration. I wished I could. But I didn't have a lick of her talent.

Or did I? It'd been a long time since I'd tried. Was it possible things had changed? Two words came to me then: *Cadmium Yellow*. I had the paint case. I had the desire. All I needed was the paper. Faster than I'd moved in weeks, I went for my piggy bank, shook out a 5-spot and hopped on my bike for the corner store. The route, unfortunately, was past the church, but I went for broke, standing tall and pumping the pedals—look Dad, no stomachache!—and must have passed without notice.

The only paper they sold at the store was cheap, but what could I do? I paid for it, plus two Hershey bars and a fistful of Jolly Ranchers, then I straddled my bike and sailed home. By the time Dad and Jimmy came in, I was at the dining room, my art supplies spread out. It helped that I'd eaten all the candy. I didn't have to fake the stomachache.

"We missed you in church," Dad said, closing the door.

"Not really," Jimmy added with a smirk.

"James Thaddeus," Dad said as he ran off.

"Yeah, well," I fiddled with the paint case as my father stood there not noticing, apparently, the new paper.

"You know," he said, "you can't be mad at God forever."

"I'm not mad at anybody," I said, choosing a brush. "I'm just trying to paint." But he didn't budge. I stared at the table and waited. I could have painted the Sistine Chapel in the time it took him to leave.

Finally alone, I ran my fingers over the tubes of paint. The colors I pulled out were exciting, like the masterpiece unfurling in my head. I held the paintbrush and started small, a flower and the ball of a sun. Then I tried a mighty evergreen—that buckled the paper. Crap. I remembered how Momma stood back when she checked her art. So I stood back. It still looked like crap. I crumpled the page and started over, crumpled the next and then the next. When the balled-up pages built a soggy pyramid, I quit trying.

The truth was I didn't like using my mother's paints. It felt like trespassing over something sacred. It was the word she'd used to describe her art wasn't it, *sacred*? I screwed the lids on the tubes and washed the paint brushes while my thoughts returned to her letter.

She'd said a lot in this one, about Sal and her life, the something exciting about to happen. But what? Then Sandy came to mind. She had good instincts. I went to the phone and dialed her number, and the minute I recounted the letter, she spit it out, just like that.

"Sal kisses her."

"What?"

"The next thing that happens. Sal *kisses* her." Even coming through the phone it sounded ridiculous.

"That's stupid," I said. "He's way too old." I thought of my father then, how much older he'd been than my mother—15 years?—and my throat went dry. "Besides," I said, "she's talking about *after* he left the ranch. Something happened *after* that. They can't kiss if he's not even there."

"Well, I don't know. How would *I* know?"

"You wouldn't—jeez."

Chapter 23

There were clues over the years to my mother's secrets. Some of them big enough to clobber me over the head. Still, I missed them. The biggest came not long after Apple treated us to that song on the lawn. It was the summer of '67, the summer of love. You could stick flowers in your hair and dance around Pardee Park. I even heard a whole new meaning for the word *grass*. At Sandy's, I learned to dance The Monkey and shout along with The Beatles: *We're Sergeant Pepper's Lonely Hearts Club Band! We hope you have enjoyed the show!* It was all supremely fascinating to the daughter of the preacher and his Sunday school-teaching wife.

At church, change happened more slowly: interpretive dance came to worship and we sang to acoustic guitar. *Kumbaya, my Lord, Kumbaya....* But the closest we ever got to communal living was bunk beds at family camp. An old diary I kept chronicles highlights of that long, hot summer: the big swing at Camp Magruder, swimming with Momma, playing dodge ball in the neighborhood with the boys down the street. If one of them pegged you, he had a crush. By the end of the week, it was over.

My mother was fickle too that summer of love. She'd been kind to Apple McEgan, but was oddly unnerved by the stranger who showed up at our door—which should have been my first clue. When the doorbell rang that now-infamous afternoon, I was the one who went to get it. There on the porch stood an old man, covered in grime from head to foot. He wore overalls and a floppy hat and held a bedroll under his arm. A hobo? You didn't get hobos on your doorstep every day, even when you lived in a parsonage. He had a short, white beard over wrinkles baked by the sun, and the wrinkles lined up when he smiled, which made him look harmless enough. What he looked like, more than anything, was a long story. It was July 27th, the day I turned nine, which I remember because of the first thing he said to me.

"Well, happy birthday!" He pulled off his hat, revealing hair as white as his beard. I got a whiff of body odor next which only fired my curiosity. Did hobos shower?

"You sure look like mercy to me," he said.

"No—I go by Grace."

He hesitated, then stuck out his hand. "Well howdy do, Grace. The name's Russell Pet—"

"Oh my God, oh my God." This was Momma, rushing up as I shook his hand. She'd taken the Lord's name in vain, in front of a stranger no less. Was it his getup? The body odor? The two adults glared at each other for what felt like a generation.

"What is it?" she said to him, not very Christian-like. And this was the same woman who felt sorry for Appoline? In the past when strangers stopped at our door, she'd been gracious, like Jesus said *For I was hungry and you gave me food*. Maybe for Momma, I thought, the rule didn't apply to hobos.

The old man shuffled his feet. "I was just tellin' sis here my name," he answered. "Russell Pearce Malson Hiram Evergreen Hobart, the THIRD." He winked. "And don't you forget it."

"Is that *really* your name?" I wanted to know. "All of it?"

"I told yeh it was now, didn't I?" He tweaked my nose. "But you can call me Russ, what my friends call me. Ramblin' Russ if we meet on the road."

"Is there something we can *do* for you, uh… Russ?" Momma had crossed her arms over her chest.

"Matter of fact, I'm in town lookin' up relatives," the old man said. "Till I find 'em, I'm in need of a place to stay. I figured the pastor's wife might take pity, long as I mind my own business. And I will. Mind my own business. Of course."

I turned to Momma. Why *couldn't* we have a hobo? But she

was so slow to answer it made me squirm. "How'd you know it was my birthday Mister—um, Russ?" I said.

He squatted to my eye level. "Well, for one thing, it says so right there." He pointed to the button Momma had pinned on my dress, which read: *Birthday Girl.*

"Oh," I said, disappointed.

Then he dug in his pocket and pressed something cool into my palm. It was a beat up old nickel and some lint. "It's an Indian Head, sis. A little gift for turning 9."

There was an Indian's head on the coin, all right, and on the flip side, a buffalo.

"Is it worth something?"

"You bet. It's almost 50 years old."

Grinning, I held it up for Momma to see. "Fifty years!" But she was unimpressed. More than anything, she seemed distracted. After a silence that nearly killed me, she said, "There's a bed in the basement—and a shower—but I don't want you taking advantage. One or two nights, then you need to move on. First off, into the kitchen. We'll get a few things straight. Grace, you run on up to your room."

"Do I have to?"

"Right this minute."

But I didn't go to my room. I hovered in the stairwell, squeezing my nickel. It was hard to hear what they said from the kitchen, but I did pick up something—a laugh or a cry, I couldn't tell which. When they moved back into the dining room, I snuck up the stairs.

Ramblin' Russ stayed through the weekend and then, miraculously, into the following week. Momma, somehow finding some tolerance, made him work for his keep, mowing the lawn and watering shrubs as he entertained Sandy and me. He reminded me of someone, though for the life of me, I couldn't tell who. He said the "kinfolk" he was tracking had been lost to him for years. He'd taken the life of a Nomad since, hopping box cars on freight trains when he decided to move on: Seattle to San Diego, Phoenix to El Paso. But it was "high time," he said, to find his relatives. As he spoke, he swung the hose to the azaleas.

"They could be anywhere around these parts," he mused, as if he might flush a cousin from the bushes any minute. He spit juice from a wad of tobacco and squinted at me. "I'll be damned if they didn't swap sides." I had no idea what he meant, though I took a guess at a family feud.

He put a finger under my chin then and tilted it up. "Them eyes of yours—not too many kids have eyes like that."

"Tell me about it."

"It's different. You ought to be proud."

"In about a million years."

"There are plenty of worse things, you know."

Sandy and I liked the old hobo with the string of names. Russell Pearce Malson, Hiram Evergreen Hobart, The Third, as he liked to say. By any name, he was a gifted storyteller, weaving yarns of his railway adventures and the bandits who chased him along the way. His stories were so fascinating, I wanted to believe every word.

"I didn't know I could fly till they cotton-pickin' made me," he said, halfway through the first whopper. "They up and threw me from that train, those same three outlaws."

"But how'd they get to you?" Sandy said, wide-eyed with faith against her better nature. "You fought 'em off, remember?"

"I did. But they came back in the dark of night. Only way they could, see? A movin' train and three against one. They chucked me out of that car over a hundred-foot gorge."

"A hundred foot!" I exclaimed, "Didn't it kill you?"

"It was meant to, sure as shootin', and would've if I hadn't caught that gust of air."

"And that's when you flew?" Sandy said.

"Just like Superman. I had the wind sheer from the train and would've kept goin' if not for that tree. It snagged my belt, seventy feet up if a foot. Took me a full day to get down and three more to find a town."

"Wow. What'd you eat?"

"Oh, I don't need much. I'm like the birds in the Bible. They don't sow or reap but God feeds 'em." I figured that line was for my benefit, since he hadn't bothered to step foot inside the church, not even on Sunday. He leaned forward, offering us a drink from the hose. "Take all you want," he said, "The Lord provides."

After a while, I started to wonder about Russ's relatives, since he never bothered to look for them or even open the Portland phone book. I decided it was another of his tall tales. But I was glad to have him around. He was showering by then and wearing second-hand clothes from the church basement, so he smelled halfway decent, even grandfatherly. Since one of my grandfathers was dead and the other who-knew-where, the old man was all right by me. But Momma never warmed to Russ. She grew quiet when he came around or would start to fidget and leave the room. Dad, on the other hand, considered him useful, especially with yard work. Far from showing him the road, he encouraged Russ to stay, long enough at least for the next Sunday's worship.

"You might find something worthwhile," he told him. "What the good Lord has in mind, you never know."

Come Sunday, as my father prepared to deliver a sermon—on the virtue of humility of all things—Russ showed up in a church-basement suit, the finest picture of humility you ever saw. Since Momma looked away when he came up, I patted the pew and he sat next to me.

Chapter 24

I grew up quickly after my mother died, especially when you measure time by the arrival of her letters. Three per year and I was suddenly 13, waiting on her tenth. I'd given up hope for any pattern, so when I spotted an envelope on a Sunday morning, I wanted to wrench that mailbox from the siding. *Sunday? He was back to Sundays?*

"Uuuuuh!" I roared at the sky, which brought my father out in his robe.

"For heaven's sake, Grace, you'll wake the dead!"

If only. When he saw the letter—and that I hadn't been mutilated by wild animals—he sighed. "It's three years today, you know."

"Huh?"

"Three years." Since her death he meant, and I wanted to roar all over again.

"I'd like you to be in church today." When he shuffled away, I kicked the doorframe and jammed my toe. Then I limped to his desk and checked his calendar. Three full years, sure enough, to the day. Plus, it was the first time the anniversary had fallen on a Sunday. *Way to go Miss Brilliance. You couldn't anticipate that?* The messenger had come and gone I'd slept right through it, to nobody's fault but my own.

It was just after services that morning, in the church bathroom, that I found the stain on my underwear. It took me a long, forever-second to realize what it was: menstrual blood. *Sure God, why not? Might as well bleed me to death.*

I cut straight through the church for home and locked myself in the bathroom. Were any of my mother's supplies still around, what the magazine ads called feminine protection? I searched through drawers and under the sink, finally locating a collapsed box. Inside was one sanitary napkin and a flimsy belt. I had only the vaguest idea what to do with them, a hazy memory of my mother in the bathroom. Hadn't she worn the belt at her hips? I undressed and stepped into it, struggling to connect the napkin to its dangling tabs. In the mirror, I looked ridiculous, just exactly the way I felt. What was worse, I had no idea how long one napkin would last—one hour, one day? Where was my mother when I needed her? Dead, idiot, that's where.

Shrinking from the bulk between my legs, I pulled on my clothes and considered calling Georgia. It's what my mother suggested, wasn't it? *Georgia Johnson is your Hazel Clayton...* The problem was, I didn't feel like calling her—or anyone. "Hi Georgia," I said in the mirror. "Guess what? Just started my period, wanna come over?"

Right.

I sat on the toilet and sighed. Couldn't I walk to Eastport Plaza, buy what I needed on my own? When I thought about it, though, standing in line with feminine products didn't sound like a picnic either. Still, I hadn't seen Georgia in so long, how could I call her now? A feather of a thought floated in then: could she have drifted away on purpose? To keep me from thinking she had the letters?

I sat up straight. Georgia wasn't the man on the lawn, that was clear, but it didn't mean she wasn't in cahoots with him. I hurried from the bathroom to find her number.

"Grace? That really you?" she said from her end. My voice had grown up with the rest of me. "Ah'm so glad you called!" I told her what I was calling about and she promised to hurry over, soon as she got somebody for her mother. "Ah'll be there quick as Ah can," she said and hung up.

Waiting for Georgia on the front porch, I considered how much I'd changed since I'd last seen her: taller with a few more curves, my eyebrows too thin after a botched session with a pair of tweezers. Not to mention the new braces to correct my overbite. More than anything, I'd grown cynical and sassy: the Preacher's Kid with the string of X's after her name. No subject was safe. If Dad asked me to do the dishes, I had a comeback. "Why not let God do 'em, since he takes care of everything."

Then again, hadn't the whole world changed? Hadn't our innocence left with 1960s? I thought of Kent State, all those guns turned on students; then Portland's riots that injured dozens. And who could forget Charles Manson? His so-called family had stabbed a pregnant woman to death. It's hard to ignore that kind of news, even when you're 13. When Manson carved an X in his forehead, it damn near stopped my heart. The X's it seemed were everywhere.

I pushed those thoughts from my mind and tried to focus on Georgia, her beautiful smile with the sliver of a gap. "Miss Brilliance, you must be psychic," I mumbled, for here came Georgia's Fairlane up our drive, showing the wear of three more years. Pardee dust engulfed the car as the door flew open.

"Grace" she called, waving an arm to clear the air. "Lookie you!" She was slightly heavier and her Afro shorter, but her smile just the same.

"Da-ad she's here!" I yelled over my shoulder. Then I was on my feet, closing the distance between us. It wasn't until I buried my face in her familiar softness that I realized how much I'd missed Georgia. Not just her personality, but her touch, the touch of a woman so close to my mother. A pinch rose in my throat as she hugged me, and I choked it back.

"Look how pretty you are," she said, pulling back to see me. "Getting your teeth straight too—and look at that hair!" The whole mop of it hung long and free, 70's style.

"Listen," she went on, "Ah got to worrying on my way over. You need somethin' right away?"

"Naw. I found stuff in the bathroom. I'm okay."

"All right, then. Lookie you, girl, how you've grown! You're about as tall as your mother now." We both knew it wasn't saying much since Momma had been petite. But I had to hand it to Georgia. In the first minute, she'd dared what most people couldn't in a month: She'd talked of Momma.

"You look so much like her. You know that, don't you? Ah hope you know that."

I shook my head and felt the pinch again.

Dad and Jimmy appeared on the porch, so when Georgia turned to say hello, I snuck to her car. In the front seat, behind the Pardee-dusted windshield, I could hide my tears.

Not five minutes later, we were sailing down Holgate hill, to the drugstore and then to a hamburger joint on 82nd. We must have been quite a sight ordering our food—the tall black woman with the short white girl—because people stared.

"What kind of shake you want?" Georgia asked. "Your mother said get her a shake."

I knew what that was about: my mother recreating her day with Hazel Clayton and the malted shakes. I would've bet no one stared at the two of them. On second thought, what did I care?

"I'll have chocolate," I said, "*malted.*"

Georgia chuckled. "Ah don't think they have that, Grace."

"Okay. Plain chocolate then."

Georgia did most of the talking as we ate our lunch. She asked about my father and the new church janitor, which was a good story: we'd burned through two already and were well into a third. When I described his sensitivity to floor wax—that he broke out in a rash—she almost choked.

"You're pullin' my leg."

I bit into my burger. "No I'm not. I swear."

"Ah bet Honey *loves* that!"

"You should see her. You know the look."

Georgia shot me the sidelong squint and we exploded in laughter. She was still chuckling when I got the question out. "So, why haven't you come around?"

She stopped chuckling. "You always had spunk, didn't you child?"

I shrugged. "Is it your mother, because she's so sick?"

"That's part of it," she admitted, her eyes going glossy, "but only part."

"And the other part?" I looked her straight in the eye, practically staring her down. *Did she have the letters?*

"Ah'm ashamed to say it, Grace, but you remind me of her. *So* much you wouldn't believe. It's hard for me, honey. It hurts so much I can hardly stand it."

This wasn't the conversation I wanted. I dug into my back pocket, whipped out my mother's letter and flicked it to the table.

Georgia's hands flew to her mouth. "Is that—"

"It came this morning. The tenth. You know what day this is?"

She looked to the letter and back to me. "Sweet Jesus. The anniversary?"

"Three years."

"Glory be."

"You can open it if you want."

She hesitated, then picked it up. "It feels like yesterday… and a lifetime ago." She turned it over and slipped out the pages, her eyes welling up. "Ah remember her handwriting. Ah'd know it anywhere." She wasn't reading so much as gazing, remembering that yesterday of a lifetime ago. She unfolded the pages, ran her fingers along the writing as her tears spilled over. A busboy came through and cleared two tables before she spoke.

"She arranged every bit of it, you know Grace," she said, dabbing a napkin to her eyes. "So when God called her home there'd be somebody to keep these, somebody to give 'em to you. Every bit."

I watched her closely, waiting for the courage to say the words. "Are you the somebody, Georgia? You with some runner?" My heart thundered. "Do you have my mother's letters?"

She sat back, hard. "Oh no, Grace, it isn't me. It would've killed me to keep these—a constant reminder—and your mother must've known." Her voice broke. "Ah adored Sharon, see? She was decent folk, the kind who can see past the skin you're in or the way you talk. The best friend Ah—" she stopped again. "Ah bet you don't know this, but when Ah first came to Good Shepherd, Ah needed that job somethin' fierce. Ah was about to lose my house! If it hadn't been for Sharon, they'd've run me away before you could say A-men." She stiffened, remembering. "We didn't have much in common, your mother and me, but we laughed at the same things, stirred the same pots. We found it easy being friends."

I sighed. "Georgia I knew all that, how you and Momma got

along. But the letters. If it isn't you, then who—"

"Oh, no." She dropped a palm to the table. "Ah don't have any idea, and even if Ah did, wild horses wouldn't drag it out of me. Your mother had reasons for the way she did this. She told me herself you'd be growed when the last one came. So what you got your period child, you're still a girl! You'll get your mother's letters when she meant, and not a minute sooner!"

"But Georgia—"

"But nothin'! It was her last wish, haven't you thought about that?"

I hadn't and the truth was, I didn't want to. Momma's story was more important to me than any wish of hers about timing.

"My mother's dead, Georgia. What do you think, if I find them tomorrow God'll smite me with lightning?" I had her attention, so I socked it to her. "Besides, there's probably no such thing as God anyway. We prayed our guts out when she was sick, remember? And what did that do? Not a damn thing!"

Georgia's head snapped, like I'd reached out and slapped her. It was her fist that hit the table now. "Don't you dare go saying that to your father. After what he's been through? It'll tear him apart. Ah don't doubt for one second God is watching this minute—your mother too—and Ah swear, Grace, if you go sniffin' around against her wishes for that shoebox full of letters Ah—" her eyelids fluttered.

Shoebox? Is that what she'd said? *Shoebox full of letters?* Since I'd last seen Georgia, I'd learned to play poker—at Sandy's house of course—so I slipped on my best poker face and glanced away, as if I hadn't heard a single thing.

"Anyhow," she went on, snatching up our lunch garbage. "The point is, Ah *know* what your mother wanted, what she wants to this day."

"Care to tell *me?*"

"Oh you're exasperating! You think Ah know what's in those letters? Ah never asked to know!"

She wasn't exactly *denying* she knew...

"But here's one thing Ah'll say," she went on. "Those letters are important. Your mother gave everything she had to write 'em. All her strength in the world." She pointed her finger at me. "And you, young lady, had better not mess it up!"

I held my poker face and promised nothing.

Chapter 25

On the way home with Georgia, I stared out the window at cracks in the sidewalk. Wild flowers had pushed through some of them. "Step on a crack, break your mother's back," they sang. I could step on all the cracks I wanted to now, since I had no mother with a back to break. I could do a jig on every one.

Georgia depressed the gas pedal and the cracks blurred, cutting my mind loose for other things, like the shoebox that held my mother's letters. It wasn't exactly the breakthrough I was looking for, but it was something, better than nothing. I imagined what it might look like: small and sturdy, like a box for ballet slippers? No, big and bulky was better, like something for Go-Go Boots; you could fit your whole life story in a box for Go-Go boots. As the sidewalk rushed by, I imagined where you'd hide such a box: under a bed, on top a refrigerator, on a bookshelf right out in the open...

"You wanna tell me what's in it?" Georgia said.

"Huh?"

"You wanna tell me what's *in* it?" Had she read my mind?

"In what?"

"The letter in your pocket, Grace. Ah didn't read it." Her voice had softened since the restaurant.

"Oh that."

She adjusted the rearview mirror. "You certainly don't have to. Ah know it's personal and everything. Ah just thought..." She missed my mother. I could hear it in her voice.

"Fine with me," I said. And it was. She hadn't tried to snoop like my father had. "She talks about you sometimes," I offered. "In this letter too."

"She does?"

"Mmhm."

"Well, since Ah'm driving, maybe you could read it to me?"

I pulled out the pages:

My dear Ace-face Grace,

She chuckled. "Ah forgot she called you that."

"Yeah, me too. For a while."

"Well, don't let me stop you."

"Okay…"

My dear Ace-face Grace,

I haven't said much about the cancer lately, have I, ol' General Hodgkins? He's a spiteful brute, that's for sure. Remember when we had him whipped, after the Cobalt treatments and all the tumors melted away? Your Dad sent you to the church for the glass punch cups to throw a party. No more cancer! I can still see you with that smile as we danced together around the living room. Heck, Honey and Georgia danced together! We were happy. All of us. So happy.

Georgia's eyes were on the road but that day was on her face, at the corners of her mouth where her lips quivered.

And then, a few weeks later, my swelled-up belly. I would've tried the Cobalt again, nasty as it was. But the cancer was back in my lungs too, and the way the doc put it, you can't radiate if it won't leave lungs to breathe.

So we're pinned up together now, ol' Hodgkins and me, sparring for whatever body parts I have left. The good news is I can still get around, so I'm set on staying home as long as I can. The bad news? It's hard to eat when your gut is crowded. If it wasn't for Georgia, I'd be weaker than I am, no doubt about it. She was here today, by my side and back to the kitchen, making this fabulous homemade soup for me. It had to be good, she put so much in it. But I was a louse, Ace. After a few spoonfuls, I flat out couldn't swallow another—

A small choke broke my concentration: Georgia was crying.

"You want me to quit?" I was surprised to see we were on Pardee.

"Oh, don't mind me." She wiped her face. "Ah was just thinking on that soup. If chopping vegetables could've saved your mother, Ah'd have chopped my way to Miss'sippi." She sniffed. " And *you*, Ace, you sound so much like her."

I took a breath. "Well I don't have to keep reading. I could—hey, where're you going?" The Fairlane zipped past the parsonage.

"You still got plenty of letter, right? Then Ah'm still driving. Now tell me more about that pot of soup."

"Let's see…"

—It had to be good… but… after a few spoonfuls, I flat out couldn't swallow another bite. I knew she'd be disappointed—

Georgia sniffled but she looked fine.

—she'd worked so hard. But the thing Georgia doesn't realize, it's her company I love most. She makes me laugh till I'm short of breath and glad of it. It's one of the best ways to fall asleep, I know that, after a good laugh with Georgia.

She was smiling now, grateful for my mother's words.

Your Dad, bless his heart, he's overwhelmed with his own pain, and hardly knows what to do with himself besides work and pray. He'll come around to be my rock, I know he will, but for now I count on Georgia to bridge the days. Quiet is fine, until you get too much of it. I learned that lesson a long time ago on the ranch…

The ranch, the ranch. Time to get back to it, I'd say. The last I wrote, Sal left for the city and the quiet settled in again. School was on us, which was good. Between that and Astrid's orders, we stayed busy. Weekends were hardest, believe it or not, because I had time to burn. Now and then girls from school called, inviting me to town for a coke or a movie. But when Astrid chewed them out, they quit bothering. She was tighter than ever with money in those days.

I thought about ways to earn a few bucks myself, the way Doug did raising a beef calf. But I needed a change of scenery, a job in town, not another animal to take care of. I figured Astrid would like the idea, until she practically burst a seam cackling at me. "Sure, Cauliflower," she said, "soon as you finish your ranch chores." She piled the work on after that, unloading hers on me too so there was no way I could get away. It was weeks before she let up, just after I gave up looking for a job. If I hadn't had Lady during that time, Grace, I don't know what I would've done.

The saddle turned out to be a boon, once I had my weekends back. I could strap things to it, which gave me freedom to pack my art supplies out on the trails. And since that ranch stretched five hundred acres, I had a whole new world to sketch. I had some paper too, good quality stuff, thanks to a teacher at school. She caught me drawing on an old lunch sack once and brought notebooks the very next day.

As for Sal, he came to the ranch only once that fall, and by the time I found out, he was gone. It was Thanksgiving, and we'd left the animals in Mrs. Clayton's care to head for Astrid's mother's place in Lodi. Doug called it Turkey with a side of claustrophobia. When we came back three days later, I found a rose propped in the barn. It was already wilted, with most of its petals gone, but I tore across the grounds anyway, past the gardens to the back of the castle, not thinking what I'd do if I saw Sal's parents. Turns out it didn't matter. The Jeep was gone and the kitchen blinds drawn. I turned back and tossed what was left of that rose.

It was sometime in December that I discovered it... the thing I wanted to tell Sal. I remember every detail of that afternoon, in the barn, getting ready for a ride. I had the saddle on Lady and had just started to cinch it when she whinnied and shivered, head to tail. It wasn't like her. I figured the blanket underneath must be creased, so I loosened the cinch and lifted the saddle. But the blanket was fine. I smoothed it again and adjusted the fit, and this time she was really mad, stomping and twitching like she was ready to buck. I circled around, looking her over. She wanted that saddle off, no question about it. I slid it off and crouched down. And that's when I saw it, just a vein and a bit of fullness, but I knew.

I ran, clear to the cottage, yelling, "Lady Agate's got a bun, Lady Agate's got a bun!" And Astrid looked at me like I'd lost my mind. "Lady who's got a what?" she said. I never talked about the horses around her, so she didn't have a clue what I meant. "The mare," I panted, "and remember the stallion's fully loaded!" She stared, wondering where I'd heard this. "Are you sayin' the mare's knocked up? You sure?" Now that she asked... I wasn't.

"Maybe her gut's tied up," she said. I hadn't thought of that. Could Lady be sick? Either way, Astrid was worried. That horse was worth a pretty penny. She called the Rossanos and it was all I could do not to ask for Sal. "Who'd you talk to? What'd they say?" I pleaded when she hung up. But she was already dialing Mrs. Clayton. Hazel would know what to do. She had horses of her own.

Half an hour later, that dear woman met me in the barn and I took her to Lady. "It's hard to tell with horses," she said, "since they carry their young almost a year." She looked over every inch of that mare, running her hands over her girth while I stood watching. "She could be in a family way," she said, "if Cesare's been at her like you say." She went around to the other side. "If I had to bet, I'd say yes." By the time she stood up I was a nervous wreck. "She looks well-cared for, Sharon, you can be proud of that." "What do I do?" I asked. She patted Lady's rump and smiled. "Same as always, just take good care of her." I gave Hazel a hug and said, "You know I will!"

And that's how I filled my days, Grace, pampering Lady as much as I could. The vet came and confirmed our suspicion. He said I could ride her, that exercise was good for a pregnant mare. "Just take it easy." I didn't use the saddle since it bothered her so much, and she was happy. Between rides, I gave her rubdowns and handfuls of oats, plus her favorite apples we had stored from the orchard.

But the waiting was hard. Time moved with a terrible slowness that winter, especially around the cottage. Finally, just before Christmas something happened that stirred things up. A package arrived. We hardly ever got packages. Still, when Pops carried it in, Doug and I didn't get too excited. We figured it was for the Rossanos and would lay around collecting dust until they claimed it. But Pops looked confused.

"It's from Oakland," he said." And what does that say there? Sh... hmph." He glanced my way. "Can't quite read it, Sis. Can you make this out?" The package was fairly big, about the size of our Atlas at school, and neatly wrapped. What it said was plain as day: Sharon Peterson, the ranch address. I almost fell over. "For me?" It was clear no one in my family expected it, because they all looked as surprised as I was. "What're yeh waiting for?" Pops said.

I tore through that paper fast as lightning and flung it aside, and there in my lap, was the most curious thing, a leather case, cool and smooth. I turned it over and propped it up. It had gold clasps and initials stamped in the leather—my initials! What was it? But I don't have to tell you, do I Grace? Since you saw it, years later. There was silence, though, when I popped those clasps the very first time, everybody leaning over me.

"What's all that?" Astrid barked when it fell open. I didn't have the slightest idea. Tubes and things. Then I spotted the brushes. "Paints!" I shouted. "It's paints!" "Who the hell would send you paints?" she snapped. In the next instant I knew, because of a card that had slipped to one side. On it was a picture of a rose. I tried to cover it with my arm, but Astrid demanded, "Open that card." Nothing got past her. I hesitated until Doug grabbed it. "Hey!" I yelled, trying to get it back, but he dashed away and waved it over his head.

My heart pounded as I tore out after him, around Pops and around the room. "It's from nobody," Doug laughed, "Sharon's best friend!" Sure enough, when the ruckus stopped we saw what he meant: the inside of the card was blank. I closed *my eyes, relieved. Thank you Sal for being smart.*

"Oh, I know who it's from," I said and Astrid whipped her head around. "Who?" I smiled and tried to stay calm. "Mrs. Stone, of course, you know, that teacher who gave me the paper? I'm sure she sent this too."

"That's perty nice of her," Pops offered. But I could tell Astrid wasn't buying it, at least not yet. Her shoes murmured and her forehead twisted up. "You mean that artsy-fartsy gal?" I sat down with the case, trying not to look rattled. "Yeah, the one you don't like—this must be her Christmas present." I hoped that would help, about Astrid not liking her. She never liked anybody.

"Cauliflower," she said, "it didn't come from St. Helena, it came from Oakland." My heart jumped but I tried not to show it. "Oh," I said, grateful Sal hadn't mailed it from San Francisco. "Well she probably took a drive into Oakland." Across the room, Doug shot me a look and I saw he knew.

"Then why the hell wouldn't she sign the card?" Astrid said. "That don't make sense." I lifted a tube of paint, fighting to keep my hand steady. "Who knows?" I told her, "She's so scatterbrained half the time, she probably forgot." I screwed the tops off some of the tubes to check their colors while Astrid stood over me. Finally she harrumphed and, to my relief, turned away. She turned away! "First mess you make with those paints," she said, over her shoulder, "they're gone."

After that, it was almost torture, Grace, the way I wanted to talk to Sal. About Lady Agate and her condition, and now the beautiful paint case he'd sent me. It was the only thing I got for Christmas my whole youth worth remembering.

I dropped the letter. "I guess she never got much of anything."

"Guess not," Georgia said. She steered the Fairlane around a corner. We were circling Pardee Park.

"Were you as poor as my mom growing up?"

"Probably worse. But there's no shame in it—long as you ain't afraid to work."

"Were your folks mean too?"

"No Grace. Just poor."

"That's not so bad." My mother could have lived with poor. "The letter's almost done. A couple more lines is all. You want me to finish it?"

"You go right ahead, child."

It was June before I saw Sal again, wouldn't you know? And what a year. So much would happen, Grace, with Lady, with me, so much would change. But that's another story, sweetheart... meant for another day.

"That's pretty much it. She just says goodbye after that."

"Hmm." Georgia suddenly seemed preoccupied.

"I think it's pretty obvious what happens, don't you?"

"Oh?"

"She has a baby."

She hit the brake and we flew forward, neither of us wearing seatbelts. "Jeez Georgia!" I'd smacked the dashboard.

She gripped the steering wheel and stared at me. "What do you—"

"A folt or whatever! You don't have to freak out!"

She looked confused. "You mean a *foal?*" she said. "A horse?"

"What else?"

She eased off the brake and resumed driving.

"Well?" I said.

"Well what?"

"*Is* there a foal?" I held up the letter. "She said Lady was pregnant."

"We gonna do this all over again, Grace? She's the one telling the story, isn't she?" She gunned the Fairlane and darted onto Holgate. "Wouldn't you rather hear it from her?"

"No," I said. "I'd rather know now. Why shouldn't I?"

"Gee, Ah don't know, because it's your mother's wishes?" She drew in a breath. "You want to know what Ah think? Ah think it's selfish and you should be ashamed."

From Holgate we bumped to the grittier surface of Pardee, a minute later pulling up in front of the parsonage.

"Georgia?"

"Mmm?" She shoved the Fairlane into Park then sat back, her jaw set. I almost asked about the shoebox, until I thought better of it.

"I found Momma's paint case," I said instead. "In her closet."

"You did?"

"Yep. But I'd already seen it, you know."

She was somewhere else again.

"Don't you remember? She showed it to me. She said that in the letter."

She didn't answer.

"Georgia?"

"Hmm?"

"Why didn't she tell me back then who gave it to her?"

"Ah don't know, Grace. Maybe it wasn't important at the time."

"Is it important now?"

"Lord child, there you go again. Have *patience*." She reached to the back seat, brought forward the bag from the drug store. "Besides, we ought to get a move on. Look who's waiting."

It was Dad, at our living room window.

"Ah'm sorry Ah yelled at you, Grace. Ah know it isn't easy."

I felt the pinch in my throat again. "It's okay."

"No, it isn't." She leaned over and wrapped an arm around me. "Call me anytime. For any*thing*. We'll get together soon as we can. Heck, maybe we'll play a prank on Honey for old times' sake. What do you think?"

"You could tell her you got your old job back."

Oh, how I loved Georgia's laugh.

Chapter 26

I didn't think much of it, all those years ago, when Ramblin' Russ got up from the pew and went straight to the stained glass. It was 1967, right after church, and he and Manny stood looking it over, one hobo in a moth-bitten suit and a simpleton genius.

"The plastic p-pealed up from the hole," Manny said. "What ha-happens when the rain comes?"

"What happens," Russ said, "is somebody oughta fix it, that's what."

A few days later, I knew the old man was up to something, the way he whistled a grand entry through the parsonage front door. I was home alone, with a cold, sneaking a show on the TV.

"Can't say it no more," he announced coming in, "that ol' Russ is good for nothin'."

"Huh?" I croaked. He had interrupted Bewitched, a terrible crime. Dad was across town for a meeting, and Momma and Jimmy had gone for groceries while she waited to pick him up. I didn't get many chances like that.

"This is a good show," I tried. "Wanna watch?"

"Been ten years since I welded something," he said. "But I haven't lost it. Check it out."

I tried to wiggle my nose like Elizabeth Montgomery to make him disappear, but I ended up sneezing instead.

"Gesundheit!" Despite my effort, he was still standing there.

"What do you mean welded?"

"Over at the church. Take a look."

I pushed myself up from the couch. Bewitched had gone to a commercial anyway. Maybe I could get back before it was over. Forgetting my cold, I raced outside, across the lawn and through both sets of doors. The stained glass was different. I knew it right away.

"By golly," I said, going closer.

In the spot just over Christ's head the hole was replaced with a pane of glass, not stained like the rest, but crystal-clear like regular glass and cut perfectly to size. The welding along the edges was a bit thicker, but it looked… right. The new pane shone clear and bright, like a crown, like it was meant to be. I knew my father would love it.

"What the good Lord has in mind," I said.

When I came back in the house, Bewitched forgotten, Russ was in the kitchen.

"Not too shabby, huh?" he said, pulling his head from a cupboard.

"How'd you do that?"

"Getting the glass cut was easy," he said. "But then you gotta install it. I found those welding tools in the barn like I figured. Just borrowed 'em for a bit." He winked.

"Barn? What barn?"

"The one out back."

"You went in *McEgan's barn*?"

"So that's her name, huh?"

"Who?"

"Never mind. Anyhow, Manny warned me about that old farmer. Quite a character, I hear."

Look who's talking, I thought.

"I slipped inside when he wasn't lookin', and slipped back again when I was done. The worst part of the whole affair was them damn thorns." He held out his arm where scratches marched like red ants. "You don't sound too good, by the way," he added.

I shrugged. I didn't feel too good either. "What was it like in that barn?"

"Very interesting. I'll have to tell you about it sometime. But, sis," he pulled out a drawer, "there must be a bottle 'round here somewhere. For your throat and mine—I'm awful parched."

Somehow knowing he didn't mean cough syrup. I climbed the counter to the narrow cupboard above the spices. One of the bottles my mother kept, a flat brown one, was three quarters full.

"You mean this?" I shook it at him.

"Mister James Beam," he said, grinning. He unscrewed the lid and held it out for me. "For medicinal purposes?"

"No thanks." I said hoarsely.

"Probably wise." He tipped the bottle and took a swig, just as we heard the front door opening. "On second thought," he said, wiping his mouth. "I think I'll hold off. Hop down now, sis, hurry up."

The next morning, feeling much better, I came downstairs to the smell of bacon, expecting to find Dad at the stove, but it was Momma, busted loose from her blue hour.

"James Thaddaeus keep your hands off that plate," she said. Jimmy was in his high chair—the one he'd nearly outgrown—with a slice of bacon in each fist. I didn't see Dad or Russ. Next to the plate of bacon was the bottle, the flat brown one from the night before, a yellow dandelion stuck in its neck.

"Dandelions drink liquor?" I asked.

"What do you think, Mercy Grace?" She was not in the best of moods.

"I don't know, but—"

"It's water. And I'd like you to take it to the basement," she said cracking an egg over the skillet. "Tell Ramblin' Russ his last meal at the parsonage is about to get cold."

I went down and found the white-haired man asleep in his bag, a sickly-sweet odor about the room. I set the bottle next to the boots that had formed to his toes. "Breakfast," I said, nudging his shoulder. A few minutes later as I dug into eggs at the dining room table, he emerged, his hair wet from a shower, and Momma immediately thrust a plate at him.

"After breakfast," she said. "We'll talk."

I scooped another spoonful of Tang and pretended not to hear. "Mornin' Mr. Russell Pearce Malson, Hiram Evergreen Hobart," I said, as he shuffled over. "Did I get it right?"

"Add a third and you're there." He winked and eased into a

chair opposite mine. "Did I ever tell you the story of Desert Fox and the Scorpion?"

I shook my head; the old man had an endless supply.

"Well, it happens after this big desert rain, see, and there's this scorpion…" He proceeded to tell me a silly tale, about a talking scorpion at the edge of a flooded wash. "Scorpion needs to get to the other side, so he begs a ride from a fox who paddles out into the current."

"Do they make it across?"

"Point of fact, sis, it's smooth sailing for a while, with Desert Fox paddling hard and Scorpion on his snout, a grand view of the desert with sand and rock and prickly pear. But when they get to the middle of the wash, look out."

"What happened?"

"You sure you wanna know? It ain't perty."

"'Course I'm sure."

"Well there's this yelp from Desert Fox. He's quit paddling, see, 'cause Scorpion's gone and bit him. 'What the hell—" He glanced at Momma, "'heck, I mean, did yeh do that for!' Fox says, 'Now we're both gonna drown!' And just like that Desert Fox is going down with Scorpion right there on his snout. There's splashing and coughing and all kinds of hullabaloo, until just as they go under, Scorpion says, 'It's simple why I done it, 'cause I'm a scorpion.'"

"That's it?"

"That's it." The old man slurped his coffee.

"They drowned?"

No answer.

"Seems to me Scorpion could have showed some restraint." Momma said, taking a chair next to me.

"Oh lots of folks have trouble with that." Russ locked eyes with her. "But it don't prove they're not sorry, now, does it?"

It wasn't an hour later that Sandy and I said goodbye to Russ on the front porch. I'd picked up the phone to call her, and the two of us stood under the eaves with Russ on the walk, his floppy hat and Levi jacket, ever darkening in a summer rain.

"But where will you go?" I asked.

"Oh, don't you worry 'bout me, I got places." And then he

sang, "*California, here I come, right back where I started from...* You girls know that one? ...*where bowers of flowers bloom in the spring?*"

We shook our heads.

"You're too young, I suppose."

We stood a while, listening to the rain, until Sandy said, "Hey—you find anything good in McEgan's barn?" Naturally I'd told her the whole story.

"Point of fact," Russ said, "that's something I been meaning to talk to you two about."

"What?" I said.

"Well, I heard you two know full well..." he shifted his bedroll. "What I mean to say is, I bet you don't know they got rabbits in that barn."

"Rabbits?" We said.

"A whole slew of 'em. So many, you could take an armload and nobody'd notice. And by the looks of the choppin' block, I'd say they eat 'em for dinner."

"Rabbits?"

"It's what I said, ain't it? They probably use the meat *and* the fur."

Sandy and I gawked at each other, then a picture flashed into my head: Appoline's white-fur pouch. Now that I thought about it, it sure could have been rabbit fur. Russ was still carrying on "—venture to say you can eat a whole lot worse than rabbit. Rattlesnake for one, which, I can tell you first-hand is no worse than an old chicken." He knitted his eyebrows, scuffed his boot against the walk. "Aw, heck," he said, "I never should've told you about them rabbits." I could have sworn then a look came over him, the kind he wore for his tallest tales. But why would he lie about rabbits?

"You go pokin' around that barn, you'll get yourselves in trouble, you will. Promise me you won't do that, girls. It ain't worth a free rabbit, no matter how soft they are—promise?"

We mumbled our assents, trying to process the rabbit tale as he backed toward Pardee. When he reached the rope swing, he gave it a whirl and tipped his hat.

"Adios then."

"Adios," we muttered back.

As he turned to go, the rain picked up, coming hard now

from a blue-black sky. I figured he was headed for the bus stop at Pardee Park, then on to Union Station to hop a freight train. The melody he sang flitted around in my head: *Where bowers of flowers bloom in the spring...* Such a strange old man. And what an odd note to leave on—rabbits!

But standing there, watching Russ go, what I felt more than anything was sad. Would I see him again? Would he be all right? Never would I have guessed that I'd follow his footsteps one day to the bus stop and beyond, that same old tune haunting me: *California here I come, right back where I started from...*

Chapter 27

People keep interesting things in shoeboxes: treasury bonds and photographs, buttons and spools of thread, or in my brother Jimmy's case, a dead turtle. He was a kid then, no more than six, which explains plenty. He thought the turtle needed a new house so he put him in the box and "accidentally forgot." So much for boys and their pets. The stench made me gag when I poked my nose in.

I didn't expect to find my mother's letters at the parsonage, but I couldn't help looking. I opened each shoebox I ran across: at church, at friends' and neighbors' houses, sometimes even at shoe stores. I was fascinated with them, the soft-air poof when you opened and closed their lids, like whispered secrets. I dreamed at night of finding *the* shoebox, which would smell not of algae and death but of ink and Noxzema skin cream. When I slipped off the lid, letters would fly out like a flock of doves. One day soon I would open that box, I knew I would.

Until then, I took up guitar. Didn't everybody in the 1970s? *If I had a hammer, I'd hammer in the mo-or-ning...* Hammering was something my beat-up psyche could relate to. Grandma Carsten had stumbled on the instrument at an estate sale and thought of me. But I saw a problem right away. Besides the fact that it was out of tune, the guitar was right-handed and I was left. I'd either have to flip it like Jimi Hendrix and reverse the strings or hold onto it like a right-hander. I tried the second option, the right-handed way, and—

whad'ya know?—it felt fine.

"Don't let it turn you into a pothead," Grandma warned, fearing a direct connection.

"No, Grandma."

I messed around with those strings for a couple of days until I realized Manny could tune it for me. It took three seconds more to talk him into regular lessons. Playing by ear or straight from memory he wrote sheets of music for me with simple chords that I could practice. Even better, I got to choose tunes I liked from The Beatles and Cat Stevens, sometimes straight off KISN-FM. The guitar became for me what my mother's art was for her, or at least that's the way I saw it. Alone in my room, I pounded the strings for hours, to drown out my frustrations.

The biggest was still my mother's messenger. Every few months, another letter arrived: now Thursday evening, next Tuesday dawn. It was impossible to pin down. Three letters later I was a year older and heading to high school without a clue how to track him.

I refused to give up, though, always searching for leads in the people around me and in my mother's letters. Most of what she wrote about that year was Lady and her pregnancy. I hate to admit it, much as I loved her story, but those letters were a bore. A growing pregnancy, like anything growing, is slow, especially when you're 14. What's worse, after the long build-up, she couldn't even describe the birth. She said she got to the barn one morning and found the colt, already standing. I wanted to be happy for her, for the way her legs went to jelly in that moment. But how could I? I wasn't the one with a new colt.

My boredom vanished with the letter that followed the birth. Not right away, with the first few pages, but by the end, it took the legs out from under me.

Dear Ace,

I wish you could see it with your own eyes: how fast a foal changes. Faster than human newborns, that's for sure! From the moment he was born late that spring, Lady Agate's colt grew agile, walking and suckling, the way the vet put it, like a champ.

In the attic, I leaned back against the two-by-four, trying to picture it.

It's the reason I called him Champ and felt so proud. Sure he was beautiful, anybody could see that: a rich molasses-brown with never-ending long legs. But even better, he was healthy... and Lady Agate too, after giving birth.

You could hardly keep me from the barn in those days. When school got out, I didn't walk home with Doug, but raced ahead, the whole two miles to the barn. Most days I kept Lady and Champ in the corral, to run around in the fresh air. So when I got home, I'd hop in to say hello and try to pet the little guy before he'd scamper away. Then I'd bring the two of them in and switch out the stallion, restless from being cooped up. I couldn't stay long, though. If I lagged too far behind Doug, I'd be asking for it with Astrid.

In the evening I'd head to the barn again, when I was done with my chores. It was my favorite time to draw, when the shadows stretched out over the hills. Even when the school year ended I kept this routine, slipping out to sketch the horses in the last light of day... and wondering when I'd see Sal again. Champ was growing so fast. He'd gone from a starry-eyed newborn with a tail like a squirrel's to a rowdy youngster I could tether to Lady for easy rides.

I have no doubt my drawing improved during those weeks. I drew from the corral fence or climbed to the hayloft to dangle my legs from the back of the barn. My perspective was a bit off from so high, but it was worth it for the view. I could see north and east and far to the west where the hills marched off to the ocean.

But I never saw Sal. The Rossanos were so late to the ranch that year I'd stopped expecting him. Plus, I was deep in thought, trying to show movement on paper. I finally had something going with shorter lines and quicker strokes when the page went black, when everything went black.

"Guess who?" a voice said. Somebody's hands had covered my eyes. It wasn't Doug. He would've faked pushing me from the

loft. In the next breath, I smelled it, the fog and the sea. "So," I said, "you finally got tired of the city huh?"

The hands tugged me to the floor, and there he was, staring down with that coyote grin. "How'd you know it was me?" There were olive-green flecks in his eyes that I hadn't noticed before. "I smelled you," I told him, and he threw his head back and laughed.

"How are you," he asked as I scrambled up. "Fine, until you knocked me over and made a mess." A lock of hair fell in my eyes and he brushed it free. "But you look good messy," he said. I couldn't stop smiling. It was so wonderful seeing my friend.

He asked about the colt then, since it was the first time he'd seen him. The Rossanos had gone to Italy that winter, according to Astrid, to celebrate Sal's upcoming high school graduation. He hadn't even seen Lady pregnant. "He's something else," he said. "Isn't he?" We stood at the loft door, watching the colt hop around, chasing a gnat or a fly. I picked up my notebook and showed it to him. "I drew pictures. You can see what he looked like from his first day."

"I saw you drawing when I came up. I watched you a while." It surprised me, Grace. He said there was this thing I did with my mouth, like a pout, so I smacked his leg. "You're lying!" Then he did the craziest thing: he grabbed the notebook and hopped into the loft doorway, leaning out so far my stomach dropped. With one hand he hung on and with the other, flipped through my sketches.

"This one's best," he said, holding the sketch I'd been working on. "You going to paint it?" He swung close to me then and lowered his voice. "I don't see the paint set, didn't you get it?" I could tell by his eyes he knew I did. But what was I supposed to say, that I'd wanted to thank him a thousand times? "It's beautiful. I loved it the minute I got it, but..." "But what?" he dangled over me. "But I'm not very good painting yet. Actually, I'm awful, so I'm working on my drawing first."

Sal hopped down. He didn't look mad. "You want to practice on me? You know, draw my picture?" Well, Grace, that took me off guard. The truth was, I did want to draw his picture. I'd tried lots of times without him around but never seemed to get it right. "You sure?" I asked and he smirked. "Would I ask if I wasn't? Tell you what—I just got my diploma. You could make it my graduation present." I must have been beaming. "You got a deal."

For the next half hour, Sal sat cross-legged in a patch of sun, dust motes framing him as I sketched his image. The evening light gave me lots to work with, the waves in his hair, the glow in his eyes. But it's always easy to draw something you've missed. Sal talked as I drew, about his trip to Italy and his plans for the coming fall. "I'm headed to USC for pre-med," he said. "And that's what you want?" "Sure." He laughed. "Unless I can find a race track on the way." He smiled a sad little smile then that reminded me of his dad.

When I'd almost finished the portrait, we heard voices in the corral below. "There he is!" And, "Hello little guy!" Sal stood and brushed himself off. "My folks are here. What'd you say you call the colt?" "Champ," I reminded him. "That's right. How could I forget?" He was halfway to the ladder when I held up my sketch. "Hey, don't you want to see it?" "Of course, beautiful, but we'll have to catch up later." Then he disappeared down below.

From the loft door I watched as he went out to his parents. Mrs. Rossano had a camera and a smile on her face. Dr. Rossano caught my eye but looked away as I waved. I'd learned not to take it personal. It's the way he was. Besides, Sal had distracted him, darting through the corral after the colt. I had an image of him, finally, in my notebook, close up and detailed. The half smile, the wild streak. But as I studied it, there in the loft, I wasn't sure if it was any good. Would another person even recognize it as him?

Two days later, I got my answer. I was sitting at the kitchen table, peeling potatoes, when Astrid thrust the drawing under my nose. "What the hell is this?" she said, hissing so hard her spit hit my face. She must have found it in my room. I put the potato down. "He asked me to draw it," I told her and her hand came so hard, it knocked me off my chair. She was shouting now, that I "had no business!" that I'd "get us fired!" I put my hand to my mouth and it came away bloody. Where was Pops? Where was Doug?

"What you gonna do now," she said, "cry? Well go ahead you goddamn baby!" I glared at her. She could slap my skin off and I wouldn't give her the satisfaction. "You're lucky I didn't break your jaw!" she yelled, leaning closer. "You go anywhere near that boy again, you better believe I will! Know your place, Cauliflower, know your place!"

Her murmuring shoes pivoted to the stove next where a pan sat on the burner. Hot grease to fry the chicken. She picked it up and swung around as my chest flooded with fear. "If I throw this in your face, if I melt it off, it won't be a problem, will it?" The grease spit as I dove under the pan and ran.

The next morning, I was in the stall with Lady and the colt, when I heard Sal's voice. "Hey, Sharon," he said, from the front of the barn. "You'll like this. I told my folks what you said and they're already calling him Champ." I stepped behind Lady to hide my face. "You turning shy on me?" he said, coming up. "I got here early," I answered, keeping my head down, "hoping I'd miss you. Astrid's orders. I'm not supposed to talk to you ever again." He took hold of my arm and pulled me around the colt. "My God Sharon, what happened?" I wanted to smile, to reassure him, but my mouth hurt. I knew how I looked, the split lip, the ugly bruise.

"Who did this? Your mother?" He wouldn't let up until I told him the truth. All of it, except the part where she'd threatened to burn my face. I was too ashamed to tell that. By the time I finished, his hands were in fists. He was going over there, so she'd never touch me again. "If you do that," I pleaded, "she'll flip. She'll hit me anyway, then run me off. She's threatened to plenty of times. She doesn't care about me, Sal, don't you see?"

The next thing that happened, Grace, changed everything. His eyes went from mine to my cut. "But I care," he said. Then, with a tenderness I'd never known, he brought his lips to the wound and kissed me. Even with my eyes shut, I filled up with light, spinning like the dust motes in the barn. When he pulled *away, I was breathless, out of my skin. "We're going riding," he said, "on the trails fast and free where no one, especially not your mother, can find us."*

The idea was so wild, Grace, my heart pounded. Did I dare defy Astrid? Champ nuzzled his mother then and I remembered. "We can't ride Lady. Champ's too young, we shouldn't leave him." But Sal wouldn't take no for an answer. "Then we'll ride Cesare," he whispered, "in the saddle together." There was a sting when he came at me again, and with this kiss, I tasted the sea.

I threw down my mother's letter. For the first time, in four years, I threw it down. Why the hell was she telling me this? What did I care about her doomed romance? My mind flashed to Sandy and what she'd said: *Sal kisses her.* Damn that Sandy. Did she have to be right about this too? I bolted from the attic, in need of air. My guitar was close, propped at the side of my bed, and I grabbed it, driving my fingers over the strings hard as I could. I didn't need a song, not even a chord, just violence and noise.

Chapter 28

I don't remember how long I sat there, pounding on that guitar. My fingers were numb by the time I quit. Afterward, I didn't really find the courage to go back to the attic. It was more like wandering through the door and letting my butt hit the floor. Maybe I was wrong about her story, I thought. Maybe whatever scared me was just a lesson about boys. She was my mother, after all. Isn't that what mothers do?

I picked up the pages and went back to it.

I can hardly explain my feelings that day, Grace, in the saddle with Sal at my back. My skin came alive next to his.

Oh boy…

I couldn't speak for so many emotions. We were full of innocence, the two of us, riding from our parents to the freedom of the hills. I felt safe with Sal, even skittering over a rocky patch on that crazy stallion. He didn't kiss me again or say much on that ride, but he didn't need to. The way he wrapped his arms around me said enough.

Okay, okay, I told myself, remember how lonely she is…

We arranged to meet like that a number of times, later that week and come the next. To stay out of sight, I met him on the ridge and climbed into the saddle with him. But it was a walk to that ridge, so after a few days, we got lazy and started leaving from the barn instead. We rode wild, like bandits running from the law. I won't pretend it wasn't fun, Grace, thundering over the trails. We were carefree at the start of that summer, and, as it turns out, foolish.

It was on the ridge that he found us, dismounted from Cesare and sitting side by side. The Rossanos had been on the ranch only a few short weeks by that time. I knew something was wrong by the look on Sal's face. One minute he was telling me how his Dad promised him a car, and the next, he froze up. I turned, completely surprised to see Lady. Why was she away from Champ? Then I realized Dr. Rossano was in the saddle. His eyes were locked on Sal, and he pulled Lady up short.

"Take Cesare back to the barn and meet me at the chateau," he said, his voice cold and hard. Sal got to his feet and started to say something, but his father nearly growled. "The girl can walk!" The color had drained from Sal's face and he moved slowly, swinging a leg over Cesare and glancing at me before he rode off.

It was only then that Dr. Rossano turned to me. "I expect you know how to get back," he said, twitching with fury. "Yes, sir," I told him. I saw disgust in his eyes too, at the bruise on my face and my cut lip. He pulled Lady forward so his boot brushed my arm. "From now on," he hissed, "as long as a single Rossano is here on this ranch, you will not step foot near that barn, you hear? Your brother will tend the horses. And if I find out you've come near my son, if you so much as speak to him, your family is gone, understand?" I was stunned by his intensity.

"Do you understand!" I couldn't find my voice, so I nodded and the tears broke free, tears I hated. They made me look weak. Dr. Rossano whipped Lady around, slammed his heals in her flanks and rode off. It hit me then how blind I'd been. Astrid was cruel, even dangerous, no question about that, but she wasn't the one in charge. In one terrible minute, Dr. Rossano had cut me off from everything I cared about: Sal, the horses, everything.

The ranch was torture after that. I missed Sal, I missed Lady and Champ. I even missed the barn. Sometimes, when it was too much, I snuck there late at night, to spend a few minutes. It was hard, Grace. Even Doug was mad at me for the chore of the horses, so I promised to do his part of the rose garden for him. That turned out to be a mistake. I'd set myself up to work in the shadow of that castle.

What was worse, the Rossanos made a point to entertain guests the rest of that summer. Rich guests with college-bound daughters. The point wasn't lost on me. I heard them splashing in the pool and tried not to picture them with their cokes and martinis. I finished my work fast so I could escape to the ridge with my art. It might've been easier, Grace, if Sal had talked to me, but from the moment his father caught us, he kept his distance. I knew how he looked up to his dad, how much influence the man had, but still it hurt.

It was late July before I saw him again. I was outside raking pea gravel when I heard his voice, and here he came with a tall brunette. He was smiling at her the way he'd smiled at me. As they went by, he looked right through me like I didn't exist. That very minute I told myself I'd never trust him again.

The next time I saw him was only days later. I was at the roses and there he was, strolling toward me. He was tan from the pool and his white teeth flashed. I tried to focus on the roses and steady my hands, but my heart hammered. When he crossed the footbridge, I couldn't help looking up, into his eyes.

"Everyone's in town," he said, "and I don't have much time." The Rossanos still had their guests. I pinched off another bloom and turned away. "Sharon, listen," he said, pulling me around. "I have to see you, we have to talk." Under the tan his face looked flushed. "Do you know the side cellar door, the one that leads to the old winery?" I shook my head. If I'd seen it, I didn't remember.

"It's there," he said, "around the corner." He pointed to the side of the castle, opposite the drive. "So?" I said. "I'll make sure it's unlocked. Meet me there tonight, just after dark." What was the point? I wondered, so he could explain away his stupid

behavior? So he could tell me about the brunette? "I don't think so, Sal." He looked around, checking the grounds, but there was nothing besides the castle, the roses and thorns.

In the next breath, he came close enough to see the flecks in his eyes. I couldn't force myself to look away. He leaned in and kissed me, and in that moment I forgot everything: the brunette and his father, my place on the ranch, but worse than anything, my own instinct not to trust him. He was the boy who liked me again, the Sal I knew. If it hadn't been for his arms at my back, I would've collapsed into the thorns.

I quit reading, my stomach churning. Sal Rossano, the boy who liked her? How about the jerk who looked through her! I dashed the letter to the plywood and burst into my room. Beside the bed, on my knees, I crawled, thrusting my arms underneath. By the handle I yanked it, stirring dust to my face. The paint case. That beautiful horrible paint case. From my knees I lifted it and flung it to the floor, so it hit with a satisfying *thwuck*. Again, and again I lifted it. *Thwuck. Thwuck.* My kneecaps burned against the hard surface, but it felt good. It felt wonderful.

"Gra-ace?" My father called from downstairs.

"Go back to your Bible," I spit. "Might as well read it to The Cyclops."

I swung the case again, surprised by the Linoleum. Hard as I tried I could barely scratch it. But the case split nicely—Sal Rossano's surprise gift!—one latch open and the paints spinning across the floor.

"Grace! Answer me!" His heavy footfalls were on the steps, so I flung the case with everything in me. I was breaking it up, my mother's story and Sal's gift. It was a crooked maw now, half-open and grinning, the lining jagged like sharp teeth.

"Grace, what in Sam Hill!"

I stopped and got to my feet. Beneath the lining blinked something white. A piece of paper? I depressed the second latch and it came open. A stitch of thread dangled too and behind it was some kind of paper. Someone had pulled away the fabric and sewn it inside. I took hold, pulled at the string and slipped it free. What I saw on that sheet of paper knocked the air from my lungs: my mother's sketch of Sal Rossano, no doubt about it.

The landing groaned. "Grace! Why won't you answer me?" What I realized in the next instant made me drop the case one last time. The mouth, the face, and more than anything, the waves running through his hair, were *just like mine.*

The door flew open. "Grace!" Standing there, Pastor Thaddaeus James Carsten, the man I'd believed all my life to be my father. His height, his coloring were *nothing* like mine. How had that escaped me? When he saw the paint case and the drawing, the blood left his face.

"Grace," he said.

"He's my father isn't he?" The pastor stood motionless, a face and body cured in concrete. Then, soft as a sigh, he nodded. I lurched forward and vomited on his shoes.

Chapter 29

The summer of '67 is the "before" photo in my mind, before we knew what "after" looked like. We still had Momma and our innocence, and Ramblin' Russ was still a hobo, just a hobo. Looking back, I know this much: Russ didn't mean for us to destroy the McEgan barn. His true motive in getting us over there, wasn't devious. He thought he was helping. He thought it would open our eyes. But his rabbit tale had started a chain of events two young girls were powerless to stop.

"Rabbits," he'd said, "a whole slew of 'em." And from that moment, it was all Sandy and I could think about. How soft they were, if they were black or gray or tawny-brown. Hundreds hopped around in our brains, and hundreds more, for all we knew, near a chopping block in the McEgan barn.

We made a habit late that summer of climbing the Tree of Heaven to worry about it. We'd only known each other about a year by then, but we were blood sisters forever, having pricked our fingers to seal the deal. From high up in the tree, we had a view of the barn and the route Russ must have taken through a forest of blackberry thorns.

"Do you really think they cut 'em up and eat 'em?" I whispered, picturing soft, furry rabbits behind those sagging walls.

"I think the McEgans could eat anything," Sandy said, snapping a leaf frond for a better view.

Now and then, strange sounds came from the barn. I heard chopping once, and Sandy swore she heard a squeal.

"Do rabbits scream before they die?"

"I don't know, wouldn't you?"

We decided we were called on to rescue those rabbits, the way Methodists rescued the poor or boycotted grapes for migrant workers. We would free the rabbits from the McEgans' tyranny. It was our mission.

"And our revenge," Sandy said, "to settle the score over the church window."

"My Dad'll kill me if we get caught, you know."

"So we'll go at night, in the dark."

And we would have gone that summer—one of the many nights Sandy slept over—if not for a slight hitch along the way. We were over the fence already, with the flashlight, discussing McEgan's shotgun when it happened. I'd been thinking that Sandy was the biggest target with her blonde hair. On the other hand, I was the one carrying the light. "You don't think he'd shoot, do you?"

"'Course he would." Just as she said it, the top popped off my flashlight and we screamed. *Were we shot?* It was several minutes before we calmed down, when we finally connected the "pop" to our newfound darkness. "Crap, it's only the flashlight."

The final straw was Momma's voice from the back of the house. "Girls! Root beer floats!"

"We can always go some other time," Sandy said and I agreed.

A new year rolled in before we found the courage. It was 1968, the year that took Martin Luther King, Bobby Kennedy and, eventually, my mother. At the time of King's death, in April, we assumed Momma had a chest cold, a nasty hack she kept fighting with cough syrup. I remember because of the visit the two of us made to Georgia's. It was the day after King's assassination, and Georgia's street, despite all the parked cars, was ghostly quiet. We'd been to her place once before, but this time it was packed: there were more Negroes in her living room than I'd seen in my entire life. We were the only whites in the place, though nobody seemed to hold it against us. In the thick of the crowd stood Georgia, her beautiful smile turned upside down.

"Ah can't believe it," she said as we came up. "Ah just can't." Momma held her hands and would have kept holding them if not for the coughing fit that had her swigging more cough syrup. "I's so sick of thiz cold," she said, drunk on Vicks.

By early June, around the time Bobby Kennedy was shot, my mother's fate was set too. We'd suffered a whiplash of emotions since that day at Georgia's, tumors in Momma's neck and chest, the six weeks of radiation and then remission. But before long the cancer was back. I only found out when Momma showed Dad as I listened in from the other room.

"It doesn't feel like a pregnancy," she said with hesitation. "It feels *wrong*."

"Now, Sharon," Dad said, "Let's not jump to conclusions. Wait for the doctor—wait and pray."

They never told me what the doctor said, or Jimmy either, who was only three. But by mid-summer, around the time of my tenth birthday, I knew it was bad. The way she moved, so listless and slow, like her demons had finally tracked her from her room.

"Grace?" she said, dragging her sewing machine out one day.

"Yeah?"

"I'm not feeling too good—"

"Sorry Momma."

"—and I have to alter some clothes to fit this tummy of mine. Your Dad took Jimmy to Honey's. You think you could go to Sandy's, maybe spend the night?"

"Sure."

"Okay sweetheart, go on then. Make sure it's all right with her folks."

"Momma?"

"Hmm?"

"What's wrong with your tummy?"

Her eyes came up, soft and shining. "There's a mass in my abdomen and new spots on my lungs."

"But the doctor can fix it right?" My voice sounded like a cartoon girl's. "Can't he?"

"It doesn't look good, honey."

I ran to her then and flung my arms around her waist. Below

my sternum I felt the bump, not a baby, not a brother or sister, but the demon that had burrowed in. I wanted to tear it loose and squeeze the lifeblood out of it.

Ten minutes later, when I left for Sandy's, I grabbed the flashlight. I don't know why. Maybe my hand craved its weight or I thought I could smash something with it.

I talked Sandy into sleeping outside that night, our pillows and sleeping bags right on the grass. Outside we could talk for hours and stare at the sky. There was no moon that night, and the Big Dipper sparkled in a dome of stars. Some were already burnt out, I knew, from a book I read, but we saw them as they once were, the last of their light racing to crash at the backs of our eyes.

"Let's do it now," I said.

"Do what?" Sandy lay next to me, her sleeping bag pulled to her chin. It was chilly enough that we'd crawled in with our clothes on.

"Do what?" she said.

"What else? What we've been talking about for a whole year, bonehead. Storm the barn, rescue the rabbits."

"Really?" She sat up. "Why tonight?"

I hadn't said anything about my mother and I didn't intend to yet. "Why not? We always say we're going to, but we're such chicken shits, we never do."

"You're serious!" She said, since I wasn't known for cussing.

"Damn right," I added for good measure.

She had her deck shoes on before I could shuck myself from my sleeping bag.

Chapter 30

It was odd sneaking past the parsonage, where I usually slept, where my parents were. When I saw the light from their bedroom window, I aimed the flashlight at the grass, throwing shadows through the blades. This time, I had the top screwed on tight.

We made short work of the blackberry jungle, finding tunnels through the vines we couldn't see from the tree. We stepped over cut and trampled vines too and then a footprint dried in mud. I shined the flashlight on it.

"Old man McEgan's you think?"

"No. Butte or Appoline's, or maybe some weirdo peeping Tom who looks in your window."

"Very funny," I said. "So funny I forgot to laugh."

A few minutes later, we were alongside the barn, the flashlight pointed at one dusty window and then the next. They were yards apart.

"Where's the door?"

"I don't know. There's thorns here—ouch!"

I cast the light over the wood where the only paint left was deep in its grooves. If you ran your hand over it, you got a million splinters, just ask Miss Brilliance who tried it first thing. Around the corner was a huge door, the kind that opens the whole front of a barn. But it was padlocked shut.

"Over here," Sandy called.

"Shh!" I warned. "The farmhouse!" I could see it in the distance, a huge white ghost in the dark. No light came from the windows, but it was possible somebody was in there, looking out.

"Where'd you go?"

"I'm here," she called, and her blonde head darted from around the barn. "Hurry!" Something rustled at my ankles and, in a flash, I was next to her. I shined the light and there it was, a standard-sized, crooked-on-its-hinges door.

"You found it."

"Count on me, chickadee."

The door stood open several inches, so I moved the light through the crack. Nothing but air.

"Just think," Sandy said, "rabbits!" She had a hand to her face, stringing hair under the tooth. "You ready?" I wanted to go in, I really did, but something made me hesitate—a noise, a hunch? I should have said something, about McEgan's shotgun or trespassing or JDH. *Something.* But I didn't want to be called a coward, or worse: a Goody Two-shoes.

"What's up?" she said.

"Nothing. It's nothing."

"Then what are we waiting for?"

Inside, it was even darker than the moonless night. The air smelled foul: something oily and rank, and something else, just as bad but somehow familiar that I couldn't quite place.

"You spy any rabbits?"

I strained to see. We saw each other faintly, in the back glow of the flashlight, but the beam, at any distance, fell weak.

"Not yet." I moved the light to the floor, wooden planks under a layer of scattered hay. "Rabbits eat hay, don't they?" The light picked up dirt clods and several candy wrappers.

"Yeah, but I don't think Mike and Ikes."

I swung the beam to and fro and hit on a lump forty or fifty feet away. It looked like a body.

"What's that?"

"Beats me." Sandy's voice shivered like jello. "But it sure ain't rabbits."

"Is it somebody?"

"I don't know."

In lockstep rhythm, we inched forward. Ten feet, twenty, over the scattered hay. Here and there, a floorboard thumped, and then, suddenly, behind us.

"D'you hear that?" I spun around and the circle of light hit the door. It was open, just as we'd left it. Against the wall was some kind of bench and a cabinet where shadows wavered. I lowered the beam and brought it back, and they wavered just the same.

"Maybe the wind?" Sandy said.

"What wind?"

When nothing happened, we pressed on. The closer we got to the shape on the floor, the more it looked human. Finally we were close enough to make it out: a coat and some blankets beside an unlit lantern.

"At least it's not a body," I said.

"Yeah," Sandy whispered, "But somebody sleeps here."

"Who?"

The flashlight shined on a patch of white: a fur pouch.

"Apple," I said.

"You mean Athole." She'd run her hand over her mouth for the sound. "It's what she is, you know, an asshole."

"Yeah, but where—" Suddenly, I knew the smell that I hadn't been able to place: *mildew*. I froze, listening, but the barn was eerily quiet.

"She must hang out here," Sandy said.

"Hold the flashlight," I whispered. I spilled the contents of the pouch into my hand: loose coins, a stick of gum and a tiny doll in a print dress.

"Apple plays with dolls?"

Sandy snorted. "Figures, doesn't it?"

Skshh came the sound and we whipped around. There in the dark, lit up by a single match, was a floating head. Our screams could have flattened a forest. The eyes were wide, the face, gaunt and dirty. Then it spoke. "Scared you, huh?" and I marveled how a severed head could talk. "Serves you right," it said, "since you both think you're such hot shit."

I caught my breath and tried to speak, but it came out like a squeak. "Hi Apple."

"Hi Apple," she mimicked. We stood there watching her, the

flame at her face, the glow of the flashlight dimly lighting the rest. She was thinner than I remembered and wore a clingy blouse with a band of ruffles at the neck. She looked like an apparition, a pale and sickly apparition. When the wooden match died out, she lit another.

"I bet you don't have the guts to do this." She lifted a strand of hair to the flame and it flared, halfway to her head.

"You're crazy!" Sandy said.

"No I'm not. I'll do it again." The laugh that followed was a rusty hinge.

"Don't Apple, it's stupid," I said.

"You're stupid." Apple took out another match, the box rattling as she scratched it alongside. This time when it flared, she brought it to her neck where the ruffles bunched. The flame sputtered at first then surged into a bright ball that lit up the barn. For a long second, we could see everything: the walls, the rafters, the door we'd come in. We all stood perfectly still, including Apple, until the ball flamed out. Then her arms shot up and she screamed, a fleet of rusted hinges. I don't remember how she got to the floor, only running with the flashlight, seeing her down, the hair on one side of her head gone, the ruffles melted and the skin angry with burn. I wanted to scream. I wanted to run.

"Get back!" she roared. She had another match lit before I understood, touching the flame to scattered hay. It caught and poured like water toward us.

"Nooo!"

We tried to run around it, but she kept lighting more, her match still alive, finding hay. The door we'd come in was blocked by fire. When it licked Apple's clothes, I turned and ran. A tractor was ahead of us, along the side of the barn, then a row of cages. Rabbits? Rabbits! every one of them white, a possibility that had escaped us. Was there another door out? At some point I heard footfalls and realized Sandy was at my side. The flames were on us, the heat at our calves, crisp and stinging. I glanced back. The barn was burning—*burning!* I ran. No exit in the back that I could see. A few more steps and we'd be trapped.

"No God!" Then I spotted it: a sturdy table near the back wall. Could we jump there and escape the flames? Something covered it, clotted and staining. Hunks of rabbit fur, dried blood: the chopping block. The smell came next, but it was nothing compared to the heat lashing our heals. We scrambled on the block as the fire raced under us to the back wall.

"What now?" Sandy yelled.

"I don't know!"

"Look," she said, "no fire!" While angry sheets tore up the walls and pooled below us, the front of the barn had gone dark. The dry hay had burned too quickly to ignite the floorboards. Slowly but surely, the darkness was inching our way.

"It's not coming fast enough!" Sandy shouted. The wall behind us was burning now, searing our backs.

"We have to run for it!"

Sandy yanked up her pant legs. I'd worn shorts, and the backs of my bare legs screamed.

"On a count of three!" She yelled. "One." I couldn't wait. "Two-Three!" We jumped into the flames, shrieking at the sting on our shins. I don't remember seeing the rabbits—or Apple—on the way out, only flying over that lake of fire, through the flames, then over the blackened floor, my feet running and running, and the flashlight lighting charred floorboards and hay, then packed earth, berry vines and, finally, fence.

We were in my backyard when it blew—the tractor we learned later—an ear-splitting explosion that released the fire into the night. Seconds later, trailers tumbled, raining embers from a coal-black sky. The roof of the barn was gone and the walls a raging inferno. The sound of the blast brought people running, my mother and father too, their faces blazing like the fire as they pulled us back, retreating to the cool of the churchyard.

"You okay? You okay?" they shouted before turning back to stare at the glow. You couldn't blame them. It was so bright, so blindingly spectacular, it extinguished the stars. I stared, along with them, and pictured the white rabbits in their wire cages. The stinging heat, the unimaginable pain. Sirens on the street wailed in sympathy. We'd gone in to rescue them and now they were burning up.

I didn't realize my mouth was open, let alone what I was screaming until my father shook me.

"What about her? Is she in there? Is she inside?"

I screamed it again, "Appoline!"

Chapter 31

All those years I tried to be the preacher's daughter. After the fire. After Momma was gone. Years of Sunday school and worship services, vacation Bible school and church camp, carrying the acolyte torch to the altar candles more times than I could count. At least I'd tried. I'd even set Sandy straight on the 23rd Psalm, which wasn't easy, considering she thought "I shall not want" meant the Shepherd himself.

"It means *things*, you big goof brain. The Lord is my shepherd, I shall not want for *things*. Get it?"

"Well I wondered," she'd said.

Now even that was slipping from me. I was a cynical 14-year-old, a high school freshman, which would have meant higher status in the church youth group if I'd bothered to go. When our youth leader confronted me and encouraged me to bring my guitar, I made excuses, preferring to pluck the strings alone in my room. I was forgetting my mother—the way she moved, the fine points of her face—and it terrified me. Now the Preacher wasn't even my father, a fact that shocked even Sandy.

"That's impossible," she said when I told her. Sandy had changed over the years too. She had an hourglass figure, wore black mascara, and parted her hair not from the side but straight down the middle. But she was still tactless as ever.

"If your mom is gone and your dad's not really your dad,

doesn't that make you an orphan?"

"Gee thanks, Sandy. I hadn't thought of that."

I continued to punish the preacher for letting me believe all those years he was my father. It made him a liar as far as I was concerned. "You don't deserve to be called Dad," I told him. "You never did."

He sighed. "There's a reason we did it, Grace. We thought you'd be happier."

"And that gives you a license to lie?" He didn't respond, and I had to laugh. Here he was, Mr. Eloquent Preacher, at a loss for words. But he always had a word about church. "You missed worship again," he'd tell me after services.

"So?"

"So, it isn't right, Grace. Here you are, the Preacher's Ki—" he caught himself.

"Try bastard child."

"For heaven's sake, it's not like the whole world knows, and, besides, it's none of their business. The least you can do is show up. Where's your relationship with God?"

"Where's yours?"

I thought about Sal Rossano constantly in those days, climbing to my room to stare at my mother's sketch. Where the hell was he now? Did he know I existed? I hadn't lifted a finger yet to find out, hadn't even tried California directory assistance, because the truth was, I couldn't imagine what I'd say: Here I am, your long-lost daughter?

Still, I couldn't stop wondering, sometimes staring in the bathroom mirror at features I knew were half his. It reminded me of a bizarre game Sandy and I played once, with an armoire vanity in her parents' bedroom. Sandy got us going first, touching her nose to the edge of the mirror while I stood in front of it. What I saw from my perspective was half of her face grotesquely doubled. It was scary funny, like her inbred cousin had just stepped in the room. The next minute she had two noses, then none as her face ballooned.

"Stop!" I said, laughing. "You look like a freak!" When she tilted her chin, the eyes spaced out hideously wide.

"You try it," she insisted.

I took her place and touched my nose to the edge of the glass, but she didn't laugh. "Holy shit," she said.

"What?" I tried to turn, but couldn't see from my angle.

"Your eyes are brown."

Of course. My blue eye was behind the mirror, so the brown was repeated on the other side. For the first time in my life, I had matching eyes, and I couldn't see them!

"Go to the other side," Sandy said, "Hurry, hurry!"

I went around.

"Freak out! Now tilt this way, a little more—Holy shit!"

"What?"

"That's *so* freaking cool. It's like there's two of you."

"I wanna see." Each time I moved, though, trying to peek into the glass, the blue-eyed girl became the lop-eyed me, the mirror image I always saw. It was opposite what everyone else saw when they looked at my face, a fact that took me years to figure out. In the mirror my blue eye was on the left, while everybody else clearly saw it on the right.

"Dang it, Sandy, I have to *see.*"

Her eyes lit up "*I* know!" and she ran out. When she came back a minute later, she had a hand mirror and she thrust it at me.

"Hold it up, use that to see!"

I did as she said and sure enough, there she was in the mirror, a girl with two blue eyes.

"Wow," was all I could say. Momma was still with us then and I saw her instantly. The girl in the mirror looked so much like her. She looked... pretty. I crossed to the other side and Sandy was right, there *were* two girls. The first with two blue eyes and now this one, strangely dark—exotic even. The dark girl had an edge. She seemed anxious to talk, like there was some kind of secret.

"Do you ever get the feeling," I said, staring at her image, "that there's somebody out there just like you only different?"

"That doesn't even make sense," Sandy said.

Standing at the bathroom mirror now, I wondered how much the dark girl resembled Sal. Was *he* the somebody like me only different? I covered my blue eye and pictured brown on both sides. All I had was a pencil sketch. How much did I look like him? I didn't know a lot about him or his personality, which made me wonder: Had the preacher told me everything? Much as I hated to, I went after him. It was easier than calling California. I found him downstairs at his desk.

"Dad?" I said, immediately wincing. I hadn't decided what else to call him.

"Hmm?" He didn't look up.

"I was thinking…" It took me a while to work up the courage, but then I peppered him. Had he ever met my father? Did he know what he was like? What had Momma said? The answers were No, No and Not Much. Finally I asked the question I'd been working up to: Had Sal ever tried to contact me?

"I don't believe so."

"Not my whole life? Not even through Momma?"

He shook his head. "Not that I know of. Your mother didn't talk about the man, Grace, and I didn't ask."

"Right," I said, folding my arms over my chest. "Or you were jealous." His jaw tightened. Knowing him and his feelings for Momma, I'd hit the bull's eye.

Before long, I knew the preacher was snooping through my things. There were fingerprints in dust, my drawers messy, and my mattress moved an inch or two. The truth is I got a kick out of it. He was desperate for the letters, and I was confident in my hiding place: in the attic, practically in plain sight but out of sight. If he thought to go in there, he'd see the flashlight and a couple of books. If he poked around, he'd find nothing under the blanket or in the rafters or past the floor. I had over a dozen letters by then, too many to fit in a book, so why bother looking in them? For once, Miss Brilliance had the perfect place. I'd seen it in the movies: the secret tome on the shelf hollowed out with great care. It looked like all the other books until you opened it to pieces of gold, the key to a safe, or a loaded gun. Mine, of course, held my mother's letters. The book I'd chosen was a hardcover copy of Crime and Punishment, for the simple reason that it was big enough for the job. With an old blade from the preacher's razor, I'd cut through hundreds of pages, past each fever of Raskolnikov, until my fingers bled. It was a small price to pay to keep the preacher out of my business. And it worked. As far as I know, he never did find my hiding place.

The problem was, I'd overlooked the obvious: our mailbox. I'd forgotten how enticing it was. The day he gave in to temptation, I happened to be over at the church.

"Shoot." I said, slogging through a guitar lesson with Manny. "I left Jim Croce in my room."

"B-but, you already know it. Ta-time in a Bottle."

"Naw, Manny," I laughed. "I'm not like you. I gotta have the music on paper. Tell you what, let's both go over. I'll make us a snack."

Not two minutes later, when we came through the entry, the preacher froze. He was in the kitchen, his face instantly terrified, as though we'd caught him with a prostitute. I didn't understand till I saw the envelope in his hand—and how he held it over a steaming pot.

"Oh my God!"

I threw my guitar at Manny and a second later was on him, grabbing and flailing, beating his chest. "How dare you—how *dare* you!" I kept beating and beating, forcing him back as his forearms rose in a half-hearted defense. "When did it come? When did it come?"

"S-stop," Manny hollered from behind me. "S-stop!" But I'd already scratched the preacher's face.

"How could you?" I screamed. "How *could* you!"

"I'm sorry, Ace…"

"Don't call me that. Only Momma calls me that."

The envelope was in my fist, half crumpled, but sealed. Still sealed.

"How long have you been doing this?" I hissed. "How many letters?"

"Grace, I—" Blood dripped from the scratch on his face.

"How many?"

"I haven't—" he sighed, "this is the first."

"Liar!"

"It's the truth, Grace. I've only read one before this. You remember," his voice shook, "when you were at Grandma's."

"You're pathetic. Look at you, a grown man, a *pastor* for God's sake, snooping around, steaming my letters. What a joke!"

"Please, Grace. I miss her too." He wiped his chin, smearing the blood.

"You want to know something?" I shook the letter, making it up as I went. "I thought about letting you read these, how *much* she adored my father. But not anymore, not to a liar and a sneak."

He was flat-out bawling now, a grown man in a 6-foot-four-inch frame, looking like Jimmy the day he smashed out his baby teeth.

"Grace, please," he blubbered, "you have to forgive me."

"Dream on," I said, turning to go.

Manny held out my guitar as I passed, but I ignored him. He was a retard, like Sandy said. He had no clue what was going on.

"Go home, Manny," I told him. "I'm done with guitar today."

Chapter 32

I crawled into the attic and released my own flood, wave after wave crashing over me with the power of a coastal storm. It was anger more than pain, and not all of it for my father. My mother had lied to me too, all along. As the preacher said, "We thought you'd be happier." *We*.

How long I sat there, in the dark attic, I don't know. Finally I flipped on the flashlight, the batteries rattling along with my brains. On the envelope was a smear of the preacher's blood. I tore right through it to my mother's pages.

My Dear Grace,

Would she call me that now if she could see me?

I can't help wondering what you'd have done if you were me and Sal said meet me in the castle cellar. Well, I'll tell you this: I had to fight to keep from smiling the whole rest of that day.

After dinner and the usual stack of greasy dishes, I went to my ridge, to roll the prospects around in my head. After dark, he'd said. I knew it wouldn't be long since the sun was low. I had to admit, I was flattered and excited. Sal wanted to see me! I sat with my bare feet over the edge, dangling free. In loose ground at my thigh, I wrote his name, Salvatore, then drew Sharon over it, spooning the S's. Was it possible for the two of us to be more than friends?

Yes, Momma, it is possible.

I looked to the sun again where it sank toward the hills and tried to picture it. But every thought that came to mind, the two of us at the rose garden, in the barn, or riding the trails, was quick as lightning covered by Dr. Rossano. I saw him on Lady with his nostrils flared. I saw Astrid too, creeping up in her murmuring shoes, and Mrs. Rossano with her cool-blue glare. As long as they were around, I didn't think I had a chance with Sal.

My dangling feet felt different then, bare as the rocks and just as filthy. I saw my clothes, old and worn. Was that why Sal wanted to talk, to explain my place, like Astrid had? The fact was, I'd never fit in with his castle crowd, the cokes and martinis by the pool. I was the hired help, the caretakers' girl. Isn't that why he'd ignored me?

The dust in the air promised a beautiful sunset over the hills, but I left the ridge early. At home, one of my favorite programs, Truth or Consequences, was on the radio. I sat next to Pops to listen, but the stunts fell flat. "You getting' sick, Sis?" he asked. "I'm fine," I told him, though I wasn't. I couldn't stop thinking about Sal and the castle cellar. Was he there, waiting for me? I went down the hall, filled the bathtub and eased in. It was dark outside. By the time I got out, it would be too late, so I wouldn't be tempted. I didn't need to hear I wasn't good enough.

I washed my hair and laid back in the water, trying not to think. But it was no good. My mind went to Sal in the rose garden that day, and I suddenly wondered: why would he kiss me if he was finished with me? There was something else too. When he held me his arms shook. I could feel them shaking still. Why would he shake like that if he didn't care? I sat up, sloshing water.

And this is where things get tricky, Grace. The decision I made next was the wrong one, no question about it. I should've stayed away from Sal Rossano. I should've waited to build my own future and confidence. I want you to know that, Grace, I was too young. Sometimes when you make mistakes there's no turning back. I should've taken the time to finish growing up...

But you didn't.

...but I didn't. When I remembered his arms and the way they shook, I jumped from that bath like fish from a lake. Had I missed him? Was I too late? I grabbed a towel and ran to my room, shaking water from my hair. I dressed and climbed out the window, hoping nobody would notice.

The moon was bright, which helped. I dashed over the drive and found grass, turning on speed to jump pea gravel. It was darker in the orchard, the glow of the moon blocked by trees, so I slowed down when I got there. From the far side of the orchard, the castle towers glowed where the bedrooms were, both towers lit up. I didn't know which was Sal's. Had he given up waiting? Most of the castle was dark, the cellar especially, since it didn't have windows. I stared at the blackened walls, hoping with all my heart Sal was behind them.

I hope he is too, Momma. If he cares about you, really cares, then there might be hope for me.

There was only one way to find out. Staying low, I made my way over the stone bridge and to the left. I didn't go that way much, since it was opposite the castle drive, and I tripped in the shrubbery. I stopped to listen, but it was clear nobody had heard. When I came around the stone wall, I saw the door Sal described and gently pushed it. It wasn't latched, and when I pushed it again, it came open.

Inside, the light was dim, only a single candle, but he was there, all right, on a couch or settee of some kind. He hadn't heard me, so I shut the door hard and he looked up. "You came!" he said, standing. "I wasn't going to," I told him, but..." I clammed up, not sure what to say. I thought his smile faded, but it was hard to tell in the flickering light. "I wouldn't have blamed you," he said, taking a step toward me. We stood a while, his face unreadable.

I could make out the settee and shapes that looked like wine barrels, but not much else. "No electricity in here?" I asked. Sal took another step. "I could probably turn the breakers on, but I kind of like it like this. Besides, there's cracks in the back wall where it comes up near the pool. Your father patched it, but it keeps crumbling." I looked him over, not sure if his point was about Pops or the wall. "If I turned the lights on," he explained, "somebody on the patio out back might see." "Oh," I said. He was worried about his parents.

In the rafters over our heads, something fluttered and I looked up. "What was that?" It came again. "Bats," Sal said, "they like it in here." "Bats?" I repeated and he laughed. "There's hundreds. They get in through those cracks, but don't worry, they won't hurt you. Come and sit." I stood at the door and shook my head.

For a while we just listened to the fluttering bats. Then Sal came closer and when I heard him breathe, I knew he was nervous just like me. He ran a hand through his hair. "Sharon," he said, "I need to explain... I owe you that much... " Oh no, I thought, here it comes. It sounded like the start of a letdown. He kept talking as he moved closer. "I know I hurt you..." But the tone was wrong. My chest went tight and I fumbled behind me, feeling for the door. He moved closer and I couldn't speak. I could hardly breathe. "I kept avoiding you," he said. "I know it was hard, but I —"

"Don't!" I blurted. I'd found my voice and the door at the same time. I couldn't let him say it, that I was the hired help, that I wasn't good enough, I just couldn't. "I never should've come," I said. I tried to leave, to twist the handle behind me, but Sal pushed me against the door. "Let me go!" I demanded.

But he begged me, "Please, Sharon, please!" I felt the heat off his skin, his face near mine, and those eyes, the dark pupils, were they filled with tears? I struggled as he held me and felt like crying too, but Sal said, "Shh, Sharon don't." He touched my cheek and exhaled with a shudder. "Your hair is wet," he whispered, "is it raining?" I couldn't stop shaking. "Are you cold?" I shook my head and he drew back to look in my eyes.

"You lived on this ranch a long time before I noticed you, just the caretaker's girl—a beat up thing, running wild half the time. Do you know the first time I really saw you?" He smiled and a tear fell to his cheek. I shook my head, fighting my own tears. "That day I caught you on Stella, your Lady Agate." Here came the coyote grin. "That great big mare and here you were, what, a hundred pounds? You knew you were in trouble, but you should've seen your face! Remember? Like you were some kind of warrior."

"I remember you weren't very nice," I said. "No," he agreed, "I guess I wasn't. My feelings for you started then, Sharon, that day in the barn. I knew you were younger—not by three whole years, but younger—and that we came from different worlds, so the whole thing seemed impossible. I tried to tell myself not to look at you, not to think about you. But when we talked, you seemed so mature." He came so close I felt his breath. "And your drawing, Sharon. You have no idea how talented you are. It's not your fault you were born into—"

"Born into what?" His eyelids fluttered. "Here's the thing," he said. "My parents told me to stay away from you a long time ago. Don't talk to her, they said. They even convinced me: They said the two of us were... well, that I have so much ahead of me and that you—"

"What? That I don't?" He didn't answer. "It's okay Sal," I said, jerking away. "You don't have to explain." I turned to leave, but he pulled me back. "No Sharon, that's not what I mean." I had the door partway open, but couldn't get through. "Please, listen," he begged. I struggled to get free, but he had my shoulders and held me there. "I can't pretend anymore." Then he kissed me, my mouth, my face, the tears that had splashed over.

"I tried to forget you, to ignore my feelings," he said, pulling back. "That girl you saw me with? The others? You know what I did the whole time they were around? I thought of you. I don't care if we have to hide from my parents." He put his hands on my cheeks, lifting my face up to his. "When I see you I want to *be with you, and when I get close..." He put his thumbs to my lips. "I want to touch you." His arms circled my back and he kissed me again, and the truth is, Grace, I was glad. In that moment, I could've stayed in Sal's arms forever. Minutes passed before he broke free. "Please tell me you feel the same."*

My body told him the answer, Grace, every inch of it. But I wasn't as wild as Sal, and my mind raced. I thought of his parents and mine, of my family losing the caretakers' job, losing everything! I thought of Astrid too: she would kill me if she knew about this. But he stood there, his eyes pleading. "Tell me, Sharon!" I broke away before I said it, got the door open and one foot out. "Yes!" I said. Then I ran, through the shrubs and past the roses, flying on a fevered passion. I flew all the way back to the cottage and to my bedroom, which, lucky for me was still empty.

And that's how it started, Grace, the two of us meeting in the old winery. Maybe you think I'm crazy for telling you this. You're a child. I'm your mother. But I want you to understand the power of first love. You'll fall one day too and, though I hate to be the one to tell you, it probably won't last, especially if the odds are against you like they were against Sal and me. If I can spare you an ounce of the pain I went through, then it's worth it.

What happened, Momma?

For now, Ace, remember this. I may have been brave, as Sal said, but I wasn't mature, not even close. The truth is, I was still a child, which I see now isn't such a bad place to be. Stay innocent as long as possible, dear daughter, because once it's gone, it's gone forever.

My love,
Momma

Finally, I understood one thing: the reason for the delay between the letters. She didn't want to taint my innocence. She was waiting for me to grow up, so I could handle the truth, so I didn't freak out. Every few months, another piece of the puzzle until the picture of my real father emerged, the lie she'd hidden all my life.

It explained everything…

Or did it? I sat a moment, suddenly remembering her own words from years before. "Sometimes it's better not to know." I was back in that moment then, a child at her bedside. I'd been happy in that world, I had to admit, the world she and the preacher had created for me. I'd been secure. And hadn't she said it herself: *Sometimes it's better not to know?* So why tell me now, Momma, why tell me at all?

I didn't make sense.

Whatever her reason, though, there was nothing holding me back now. I knew Sal's name, didn't I? I could use a phone. I yanked open the attic door and marched across the bedroom, determination driving me. I continued down the steps and picked up the phone, my breath hissing into the mouthpiece. I checked the phone book for the area code—California directory assistance—then whipped the rotary dial around, again and again. Each time it hummed into place, my chest grew tighter. Finally, I heard the ring, then the soft clack of a connection.

What city please?

"Uh…" My brain froze.

Hello, what city?

What *city?* I couldn't think of any cities let alone say his name.

Hello?

I couldn't speak.

Hello-o?

Breathless with fear, I drew the hand piece from my ear and hung up.

Chapter 33

The fire in the barn haunted me for years, smoldering through my waking hours and rising up in my dreams. Except, instead of Apple or the rabbits I see my mother in those dreams. She's there as I reach for her, my feet sliding back as the flames climb higher. "Grace!" she calls but I slip farther and farther still, until a wall of fire comes between us and I can't see her anymore. Then Sandy and I are in the churchyard as the barn explodes, shooting comets over us, over me, a girl in that summer my mother died.

Apple McEgan survived the fire, with nasty burn scars on her face and scalp. Sandy and I saw her weeks later when the bandages came off, when she smelled like mildew *and* disinfectant. It was hard not to react, and Sandy was hopeless, her gray eyes swelling to the size of jawbreakers. Hair would never again grow on the right side of Apple's head and the skin from her scalp to her mouth looked like a helmet melted in place.

"Butte said I never cried," she told us, half of her lips stiff while the other half smiled. At my parents' insistence, Sandy and I braved the farmhouse to visit her, carrying clothes from the church basement and fistfuls of bubble gum from the corner store. The minute I saw her, I knew I should feel sorry for her, the pain she endured and that hideous face. But the way I saw it, she was still Apple McEgan and rotten to the core.

She was chatty that day, more comfortable in her burned skin than the skin she was born in. When we stepped into her room, I knew why. It was filled—from one mildewed wall to the next—with gifts. Flowers and boxes of chocolates, stuffed animals and store-bought clothes. It made the bubble gum and second-hand clothes we'd brought over look lame.

She led us around the room. "These are from Van Duyn's... This is from Lipman's," and as she did, I got nosey, checking signatures on cards. Most were members of our church, which didn't surprise me. It was the only thing Good Shepherd had talked about for weeks: that poor McEgan girl and the way she'd been forced to live in a barn until it caught fire. It hardly mattered that she'd set the fire... or that she'd had put us in danger too. I was tempted to tell them she also broke the church window.

As we circled the room, the part of Apple's face that wasn't a helmet head downright glowed. She had a subscription to Glamour Magazine. She got telephone calls and visits. Heck, *we* were there. And that's when I put it together: Apple liked being pitied, it was better than being ignored.

"I love bubble gum—Thanks guys!" She said when Sandy offered it. "I'll chew it when my lips aren't so tight."

"Oh." We hadn't thought of that.

The fire that dark, summer night had changed her parents too. They accepted the goodwill of neighbors, and some of the farmhouse shutters came unstuck. My mother was one of many who cooked them dinner, even if she was too sick to deliver it. When Dad and I walked it over, Mr. and Mrs. McEgan surprised us, sitting down to confess their mistakes. They said they didn't force Apple out to the barn, not exactly. They ignored her—as punishment for her behavior—and it went on so long she moved out on her own.

"We both figured she'd come in when she got hungry," McEgan said.

"I didn't." Mrs. McEgan had jolted her husband from his hangdog look. "I snuck some food out now and then."

Apple denied any intent to hurt herself—or Sandy and me. She told us what she told everybody. "I just wanted to give you a scare." Luckily for her, the judge in Juvenile Court bought it. She got a counselor and a new school.

The Sunday Apple showed up in church I almost fell over. Nobody had warned us she was coming, not even Dad. But there he was, escorting her to the altar like the bride of Frankenstein. As she passed, in one of her many new dresses, the congregation practically flew into raptures, equally drawn to and repulsed by her scars.

Dad took her to the podium and she spoke into the microphone, though only the last words came through, "...thank you for everything." Then she smiled and did a little curtsy. I was counting on that being the end of it until the organ started. The next thing I knew the girl was singing, in front of the stained glass she once broke, in front of the choir she still sings with to this day.

"...With heal-ing balm my soul he fills, and ev-ery faithless murmur stills..."

It was painful to watch her, the way her mouth stretched for the high notes.

"...both soul and body bear your part! To God all praise and glo-ory."

When she finished, no one clapped and no one moved, except to sniffle or wipe their eyes. The blueberry bonnets had their hankies out, flying like doves around their faces. What was worse, Apple stood there, basking in the attention, like she might as well bask forever.

Momma wasn't in church that day. She'd grown sicker after the fire and took to staying home half the time. So we did what people of faith do, diving full-bore into prayer, my father, the congregation, Jimmy and me: *God don't let our mother die. Kill the cancer, hurry up.*

But He didn't kill the cancer, not by a long shot. Georgia was first to notice, on a day we'd gone over to the church.

"You forgot to ask me," she said, lugging a mop into the Sunday school classroom.

"Hmn?" Momma sat on the edge of a low kid's chair sorting tissue paper, the belly we were trying to ignore between her knees.

"When you came in a while ago, you didn't ask," Georgia repeated. "Y'always do."

I knew what she meant. It was a running joke between the

two of them over the long drive from Georgia's house. "How much gas money it cost you today Georgia?" Momma would ask, and Georgia would say, "'bout a buck more than Ah make."

But that day Momma was quiet.

"You feelin' all right?"

She quit with the paper. "Now that you ask, I think I need to lay down."

Fast as she could prop that mop, Georgia was there, helping my mother from that chair.

From that day on, Momma rested more and ate less. What the cancer stole from her body, it sent to her abdomen, and the tumor grew. She needed pills for the pain, pills for her stomach, pills for sleep. By early August, Georgia was coming to the parsonage every day, the minute she finished her work at the church. It was a comfort to Dad who was beside himself with worry. Not to mention he had Momma's shoes to fill too, at least until she got better.

Until she got better. That's how we all thought. Even as her skin yellowed and her belly grew—she was going to *get better.* For the longest time, I was sure of it too, until an unusual circumstance finally knocked me to my senses: a voice from her bedroom. I hadn't heard it in so long, yet I knew it in a flash. I'd just come in from the backyard and I raced down the hall. Her door was open, and sure enough, there he was with that beat up old hat.

"Russell Pearce Malson, Hiram Evergreen Hobart—the third!" I said, grinning. Russ jumped at the sound of my voice, which made me play back what he'd just said.

I got your letter.

And Momma had answered *Thanks for coming.*

She'd sent Russ a letter? I looked at her with new eyes then, my mother, so pale and weak, and I knew. She was dying.

"Hello, sis," Russ said. "Tell you what, your mom and me are talkin'. Go outside and play a minute. I'll be right out."

"But I just came in!" I kept wondering why my mother would want Russ.

"Grace, honey," Momma said, her voice thin, "just for a minute."

Then Russ backed me out and closed the door.

The old man slept in the basement that night, like before, so I figured he'd stick around a while doing yard work and telling tales to Sandy and me. I was looking forward to it, especially since Momma was sick and Dad distracted. But the next morning when I came down, he had his bag rolled up and ready to go.

"You're *leaving*?"

He sat on the couch, playing a game with Jimmy: which fist is hiding the quarter? "Your mother's real sick, Grace," he said. "I don't wanna be a mouth to feed."

"But you can mow the lawn and stuff." I was emphatic. "Do chores and everything, like before."

Jimmy smacked Russ's fist and he opened it to an empty palm. "I appreciate the thought, sis. But there's some things I need to look after." He unclenched the other fist and gave Jimmy the coin anyway.

"What things? You're a, a…" I couldn't think of the right word, "a *train* rider."

Russ laughed. "Even an old train rider has things to do." To Jimmy, he said. "Take care of that sister of yours." Then he stood and picked me up "You be good, sis" and planted a kiss on my cheek. His eyes went glossy before he put me down, but all I could do was stare. My mother never even liked Russ. Why the heck would she summon *him*?

The question would haunt me in the days that followed, for not 24 hours after they talked, my mother was gone.

Chapter 34

I look back now and realize how young I was when my mother died, just ten years old. And despite what I thought, still a child when I found her letters. *All* her letters. It took longer than I expected, longer than I would have guessed my sanity would hold out.

But it could have been worse—and I have the preacher to thank for that. If he hadn't been so sneaky and tried to steam open a letter, I might never have sniffed out the messenger. But, as it turns out, the preacher had spooked him. I didn't know it at first, not until the shadowy figure—the same I'd seen on the church lawn—slipped into our house one night as we slept. I was a few months shy of 15 that spring and sound asleep when he made his move. It was a noise that woke me: a faint scratching at our front door. I'd left my bedroom door open and the sound drifted up the stairs. Was an animal trying to get in? A dog or a cat? Or was it a key in the lock, one of dozens floating around? The next sound I heard erased all doubt: the slow whoosh of the front door opening. I knew the sound well since I'd opened that door a million times myself. The suction came first, then the slip of its base over the rug—the way I heard now. Ever. So. Slowly. No dog or cat could do that.

Wide awake now, I sat up. Dim light from the street fell like a spell over my room. Did the preacher just come in? Maybe he couldn't sleep for thinking about the letters and went looking for one.

Now the door closed with a delicate click. It *had* to be the preacher. Then came a footstep, very faint, followed by a second and two more. Something was off; I felt it first before I understood. The preacher's footsteps were heavy but these were light and more like a two-step. My skin went cold.

And why would the preacher use a key?

The lights downstairs were out. In my room, in the faint light from the street, I could make out crumpled socks and a pair of sneakers, but outside my door it was pitch black. Why would the preacher walk around in pitch black?

Now there was nothing but the thudding in my ears. My pulse, rattling fast. Had I imagined the footsteps? Or dreamt them? I almost convinced myself I'd been asleep when I heard a creak, a sound I knew like my own heartbeat. It was the second step from the bottom.

Cri-eek it said again.

Someone was coming up—Oh God, who? The footsteps weren't the preacher's, as much as I wanted them to be the preacher's. The rhythm was wrong: one and a quick two. One and two. I'd been up and down those steps a zillion times, and it was impossible to keep them quiet. Every step gave way, a little or a lot, and every third or fourth made noise, like the one I heard now.

Raah-ick. Halfway up.

Panic shot through me. In my mind I was screaming, but my body froze and no sound came out. *What could I do?* I couldn't take the stairs, I'd run right into him, and there wasn't time to crawl on the roof. *Could I jump out the window?* Sure, if I wanted to break my neck.

Uooh-ock.

I yanked up the covers. My mind raced. I thought of Jimmy, in the next room, and wished he would talk in his sleep—anything to make the footsteps stop. But there was nothing, just the steps—one and two—coming up. Now my breath was loud as my heartbeat.

Could *he* hear it too?

I started to get up, but the bed whined, and the climbing stopped. I could feel him there. Listening. The next sound I heard was the tap of a shoe, ever so lightly, on the landing. One—and two.

I eased back to my pillow, trying to hear over my heartbeat. One and two. Tap, tap. He was coming toward me! I shut my eyes. *Please oh please.* Could he hear my heart?

Tap, tap.

Who was it? What did he want? I couldn't stand it, so I cracked my eyelids, just a slit, and there he was, not three feet away! It definitely wasn't the preacher. This man was short with a wide-legged stance. And he was looking at me! Through the veil of my eyelashes I watched the blur of him watching me. I sucked in a breath and would have let loose a scream except it hit me in that instant who it was. The messy hair, the slumped shoulders. I could make out his features too, and, most of all, the envelope in his hand. Air rushed from my lungs—louder than I intended. I had to fight to keep from giggling or jumping up to say *boo!* Heck, knowing him, he'd crap his pants. I lay there for what seemed like forever, trying not to laugh, as he tapped closer and put the envelope on the nightstand, just inches from my head. When he squared it to the lamp, I gave in and smiled. It had to be just so. He stepped back and looked at it, then turned and creaked back down the stairs. The last sound I heard was the scratch of the key in its slot again: good old Manny had locked us in, safe and sound.

Manny! I jumped up, careful to leave the lights out, and grabbed the envelope then shot through the dark into the attic, shoving the midget door shut. I pawed the floor for the flashlight and clicked it on. It was Momma's letter, all right. *Nice going Miss Brilliance—Manny all this time.*

Part of me wanted to celebrate and the other part kick myself. Manny? Manny! It seemed so obvious now. He'd adored my mother, he was trustworthy and reliable, and look where he lived: right across McEgan's woods. No wonder I'd seen the messenger behind the church—he was headed home! I pictured the runner again, the jerk of his legs, and all at once I remembered the slight hitch in Manny's walk. I'd known him so long I'd stopped seeing it. Manny, Manny, Manny: the simpleton genius, perfect for the job. I imagined my mother explaining the task to him. "Three letters a year is all, Manny, so they'll last, you understand? And be sure not to let her see you. If she figures out who's got the letters, she'll look for the rest."

"Da-don't you worry," I imagined him responding. "She'll

never see me."

Even now—*especially* now—I knew better than to approach him about the rest of the letters. He'd stay loyal to my mother no matter what. It was why he came in the night and changed his pattern. It was the reason I'd been fooled for so long. Then I realized why most of the letters came on Sunday mornings, suddenly I realized why. It was something Manny had said once, that he had trouble sleeping Saturday nights. He worried about the worship music is what he'd said. If he couldn't sleep, why not deliver a letter? The one I held now looked like the others: my mother's writing at center, and what I now knew was Manny's penciling in the corner: the number 15.

Had that much time passed? Was it really her 15th letter? I ran my finger over the pencil marks, squat and square, just like the numbers on my guitar music—and I'd missed that too! But it was okay. It was all okay. Finally, at long last, I knew the messenger. It was the same man, the only man, who'd witnessed my father steaming a letter and delivered the next one straight to me. Heck, he'd busted into the parsonage to deliver it to me. I would find the stash of letters now, no doubt in my mind. If there was anybody I could outsmart, it was Manny.

Chapter 35

I'd been to Manny's place before, but only a couple of times. It was a one-story home he'd inherited from his mother, and I pictured it as I sat in the attic, the cozy furniture, the handful of rooms. The letters had to be in one of them—in a *shoebox* in one of them.

Dreaming of shoeboxes and crazy schemes to distract Manny, I plied open the 15th envelope.

Dearest Ace,

From the second I left the cellar that night, I was flying high. Sal cared for me, he really did! He was handsome and rich, gentle and wild, and a mistake I would pay for the rest of my days. Lives were traded for that short happiness, Grace, it's taken me years to admit that. His attention may have been intoxicating, but like the stuff Pops poured down his throat, it had its consequences.

Like me, Momma? Like me?

At the time, though, I didn't think about any of that. I was giddy over Sal, just the idea of him. The cellar became a regular habit for us, once we worked out a signal. We needed one, because Mrs. Rossano would read late in the chateau library. Since it was sandwiched between the two towers, Sal couldn't get past her, so he came up with an idea.

The minute she went up to bed, he'd put a lamp in his tower window. "The light is small," he said, "but I think you'll see it." Later that night, we gave it a go, and from my bedroom window, I could make out a glow, just barely, in the south tower. The rest of the castle was dark except for that light. It was only a test, but it made my heart flip, seeing that lamp and knowing Sal was behind it.

I pictured my mother, staring wide-eyed out her window and lost myself in her story…

I watched that lamp for a long time from my bed, thinking about Sal, until sleep finally got hold of me. The next morning when he found me at the chicken coop, I told him right off how I saw it, and he checked behind him, then grabbed me by the waist and spun me around.

"Look for it again tonight," he said. "Then come straight to the cellar." His excitement was contagious, and I grinned as he yanked me close, kissing me so hard it stole my breath.

That night, after Doug and I turned out the light, I could hardly lay still. Good thing I had an easy view out the window. I must've watched for more than an hour before I saw that light. But this time, it was clear as the moon. I checked on Doug, on the other side of the sheet—he was asleep—then slid open the window and ran fast as a deer over the grounds.

Sal had beat me to the cellar, but only by a few seconds because he didn't have the candle lit. When we heard each other, in the dark, we ran together, laughing ourselves silly. We were young and stupid, Grace, and falling head over heels in love. I can't tell you how often we met like that. Not every night, but almost, often enough to get tired from lack of sleep. I have to admit I lived for those nights, to hold Sal's hand and stare into his big dark eyes.

It seemed like a miracle we were together. The rich city kid, and the caretakers' daughter with barely a dime to her name. We used to marvel about it, sitting there on that old settee with the bats overhead. Heck, the Rossanos bumped elbows with the high society of San Francisco. And who did the Petersons mix with? The ditch diggers and prune pickers of Napa Valley, the kind of people his parents didn't even notice. I laughed about it until I remembered how Sal once looked through me. I tried not to think about that, when Lord knows I should have.

Every now and then, on those quiet, candlelit nights, we ducked out of the cellar to stroll through the orchard or up to the pool while his parents slept. Sometimes we dangled our feet in the water and watched the stars, and once or twice, on very dark nights, we shucked our clothes and slipped in to swim, quiet as fish in a stream. But it was a big risk, so most of the time we kept to the cellar where there was little risk somebody would see us.

I didn't know how big that cellar was the first time or two, but after a few nights, Sal took the candle and showed me around. Some of it was huge wine barrels, side by side, and in the back there was a set of stairs to the living quarters, the way Sal got to the cellar.

"Do your folks use them too?" I asked, and he said, "Not much. To get to their wine once in a while, but that's about it." It was just when he said it that I noticed the racks of bottles. Rows and rows of them, some thick with dust. "From the old winery," he explained and dusted one off to show me. The faded label said: *Chateau Genevieve.* It was over 60 years old!

Sal handed me the candle next and flipped the bottle to his other hand. "Maybe we'll drink it." I'm sure my eyes went wide. "Are you crazy? What about your folks?" But Sal only shrugged. "I'll tell them my buddy and I drank it way back when."

The next time we met in the cellar, sure enough, Sal pulled a corkscrew and a wine glass from his jacket. It made me jittery, Grace, since I'd never had a drink in my life. But Sal said, "Don't worry, just have a taste." He wrestled with the old cork, then filled the glass and held it out to me. I couldn't tell you if it was good, just blood-red and tart on my tongue. I smacked my lips, and he laughed, saying, "I can't take you anywhere."

Sal led me to the settee then where we shared sips and talked, about the ranch and the old winery, the way it must've been at the turn of the century. He knew the history too, and since I loved the old story, I piped right up. "I think Genevieve made a mistake," I told him, "She should've come to see what the wine master had built. She would have known how much he cared." Sal put the glass down and answered me with a red-stained kiss. Then he pulled me from the settee and led me around in a silent dance. "Maybe with Genevieve," he said, "it wasn't meant to be." Candlelight flickered in his eyes. "Maybe this is." He whispered my name then and, for the first time, there in the cellar, told me he loved me.

Moments like this came in my mother's story when I stopped reading, trying to picture them together. I was going on 15 then and no longer put off by their romance. The last few months had changed me, and I was curious: what was it like to be kissed by a boy or to have one say he loved you? I'd held hands with a boy, I'd had a few crushes, but nothing more. I knew my mother wouldn't go into detail. She was my *mother*.

But I was curious, so I let my imagination fill in the blanks.

I found myself staring, not at the words on paper, but at the attic rafters as I imagined the two lovers growing bolder with each rendezvous. I saw them dancing by candlelight, feeling the warmth of each other's skin. I saw her hands around his back as he reached up to caress her cheek, then his fingers as they trailed down. I saw him carry her across the room to lower her to the settee... as I fell into the fantasy with them.

Chapter 36

Early the next morning I woke, my back stiff against a hard floor, an eerie eye glaring at me. *Good morning, Miss Brilliance. You let the batteries in the flashlight die again.* I crawled on my knees and pried open the midget door. Daylight stung my eyes. It was quiet in my room, the pale light of sunrise flooding the windows. *I'd slept in the attic all night?* Slowly, it came back to me: the middle-of-the-night delivery and the revelation about Manny. I turned for the letter, and there it was, still on the blanket. I remembered the cellar then, my mother and Sal in a silent dance. I hadn't finished reading it, had I?

Leaving the door open, for the light, I crawled back to find my place: the flickering of candlelight, Sal whispering her name. Here it was:

It was near the end of that summer, Grace, when Sal got a big surprise. Dr. Rossano showed up at the ranch and guess what he drove? The new car he'd promised Sal. He'd revved the engine so hard, we all came running—Doug and Astrid, Pops and me—and spotted it from the rise: a cream-colored Plymouth with gold stripes. "It's the '57 Fury," Dr. Rossano said as we came up, "What do you think?" He wasn't talking to us.

"Wow," Sal said, grinning. Mrs. Rossano stood next to him in her capris and matching shoes. "You'll need it to get home from college, darling," she told him. "It's a long drive from

USC." Sal ran his hand through his hair. "It sure is beautiful," he said. The car was something, all right, with panels at the back that reminded me of wings. The way Sal drove, he'd have it flying in seconds.

Doug practically drooled. "Is it a V-8 under the hood?" But Dr. Rossano ignored him. "Well, go on son," he said, "give it whirl." Sal glanced at me as he slipped into the driver's seat, so I scooted behind Pops to hide my smile. The next minute he turned the castle drive into a cloud of dust while we all laughed.

In the wee hours of the next morning, Sal and I crept into the front seat of that Fury and he pulled me close. "One of these days. I'll take you for a ride," he said, "I promise." We both knew it was impossible with our parents around.

Sal kept his promise come November and Thanksgiving weekend. It was an idea we cooked up together. After a holiday dinner in San Francisco, he would pretend to drive back to school but head north instead. My part was harder. We were supposed to leave for Lodi, but at the very last minute, I would fake getting sick. Astrid's mother was prone to bugs, so it was my best bet for staying home. As we loaded the car Wednesday, I covered my mouth and ran inside. I'm not proud to say it, Grace, but the trick worked. When I came out of the bathroom after making plenty of noise, Astrid said, "You ain't bringin' that to Lodi, no way, no how."

I was all alone for Thanksgiving and happy as a clam. One can of pork and beans tasted delicious—Sal was coming the very next day! On Friday morning, I got up early to wait, sketching the castle towers and the view east over St. Helena. It was quiet that morning, only me and the birds and cottontails.

It was still early when I heard the sound of tires and stood up. Then I realized it was only a bike, the kid Astrid had hired to tend the animals. There was no sense letting him know I was there. Half an hour later, I heard tires again, and this time I knew, the way the gravel spit on the castle drive. I dropped my art pad and ran, past the orchard, all the way to the rose garden where the Fury skidded to a halt. When Sal jumped out,

I raced into his arms. "I missed you so much," I said, trying not to hyperventilate.

The rest of that day is locked in my memory, Grace. Sal took me on a wild drive as we made our way up to Calistoga. "Everybody's a stranger there," he said. It was a nice day, nice enough to have the windows down. After a while, he pulled off the main highway and let me drive, and what a thrill! I was barely 15, and I'd only been behind the wheel of the Chevy a couple of times. I couldn't help grinning, especially the way he kept telling me how beautiful I was.

By the time we pulled into Calistoga, I was so hungry my stomach growled, so he said, "Pick a place to eat lunch." Well, Grace, I almost never got to eat in restaurants, which meant anything was a treat. I chose a quaint little diner and we walked in, smiling and having so much fun even the waitress giggled.

We fit a lifetime in that afternoon, the two of us, walking through town, holding hands, buying bread and cheese for dinner later. I'd never done anything like that before, and it was heaven. But the best part was being together in a place where nobody cared that he was rich and I was poor.

It was late afternoon when we roared up the castle drive to the back patio. I was tired, but excited to go inside. Remember, I'd only been inside only once and only in the Great Room. I wanted to see everything—especially the rooms that still looked the way the wine master left them.

Sal took me to the dining room first. It was gorgeous, with dark cherry walls that sparkled under an antique chandelier. I tried to imagine the wine master there, brooding over his long-lost Genevieve. But Sal sighed and pulled me along. It was all old hat to him. "Most of the rest is remodeled," he explained as he tugged me through the kitchen and guest rooms. The tour of the main level was quick, then we climbed a staircase at the rear of the chateau to the library.

It was where Sal's mother liked to read, and now I knew why. The room was cozy and quaint, narrow and long, running *the full width of the castle. I started to look through the stacks of books, but Sal was anxious. "Come on," he said. "Let's head up." Staircases at each end of the library led to either tower. "My mother calls them the bedroom suites," Sal explained, and I was glad when we skipped his parents' side.*

"This whole thing is yours?" I asked after we'd climbed the south tower. "Yup," was all he said. The space was huge and brighter than I would have guessed, with windows on three sides. Behind us, a door opened on a bathroom with a gleaming floor. "And your own bathroom too?" I skipped to a leaded window with a view of the pool. "You get used to it," he said.

We were hungry again, so we made a picnic on the bed and talked, mostly about his college life in Southern California. I'd never even seen a college. Heck, I'd hardly been anywhere. "What's it like?" I wanted to know. "There's loads of people," he said, tapping a finger to my nose, "but nobody just like you."

When the daylight began to fade, I went to the big window facing front. Sal's view took in the rose garden and the grounds beyond, more enchanting than ever from the castle tower. I could see past the orchard too, to the little box we lived in. "It looks like a shack from up here," I said. "You can hardly see my window." Sal put his arm around me and kissed my neck. "But I could feel you there," he said, pulling me close, and then he reached over and turned on the lamp.

I spent that whole night in Sal's arms, Grace, a fact I'm not proud to admit. But please believe that I'm not trying to excuse it, only to tell you my story. There was a painful price to pay later, a price you'll understand when my story is through.

Was it me, Momma, was I the price? I fell back against the two-by-four and continued reading.

The next morning started out foggy but as the sun burned through, we decided to take the horses out. The kid up the road would've been finished by then and Champ was old enough to be left alone.

"Boy he's grown!" Sal said, the first glimpse he got. I had to laugh. "What'd you expect?" He followed me to the tack wall, so I figured something was on his mind. "I wish we could talk somehow after I leave," he said, "at least write to each other or something." I threw Lady's blanket on and turned to face him. "I thought about giving you my address," he went on, "but how can we write with your parents here?"

"We can't," I agreed. "But I won't see you in so long," he said, coming close. "We're going back to Europe for Christmas and then... who knows? I'll have to memorize your face again." I looked into his eyes, already feeling how much I'd miss him, and then he leaned in to kiss me. Entranced as we were, we didn't hear any footsteps, just the sound of a throat clearing and then, "Well, well, well."

We jumped apart. Standing there, big as life with a bag of oats in her hand, was Hazel Clayton. "Well, well, well," she said again. "Hazel," I started, "what are you—?" "I came for the horses," she said, "since that jug-head your mother hired isn't too reliable." For a long minute, nobody spoke. Then Sal stepped forward. "I'm here to see Sharon. I care about her." "I can see that," Hazel said, dropping the bag of oats, "and I can't say I blame you." Oh, how I adored that woman!

It turned out to be a relief Hazel caught us that day. She agreed to keep our secret, at least for a while. But even better, she offered to let us send letters through her. She'd heard us talking. "I'll put your mail in my box," she explained, "then nobody has to know." "Oh Hazel!" I shouted, throwing my arms around her. "You're a saint!" She patted my back. "Oh, honey. It's the least I can do for love."

For weeks after that, I took letters to Hazel, and she gave me Sal's that he'd sent from school. It was exciting, Grace, but risky too. Hazel's house was a trek from the cottage, so I had to ride Lady to make up the time. Every week I'd trot over there and she'd have a stamped envelope ready to send what I'd written. And almost every week there'd be a letter from Sal. Soon as I had it in my hands, I rode hard back to the barn, climbing to the loft to read it in private.

And it was wonderful, sitting there, hearing his voice through his words. I loved every minute of it. As long as it lasted that is... A couple of months into the new year his letters stopped coming. I'd ride to Hazel's with one for him and she'd shake her head. I kept writing, kept trying to figure out what was wrong, and nothing came. He'd been in Europe, I knew that, but the trip should have been over long before.

Then, finally, sometime in February a letter arrived. It was different though, just a few words about school and how he was so busy. It felt strange. I felt strange. I wrote once more and asked him point-blank to be honest with me, but I never saw another letter. My heart ached, Grace. I felt desperate and sick. More than anything I needed to see him.

But it wouldn't happen until spring, when Sal got a break from school, and even then it would be next to impossible for us to talk. The Rossanos had invited another family it turns out. I hid on the rise and saw them pull up in a caravan that day: another couple and their daughter, their stunningly beautiful daughter. What was worse, she rode in the Fury with Sal, and the first thing she did when she stepped out was sling an arm around him. I hadn't eaten much that afternoon, but I ran off that minute and lost it all behind a tree.

I dropped the letter to my lap. There was no more story after that anyway, just a weak sign off. Was it the end of my mother's romance with Sal—already? There were hints she was pregnant if you looked close enough. She was desperate and she'd thrown up. I thought about the other girl, the one my mother called stunningly beautiful. Had Sal fallen for her instead? Heck, for all I knew, the two of them were still together somewhere. I considered the step I'd been too scared to take and worked up the nerve. Grateful the preacher wasn't up yet, I headed for the phone. Without stopping to think, without giving myself an out, I picked up the receiver and dialed.

What city please?
This time I was ready.
"San Francisco."
For what name?

"Rossano." My heart thundered. "Salvatore Rossano."

Can you spell the last name?

I saw my mother's handwriting. "R-O-S-S… A-N-O."

I tore off a sliver of fingernail. I'd developed the habit lately, and now most of my nails were nubs.

I'm sorry, there's no listing for that name in San Francisco.

"You sure?"

Static crackled. *Yes, ma'am, I'm sure.*

"What about St. Helena?"

A pause. *No—sorry.*

"Then how about Sal—just *Sal* Rossano?"

I'm sorry, I have no Rossanos at all, listed or unlisted. Would you like to try another name?

The question confused me. "Did he change it?"

Ma'am?

"Never mind. Thanks anyway," I said, slipping the receiver back to its hook.

I paced the floor. If he wasn't in San Francisco or St. Helena, where could he be? California is a big state. I pulled out our encyclopedia, found a California map, and burned up the phone checking Santa Rosa, Calistoga and half a dozen other places. I practically begged one operator until she came up with something, a Gregory Rosano, with one "s" outside of Fresno. I didn't bother to write down the number.

Where was he? How could I find him? Then a thought blew over me like a draft through a door. Could *that* be the reason for my mother's letters? To tell me where he was? I could almost hear her now, instructing Manny. "Don't give her the last letter before she's ready, Manny, before she's old enough. The minute she has an address she'll leave home to find him."

She would have been right about that.

Chapter 37

I expected to find the shoebox as soon as I talked my way into Manny's house. Innocent as an angel, I would open it before he knew what was happening. "What's in *here*, Manny?" I'd say as he stuttered "Da-da-don't!" to my "Oh gosh, my mother's letters!" How could he stop me with her story at my fingertips?

But first I needed to get inside the Mankiewicz place. It didn't take much, one suggestion to change the scenery for our guitar lessons and I was in. Except for a new air conditioner in the window, the living room hadn't changed since his mother had passed. Her knickknacks and doilies still decorated every surface. All of it was in its place, but covered in dust, just as you'd expect from Manny.

I sat down, mindlessly strumming my guitar strings. The most interesting feature in the room, for somebody looking for a shoebox, was the console record player against a wall. It was big enough for my mother's letters, for several shoeboxes full of letters. And the fact that Manny wouldn't touch it, even when I begged him to play some records, only increased my suspicion.

"The thing is," I told him. "I should hear more guitar. You know, stuff like James Taylor and Joni Mitchell."

"Sa-sorry, but even if I had their records. I couldn't pa-play them. The needle arm is broke."

Sure it is, I thought. I stared at the console, wishing my eyes actually had X-ray vision. When Manny left for the kitchen, I got up to peek inside, encountering, as I did, the heavy vase on its lid. Damn. Not enough time to move it and get inside. That's when I spotted the fingerprints in the dust. If the record player wasn't working, why would Manny lift the lid? Better yet, what excuse could I come up with to lift it myself?

"Won't it be fun?" I said, at his door the next day with a can of Pledge. "We'll wax the furniture!" And remove that stupid vase, I thought. Manny started to object until I sashayed in, singing the commercial jingle: "Lemon Pledge, ver-y pretty, puts a shine down lem-on good... Lemon pledge as you're dust-ing brings new lust-er to the wood!"

How could he say no? Like the TV blonde in blue chiffon, I put my rag to an end table first, but the army of knickknacks was intimidating. Manny was at the bookcase, so I decided to go for it, slipping to the console and shifting the vase to the floor. I went ahead and gave it a spray for good measure. *Lemon Pledge, very pretty...* One swipe picked up a wedge of dust no TV blonde had ever seen. I checked Manny again, then yanked up the lid. Inside was a bent needle arm and some albums. No shoebox and no letters. In desperation, I felt around for hidden panels or secret compartments. Nothing.

Crap and damn. The console was a bust.

I lowered the lid and jumped when a face glared back. It was my own reflection in the patch I'd waxed, the face I'd seen a million times, but somehow now it drew me in. The features were warped in the wood grain, like another me in another world, and I shivered. Maybe we all have doubles, I thought, who live in opposite realms. What's on our right is on their left and vice versa. I watched the girl in the wood. When I moved, she moved. When I stuck out my tongue, she stuck out hers. I wanted to crawl in next to her and look back into this dusty room, to see my world from hers. What would happen if I tried? I leaned in closer. Was it possible for our worlds to flip?

"You wa-want a pop?" I practically flew out of my skin. "I'm thirsty. You want a pop?" He'd dusted two shelves already and replaced the books according to size.

"Might as well," I said, giving up on the console. I finished dusting it, then slipped the vase over the girl from another world.

In the weeks that followed, I learned to distract Manny, buying time to search places I could check behind his back: the kitchen, the hall and bathroom. I even pawed through his laundry basket, ignoring, as much as I could, his dirty laundry. But I didn't find any letters. I figured they had to be in one of the bedrooms, and I racked my brain for a way to search them.

"Leave a window cracked," Sandy said later, "and we'll go in when he's not home."

"You think?"

"Why not? He broke into your place, didn't he?"

She had a point. Two nights later, on a sweltering August evening, we waited for choir practice, and the minute Manny stepped in the church, we raced to his place, laughing like banshees all the way. We were fully developed that summer of '73, and—after my birthday in July—both 15. But unlike me, Sandy had boobs, not the poached-egg kind like mine, but real, fill-up-your-bra boobs. It was a bathroom window I'd left cracked at Manny's and she had a hard time getting them through.

"Thanks," she said, as I pulled her in, and she wiggled her cutoffs back into place. "I feel like a cat burglar."

"Me too. Remember, we only have an hour, then everything goes back the way it was. Let's split up and hit the bedrooms."

"Yeah, yeah. Hey, can we look in the fridge? I got the munchies." Sandy had become fascinated with hippie lingo, and dropped phrases like "Can you dig it?" and "Far out" whenever possible. I knew she didn't really have the munchies, not the marijuana munchies anyway.

"Are you nuts? If you eat his food, he'll know we were here."

She popped her gum. "I'm only kidding, man."

The first bedroom I entered was sparsely furnished, a bed and nightstand. The closet was empty but for some old clothes and Christmas decorations. I got through it in a few minutes. But the next room looked promising. With floral bedding and crocheted pillows, it was clearly his mother's old room. When I opened the closet, I spied a tower of shoeboxes and fell on them, throwing off lids and dumping contents. Ten seconds later, I wanted to cry. The shoeboxes held shoes, ugly old-lady shoes. I kicked one particularly hideous pair and growled. "Why didn't Manny throw this stuff out?" A memory came back to me then, the day we packed up my mother's things. Everything I touched that day reminded me of her, her shoes, clothes, all of them still smelling like her. We had two piles going, things to keep and things to give away. Just two piles, until Grandma came in with a garbage can. At the sight of it, I ran from the room to the farthest corner of the churchyard and cried.

"Gra-ace!" Sandy was calling me.

"Yeah?"

"Come quick!"

I sprinted down the hall. "Did you find something?" It was Manny's room. There was his music and his guitar. Sandy was on the floor, some kind of box in her lap. *Oh God please.*

But the minute I came up, she said, "False alarm."

The box held pictures. Mankiewicz family photos. "Why the heck did you call me?"

"I thought I had it. Did you find anything?"

"Just some old-biddy shoes." I knelt beside her and picked up a snapshot, a faded black and white. The boy in the frame was too big for his tricycle.

"Same dorky face," Sandy said. There was no mistaking Manny.

I had an acute sense of where we were then, how we'd torn up his place. "We'd better hurry."

In less than an hour, we had combed through the entire house, even checking the crawl space underneath. Eventually out of places to look, we straightened things up and slipped back outside.

"I just don't get it," I said. "I was positive we'd find the letters in there." The sun was low, the warmth nice after Manny's air conditioning.

"The thing is…" Sandy quit walking.

"What?"

She spit out her gum to loop some hair under the tooth. "Maybe you're wrong."

"About what?"

"About Manny, you big honky." There she was, with her sun-streaked hair and freckled face, so pink next to my summer tan. And she called *me* honky? "That guy that came into your room?"

"Yeah?"

"Maybe it wasn't Manny."

"Right. It looked like Manny and moved like Manny, but it wasn't Manny, because there's somebody running around the neighborhood who's his perfect twin."

"It's not unheard of, you know." We resumed walking until the church came into view. "Besides," Sandy went on, "Isn't it about time you gave up on all this?"

"*Excuse* me?" I stopped again.

"I mean, it was fun breaking into Manny's pad and all, but what's the point?"

"What's the point? *What's the point?*" I got in her face. "So I can find the damn letters you idiot!"

She turned and mumbled something, so I grabbed her and whipped her around. "What'd you say?"

"I said it's all you ever think about, those stupid letters, every stinking minute!"

"It's *not* all I ever think about, and even if it was—"

"It's a waste of time. So what if you find them early. So *what?*"

"You don't get it, do you?"

"No, I don't."

"I don't have a dad like you do!" I yelled. "Not a *real* one. Maybe my mom's gonna tell me where he is! Maybe that's the reason for the letters. Have you thought about *that?*"

To my horror, she burst out laughing.

"What's so funny?" I wanted to hit her. I wanted to hit her face off. "What is so *goddamn funny?*"

She laughed even harder. "You are, Grace. *You* are so goddamn funny. Your real dad doesn't give a crap, don't you see? He never did. *That's* why you don't know him or where he is."

"Shut up!" I hauled back and slapped her. "You don't know! You don't know anything!" A bright imprint rose on her cheek and she staggered back, her eyes brimming. Then she took off, toward Pardee, running home to mommy and daddy. My palm stung where it met her cheek and I stood there, fuming, desperate for my room and my guitar. I made a bee-line behind the church, straight for the parsonage, running over the grass the whole way. But when I hopped the porch and stepped inside, the preacher blocked my way.

"You're in big trouble, young lady."

Had Sandy's parents already called? Had somebody seen us in Manny's house? My palm still tingled where it had hit her cheek. "I am?"

"I've been looking for you for hours." In his fist was a sheet of paper. "Where have you been?"

"The neighborhood," I lied. "You know, Sandy's house."

"No, I don't know. Mrs. Shelby hasn't seen you all day. I called over there twice."

"Oh." I tried for the stairs, but blocked my way. "Why should I have to tell you anyway?" I spit. "You think you're my father? What a joke."

His jaw clenched. "That's part of it—"

"No it isn't, because you never were."

"I was trying to find you, because—" He held up the paper and his lip started to quiver. "I got this and…" Once again, the eloquent preacher was at a loss for words.

"And *what?*"

"It's the phone bill. All those calls to Directory Assistance."

Uh-oh. I tried to get past him, but he blocked me again. "So? There's no law against it."

He rubbed his mouth in a lame attempt to stop it from quivering. "'Course not, Grace. The truth is—" he pivoted away and back again. "Just tell me, will you? Did you find your father? Did your mother say where he is?"

I stared, amazed. He also expected her to tell me.

"Wouldn't *you* like to know," I said and darted around him.

Chapter 38

The preacher and I walked around with hair-trigger emotions after that. I was itching to pick a fight and he seemed ready to take me on. He was on me constantly about church that summer, as if that would bring back his compliant child. It was also the summer Jimmy figured it out. He heard me say "my California father," then cornered me to ask if we were really brother and sister.

"We are," I said, sorry he'd overheard. "But only half."

I expected it to hit him hard. He was eight years old. Heck, he almost cried in Little League games when he struck out. But the news hardly fazed him, and that's when I realized it had been almost five years since our mother's death. She'd been gone more than half his life.

"A half-sister is still a sister, huh?" he said, tossing his baseball my way. I caught it in my chewed-up fingers and tossed it back.

Sometimes I suspected people at church knew the truth, the way they stared at Jimmy and me. He was an ox for his age, the spitting image of the preacher, while I was darker and petite, not to mention lop-eyed. But if the congregation didn't already know, it would soon, since I was too hotheaded to keep my mouth shut. It was a Sunday when it came out, after I'd been coerced by threat of punishment to show up for church.

"Great to see you Grace!" one of the blueberry bonnets gushed when I came in.

I kept to myself during the service, which happened to feature—joy of joys—another solo from Apple McEgan. When it was over, I got up quickly and would have been gone in the next minute had I not heard the preacher yammering.

"She'd love to go," he was saying at the sanctuary doors, "Sign her up."

"Shouldn't I talk to her first?" This was the youth director and I knew she meant me. Her name was Debbie, the gal I'd worked so hard to ignore.

"Nah! It'll be good for her, get her out of the house for a change."

And wouldn't he lo-ove that? "Hello Deb." I stepped in.

"Grace!" I'd startled her. "We were just talking about you."

"Planning my life, it sounded like."

"Well I—" her face went red.

"Watch it, Grace." Here came the Preacher Eye.

"It's the mission trip over Labor Day weekend," Debbie enthused. "I thought you and Sandy might like to come." Sandy and I knew all about it, of course. All the Goodie Two-shoes were going. "Up to the Yakama Reservation," she added. "We'll paint houses and have tons of fun."

"Not me. I wouldn't be caught dead."

"Grace!" The preacher said under his breath.

"But your dad thought you might—"

"My *dad?*" I leaned into the space between them. "My DAD?" I said it so loud heads turned. Plenty of people were milling about, and I couldn't resist. "Do you mean my REAL DAD IN CALIFORNIA? Because that's where HE lives!" Every eye in the place was on me, the blueberry bonnets' widest of all.

"Knock it off," the preacher said.

I backed away, toward the entry. "Here's an IDEA," I said loud as I could, "if you happen to FIND MY REAL DAD, let my FAKE DAD know, would you? Sal Rossano's his name, THE GUY WHO KNOCKED UP MY MOM."

The preacher was coming now, so I turned, breaking into a run. I figured I had a good lead until halfway down the outside steps when I heard shoes behind me. I raced over the grass, faster than I thought the preacher could move, and flew up the parsonage porch, reaching for the doorknob when a hand slapped mine. But the fingers weren't his. They were small and stick-like. I turned to follow them to the hand, the arm, the hideous face of Apple McEgan.

"What do *you* want?"

"I'll help you find him," she said.

"*Who?*"

"Your real dad," she panted. "I'll help." She smiled her grotesque smile, and I jerked back my hand.

"Get away from me, Apple, you're disgusting." Then I ran into the house.

That very night, after I'd cried myself to sleep, another letter arrived. Number 16. I found it the next morning, slipped under my bedroom door, which made sense, since I'd slammed the damn thing shut. *Manny.* He'd seen my outburst at church. Was that why he'd delivered another one—right to my bedroom? On the other hand, it was near the anniversary of my mother's death. I always got a letter near the anniversary.

On the way to the attic, I studied the envelope, wishing I could sense where it had been, where the shoebox was. The usual markings were there with the same rubber band dents. I turned it over to the flap at the back, which took a while to get open since I'd chewed my fingernails to bloody nubs.

My Dear Grace,

It was clear from her writing she was growing weak: the anemic penmanship, the shaky strokes. I shuffled the pages, three of them, not an unusual number, but her words were bigger and farther apart, the lines at a slant. She wasn't just weak. She was frail. I tried to remember when that had happened—a couple of weeks before it was over? Would she have enough time to finish her story?

My Dear Grace,

All this time, all these letters about my days on the ranch, and hardly a word about my life with your father.

You mean Sal?

It's high time I fix that, because Thaddaeus Carsten was a Godsend.

Oh, that *father.*

It's the honest-to-God truth, Grace. If our paths had never crossed, I don't know what I would have done. I met Thad, all six-foot-four of him, at the lowest point of my life, when I didn't have a soul to turn to. I'd run away from the ranch by then to San Francisco and been on the streets several weeks. I'd burned through my cash, not a red cent on me. So imagine how I looked, covered in grime and scrounging for food. Here was this towering man with such conviction, and there I was, no point in sugarcoating it, a filthy sinner. But you want to know something? From the very start, he overlooked that, and he's been by my side ever since, my Godsend, my rock, my Preacher Man.

But let me back up, sweetheart, and say outright what you probably already suspect. Thaddeaus Carsten, the man who's loved you and supported you all your life, is not your father. Not in blood, I mean. If this comes as a shock, precious child, I'm so sorry. But I'll guess by now that you've already figured it out— your natural father was Sal Rossano.

There it was. Finally. The truth about dear old dad. A wave of emotion rolled through me. I'd known it, of course, for a long time, but hearing it from my mother still shook me. I put down the letter. Sal was my father, my *real* father. What did I feel? I wasn't sure, but for the first time, I wondered: Was it possible I had memories of him that I'd buried long ago? Then I saw it, in my mind's eye, my parents' marriage certificate. Oddly, I'd never bothered to look at the date. I'd never figured out how old I was when they got married.

I sailed downstairs and there it was in my father's desk: the document joining Thaddaeus James Carsten and Sharon Louise Peterson. The year... the year... where was it? There: 1958. It whipped me like a bitter wind. I was born in July of that year and they were married on the 17th of October. Three months later. I'd been too young for any memory.

I put the papers back in the drawer and returned to the attic. What she wrote next confirmed it, when she met the preacher, I was a baby still swaddled.

Their first encounter was far from romantic: at a restaurant as she scarfed food from an abandoned plate. The letter went on and on about him, how he was the perfect gentleman who bought her a meal and a private room, blah blah blah. I skimmed forward until she went back to what I wanted to hear, more about Sal.

How things got to that point, Grace, is so complicated. So much happened before you were born.

Tell me, Momma.

Do you remember where I left off? It was spring break when the Rossanos finally showed up again, with another family, remember?

Yes. And the stunning girl.

Well, let me tell you, Ace, I was a wreck. Anxious and scared with my belly growing, the way I'd watched Lady's grow. I wore Doug's old shirts. I didn't tuck anything in. Still, it seemed impossible nobody had noticed. I was sick to death with fear. I'd gotten myself in a terrible fix. Most of all, I needed to talk to Sal. But every time I saw him, he was with somebody else, and usually it was her. The nagging feelings I'd had were crushing now. I had to see him.

But how? I had no heart to go near the castle, and Dr. Rossano had banned me from the barn. Then one day, as I left the chicken coop, I heard his voice. What I saw next was hard to watch: Sal and the girl, on horseback, heading out for a ride. She was on Lady, of course, and I could tell right away something was wrong. Lady circled and stomped with that girl on her back. Finally I saw the reason. She had a stick.

"You don't have to do that," I told her, running up. It was so strange, Grace, the whole time I explained how the stick scared Lady, Sal kept his eyes in the distance. Why wouldn't he look at me? Why hadn't he done something himself about that ridiculous stick? When the girl admitted she didn't know much

about horses, he finally caught my eye.

"Did you get my mother's orders?" he asked, yanking Cesare's reins. I frowned and shook my head. "About the cellar? She wants you to go down and clean out that junk for once." I stared at him. Mrs. Rossano never gave a hoot about the cellar, and what junk could he mean? Was he sending me a message? I looked him over and said, "Okay," and then they rode off.

It had to be a message, Grace. There was nothing but barrels and racks of wine in that cellar. Did he plan to meet me? I was part keyed up and part relieved. Finally, I could tell him about my predicament, our predicament. I knew he'd be scared, like I was, but I hoped he would come around.

Those were my thoughts when I slipped through the cellar door hours later. I thought I'd beat him there at first, because it was pitch black, no candle and not a drop of light. "Sal?" I called, and he said, "I'm here." I don't know what came over me, Grace, but I ran to him in the dark, all the emotions of those lonely months pouring out. I wanted his touch, his arms around me, I needed the reassurance so desperately. I found his shoulders and whispered, "Sal," only his name, wanting his kiss, to lose myself in it. But the instant our lips touched, terror struck.

It wasn't Sal. It wasn't him! I still remember the sound I made, the horrible, animal-like groan when I stumbled back. It was his father, Dr. Rossano. A long, black silence filled the space between us. I expected him to come after me, slap me or beat me, and then he spoke. "You will leave the ranch tonight, forever. If I ever see you again—ever—I swear I'll—"

"Please, Dr. Rossano," I cried, "I have to see Sal." He stepped closer and spoke in the ugliest tone. "Sal was here tonight, all right. I followed him. I figured him out soon enough." He came toward me, step by step, and I started to shake. I started to sob. "Please, Dr. Rossano."

He lunged at me and grabbed my wrist. "He won't see you again, not some damn hired worker, not while I'm alive." He squeezed my wrist so hard I thought he'd crush it. "He knows now what he'd throw away: his inheritance, his future, everything!" He whipped me around and cursed me. "I won't let you ruin his life. I won't. I want you out of here tonight!" I tried to wrench free but he twisted my arm back. I'd never been so scared, Grace, in all my life.

Finally I pitched forward and he lost his grip, just long enough that I scrambled away. I got out the door and ran. I wasn't thinking, only running, over the grounds and through the orchard. I ran and ran, stumbling in the dark, not knowing where I'd go. There was no way I could go back to the cottage. Astrid would know, soon enough, what had happened and beat me too. I kept running and running, not thinking where I'd go until I saw the barn, its broad shadow in the dark.

What I did next, Grace, was stupid. I went straight to Lady's stall and jumped on bareback. I don't even know why. I was in no shape to ride, sobbing the way I was, pregnant and scared, but I did it anyway. My life on the ranch was over, Dr. Rossano had made that clear.

Out the gate we went and toward the hills, fear and anger driving me. For the first time in my life, I slapped Lady's butt. I slapped her hard and made her run. It was dangerous because it was so dark, overcast with no moon. But I pushed her anyway. I pushed her and pushed her, through the hills and toward the ridge, into the blackness of the night.

It was bound to happen sooner or later. Lady's front hooves caught something and I flew, hitting the ground as she stumbled and crashed against me. There was nothing but her weight then, that huge, solid body. I couldn't breathe. When she shifted to get up, I felt my chest collapse and bones snap.

Every breath was a stab of pain. I tried to stand and nearly fell. My ankle was on fire too. I couldn't put an ounce of weight on it. It was so dark, I couldn't even see Lady. When I finally heard her panting, I lurched forward on one foot, sucking air and fighting panic. Was she hurt? I felt her neck and her side, hopping around in the dark and running my hands down her legs in a terrible panic. Thank God, she seemed okay.

But I wasn't. I could barely get air, and there was so much pain it made me dizzy. Was the baby hurt too, I wondered? I had to get help. I called out but my voice vanished in the blackness around me. We were so far out in the hills. I grabbed hold of Lady's mane and tried to swing a leg up, but the pain was like hot knives. I bent over and threw up. There was no way I would ride again that night, out of the hills or anywhere else.

So there I was, Grace, in the pitch-black night, terrified and hurt like I'd never been. Lady was all I had. I took her by the mane and turned her in what I guessed was the direction of the barn. "Go on, girl," I gasped. Then, for the second time in my life, I slapped her butt. I heard her hooves trotting away, not knowing if I'd see her again.

That was the longest night of my life, Grace. My foot throbbed and pain shot through me with every breath. I couldn't think about Sal or what had happened with Dr. Rossano. It only made things worse. I sat on the ground and tried to rest, but there wasn't much rest in it. My thoughts went to my brother Doug and our cramped but cozy bedroom, and then, strangely, to the girls from school who used to invite me to town. What I would've given that night for a friend!

But I was alone, Grace. Desperate and alone. When I lay back against the hard, dry ground, there was nothing to look at but a cold, empty sky.

That was it. The end of the letter. I tried to imagine what it must have been like, alone, in the dark like that. No wonder she had craved a friend. A friend... I saw Sandy in my mind's eye then, walking through the churchyard the night before. Had I really slapped her? I remembered my hands stinging, the way she'd looked—so hurt—and my cheeks burned. She was my friend, my best friend, and I hadn't talked to her since. I sat there a minute then ran for the phone.

Chapter 39

It rang forever before anybody picked up. Mrs. Shelby, just my luck. I asked for Sandy and when she said, "Mmhmn?" I knew she knew I'd hit her daughter. But she didn't seem angry, it was more like amused. "If it isn't Mercy Grace Carsten," she said. Mrs. Shelby got a kick out of calling me that, what she'd dubbed my "righteous name."

"I don't think she's real keen on talking to you right now."

The preacher was in the living room watching the TV, so I stretched the phone cord into the alcove. "I know. But can you please put her on?"

On the other end, the phone clanked to the counter, and I heard *Sa-andy!* then footsteps clopping away. I pictured the Shelby kitchen with its dishwasher on wheels, nothing fancy, but it beat the way we did dishes by hand. The phone rattled again and I waited.

"I know you're there," I said. The receiver brushed against something. She was stringing a lock of hair.

"Look Sandy, I've been thinking. I shouldn't have slapped you. I mean, all you did was say what you thought."

A snort hit the receiver.

"The thing is," I burrowed deeper into the alcove, "I'm sorry, okay?" Only silence on the other end. "Hello?" The phone crackled as I wrapped myself in the cord. "Sandy?"

"I heard you."

"Oh. Well, if you're not doing anything, maybe we can—"

"We're going shopping for school clothes. In case you forgot, school's only a couple weeks away. You know, our *sophomore year*?"

I hadn't thought about it. My sights were set on finding my father before the summer was over, and there wasn't much time left. "I know, but—"

"Grace?"

"Yeah?"

"You know what you said just now, that you're sorry?"

"Yeah."

"So am I."

It must have killed her to say it. Sandy never apologized. "It's okay," I said. "I probably do talk about the letters too much and you only—"

"No, that's not what I mean."

"What, then?"

"I lied to you."

"You did?"

I heard the Shelby refrigerator, the faint sucking sound when it opened, then liquid pouring. Probably Kool-Aid. Lime was Sandy's favorite. "Look," she said, "you have to promise you won't get mad." The glass clanked against her teeth and she swallowed.

"Okay."

"You're right about Manny. At least I'm pretty sure you are."

"What do you mean?"

Glass on teeth again. Another swallow. "I saw him."

"Saw him what?"

"Acting fishy, but I didn't tell you."

"Why?"

"I don't know. I didn't want you to find the letters."

I stretched the phone cord even tighter. "But that's crazy. Why didn't you want me to find them?"

"Like I said, it's all you think about. I figured maybe after a while you'd forget." She breathed into the mouthpiece. "Fat chance, right?"

I let up on the phone cord, whipping it now like a jump rope. "Sandy?"

"Yeah?"

"You still haven't told me what you saw."

"I know. It was a while back."

"You mean you don't remember?"

"'Course I do, it's just—"

"Just *what?*"

"It was way back when, when we were in school."

I wanted to scream. She'd kept it from me the whole summer? I was tempted to run over there right that minute and slap her again. Instead, I took a deep breath. "So what was it, what happened?"

More Kool-Aid. Her breath in the glass. "I went to your house after school and you weren't there. Your dad said you were at the church, a guitar lesson or something, so I went over."

"And?"

"And you'd split, rode your bike to the store or something. But Manny was there, at the organ. He didn't hear me come in."

"Yeah?" The Cyclops still chattered in the living room.

"So when I saw you weren't there I almost yelled to him— Where's Grace?—until it dawned on me what he was doing."

"What?"

She breathed into the receiver again, a long, noisy exhale. "Looking through a shoebox."

"A shoebox?" I felt the blood drain from my face. "Are you sure?"

"I wasn't at first. It's so dark in there. So I crawled to the front pew, you know, all secret-like, to see."

"Holy crap, did he see you?"

"No, and that's the best part. I watched him the whole time. It was such a gas."

"What'd he do?"

"He had the box on his lap and these envelopes in a rubber band. They even *looked* like your mom's."

"A rubber band? You sure?"

"Yep. A big one."

"How many—how many letters?"

"I don't know. Six or eight. He took one out and kept the rest in the box—and Grace?"

"Yeah?"

"It was the same night that man came into your house, the one who left the letter. When you told me it was Manny, that that's what you thought, well, *I knew it was.*"

I nearly exploded. I wanted to run over there and not just slap her but grab a fistful of that sucked-on hair. After we'd searched Manny's house, she'd tried to convince me it wasn't him. *What the hell!* I took a breath, tried to keep my voice steady. "But Sandy, why would you *do* that?"

"Oh, come on! I already said I'm sorry! Listen, I know you want to find your dad. You keep saying you want to find him, so tell you what, I'll help you."

How sweet. I could have been snotty and told her Apple McEgan had already offered. Instead I said, "Okay."

I could hear Mrs. Shelby again. She wanted Sandy off the phone. "Tell me quick before you have to hang up, is that everything?"

"No."

"Then what else?"

"I saw where he put it."

"Put what?" My heart pounded.

"The shoebox, dummy. I know his hiding place—"

"Oh my God." Had Sandy followed him?

"—or what *used to be* his hiding place."

"Where?" She was killing me. "Where!"

"You know the floor? Back where the carpet's kind of warped?"

I couldn't picture it.

"By the stained glass."

The *church*? She meant the *church*? But I'd already searched the church plenty of times. Her voice droned on through the earpiece. "...you know, you'd hardly notice... right under the stained glass... for heat or something, with all those slits in the lid."

Suddenly I knew where she meant: the vent at the back of the chancel, the one I'd stood on, years before, the day Apple broke the stained glass. I'd pushed my toe into the warped carpet.

Mrs. Shelby was talking again.

"I have to go, Grace."

"Wait—is it still there? Is the shoebox still there?"

"How should I know? I never looked."

"You never *looked?*"

"Well only through the slits once. I figured if I got into it, I'd have to tell you. So I never did." Her breath hit the receiver. "Hey, Grace, my mom says we gotta split so—"

I slammed the phone to its carriage and flew over the lawn in my bare feet, my weight never bending a blade of grass.

Chapter 40

How many times I'd passed through those sanctuary doors, who could say? As I approached the Shepherd again, in his accidental, sun-lit crown, memories flooded back: my third-grade Bible and confirmation; all the Christmas pageants and Easter Sundays; stints as an acolyte and communion helper. How many times had the Shepherd watched me, first as the starry-eyed preacher's kid, then as the orphan with the acid tongue. How many times? They all seemed trivial now, except in how they'd delivered me to this moment.

The sanctuary was empty and the vent only half a room away. As I walked, the Shepherd drew nearer, his left arm with the snowy lamb and his right open, as if to say come. *Come!* I wanted to laugh, I wanted to cry. All this time? Had my mother's letters been at his feet all this time?

Part of me wanted to fly to that vent, but how can you rush to a moment like that? If the letters were there, I'd know where to find my father. If they weren't... what then? What would I do? I imagined jumping through the window, crashing head-first through a cyclone of kaleidoscope glass.

The vent was close now. Its outline there. *Please, oh please.* I kept going, past the organ and the choir loft. The grates appeared now, as light from the window stained my clothes, bronze and sapphire, green and gold.

I fell to the floor and probed its edges, desperate for the fingernails I'd chewed to nubs. I'd have to get a whole fingertip under. But my fingers were too fat; it wasn't working. I lay down for a better angle and caught a flash between the slits. White. Then I flew into a frenzy, clawing at the grate, digging at its edges—damn!—but it wouldn't come.

I slapped my fist to the carpet where it was warped. I'd poked my toe in that bubble the very day I saw the halo. I forced my knuckles in now and flattened it. *Yes!* I got a finger under a corner. But when I pulled up, the grate jammed at an awkward angle. I'd have to work the other corners. Again, I clawed until my fingers throbbed. I fought back tears. I felt like screaming or growling or biting off my nail-bitten fingers. *Manny must use a screwdriver or something.* I looked around, but there wasn't any screwdriver. I bent over a corner and sank my teeth under the carpet. My teeth! I bit my lip along with the grate but hauled back anyway. It came up—and stuck. Did it have to be so hard? Did everything have to be so hard?

Groaning in frustration, I bent over again to use my teeth. I grunted and yanked. All four corners were up now, all four corners! I centered my weight and gripped both ends, then I heaved, not just with my hands but my whole body, roaring like a bear, and it broke free—it broke free! This was better than a dream. In the belly of the vent was a shoebox. An ordinary, everyday shoebox. It was simpler than the one I'd imagined, the one smelling of ink and Noxzema skin cream. This one was gray with a faded price tag at one end: The most glorious shoebox I'd ever seen.

I leaned in and scooped it up, passed it through a rainbow of color to the carpet beside me. I placed my fingers at the corners, took a breath and lifted the lid, and there they were: my mother's letters. *My mother's letters!* All at once I was trembling, then full-out sobbing. My mother's story lay before me, wrapped in a rubber band: every word, every letter, every word of every letter.

I picked up the bundle, grateful at last to feel it in my hands. I steadied myself and leafed through. Manny's pencil marks were there in the corners: the number 17 on the top letter, all the way to 22. From my tight, tortured throat, a laugh bubbled up. It was the answer to one question that had gnawed at me for years: how many letters had my mother written? Now I knew: 22. There was no special meaning to that number, but now I knew. In my hands were her six final letters. Whatever remained of my mother's story, whatever she'd tell me about my father, had to be in them.

Six letters. It seemed like such a small number, till I remembered only three came per year. It would have been two more years before Manny delivered the last one; I would have been a senior in high school! Instead I was just 15. I didn't even have a driver's license.

"Sorry Momma. I couldn't do it in your time."

With fingers that still throbbed, I lifted the rubber band and pulled out 17, the beginning of an end I wasn't supposed to see yet. I tugged the back flap open, right there on the church carpet under the Shepherd's gaze.

My Dear Grace,

There's no point in reliving that night in the hills. It was long and painful, and I doubt I have the strength anyway. It's gotten to the point where I have to rest every couple of minutes...

I can tell, Momma, I can tell.

But I will say this, out in the desert, all alone, I was never so glad to see a sunrise in my life. I struggled to sit up and stare at it. All I was wearing was an old shirt and a pair of jeans, and it was cold, so cold. I didn't have religion in those days, Grace, but I thought about God then, and how, in spite of everything the sun had come up. And it was glorious.

A while later when I tried to stand, it was torture. My left ankle had swelled and a sharp stab took my side with every breath. I pushed to my knees and then onto one foot, and it doubled me over. There was a boulder a ways off, a place to sit, and I was trying to hop over to it when I heard the thump of hooves. I almost yelled out until my mind flashed to Dr. Rossano. Could he be tracking me?

I started to panic, Grace. There was nowhere to hide, and I could barely move! The hooves got closer. Only one horse... was it Lady or Cesare? If Cesare was coming, it was almost certainly Dr. Rossano. For a split second I hoped it was Sal, then I forced the thought out. I didn't need the disappointment when he didn't show.

Not a minute later, Lady galloped around the corner with Doug. I was so relieved it wasn't the doctor and so darn glad to see my brother I burst into tears. "What happened to you?" he said, jumping down. His eyes were huge. "You been out here all night?" I nodded that I had, then tried to get my wits about me because the crying hurt worse than breathing. I poured everything out to Doug, telling him about the night before and Dr. Rossano.

"He doesn't... know it," I said, trying to breathe between words, "nobody does, not even Sal, but I'm... pregnant." Doug's face went white. He looked so scared it made me scared. "I was all... messed up Doug... I took... Lady out and we... fell. Now I can... barely breathe."

Doug helped me to the boulder to sit. "How'd you... find me?" I wanted to know. "I got up to milk Jersey," he said, "and Lady was outside the barn. That's when I realized I hadn't heard you behind the sheet, that you never came home last night. I hopped on Lady and she ran straight here. She knew just where to find you, Sharon." I loved that beautiful mare, the horse who'd brought me so much joy. Down her leg was a terrible scrape, a scrape I must've caused and it broke my heart.

"Does it hurt where the baby is?" Doug asked and I shook my head. "But it's... so hard to breathe." A while later, he tried to help me into the saddle, but I couldn't climb, and I couldn't bear to let him lift me. Any movement and my chest felt like it would rip open. "You have to go back," I told him, "get Pops and the Chevy... see if he can drive this far." He agreed and hugged me tight before riding off.

It seemed like forever that I waited on that rock. Then finally I heard a car. I looked up, expecting the Chevy and my blood went cold. Here came the Jeep bouncing over the rugged trail with Dr. Rossano behind the wheel. The minute he spotted me, he threw open the door and ran after me, really ran. I stood up, but what could I do? When he got hold of me, he dragged me—oh, the white-hot stabs of pain!—all the way up to the Jeep. He said nothing but forced me into the passenger side, running his hands over me like a doctor from hell. He was feeling for something broken, so he knew about the fall. I winced and moaned as he felt around... first my ankle, then my legs, then my ribs where the pain was a razor.

When I screamed in agony, he jumped, but his hands had found the bulge in my belly and they came at me again. Fear and rage washed over him as he whipped my shirt aside and stared at my bare abdomen. When he finally looked up, he had these eyes, Grace, such eyes, I thought he would kill me. I tried to scoot away, but he yanked me upright, his fingers squeezing my arms like a vise. Then he threw me back and my head hit the steering wheel. There was nothing but ringing in my ears then, and the two of us panting like wild animals. "Fix yourself," he said before he got in behind the wheel.

I don't remember the ride back, Grace, so I must have passed out, only lifting my head as we pulled up to the cottage. The door on my side opened again and Chipper nuzzled my leg. Astrid and Pops were there, but not Doug. I knew it wasn't his fault the way it happened. Dr. Rossano must've caught up with him, plain and simple.

I was dizzy and weak, but I knew this much: someone was pacing outside the Jeep. The doctor. The sound of his voice brought back the white-hot pain. "She's lucky she didn't break her neck," he roared, "trying to steal my horse the way she did!" Steal his horse? Was he crazy? "It serves her right," he went on, and then he gave his diagnosis: a sprained ankle, broken ribs and "pregnant as the town whore." Astrid gasped and Pops let out some kind of grunt. I could barely focus, but the shock on their faces was clear. "My best guess," he said, "she's already five months gone."

My parents stared at me and the swollen belly they'd somehow missed, and in my shame, I looked away. Dr. Rossano kept going, straight matter-of-fact. "I won't press charges," he said, "long as she leaves the ranch. God knows who the father is. Far as I know, could be anybody in town." Those last words shook me. "That's a lie," I gasped, fighting to breathe, "Sal is the father... and you know it. You said so yourself... you figured him out." There, I thought, they'd all heard it, they'd all heard the truth.

But Dr. Rossano laughed like I'd crowned myself the Queen of England. "You're five months pregnant, sweetheart," he said, "that means last fall when my son wasn't even here." I sucked in a breath, tried to keep from passing out. "He came to the ranch... at Thanksgiving," I said, "when you were gone... ask him, just ask him." I could see my parents thinking back, remembering Lodi. But Dr. Rossano shook his head. "That's ridiculous," he said, "don't even bother."

Astrid stepped forward then. I'd never seen her look so shaken. "Sharon may be stupid," she told him, "but she ain't no whore. Why don't you ask your boy like she says?" But Dr. Rossano turned on her. "I'll do what I damn well please! I want her out of here, the minute she can walk. Find a relative, whatever it takes." Astrid opened her mouth to say something but he practically stuffed his finger in it, jabbing at her. "You want to stay on this ranch? You do what I say."

I made myself slide out of the Jeep then and grab Pops. "Go find Sal," I cried. "Tell him to come... He has to know." I thought of the times Pops had saved me from Astrid. He was my father, he would help. "Please, Pops, please," I said, gripping his hand. But I couldn't even get him to look at me. He turned for the cottage and mumbled something. "What Pops," I said, "what?"

You want to know what it was, Grace, that he said? He said "I need a drink," and then he was gone. He never did lift a finger to help me.

Oh Momma, I'm so sorry.

After that, I let go of Pops emotionally and never looked back. Which is why, all those years later, I acted the way I did. I couldn't believe it when he showed up at our door.

Our door?

How the heck he had the guts I'll never know. You realize who I'm talking about, don't you?

Who?

Ramblin' Russ. Russ and Pops are one and the same. He called you Sis, remember? Just like he called me.

Ramblin' Russ was her father? I was stunned. All I could see was that old hobo with his hat in his hands. He called me *sis*, yes he did. That was *Pops*?

He never had a dozen names like he said, just Russell Peterson. But he made sure to invent a new last name soon as he saw me. "Pearce," he told you, remember? Instead of Peterson? He knew I wouldn't stand for it. He didn't deserve the title of grandfather, not in my book.

I chewed him out for coming when you went upstairs. You were happy and well adjusted with the father you had, and here he was, putting all that on the line. But it was your birthday and he practically begged me, "Let me stay, just a while." He swore he wouldn't tell a soul who he was, not even Thad. He knew how I felt about that too. Thad didn't need the heartache of my history on the ranch.

I have to confess, Grace, that was one of the hardest days of my life. Not just because my father had come. He had something to tell me, something I never suspected. It was terrible news and it hit me hard—

I remembered then: When Russ and Momma were in the kitchen, I'd heard a laugh or a cry though I didn't know which. Was that when he'd told her? The sound played in my mind again, a choked squeal, when an entirely different sound made me jump— this one from across the room. The sanctuary doors had pulsed. Someone had come in the church.

I grabbed the shoebox and crawled, quick as a mouse, behind the organ. Was Manny on his way in? Crap—I'd left the grate off the vent. Then it occurred to me: so what? They were *my* letters, weren't they? And I had them now for all time. I started to crawl out again, to come clean, when another thought occurred to me. If my plan was to travel, to use the last of my summer to find my father, wouldn't I be smart to keep it a secret, maybe even slip away? If Manny knew I had the letters and the preacher found out, they would watch my every move.

I stayed crouched behind the organ as noises seeped in from the hall. But the sanctuary doors stayed closed. The preacher, I assumed, had passed to his office. I exhaled in relief. He'd never let me go to California on my own to find my father, I was 15! And the last thing he'd want to do is take me himself. Was there anyone I could ask? I thought of Georgia. She'd been over again the previous week. Would she agree to take me, with or without the preacher's blessing? Would the Fairlane make it? I remembered her mother then. Last we'd talked, she was worse than ever. I needed to find another way.

I jostled the shoebox, all those envelopes sealed tight. If I didn't return them to the vent, Manny might check and figure me out. If only I had X-ray vision, I thought, I could read through the letters and put them back, no suspicion raised. If Manny looked in, he wouldn't suspect a thing. I saw it then in an instant: the preacher standing with an envelope over a pot of steam. It just might work, I thought. It just might.

Chapter 41

It took two nights to get through the letters while the preacher slept. Two nights over that stove, in a kitchen damp with steam and tears. The morning I finished, flaky with glue from resealing the flaps, I snuck to the church and slipped the envelopes back in the vent. Then I returned home to watch the clock. When I figured Sandy was up, I dialed her number.

"You know that mission trip this weekend?" I said when she picked up.

"Yeah."

"Pack your bags, we're going."

"Wait—we are?"

"Well, sort of."

The trip was easier to make happen than I could have imagined. A little lie here, another there. Thank God in the eyes of the preacher it was never too late to become a Goody Two-shoes.

"I'm glad you changed your mind, Grace," he told me.

"I'm covering the travel cost for Sandy too," I said, flashing a fist-full of bills. All the 5-spots from Grandma made for a convincing prop.

As it happened, the preacher never did check with Debbie, who would have told him she hadn't heard a peep from us about the mission trip. On the last Friday in August when the youth group boarded a bus heading east, we bought Amtrak tickets for a train heading south. With any luck, it would be days before the preacher caught on.

"This is so far out," Sandy said when we climbed the steps of our passenger car. Her fascination with all things hippie hadn't faded. It was 1973, and teenagers had been running away to San Francisco for years. Since she looked older, Sandy did the talking to buy our tickets and played the part well in her bell-bottom pants and baby-doll blouse. Another hippie-chick headed south.

"Groovy," she said as we plopped into our seats, mine next to the window and Sandy's the aisle. "California by morning, can you believe it?"

"It reminds me of that Ramblin' Russ song. *California here I come*," I sang, "*right back where I started from*." Sandy laughed. She and I had had our adventures over the years, to Eastport Plaza and Pardee Park, but always within bike-riding distance of our own front yards. Now Union Station disappeared as we moved steadily away.

"Oh, hey," she said, rifling through her bag. "That reminds me—you should have brought your guitar." She pulled out a string of daisies, the kind that grew in Pardee Park, plopped it on her head and pretended to strum imaginary strings. "*If you're go-ing to San Francisco... be sure to we-ar some flowers in yo-our hair.*"

"I'm surprised you didn't wear that to buy our tickets."

She grinned. "I know. That old fart at the counter would have loved it."

I'd stopped being mad at Sandy. She made me laugh. "We aren't exactly *going* to San Francisco, you know," I said, reclining my seat. Packing my bags and covering my lies had exhausted me. "We're getting out north of the city."

"Whatever." One of the daisies fell from her hair and she fished it up, leaned over and tried to press it into mine. She fiddled so long trying to make it stick, I lost track of time.

"Hey!" she said, and my eyes snapped open. "Where'd you go?"

"Sorry. I'm really tired."

"You can't be. You have to tell me your mom's story, all the rest." Her voice whirred like a pinwheel... "Hey!"

I snapped awake again.

"You're useless." But she reclined her chair too. "Go ahead, take a nap. Just be ready to tell me everything when you wake up."

The train was moving at a good clip now, nearly as fast as I was sinking...

I don't remember dreaming, only closing my eyes and the next thing I knew, my whole body lurched and my feet hit the forward seat.

"Good morning, sleeping beauty." Sandy was in the aisle with two cans of Dr. Pepper, some candy bars and potato chips. "Vending machines on a train," she said, sitting down. "Ain't it groovy?" She pealed off a tab and slipped it back in the can, handing it to me. "Chug this. It'll wake you up. You slept through three whole stops."

"Three?"

"Yep, a good long nap."

But it was still light outside. The train was passing a field of wheat where tall seed pods chased a breeze. I tipped the can and drank half my Dr. Pepper in nothing flat.

"I called Russ's phone number," I said.

"You *did*? How'd you get it?"

"This thing called directory assistance?"

She smacked my jeans.

"Anyhow, it was listed in St. Helena. Russell Peterson."

I'd already told Sandy the first revelation: that Ramblin' Russ was my grandfather. But there hadn't been time to go over the rest. We'd barely had time to pack.

"So what happened? Was he there?"

"I'm not sure."

"You're *not sure*?"

"Some woman picked up."

"Who?"

"She had this cement-mixer voice."

"Oh, that bitch your grandmother—what's her name?"

"Astrid. Must have been."

"What'd you say?"

"I said 'Is Russ there?' and she said, 'Who *is* this?' like I was some creep or something."

"Did you tell her?"

"'Course not. I hung up."

"You *hung up?*" Sandy turned on me, the freckles wrinkled over her nose. "You didn't ask her about your dad?"

"No."

"Gra-ace!"

"What?"

"Do you even know where he is? We're going all the way to California. How the hell are we supposed to find him?

I swallowed the last of my pop and rattled the tab. "We're not."

"Okay, now I *am* freaked out. Isn't that the whole reason we're going?"

"It's a long story, Sandy."

"And this is a long trip, Grace."

I'd planned to tell Sandy everything, once we were on the train, but that didn't make it easy.

"Come o-on," she pressed, "did he move away or what?"

"No."

"Then *what?*"

I looked around the train car. No one was listening. Outside, mountains rose in the distance. "He's dead."

"*Dead?*"

It felt like clothespins had been snapped on my windpipe.

"As in *dead* dead?"

I nodded and the clothespins clamped tighter.

"Holy shit." Sandy slumped in her chair. It was just the sound of the train then, the wheels on the track going 'round and 'round. "How the hell... I mean, *when?*"

"A long time ago. Before I was even born."

"You gonna tell me what happened or what?"

"Yeah, yeah."

"Then tell me!"

"Okay, all right. Dr. Rossano figured out that my mom was pregnant, right?"

"Sure, out in the hills."

"Then he told her to leave, right?"

"Yeah, so did she?"

"Not right off. I mean she couldn't even walk." The daisy fell from my hair and I picked it up, twirled it between my fingers.

"You gonna spit it out or what?"

"Just hold on." I wasn't in any hurry. "Not all of her letters were about the ranch, you know."

"How do you mean?"

"She wrote about all kinds of stuff: Jimmy and me, Georgia—and a whole bunch about the preacher that I didn't know."

"Like what?"

"How devoted he was to my mom. He wanted to take her to Paris after she got sick—I didn't know that. Just the two of them. He was trying to collect the money."

"Paris?"

"To see the art, all the museums, since she always wanted to go."

"But he never took her."

"No. She was afraid to leave Jimmy and me," my voice cracked. "I guess she didn't want to die over there."

Outside, the sun dipped behind the mountains, turning them black.

"Grace," Sandy said, pulling her knees to her chest, "I'm really sorry about your dad, but if he's dead, why are we going to California? There must be something you're not telling me."

I sighed and leaned my head against the back of the chair. "There is." Then, measure by measure, I recounted my mother's story, details I'd read only days before: five months pregnant and Sal nowhere to be seen. I explained how Astrid grew agitated, how the question of fatherhood had set her on fire. She drilled my mother about other boys and tried to slap their names out of her. The pressure continued until my mother finally remembered an important fact, that Hazel had seen Sal too, on the ranch that Thanksgiving weekend. Astrid was ecstatic. She even drove to Hazel's place to confirm it herself. Finally convinced Sal was the father, she cackled her conclusion: good old Cauliflower had outwitted everybody. Armed with her own plan, she marched to the castle where Dr. Rossano had stayed on, and came back the same night with an offer.

"What kind of offer?" Sandy asked.

"Money."

"How much?"

"Twenty thousand."

"Dollars?"

"Yep. It was worth a lot more in the 1950s. Ten thousand to the family—Astrid, mainly—and another ten to my mom, to get rid of her. But here's the catch: they had to promise to give up the baby and never to tell a soul, every one of them. Dr. Rossano would deliver the child, then take it to a secret home. There were plenty of people who wanted babies, who would even pay for them. As for my mom, she could stay on the ranch until she delivered, but after that never come back, never bother the Rossanos again.

"Could he *do* that?"

"He drew up papers. They had to sign or no money."

"And your mom, did she sign it?"

"Not at first. She tried to find Sal first. Hazel and Doug helped, calling everywhere they could think, but nobody would let on like they knew where he was. Then the news came to the ranch. They found him in his Fury at the bottom of a cliff."

"Oh God. What happened?"

"His car went straight off."

"How?"

"Nobody knows."

"Was it an accident?"

I shrugged.

"You mean he killed himself?"

"I don't know. My mom didn't even know. He drove so fast." I shivered. Sandy and I both had drivers' permits. "Anyway, it wasn't long after that, she finally signed those papers."

"But, Grace, she never gave you up. Something else must have happened."

"Yep. It's why we're on this train."

"You gonna tell me now or torture me?"

I stood and got my bag from overhead. "You can hear it from my mom."

"Your mom?"

I reached into the bag and pulled out letter number 22. "I figured Manny wouldn't notice if I only took the last letter."

Chapter 42

I opened the letter—the last my mother had written—and started reading it to Sandy.

Dear Grace,

The day before you were born was completely crazy. A big thunderstorm rolled in, which didn't happen on the ranch very often. It was one of those humid afternoo—

"Wait—when's your birthday?"
"July 27th, why?"
"Then it's July 26th 1958, right?"
"Right. Why?"
"Just getting my bearings. Keep going."
"You're the one who stopped me."
"Keep *going*."
"Okay, okay."

It was one of those humid afternoons. Soon as the lightning started, I went to the barn to check the horses. I was way too pregnant to ride, but I knew they'd be scared. We could keep each other company. It was such a sad time. It had been months since Sal's car crashed, but I couldn't stop thinking about him or wishing I could talk to him, especially about the baby. But there was no hope of that now. Not ever.

I'd already signed Dr. Rossano's papers. It's what everybody seemed to want: a good home for the baby, a whitewash for the Rossano name, and money to prop us all up. Even I thought it was best to be truthful. I was 15, with no husband. What could I do?

Every day I felt you kick, I tried not to think about it. I tried not to picture what you might look like. Astrid said the minute I gave birth they'd whisk you from the room. "It's better that way, then you can skip all that mothering nonsense," she said. But I couldn't imagine it, Grace, delivering a baby and not even holding it.

Dr. Rossano figured the labor would come at the end of August, which was four more weeks. He based it on the Thanksgiving date I'd told him, then said, "Unless you're lying, which wouldn't surprise me." It was hard for me to look at the man, Grace, but I couldn't let that go. "I'm not lying about any of it," I told him, "and you know it."

I didn't have a whole lot of faith in his prediction, since he was no expert in delivering babies. His training was internal medicine. Plus, I refused to let him touch me, not after everything else. It's true he was a shell of himself since Sal died, his only child killed in the car he'd bought for him. But that didn't change how I felt, despising the idea of him delivering my baby. Still, I'd signed those papers, so I let him look me over—with my clothes on.

I do remember this: I felt as big as Jersey in those days. All I could fit into were a couple of cotton dresses Hazel had sewed for me.

"Wait—Hazel?" Sandy said. "Who's that?"

"The neighbor. The one who saw her with Sal and mailed their letters."

"Oh yeah."

That day in the barn, I leaned on Lady for support. I was scared to death of giving birth, but I knew the mare had been through it, and that helped. "Did it hurt much, Lady?" I asked as I ran my fingers down her nose. But she slapped her ears back, full of jitters from the worsening storm. As night came on, it was getting harder to settle her down, the thunder crashing and banging over the roof. I could hear Cesare in his stall and Champ next door.

When Lady could no longer hold still, I left her stall, and that's when I got a good look at the lightning. It was quite a show, so I went straight for the hayloft for a better view. I was crazy to climb up there, considering how big I was, but I was young and dumb, Grace, and I did it anyway. I took one rung at a time up that ladder, glad I'd worn shoes, until I pulled myself up to the top.

At the loft door I sat on the frame and dangled my feet out, watching each flash zipping like gunshot through a purple sky. I kept watching as the hills lit up, so I could trace the trails where I used to ride... so I could remember when I left them behind.

A hard rain came next, drumming the ground in the corral, kicking up dust far below past my feet. At that point I was starting to get wet and I decided I'd better get back. But when I stood, water splashed at my shoes. How did so much come in at once? I wondered. A sharp pain doubled me over and then I knew. My water had broken.

Trying not to panic, I went for the ladder. But I had a horrible time twisting around and planting my feet. I started climbing down, maybe too slow, when another pain hit. I slipped and my feet thudded down the rungs to the ground. More water splashed. My ankle burned, the one I'd sprained months earlier falling from Lady. I limped to the front of the barn. Sheets of rain rocketed down as another contraction roared through me. My fall from the ladder had changed things. I called out, but the cottage was too far.

By the time I got there, I was drenched, hot tears mixed with rain. I don't recall ever in my life being glad to see Astrid, but I was that night. She pulled me in and went for the phone— Dr. Rossano, back in the city. I headed for my room as Doug *jumped up to help me, but I didn't see Pops, not the whole night. He'd been on a drunk for days.*

"That's Russ," I said looking up.
"Yeah I know. Keep reading."

The rest of that night I'd just as soon forget, Grace. Doug and Astrid tried to help, but they were scared as I was. It seemed like Dr. Rossano took forever to get there. "Patients at the hospital," he said, finally rushing in. It was after midnight by then and the pain had grown so intense I was wild with panic. I didn't care who he was. First thing he did was lay me bare and feel around. Then he paced the room, past the tacked-up sheet, then paced some more. The labor was nonstop, the contractions coming on top of each other. When he crouched between my knees and felt inside, the intensity of the pain nearly knocked me out.

The next thing I knew, Astrid was there and they were whispering. Doug stood a ways off, his face white as Jersey's salt lick. "Doug," I called, "come sit," and he knelt by the bed and held my hand. "The cord is wrapped around the baby's neck," he whispered. I didn't know what that meant, but by their faces it wasn't good. Finally the doctor was there again. All I remember is screaming, and then everything went black.

When I came to, both Astrid and the doctor were at the foot of the bed, their faces tense and their hands working. I heard a weak cry and then Dr. Rossano hoisted a bundle. I saw a small flash of skin and dark hair and then nothing. My baby! Doug looked stricken. "It's a girl," he said.

"It was YOU!" Sandy shrieked.

"...The thing is," Doug went on, "she's struggling just to breathe, but she's beautiful, Sharon. Tiny and beautiful." And then Astrid was over me. "We're goin' up to the castle," she said, her face flushed, "where there's more room." I heard the doctor rush out with my baby, the tiny beautiful girl I hadn't seen. "No!" I screamed, "bring her back—please!" I tried to sit up. "Let me see her—just once. Astrid! Dr. Rossano! Please! She's my own flesh and blood!" But Astrid only swatted Doug's arm. "Stay with

her. She'll pass the afterbirth in a bit, but that'll be easy. If somethin' goes sour, you know where to find us." I grabbed her arm and whimpered, "Please." But she twisted free and disappeared behind the sheet.

It didn't take long before the pain came again. Doug fed me water and stayed with me, but the next part wasn't easy like Astrid said. It was almost as bad as before. I started to pant, and it made me dizzy. "Something's wrong," I told Doug, "I know it. I feel it." Horrible thoughts raced through my head. Pain can do that to a person. I thought I was torn up, that my body parts were coming out. "You think it got blocked?"

"I don't know," he said, fidgeting with worry. I must've looked awful. Doug had me covered with a sheet, but I didn't care. There's no modesty with that kind of pain. "Take a look," I said, "Maybe you can see what's wrong." He drew the sheet to my knees and his eyes almost popped out, which scared me even more. "What Doug? What is it?"

His instincts took over then. He reached down and gave a pull as I screamed in agony, then he lifted it up for me to see. If I hadn't been so exhausted, Grace, I might've leapt straight out of that bed. It was a baby, by God. Another baby! Still blue but gasping for breath right there before us, a perfectly-formed baby girl.

"Oh my God!" Sandy said.

That baby girl was you, Grace, the surprise nobody expected.

"What does that—" The whites of Sandy's eyes shone like rings around an eclipse. "You mean *that* was you?"

"That's what she said."

"So the first—you have a *sister*? A *twin sister*?"

"I did."

"What do you mean *did*? Is she dead too?"

"I don't know. That's why we're going to California."

"Oh my God."

"To find out."

"Oh my God."

"Exactly."

Chapter 43

As the train clacked on through the mountains, Sandy stared out the darkening windows, stunned to silence. It suited me, for an old memory had crept in of a sunny day, years before, when my mother took me for ice cream. She wore an oversize dress that day, and I wore the sandals with the yellow daisies at my toes. I saw her strolling to the counter and ordering three cones, with only two of us there to eat them. Now finally, after so many years, I understood why. She had given up a daughter, a tiny girl she'd only glimpsed once. And in that moment, that carefree, Dairy-Queen moment, she'd bought a cone for her too, as though she were with us, her mother and sister, as natural as anything. When she realized her mistake, that my twin wasn't there, the grief had doubled her over. She didn't know where my sister was or whether she was happy. She didn't even know her name.

Now here I was, running away to find that girl, and the thought made my hands sweat. Was she still there? Would she want to see me? I held my breath and dried my palms on my jeans.

By the time we crossed into California night had fallen. But it wasn't time to worry yet. We'd be on that train until another day dawned. In the morning, we'd get off in Davis and hop a Greyhound bus for St. Helena. It was anybody's guess what the day would hold for us there.

The lights had been lowered on the train, but I wasn't sleepy. When we stopped in a town called Dunsmuir, I talked Sandy into stretching our legs, and we went outside.

"So," I said, a sudden updraft lifting our hair. "What do you think of it all?"

"I still can't believe it. You had a twin all those years and your mom never even told you?"

"Nope."

"Why?" She rubbed her arms in the chill.

"It's complicated. She'd signed those papers. She didn't expect to ever see her again. So what was the point of upsetting me?"

"Then your sister was adopted?"

"That's what they told her, that some other family whisked her away." I looked down the length of the train. "Except…"

"Except what?"

"They lied."

"They did?" She strung another lock of hair.

"My mom didn't know it for years, not when she left the ranch or even the whole time I was growing up. She only found out from Russ, when he showed up that summer."

"What'd he say?"

"Pretty much the opposite of what she thought. That my sister wasn't with some nice family. She was on the ranch, with Astrid."

She spit out the lock of hair. "You're shittin' me."

"No, I'm not. Astrid had been raising her for years by then, working her like a slave the way she did my mom, only my sister never went to school. She stayed with Astrid all day long, at her beck and call."

"Why Astrid?"

"She had birth defects, Russ said. From the labor, the fact that Dr. Rossano didn't know what he was doing. She had trouble breathing but he never bothered to take her to the hospital. The couple that was supposed to adopt her took one look and backed out. They tried other people, I guess, other couples, but nobody wanted—" My voice cracked and my eyes stung.

"So they just *gave* her to Astrid?"

"Not in the beginning. Mrs. Rossano took control first. She

came to the ranch to see the baby and had a fit. Her son was dead and it was his daughter, her granddaughter. She fought with Dr. Rossano and begged him to let her take her to San Francisco to raise."

"Did she?"

"For a couple of years, but not much longer. See, the baby—"

"Your *sister*."

"Yeah, my sis—" my throat caught "—she needed a lot of attention and Mrs. Rossano couldn't hack it, I guess. She was depressed. She blamed herself and her husband for everything that happened, you know, with Sal and the car crash."

"She should have."

"Anyway, Russ said she wasn't fit to be a mother. About the time my sister turned two, Mrs. Rossano had a nervous breakdown."

"Holy shit."

"That's when they dumped her on the ranch." I put my hand to my mouth, trying to stop it from trembling. "They just showed up one day and said they were leaving her there for good. And the whole time, Mrs. Rossano sat in the car and let the doctor do the dirty work. He left instructions to lock up the castle, sell the horses, said they were leaving town. He said Astrid and Russ could stay on at the ranch to raise the girl and that was that. They drove off. She was two years old and they never even said goodbye." I blinked back tears. "Russ figured they went to Italy or something. Checks came from some bank in San Francisco, but they never saw the Rossanos again."

"And your sister? She's still on the ranch?"

"That's the question. I don't even know for sure if she's alive. She had health problems with the birth defects. Nobody said what exactly. But she was alive when my mom died."

"How do you know that?"

"Russ. My mom wrote to him, remember, and had him come? Since she hadn't *done* anything herself for my sister." I turned my face from a group of passengers approaching the train. "She made him promise to stay on the ranch, you know, to protect Patsy from Astrid until I was old enough to—"

"*Patsy?*"

"Oh, sorry. That's her name."

"Patsy, huh?"

I nodded, felt my tears slop over. "I'm not used to it either. I guess she looks something like me."

"Yeah?" She wrapped an arm over my shoulders. "With any luck, we'll find out tomorrow."

I wiped my tears as the porter called, "All a-board!"

"Speaking of you, Grace," Sandy said, climbing into the car with me, "you haven't finished the story yet of the night you were born. Did Sal's dad ever find out there were two babies?"

"That's the best part. But I'm worn out. Why don't you read the rest?"

When we were settled in our seats, I handed the pages to Sandy. The lights were low, some of the passengers asleep, so she flipped on the overhead and found the place where I'd left off.

"Hey," she whispered, "you want me to read out loud?"

"Sure. I'll never hear it too many times."

Doug had you by your shoulders at first and he just held you there, in midair, while you cried yourself pink. Can you imagine? Another complete and beautiful baby? I would've been less shocked if my insides had come out. Your cry was so primal, we stared, absolutely amazed. When Doug went to his bed for a sheet to wrap you in, I started to sob, overjoyed and overwhelmed. We had no idea what to do, about you, about the cord, about anything, so Doug just wrapped you up and laid you next to me. Your little hands were still blue, but you were so beautiful, I fell in love. I wished Sal could've seen you. Your hair was like his, so much like his. How I wished he could've seen you.

A thousand thoughts ran through my head. Twins! No wonder I'd felt so big. And a thousand questions: Should I have known? Should the doctor have known? That's when it hit me, Grace, that it wasn't over yet, not by a long shot.

"We have to hide her, Doug," I said, "we can't let the doctor see her, I signed those papers!" Doug's face turned grim. "But how? How are we gonna hide a crying baby?" He was right. You were already cooing, making these sweet little noises. It seemed impossible. I held you tight and tried to think but my mind was a mess. Each thought I had smashed into the next.

"We have to find a way, Doug—please, we have to!" I was fierce with love, Grace, and scared to death, picturing Astrid and the doctor coming back any minute and taking you away too. So scared. Where could we hide you? That cottage was cramped and the barn was no good. Then it hit me. It flew out of my mouth.

"Hazel Clayton—take her to Hazel's, Doug! She'll hide her for me!" Doug stood and turned around. "It might work," he said. The color was back in his face. "She's the only thing we have," I told him. "Hurry, before they come back! Did they walk to the castle?" But Doug shook his head. "They drove the Jeep." We both knew that was bad. They could be back any second. I looked down and saw the cord. The two of us were still attached!

"We have to cut the cord, Doug! Did you see how he did it the first time?" He said he didn't and paced the room like the doctor had, back and forth past the tacked-up sheet. Then he stopped. We'd heard a noise from outside. "Do something!" I pleaded. He yanked his ratty shoelace until it broke and tied the piece around the cord. "Hurry, Doug!" Then he ran for a knife while I called, "Hurry, hurry, hurry! It's the Jeep!"

Doug was fast, but not fast enough. Just as he was about to cut the cord, the sound came through the walls, a car door slamming. "You have to go, Doug, out the window. You have to go!" He sliced the cord and whisked you up, in the bloody sheet, but I grabbed hold of it. "Don't take the sheet, Astrid'll notice it missing! Take something else!"

He grabbed a shirt and rolled you up as you whimpered, and, by then, we were out of time. We heard the front door and I just about lost it. "Go! Hurry!" It was awful, Grace. As Doug dashed for the window, I grabbed at the cord still hanging from me and cut through it as close to my body as I could. Then I threw it and the knife under my bed. He was at the window, opening it as the murmur of her shoes came down the hall. It was Astrid—alone. If she caught him with you, if she heard a peep, it was over. She'd see more money in another baby.

"Hurry Doug!" I hissed. I watched him slip out the window,

heard a small cry as he landed, and there she was, around the sheet, beside my bed. Oh God, had she heard? Had she seen? A whimper escaped my lips. "You pass the afterbirth?" she said. I stared for a minute, trying to process her words. Then I shook my head. "Not that I know of. I don't think I passed anything." She looked around, her eyes landing on the open window. "Where's your brother?"

"I don't know," I said, "I just woke up." My heart was pounding Grace, like you can't imagine. If she'd heard something, if she spotted Doug, we were finished. "What the hell's the window open for," she snapped, "it's the middle of the night!" Then she went to it as I stared. I could barely stand it. Would she see him outside with you? Would she hear you cry? I held my breath until my heart and lungs burned. The next thing I know she was closing the window, her shoes murmuring back to my bed.

Sandy whipped down the letter. "They made it? They actually *made it?*"

I patted my armrest. "Here I sit. He got all the way to Hazel's."

"Fa-ar *out!* A few more seconds and you'd be somewhere else. I wouldn't even know you."

"Nope, probably not."

"So Astrid never caught on—or the doctor either?"

"Read the rest."

"It's too long. Just tell me!"

"Dr. Rossano stayed at the castle all night, so he never saw a thing. And Astrid was clueless. The afterbirth came but she didn't notice the two cords."

"You're so damn lucky."

"Tell me about it."

"Then what?"

"The next morning the doctor showed up and played like my sister was already gone. You know, like that couple had whisked her away."

"The big lie."

"Yep. Then he handed my mom a check. Ten thousand bucks. She didn't want it. It made her feel like she'd sold her baby.

But she took it just to get rid of him. She didn't have to spend it. The very next day her milk came in and she left for good."

"To Hazel's?"

"Mmhmn. To get to her baby—to get to me. She stayed there a couple of weeks, I guess, getting her strength back, then left for the city. It would have been longer if Russ hadn't figured her out."

"Russ? How?"

"Doug was sneaking over to bring her stuff—her paint case, clothes and stuff—and one day Russ followed. That's how he found out there were twins."

"He knew and he didn't he tell Astrid?"

"It's the one thing he did right all those years. As far as Astrid knows, I don't exist, I never did."

"Wait'll she meets you! She *will* meet you, right?"

"Its a pretty good bet." I reclined my seat as far as it would go.

"Grace?"

"Mmm?"

"Did your mom ever spend that ten thousand bucks?"

"No. She didn't tell the preacher about my twin either. She figured she'd already lost her, what was the point?"

"So what happened to the check?"

"She tore it up."

"Wow."

"Yeah. Thanks to Doug, though, she had a little cash. He raided Astrid's money tin and split it with my mom. Then he ran off too, Texas, he said. They had a good laugh over it, picturing Astrid's face when she opened that tin."

"Serves her right."

I closed my eyes and heard a click. Sandy had turned out the overhead. My back was stiff and I wished we'd bought tickets for a sleeper car. "The sad thing is," I added, "my mom and her brother lost touch. She never figured out where he went."

"You've never met him?"

"No."

If Sandy had more questions, she let them rest, for it was only the forward motion and the hum of the tracks after that. I drifted in and out as the train chugged on, ever southward through the night.

Floating and dreaming, I was carried, as if on warm, placid water, toward the sister I didn't know, the twin with which I'd shared a womb and grown into being but hadn't touched in 15 years.

Chapter 44

I slept through the sunrise, the kind of sleep you startle awake from, not knowing where you are. Why was Sandy tapping my leg? Why was I sleeping in my jeans? Then I remembered: the train ride to find my twin. That's enough to wake you up quick. After we rolled to a stop in Davis and stepped out, I shaded my eyes against a morning sky, a too-bright, California sky. The air around me buzzed with excitement, but my feet were heavy. I didn't want to move forward. I didn't feel ready.

Sandy got our bus tickets as I stood in a daze, and then, while we waited, some breakfast that went down too rich for my squeamish stomach. The next thing I knew she was prodding me onto the greyhound bus. The truth was, I hadn't thought through any of it: what I'd do if I found my sister, what I'd say. Not to mention Astrid, how I'd handle her—or Russ.

On the bus I gazed out the window. California's shades of green were paler than Oregon's. I had a whole bus ride to Napa Valley to look at them. With so many distractions, there was no time to worry yet.

Then the trip was over and we were in St. Helena. Too fast, it was all happening too fast.

"Which way do we go?" Sandy asked as we stood on the sidewalk.

My teeth chattered. "North, I think."

"You *think*? You didn't you get the address?"

"We don't need it."

Sandy gaped at me like I was out of my mind. And maybe I was.

"It's fine," I said. "Follow me."

There were two roads north of town and one of them was a highway, not the sort of road my mother wrote about. So we took the slower one, which cut to the west and then northwest. Brown hills stood in the distance, studded with low, green trees. It felt right to me, the way my mother had described. I walked slowly, as slowly as Sandy would tolerate, stalling more than anything but also studying the scenery. My mother had passed this way when she was my age, 15, the same age she'd been when she'd given birth.

One foot in front of the other.

Soon the houses thinned out and the road took us through trees, tall redwoods and hearty madronas, the dust and perfume of Napa Valley. I thought about bits and pieces, landmarks I remembered from her letters. I'd read them often enough: the two-mile walk from school, the reservoir she'd spotted on horseback, and the stone bridge across a creek that Pops practically drove off of. If I let her words guide me, I would find it, I knew I would.

Sandy wasn't so confident. "You sure you know where this place is?" she asked, after we'd been walking quite a while.

"No, but I—" Sandy's timing was perfect. I looked up to answer her and just to our right, on a bushy rise, was a huge, concrete structure, like a pool... *or a reservoir.* I took off jogging, scanning the road for the stone bridge. I kept running until I saw it, up on the left.

"What is it?" Sandy panted, arriving beside me.

"The stone bridge my mother talked about," I said, my feet planted firmly on it. "This has to be it." A creek ran under the bridge, with native plants all around. I started walking, one foot in front of the other. The time to worry was closing in.

The road ahead was similar to what I had pictured. Dark and cool, it wound through evergreen giants and thick undergrowth, dipping one way and then the next. We followed it a good ways until we came out on the other side.

"Wow," Sandy said.

There it was, in the distance, lit up by the sun: an actual, flanked-by-two-towers castle. But I was speechless, stunned by the ravage of 15 years. The place no longer looked like a Garden of Eden the way my mother described, but like an overgrown jungle, the grass gone to seed and the castle bound in ivy. We went closer. A long, hushed walk. It appeared locked up, put out of service, the way Russ had said. Creepers covered the castle windows and weeds choked its base. There were no roses big as pomegranates, only disease-bitten buds and a crop of thorns. We crossed another bridge where the old winery doors leaned out, and I searched for the cellar door my mother and Sal had once used, but it was swallowed in undergrowth.

"There's nobody here," I said. "We'll have to find the cottage."

My insides roiled. The time to worry drew closer still. We picked our way through wheat-like grass and found the walking paths my mother had jumped. They flowed like hidden rivers through the seeded stalks. Finally, we crossed the orchard my mother and Sal had strolled at night. Ripe plums littered the ground, what my mother had called prunes. We stepped over and around them, and then, there it was, through the trees: a tiny cottage, no longer quite white. Beside it, as pretty as the cottage was ugly, a neat little vegetable garden, brimming with growth. Somebody lived there all right. We went closer and stood a minute, staring. The time to worry had arrived.

"What're you gonna do?" Sandy whispered.

"I don't know."

"There's a car on the other side. Somebody's in there."

All the times I'd tried to picture my sister, I hadn't come up with much. Would I know her face in the next minute? The morning was still cool, but I was sweating. "I guess I'll knock."

It was the strangest sensation getting my body from the trees to that door. My blood felt thick. Over the packed earth, I went and up the steps of the screened-in porch, right to the splintered wood framing the flimsy door. Through the mesh of the screen, a few feet away, was the cottage front door, firmly shut. The faint sound of a television leaked through. I lifted my fist, rapped on the screen door, and it rattled back.

Then there was nothing but the murmur of television. Soap opera voices.

"They can't hear you," Sandy said. "You have to go in."

I opened the screen and stepped inside, the smell of people and old cooking wafting past. I crossed the porch, stood by a couch and a beat-up chair. I took a breath and lifted my fist. One rap, another. This time, I felt the floor under my feet sigh and heard the soap-opera voices stop. I turned to Sandy, then back around to examine the mat under my feet. When the door came open, I saw the shoes first—soft soled—then the thick waist and barrel chest. It had to be Astrid, the way her presence made my stomach churn. When our eyes locked, she stumbled back, she actually stumbled and her mouth came open. "Who?—" It was the oddest thing. The last thing I expected. She kept stumbling, past the now-dark TV, into the room, staring at me like I was a demon from hell.

Had Russ said something? Had he told her about me?

I didn't care. I was finally here, and the only thing I wanted was my sister. I followed her back—almost driving her—until she dropped into an armchair, white as talcum.

"Who *are* you?" she said.

For a second I wondered if I had the wrong place and looked around. No Russ and no teenage girl. Was there *another* castle up the road?

"I think my sister lives here. I came to see her."

"Your *sister*? *What* sister?"

"My twin. Doesn't she live here with you and Russ? You're Astrid, right?"

"Impossible... *impossible*," she said. But a terrible doubt had clouded her eyes. She was Astrid, without a doubt. I could see the wheels turning, I could almost hear her thoughts. She'd gone back to that night, 15 years ago, for that all-important question: Could there have been *two* babies? Finally she looked at me, color rising in her cheeks. "Whadya know," she said. "Never suspected it. And you are?"

"Grace."

"Grace, huh? Whadya know." Then she stared at me for the longest time, the wheels still turning. "How the hell she get you out of here?"

I didn't answer.

"Whadya know." She planted her hands on the arms of the chair and, with great effort and grunting, pushed herself up.

"Where's my sister? I want to see Patsy."

Her laugh was so sharp I jumped. A succession of barks came next, the cackle my mother had described.

"*Patsy?* Who told you *Patsy?*"

"Russ did."

"You know Russ?" She shook her head. "That sum-bitch. He told yeh Patsy, huh?" She was headed from the room, so I followed. We both followed.

"Isn't that her name?" We were in the kitchen.

"Call her what you want... it don't matter no more."

"Why? Why doesn't it matter?"

She turned, her face going strangely sweet. "I hate to be the one to tell you girls, like this and all, the very minute you show up here—where'd yeh come from, anyway?"

"Portland."

She clucked her tongue. "All the way from Portland, huh? Such a long ways." She took another step and I heard her shoes, like Momma said, murmuring against the floor. "Well the fact is, you're too late." The sweetness was gone. "Your sister died a month ago."

My head went light, my body numb—except for the clothespins that squeezed my throat. "But... how—"

"She had seizures pertinear every day. Was a big one that finally got her. Russ don't even know it. He ain't bothered to come around."

"But he promised to keep an eye on her."

She turned again, her face twisted. "Promised *who?*"

"My mom."

The fact surprised Astrid; I saw the flash before she covered it up.

"The promise of a drunk ain't worth much now, is it? Anyhow, I found her, over t'the chicken coop, already passed I'm sorry to say." She was headed for the refrigerator. "It was sad, you bet, real sad and all, 'bout enough to make yeh cry when you dwell on it. I made a nice box for her and buried her that same day."

"You made a box?" I was fighting to keep my breakfast

down.

She held out thick arms. "Look around girl. You think I got money to burn? It ain't nothin' new. They been makin' boxes hundreds of years. Besides, she never had a birth certificate, so what's the point of going to town? Hell, far as the world knows, she never existed." She faced me square on, and leaned into me. "But I s'pose you already know about *that*." The look in her eyes sent a tremor down my spine. Then she straightened and opened the refrigerator, accidentally knocking a can of pop to the floor.

"You want to get that for me, blondie? I can't bend too well these days." Sandy went for the can, handing it to her and then backing away.

"The grave's up in the hills. I can take you there if you want, but it's quite a hike. I thought it best she be up in the hills." Astrid tapped the top of the can and waited a minute before popping it open. "You girls want somethin' to drink?"

I gagged and nearly threw up. I didn't want something to drink and I didn't want to see a grave. I wanted my sister. I turned and ran, out the door and down the drive, hot tears wetting my face. I ran so fast my flats flew off, my feet hitting sharp rocks, but I didn't care. *Let them cut me!* And I didn't stop, not even when Sandy called after me. *Especially* when Sandy called after me. I ran, all the way to the bridge, and when I got there, I turned around and roared in her face.

"It's all your fault you stupid bitch!"

She went crimson. "My fault? How is it *my* fault?"

"You knew where the letters were! Way back when we were in school! My sister's been dead for a month! *A month!* If you'd told me then, when you first knew, I would've been here, you selfish brat! Now she's dead, just like my mother, and I'll never, ever see her— EVER!"

I fell to the bridge, my feet coated in dust and blood. I cried and choked, on anger and spit and tears. "First my mother and now my sister," I wailed. Sandy fell next to me and reached out "I'msosorryI'msosorry" running from her mouth. But I smacked her away. What good was she? What good was any of it? All that effort, the train and the plans and the lies. All those letters, all those years, and for what? To miss my sister by *one month*? She was in the ground, buried and rotting, just like my mother.

"Does it make any sense to you?" I bellowed at Sandy. "All those years I'm up in Portland and my sister's here, stuck with Astrid?"

She shook her head, her own tears flowing.

"Then just when I'm about to find her she has a seizure and dies? A stupid *seizure*! Does that make sense? Well *does it*?"

"No," Sandy whimpered. "I mean, how do you even die from that?"

I glared at her. What the hell was she talking about? "Isn't it goddamn obvious?" I roared, "She swallowed her tongue or something and couldn't get—" I stopped, felt the blood drain.

"Couldn't get what?"

"Oh my God."

"What?"

"Oh my God." I jumped to my feet.

"*What?*"

"She's not dead, Sandy."

"Who?"

"My sister, you stupid shit!"

"But what do you—"

"The seizure story! It's exactly what Russ told my mom. It was in her last letter, the part we didn't read."

"What was?"

"That Astrid had the story ready. If my mom found out my sister was on the ranch, she was gonna say it: that Patsy had a seizure and swallowed her tongue!"

"You mean she didn't bury her?"

"Think about it, Sandy, if my sister's dead and Russ is gone then who's taking care of that vegetable garden? You saw how perfect it was, right?"

She furrowed her brow. "I don't know, Astrid?"

"Did you see her push out of that chair? Did you hear her say she couldn't bend?"

"Oh, yeah!" Sandy's eyes went wide. "And she made *me* pick up the can of pop."

"Exactly. Astrid can barely move. Somebody else is working that garden. She's alive, Sandy, I know it!" I turned and ran.

"Where're you going?" she called after me.
"To find my sister you dumb shit! Where else?"

Chapter 45

Not in my entire life had I covered so much ground on foot. Not in Pardee Park, not in the churchyard, not running from the fire in McEgan's barn. That ranch was so big, I had no idea where to start. I flew from that bridge in my banged-up feet, through the tall grass and up the hill. I don't know what I was thinking, racing around that castle, the empty pool, back through the woods and down by the creek. No, that's not true. I wasn't thinking anything. Just looking and looking, hoping, in the next second, *every* second, to see her: wading through the creek, climbing a tree, picking prunes in the orchard. A sister, *my* sister, moving and breathing and alive.

I was determined to cover every inch of that ranch, every inch that wasn't the cottage. I ran opposite its shack-like walls, checking behind me for Astrid the way my mother had. I ran to a little stone structure that must have been the springhouse. My sister wasn't there. I ran to the chicken coop. Only chickens. I ran up a beaten trail. To my left were the hills, and straight ahead, the barn of my mother's childhood.

I held up to look it over, one of the places she'd loved most. It was still in good shape, at least compared to the old McEgan barn, the walls a faded-red, but straight and sturdy. Standing near it, only a few dozen yards distance, I was moved in a way I didn't expect. I sucked in air and a chain of sobs shook me. All the hours my mother had spent there, with Sal, with the horses, on that stormy night she went into labor. How scared and how alone she'd been.

The doors to the barn stood open. Two large doors, pushed wide. Had Astrid done that, or someone else? I turned around to check behind me. No change at the cottage, and here, over the rise, came the blonde head of Sandy, bobbing along on my trail. I wasn't going to wait for her. I kept going forward, one foot in front of the other, every ounce of me hoping. I'd raced across that ranch, checking every spot I could think of. If I didn't find her in the barn—or somewhere near it—I might not find her at all. I might find instead that I'd fooled myself and she was dead.

I was at the entrance then, my hands tingling, my cheeks slick with tears, my chest aflame. At first I saw nothing but empty space. Horse stalls with no horses, just the days-gone-by smell of them, faint and earthy. Then I saw movement, only slight, at the far end of the barn. I went toward it. An animal of some kind? Brown but not large… or was I wrong? I was seeing only part of it. I became aware of something else: a small sound that might have been musical. The pulse in my ears had grown so loud I wasn't sure what I was hearing. I kept walking, over the concrete, in my bare feet. Was it a radio? No, humming? Yes, humming.

I kept my feet moving, one after the other, trying to make out a tune. The inside of the barn took a turn just ahead, and most of the animal was around the corner. I could see its hindquarters now and it was plenty big, whatever it was. Past the animal was a row of steps, the wooden rungs of the ladder my mother had climbed to the loft, I was sure of it. She'd gone up there to read Sal's letters. She'd been up there when her water broke.

I traced my fingers along the plywood wall. The animal was closer, the sharp hip bones, the tan hide—a cow? Yes, a milk cow. Part of the udders were visible too. The sound came clearer now, *definitely humming*. But the pattern was odd, as though random and ever changing. Was the voice young or old? When I turned the corner would I find Astrid, my sister, or someone else altogether?

My heart thundered. I put my hands to the inner wall, inching forward. The cow's form elongated as I eased to the edge. Her pale udders, her long mid-section, the back half of her shoulders. I caught a glimpse of fingers then, just the flash of a hand, and suddenly, there she was, born to me in that instant, more beautiful and terrifying than any creature I'd ever seen: her hair like mine, her face like mine, but so thin and filthy it scared me. Her curls were matted, her upper lip scabbed. I watched her a minute—stroking the cow and humming sweetly—before she knew I was there, before I knew what I was seeing. Her notes stayed random, like chimes in the wind, and then her eyes flashed, the accident of our birth: one light, one dark, one blue, one brown.

Just.

Like.

Mine.

No wonder Astrid had stumbled back at the sight of me.

A little cry escaped my lips and she looked up. *We are. We always have been,* passed between us. A little cry escaped her lips too, and she said, "Grayth? Merthy Grayth?" My name? She knew my name! I started toward her, just one step, when her eyes shut off. I don't know how else to describe it. She was no longer looking at me, but somewhere short of me, in the space between us. Her body went stiff and her face twitched. Drool formed at her lip where her teeth protruded. A seizure, I realized, she was having a seizure! But it wasn't violent, it was eerily quiet, as if time had stopped. And that's when the revelation came, like a curtain pulled back. The protruding mouth, the face like mine and not like mine.

My vision in the clouds.

Suddenly I was a child again, back in that weedy grass, staring at the sky over my backyard fence and that face, the blue eye on the right and brown on the left—exactly *opposite* mine. It wasn't my own face I'd seen in a sky of sno cone blue, it was *hers.*

"Oh my God!" Sandy said, rushing up. "She looks just like you!"

"Yeah," I said, "except opposite."

She moved in closer, examining my twin, then me. "Holy shit! How did that happen?"

"No idea." An odd thought crossed my mind: the mirror game Sandy and I used to play. If Patsy stood at one end of the glass and I at the other, we'd be exactly the same: two blue-eyed girls. And then, when we switched, two brown.

"Look," Sandy said. "Even her hair, the little cowlick. It's backwards from yours. But what's wrong with her, Grace? She's so dirty, and why's she *drooling?*"

"I think it's a seizure."

"Oh God. She gonna swallow her tongue?"

"I don't think so."

"Was she like this when you got here?"

"No. She said my name and—"

"She said your *name?*"

"Russ must have told her."

"Oh my God, Grace, I just realized."

"What?"

"All those times you said you were missing something. When we were little, even." Her eyes burned bright. "She's it, isn't she?"

The seizure didn't last long. I rubbed her arms and petted her hair, the matted mess of it. I talked sweet to her, saying "Patsy, Patsy." When her eyes cleared, she was back with us like she'd never left at all.

"Grayth!" she said, wrapping her arms around me. "You came—it'th really you!"

"You know about me? How'd you know?"

She pulled away, her eyes so much like mine the hair on my neck stood up. "Popth told me—on my latht birthday. He thed keep it a thecret."

"Pops?"

"He'th my grandpa but I call him Popth. He thed my real mother wath dead but I had a thithter. Don't tell Athtrid, he thed, whatever you do and she'll come. One day your thithter will come. And Popth wath right. You look like me exthept perty!"

"I'm not pretty."

"Yeth you are." She squeezed me again and leaned back, spotting Sandy. "She'th perty too!"

I couldn't quite figure her out: her expressions and the way she talked. Her bucked teeth didn't help, worse than mine were before braces, but it was more than that.

"That's Sandy," I said. "My friend."

She lifted a hand. "Hi Thandy my thithter's friend."

She dropped her hand and stepped back. Something was wrong with the way she moved. The birth defects were pronounced.

"I'm sorry it took me so long, Patsy. I didn't know about you until just last week."

"It'th okay. But I'm not Pat-thy. I'm Thpathy."

"Wha—" I tried putting the sounds together. "Th—pathy?"

"No, thilly." She laughed, the sound of my own chortle exactly. "Not like *I* thay it." She put her tongue under her teeth, leaned into me and tried again. "Thpathy."

Sandy shot me a look. I knew what she was thinking, the same thing I was.

"Spazzy?" I said. "Is that what you mean? Spazzy?"

"Yeth!"

"Is that what Astrid calls you?" I wanted to kill the woman that very minute.

"That'th it." The way she grinned past her bucked teeth, snapped the clothespins back on my throat. She was my age, she'd lived the exact same number of days I had, but mentally, she was still a girl, no more than a child. Astrid had probably called her Spazzy from the start. She giggled and I blinked, fighting tears I didn't want her to see.

"Can I ask you a favor?" I said, shuffling my feet. "Do you mind if I call you Patsy? I think it's a pretty name, don't you?"

She looked at me sideways, her gaze glued to my every move. "Pat-thy?"

"Yeah. I really like it, don't you?"

"It'th okay." Her hips took an awkward rock, tilting her shorts. "But only if you promith one thing."

"What?"

"That I can fikth your foot."

"My foot?" I looked down. Both of my feet were filthy, but dark lines stained the toes on my right. I lifted them and found the concrete underneath sticky with blood.

"Oh Jeez, you cut it good," Sandy said. "Hey, where's she going?"

Patsy was on the move, heading for a side door to our right. It was painful to watch her walk, her hips a seesaw as one sneakered foot thrust to the side with each step. It took her forever to get to that door.

"She's so… different, isn't she?" Sandy said.

I ignored the comment. A few minutes later Patsy seesawed back to us, sloshing a bucketful of water. "Go on Rose" she said to the cow and gave her a good-natured shove. Then she pulled over a stool—"Thith ith for you"—using her right hand not her left. I don't know how I noticed that, but I did. How many times had I dreamt I was right-handed?

"Go ahead," she said. "Don't be a thcardy cat."

I sat on the stool and she planted the bucket, plopping down on the floor behind it. Soon as she hit the concrete, Sandy gasped and covered her mouth. I had to lean around the bucket to see why: horrible scars marred the insides of her thighs. The skin looked melted, like Apple McEgan's head. I stared at the crotch of her shorts, trying not to imagine what was underneath. It set my own skin on fire.

"What happened?" Sandy said, her mouth still covered.

Patsy's face went pink, and she folded her legs to hide the scars. "I wath bad."

"Bad?" I asked, "How do you mean?"

"Athtrid punished me."

"*Astrid* did that?"

From the bucket of water she lifted a rag and began to dab it over my bloody foot. "When I wath in the bathtub. She had a pan of greathe—for the chicken—and she dumped it on me."

I couldn't speak, remembering my mother's words, how Astrid had threatened to burn her with grease too.

"She doth it every Thunday."

Sandy crouched next to us. "She pours grease on you every Sunday?"

"No, no, no. She *cookth a chicken*. She only burned me one time, but I got a fever and chillth. Usually it'th not tho bad. Little thtuff." She pointed to a scar on her forearm, a bruise on her cheek. Astrid's back may have been stiff, but she had no trouble inflicting pain.

"She's a monster," Sandy said.

Patsy shrugged. "You have to watch yourthelf around her, that'th all." The edges of the scar peeked out again and my stomach churned, full of acid and bile. When she picked up my foot and began to wash it, I was grateful. There was something familiar about the gesture, and deeply soothing. I closed my eyes. The longer she worked the less sick I felt. The cool water, the gentle touch, her right hand in command like my left. People should wash each other's feet more often, I thought, and then I realized why it was familiar. It was a Bible thing, a Jesus-and-his-disciples thing. But Patsy wouldn't know that, would she? Sure as hell not from Astrid. I opened my eyes to watch her, the matted hair and scabbed lip, her expression strangely sublime.

"Why'd she do it, Patsy?" I asked. "Why'd Astrid burn you like that?"

She wiped the space between my toes now, which tickled some, and shrugged. "Becauthe of a boy." Her face went pink again.

"A boy?"

"I couldn't go to thchool, I'm too thtupid, tho I never had any friendth. But I found one, on the truck that deliverth our hay." She tore a strip of cloth and tied it around my instep to cover the cut. "Rose needth hay, you know, she'th tho funny if she doethn't get it she—"

"The boy, Patsy," I interrupted.

"Oh. Well, he wath nithe. I thed hi and Athtrid heard me. It wath that night she poured the greathe."

"For saying hi?" Sandy said.

Patsy nodded.

"But why?"

"She thed nobody would make a baby with a twat like that."

A bolt of anger shot through me, so powerful it blurred my vision. Astrid was evil. Not just cruel, but evil. Patsy got up then, no longer wanting to talk about it.

"I'll dump the water out," she said and seesawed off.

"Jeez," Sandy whispered, watching her go. "What the hell we gonna do?"

"What else?" I got up from the stool and eased some weight onto my foot. "Take her home, of course."

"Are you crazy?"

"Why? What would you do?"

"I don't know. Call somebody or something. But she lives *here*, Grace. You can come and visit her whenever you want."

"No way."

"Think about it Grace. I mean, I know she's your twin and all, but she belongs at a place like this. She's filthy as all get-out, never even been to school, and she can barely walk. You saw the sore on her lip, right? It's probably impetigo. Who knows what else she's got. Ringworms—cooties for God's sake. She's worse than Apple McEgan."

I don't know why, but the thought of Apple made me want to cry. "Is Apple that bad?"

She gaped at me. "I have no idea who you are, Grace. You don't even make sense. What do you think you're going to do? Take her on a train? Buy her a ticket and put her in a seat smelling like that with that hair and those clothes? Besides, Astrid won't let her go anyway. She probably does all the work."

"What should I do then, Sandy, leave her here to be Astrid's slave? Let her burn her again?"

"She only did it once, Grace. Even Patsy said."

"So that's fine?" I shook my head. "There's no way, Sandy. I'm getting her out of here. I *have* to."

"How?"

"I'll think of something." And I knew I would. The way I felt, I could do anything. I'd found my twin, after all these years, and nobody—not a single soul—was going to keep us apart.

When Patsy came back I startled her with a hug, and her response was to return it—twice. Then the three of us went out the back of the barn, away from the cottage. I didn't worry what Sandy was thinking or what I would do next. I'd made up my mind and that was that. The details would come. The sun was high over our heads, and the sky so blue, so clear and vibrant I wanted to eat it up.

I grabbed Patsy's hand and threaded our fingers. "See that sky?" I said, "You know what I call that color?" She gazed up, her lop-eyes squinting, her bucked teeth jutting. "It's sno cone blue, sister, sno cone blue."

Chapter 46

The task ahead of me was like nothing I'd ever faced. How would I rescue Patsy? How in the world would I get her home? But the minute I put myself in my mother's shoes, the answer came. She'd been in trouble on that ranch. Desperate trouble. And where had she turned?

To Hazel Clayton.

I had no idea, of course, whether Hazel still lived on the neighboring ranch. Hell, I had no idea whether she still *lived*. Fifteen years had passed. I tried to remember how old she'd been, what my mother had said. *Old enough to have grown children. Old enough to be a widow.* But it didn't mean she was dead. People could live a long time, look at old Mrs. Crookshank.

I asked Patsy if she knew Hazel or any of her neighbors, but she only frowned and shook her head. I tried not to worry. The ranch stretched acres and acres and, unlike my mother, Patsy had never had a horse to ride. She didn't go to school either, and the truth was, with that seesaw limp, she couldn't get far, not easily. It was possible she just didn't know about Hazel. The reverse was also true. If Hazel didn't know Patsy was there, and if the horses were gone, why would she bother to steer her car up that long drive?

She might still be in that house—if I could find it.

One more time that day, I searched my memory for landmarks. How had my mother spotted the neighbor's drive? On horseback, on the town side of the castle. She'd caught a glimpse of the road from there too, near the woods with the old grape vines. And where had she started? From the corral out back, where the three of us stood now. My banged-up feet were in my sister's old boots, boots she'd pulled from a corner of the barn, and they fit to a tee, every toe in the depressions she'd made.

"Hang on a minute," I said to Patsy. Looking at her still gave me a jolt, a sudden flash of my own reflection. "If we go through the hills, which way is it to the road—the one into town?"

She held up an arm, pointing left, on a trail past the cottage. "That direction, I think. But it'th a long wayth. I never been."

"Why?" Sandy said. "We taking the long way back?"

"If we're lucky," I replied, "we'll find Hazel Clayton and get a ride."

Patsy fell into a rhythm on the trail with her seesawing hips and flailing limbs. She was slow, and it started to make me anxious, especially when we passed near the cottage. But luck was with us, and we never saw Astrid. I kept picturing my mother hurrying along the same route so soon after delivering twins. She'd had no plan beyond Hazel's, where to go or what to do, no thought about meeting the preacher, only a future on her own with a baby. Her anxiety must have been crushing.

Once we were in the hills, and hidden, I was able to let my thoughts wander. Patsy couldn't talk anyway; she needed her breath just to walk. What would it be like to take her home? I wondered. How would people respond? The thought made me sweat, especially when I pictured the preacher. Her existence would be a shock to him, my mother had made that clear. Would he resist her, the way Sandy had? I watched Patsy fling herself through another step and tried to imagine him seeing it too. But all I could see was his face, annoyed at me.

I imagined how others might react. The blueberry bonnets would be astonished but sweet, and our youth leader, Debbie, thrilled by a new prospect. Sandy's parents would ask a million questions and so would Jimmy. I thought of Manny and his music, Honey and her petty prejudices, heck I even tried to picture Apple McEgan. But Georgia was easiest. She'd welcome Patsy with open arms, despite how she walked and talked. She'd see Momma in her face, the way she'd seen her in mine.

I don't know how far we trudged through those hills. Far enough to see multiple views of the castle. Far enough that I wondered if I should carry Patsy, hoist her on my back to give her legs a break. Each step had become a strain that made her grunt.

"Thith ith tho far!" She kept saying, though she never asked us to stop.

Just as her grunts grew more desperate, we crested another rise and there it was: a thin asphalt drive to a house below, almost directly below. Patsy released a shuddering breath that cut through me. I should have carried her.

"Is that it?" Sandy said. "I'm so thirsty."

"I hope so." It had to be. I turned to Patsy, her matted hair stuck to the sweat at her temples. "You know who lives there?"

She shook her head.

The doorbell was loud, so at least we knew it worked. The longer we waited, the faster my heart beat. Sheer draperies covered slender windows beside the door, so we couldn't see much. Sandy leaned forward to peek and ring again, then one more time.

"I think somebody's coming," she said finally.

She was right. We could just make it out through the drapery, a figure moving toward us. The drapery shifted and we saw a wrist with some kind of pincushion, and then a face. It was wrinkled, with cloudy eyes that raked over us. A second later, the door came open. The woman standing before us was dressed in a pantsuit, leaning on a cane. *Hazel?* Her white hair was cut in a bob and she wore a touch of lipstick. My hands went slick. From behind her, inside the house, came the staccato chatter of voices.

"I'm sorry it took so long," she said. "I was sewing. Do I *know* you?"

I stepped forward. "No ma'am, you don't. But maybe you knew my mother? Her name was Sharon and—"

Both of her hands flew to her heart, setting the cane loose. Her eyes shot from Patsy to me and back again, as the cane clattered to the floor.

"Good Lord, you came! I knew one of these days you would, I just knew it!"

"You're Hazel? I mean Mrs. Clayton?"

"In the flesh! But Hazel is fine. And you? I never knew where either of you went. Which one are... wait—" she held up a hand. "Don't tell me, don't tell me a thing. Come this way first. Hurry, hurry. We'll do that first." She indicated the cane. "Could you get that for me, dear?" And I made a dash for it, wedging the handle under her wrist. We made our way through a long entry, Patsy's bad leg swinging, the cane tapping. "I'm so glad you came!" she kept saying. When the entry opened on a sunken living room the chatter of voices burst over us.

"Hello!"

"Watch-your-step!"

"Come in! Come in!"

Caged birds, bright as tropical flowers bobbed on their perches. Patsy laughed. I laughed. Hazel scolded them for being noisy and went to the kitchen for three glasses of water. Soon as we gulped them down, we went straight back to the birds. They were striking, bright blue, yellow and red.

"They're tho perty," Patsy said. "I never theen birdth like that!"

"Spoiled, both of them," Hazel added. "You know what they are?"

"Parrots?" Sandy tried, and Hazel winked.

"You've been around. Macaws to be exact. They're excellent companions. Know how long they live?"

We shook our heads.

"Sixty years. They may outlive me yet. Know what I call them?"

We shook our heads.

"Ask them. Go ahead—like this." She turned from the birds and cupped her mouth. "What's your name, pretty bird?"

I smiled and went for it, right into the cage. "What's your name, pretty bird?" and the chatter was instant.

"Pretty-bird!"

"What's-your-name?"

"Grace."

"Call-me-Mercy-what's-your-name?"

"Grace-pretty-bird!"

"Oh my God," Sandy said. "They said your names! They're

named after you?"

"Oh, no, no, no," Hazel laughed. "The other way around. She's named after them." She pointed to the first one, "That's Mercy," then the next, "and that's Grace—I'm an old Catholic, you know." Her eyes flashed to me, wrinkled with glee. I was sure I'd gone white. "So you're Mercy Grace, the tiny babe who was here so many years ago?"

I nodded.

"It's written all over you. My, my, my how time flies. What's it been, sixteen years?"

"Fifteen."

"That sounds right." She inspected my features. "Those eyes. When you were first born you could only just tell. Lovely indeed. Did your mother tell you how she came by your name?"

"No. Wait, yes. But it wasn't about birds. She said it came to her out of thin air."

Hazel guffawed. "Well, I s'pose that's true with these two, isn't it?"

"She's named after *birds*?" Sandy said.

"Well not exactly. More like the concept. It was a good fit. Just exactly what Sharon needed the day she got here. A little mercy and a lot of grace. I can still see her, weak and dusty, young and beautiful, just like you girls." She leaned heavily on her cane. "Those were hard times, dear."

I stared at the colorful creatures preening on their perch. Never in a million years would I have guessed.

"I taught your mother to sew, did you know that?" Hazel indicated her wrist and the pin cushion. "In the time she was here, which wasn't long, she sewed a little gown for you, so you'd have something to wear when you left." She clucked her tongue. "How I hated to see you two go."

I tried to imagine myself as a newborn, in a gown my mother had made. "She sewed all my life," I said, remembering the smell of her oily Singer. "She loved every minute of it."

"I'm not surprised. She took to it right away." Hazel's face softened, and she turned to Patsy. "And you, young lady, you must be her first born."

Patsy's lip twitched. "I gueth."

"Oh dear child how she missed you. She told me all about it." Hazel took Patsy's hands. "It broke her heart when they took you away, broke it right in two. She had so much love for you—*so* much."

Patsy gave a little smile that instantly crumpled. She dropped her head, crying now, and the scab on her lip split open.

"Oh sweetheart, what's your name?"

Patsy looked up, spit it out like a bad seed. "Thpathy," she said.

"What's that?"

"Thpathy!"

My cheeks went hot.

"But I don't—" Hazel started. "You have to say it again sweetheart because I can't—"

"It's Spazzy!" I cried, stepping between them. "Are you *deaf?* It's what Astrid calls her: Spazzy!" I roared it to the ceiling, "Spazzy, Spazzy, Spazzy!" Then I collapsed to the floor, sobbing into my hands.

Mercifully, Hazel forgave me. She wrapped me in a hug and rocked me, right there under those birds. Then she took us to the kitchen and fed us sandwiches and whole milk, before sending us to the tub, one by one while she washed our clothes. She handed us silky gowns to sleep in, which thrilled my sister to no end. She combed Patsy's hair and dabbed medicine on her bleeding lip, and then placed her before the bathroom mirror, where Patsy became tearful again.

"I look tho perty," she said, "almotht ath perty ath my thithter!"

What I remember most from that night is Hazel's tenderness. When I informed her of my mother's cancer, that she'd been gone for five years, she wept. When Patsy lifted her gown, revealing Astrid's handiwork, she wept again. We all did. You couldn't look at those scars and not feel pain.

"I'm such a fool," Hazel said, dabbing her eyes, "for not knowing you were on that ranch. All this *time.* You won't go back to that woman. She'll have to kill me first." I was overjoyed by the promise, but Patsy stayed strangely quiet. As night closed in, Hazel covered us with blankets and curled up with us on her living room furniture to make a plan.

"Does Astrid know you took her?" she asked.

I shook my head. "She told us Patsy was dead from a—" I glanced at my sister, so thin in her blanket, her eyes wide. "Anyway, I took off running. As far as Astrid knows, that's still what we think."

"But Patsy's been gone for hours, right?"

I nodded.

"Astrid will figure out you took her, I'm sure. Could she guess you came here?"

"I don't think so. I don't know."

"It'th getting dark," Patsy said.

Hazel turned to Sandy. "Go make sure the front door's locked, will you?" And Sandy hopped up.

"Let's just leave," I said. "Soon as we can. If we can get Patsy on a train to Portland, Astrid can't stop us." I put my hand on Patsy's knee. "You *do* want to go with us, right?"

She frowned. "I don't know."

"You mean you want to stay on the ranch with *Astrid?*"

Her eyes probed mine. "The ranch getth lonely but it'th not a bad plathe. Athtrid feedth me."

"We'll feed you," I insisted, "all you want, anything you want. Ice cream, candy, potatoes and gravy—anything! Plus in Portland you can go to school, you'd like that, wouldn't you?"

Her face lit up. "I alwayth wanted to go to thchool, but only if you go with me. I wanna thtay with you." Her eyes went glossy and sought Hazel. "I wanna thtay with my thithter."

"Yes, of course, dear, we'll do everything we can to—"

Patsy stood, suddenly, gasping for breath.

"What is it, Patsy?" I stood with her.

"She won't let me go," she cried. "thithter or not! Athtrid will come after me until she findth me—tomorrow and the day after and the day after." The room echoed with her fear. "She'll take me back and *beat me.*"

"Patsy don't—"

"She will. She'll come after me!"

"She's right," Hazel said. "Astrid won't give up easily. We have to think. We have to put the fear of God in her."

"How do you mean?"

"I mean we have to confront her."

Patsy's breath came ragged now.

"Oh, no, sweetheart, don't you worry," Hazel thrust herself from the chair. "That woman won't lay another hand on you, not while I'm around. If she even comes close," she said, grabbing her cane and twirling it, "I'll flat-out bust her ugly nose."

Patsy's laughter—sharp as her fear before it—shook the walls.

Later that night, buoyed by our plan and my sister's relief, I borrowed Hazel's phone to call the preacher. It was time we talked.

When he picked up, I said, "Hi Dad," knowing he would notice. I hadn't called him Dad in months. "I'm not really in Washington State, Dad, I'm in California."

"*What?*"

"California."

Silence on the other end.

"I followed Momma's letters. It's a long story, you know? I have—There's..." I took a breath. "I have a sister, Dad, a twin sister."

"You have a sis—" I heard him choke and then cough, the sort of cough that masks emotion.

"She was born with problems, see, and they took her from Momma. She's a little funny, Dad, a little different. But I'm bringing her home and I mean it. Don't even try to stop me."

He was silent again for the longest time, and then he mumbled, "What the good Lord has in mind..." Of all the things he could have asked me then, it was this, "Has she been baptized?"

I had no idea.

"Because, we can do it soon as you like." The tightness was still in his throat, but there was strength now too.

"Okay, Dad. Sure, okay."

"I—Grace, where are you? I'll gas up the car and be there by morning."

"Oh no, Dad, don't. Nothing against you. I just wanna do this the way we planned. If it's okay with you, I mean. We're with an old friend of Momma's, a neighbor named Hazel. She's a sweet old gal. You could trust her with anything."

I heard his shoes on the kitchen Linoleum, pacing.

"She's getting us tickets if it helps. On a sleeper car for the train ride back. Won't that be great, all three of us girls on a sleeper car? You can talk to her about it, she's in the other room."

"Okay, Grace. All right, I'll talk to her."

"Thanks Dad. Thanks a lot. Oh, and Dad?"

"Yeah?"

"I'm really sorry about everything. You've been good to me, you know? You've been a good dad."

"Thanks, Grace, I—" his voice cracked.

"Oh, and Dad? There's one more thing... Momma wrote a letter. To you, I mean." I hadn't told anyone, not even Sandy. "It was tucked in the last letter for me, in its own little envelope. I found it before we left."

"You did?" His voice sounded unnaturally high. "What does it say?"

"How should I know?" I couldn't help grinning. I knew how much it would mean to him. "I didn't open it. You can read it yourself when we get back. The envelope says 'To My Preacher Man.'"

I heard the cough again before I put down the phone and went for Hazel.

The next morning as we piled into the car to confront Astrid, I expected to be scared out of my wits, but it was more fun than I could have imagined, the four of us with the windows down, flying up the road to free Patsy, hooting and howling the whole way. The hooting was by design so Astrid would hear us as we approached, and it worked. She was on the cottage steps by the time Hazel pulled up.

"What the hell!" she said, her face florid as a baboon's butt. "You got my girl? I been worried sick!"

"That's a laugh," I said, poking my head out. "You told us she was dead!"

From the moment we tumbled out of the car, things moved quickly. She accused us of kidnapping, and we scoffed. She threatened to fight us, and we scoffed. When she stomped down the steps headed for Patsy, we blocked her way. And then, Bingo! Right on cue, she threatened just what we wanted.

"Give me that girl, or I'll call the police."

"You go right ahead Astrid," Hazel said, stepping forward and pointing her cane, "because we've got a few things to report too."

I had to fight to keep from laughing. Hazel was small, but she had Astrid drawing back, her eyes on the cane.

"Go ahead Patsy," Hazel said, "let's show your dear grandmother what we mean."

Sandy and I stepped apart, allowing Patsy the room.

"That burn on your legs, child—" Hazel went on "—how did it happen?"

Patsy hesitated, but only a moment, then she nodded Astrid's way. "She did it."

"Your grandmother?" Hazel asked. "The one who takes *care* of you?"

Patsy nodded.

"You sure?"

"She doethn't take care of me. She'th mean and she burned me."

"You can make that phone call now, Astrid," Hazel said. "We'll wait."

But she didn't budge, except for her neck, which had started to twitch. I don't know what made me do it since it wasn't part of our plan, but I cleared my throat and threw an arm around my sister. "By the way, Patsy, is there anything you want in the house? From your room maybe, or better yet the *money tin?*"

Astrid's head snapped. "How do you—You wouldn't dare."

"I wouldn't? You sure about that?"

She glared at me but was clearly unnerved. I was too much like Patsy—the eyes, the hair, the face. I took three steps in her direction. "You got some jewelry in that money tin, Astrid? Another ring maybe? My mom told me a-all about it. That nursing home, right? Do you still work there? There some good stuff in that tin?"

"You don't have the guts," she said.

"Oh?" I went closer, close enough to see the hairs on her chin. "Now you listen to this, Astrid. I don't care about your damn tin, but you ever bother my sister again—you even come *close* to her—so help me God, you'll end up in jail for what you did, you hear me? They get one look at that scar and they'll lock you up behind bars."

Her mouth twitched but she didn't speak, not the whole time we backed away and climbed into the car. Hazel started the engine and we tore out, a cloud of dust obscuring her through the rear window as Patsy yelled at the top of her lungs, "Go, Hazel! Go fatht, go fatht!" I swiveled forward and let loose a howl, we all did, and the car sped forward, past the orchard where my mother picked fruit, the tall grass and tangled roses, past the vine-choked castle where twin girls were conceived on a Thanksgiving weekend, Hazel's tires spitting gravel and the four of us hooting and howling the whole way.

Chapter 47

Many years have passed since we rescued my sister from that California ranch. I have teenagers of my own now, and today we're on the back patio enjoying the sun between bursts from the chimes. Their music always reminds me of Patsy's humming: ever changing, ever new. I've had to restring the silver tubes twice, but they still sound like they did when my mother hung them all those winds ago.

These days I live across town from Good Shepherd, but I've driven through the old, Southeast Portland neighborhood plenty of times. I took my own kids through it once when they were small, telling of the pranks Sandy and I played, the lessons learned, pointing out the stuff of my childhood. Pardee is paved now and there's a new lane past the parsonage. It travels behind the farmhouse, where the McEgan barn once stood, to a row of high-density homes squeezed together on tiny lots. That's something I never imagined.

But other features look the same: Pardee Park and the corner store where I used to buy candy; Good Shepherd and the stained glass, where Apple still sings on Sunday mornings. There's a funny bend in the curb now around the Tree of Heaven. It's a fine tribute to Mrs. Crookshank, who faced down chain saws to divert the street. She gave up some of her own property to save that tree before she died.

Hazel Clayton is gone now too, and many others. But Dad's still with us, long since retired from preaching these days. He lives a short drive from our home in a little ground-floor apartment. We bought him a new recliner recently where he sits with his Bible, bookmarked now by the unexpected letter he got from Momma, the one addressed: To My Preacher Man. I never had any doubt he'd forgive her deepest secret. I don't expect Dad to be with us much longer, so I hold tight to the moments, the way he looks sitting there and the way he was as a younger man, my father and my mother's Preacher Man. Years ago he told my husband something I'll never forget, that he trusts him as a father to his grandchildren "in blood and deed." Down to my core, I know exactly what he means.

They're practically all grown up now, our three progeny: two girls and a boy. That's how long it's taken me to tell this story, to be *ready* to tell it. Our oldest, with her fair hair, reminds me of Sandy. And our youngest has traits of my mother; she talks like her, laughs like her and, miracle of miracles, *draws* like her. If she doesn't pursue an art degree, it'll shock me. But of the three of them, it's our boy who looks most like Patsy—and me, I suppose. Another marvel of genetics. He has hair like ours, teeth like ours and eyes like ours, except for the color because they're both blessedly brown. But when I look at him, I see Patsy more than myself, the depth of his innocence, maybe, or his still-boyish awkwardness, even at 17. Or maybe I just miss her so damn much.

Patsy, dear Patsy.

We only had her for a while. Less than two years. It was a seizure that took her, the lies of Astrid returning to haunt me. As time went on, she seemed to have them more frequently, small and innocuous, like that bout in the ranch barn, or big enough to knock her flat, to knock us all flat. Her cerebral palsy was to blame, the damage sustained from a dangerous delivery in a cottage bedroom.

Dad took her to doctors, who referred us to specialists who did what they could. But not much helped. The seizures got worse, whatever the treatment, until it seemed like a matter of time. I was with her when the grand mal came, just outside the doors of Marshall High School, where I'd demanded she be allowed to accompany me, even if she couldn't read. "I'll teach her," I kept insisting, "I swear I will," until they gave in. The two of us were arm in arm when it happened and had just left the school alongside

Sandy. It was the way we'd taken to walking, to be ready if a seizure came. But on that day, Patsy went down with no warning, straight through my arm to the concrete. Everything after that was a nightmare...

Which is why, when that scene returns, I tend to escape to happier times. And oh, did we have them, the whole 20 months she was with us! Patsy and I had a riot together. I learned to sew on Momma's old Singer so I could make dresses for the two of us, poorly-sewn, perfectly-matching fashion dresses. Then we'd parade around in them, posing and laughing in a show of symmetry. *Look at us, we're sister twins!* We acted like we couldn't get enough of each other. And the truth was, we couldn't. We finished each other's sentences. We burst out laughing at the same, silly jokes. We curled up, side by side, and fell asleep. I started to believe I dreamt her dreams and she dreamt mine. Oh, how I loved that girl! Despite everything, despite her challenges and what she'd been through, she was sweet and sensitive, as utterly grateful to have me, to have a family, as I was to have her. And there was nothing like watching her squeal her way through a store, the shoes, the baked goods, the produce. She'd never seen anything like it.

But our best times were spent simply being together. We'd hang out at the house, styling each other's hair, putting on makeup and checking traits. We were rare, the two of us, what we found out from a book on genetics is called "Mirror Image Twins," twins in the image of each other—in the strictest sense of the word. For example, the mole on her left arm was on my right, and, even stranger, the "d" splotch in her blue eye appeared as a "b" splotch in mine. We couldn't stop looking—or laughing. It was uncanny... and deliriously fun.

Sometimes I worried it would be too much for Sandy and Jimmy, that Sandy would grow jealous or Jimmy annoyed. But thanks to the laughter—the wetting-your-pants kind of laughter— just the opposite happened. Patsy and I entertained them for hours just by aping each other. We'd practice in the bathroom until we had it down.

"Ready to start?" I'd say.

And she'd answer, "Ready."

Then we'd come out, face each other and pretend to gaze into a mirror. We'd go chin up, check our reflections, then clear steam from imaginary glass, her right hand to my left, moving in unison against a make-believe barrier. We'd pretend to shave an armpit, brush our hair, apply mascara, then check our hair again, pick food from our teeth and wipe it on the glass. We never could stay straight-faced for that last move since it wasn't glass we touched but our two fingers… the way I still touch a mirror and feel Patsy today.

Those were happy times, sure enough, and so was Patsy's baptism. Dad launched into planning it on our arrival from California, having checked it with her, of course, first.

"But I never even been inthide a church!" she said with great angst.

Dad squeezed her shoulder. "Then you haven't known the love." Despite my apprehension, he was sweet with Patsy, moved to tears at first sight of her. "She's so much like you," he whispered many times. I'll never forget that, because of the way it made him smile.

Dad wanted to show Patsy he cared, and in his book, that meant tending to her soul first. By then, the whole world knew I was illegitimate since I'd announced it at church, so all Dad had to do was introduce the idea of twins and—whamo!—another teenager was born. She was obviously the product of the same birth, so there was no gnashing of teeth. People took one look at Patsy, another me, and flew in like doves to welcome her. All the attention made her giggle and flap her hands "Okay, okay!" but I knew she loved every minute of it. They were an instant extended family.

Dad's plan for the baptism was to do it up big. He paced the floor over it, scheduling it weeks away so far-flung friends could plan to come.

"Plenty of time makes it fine," he said, marking the date on his calendar.

I hadn't heard him rhyme in years, so I blurted out, "Go too fast and you'll break your—"

"Gra-ace." He still had the Preacher Eye, but Patsy and I were too tickled to care.

The congregation would attend the baptism and many more

besides. It didn't surprise me when Hazel Clayton made plans to fly up from California. We'd been talking to her over the phone since the day she put us on that train, Patsy and I passing the receiver back and forth "Hi Hazel!" "Hi Hazel!" anxious to know if she'd run into Astrid. She never heard from that woman again and neither did we.

Russ, on the other hand, showed up like before, straight out of the blue. The minute we saw him Patsy lunged and I froze. She hobbled over to him, blubbering "Popth! Popth!" as he dropped to his knees and flung his arms around her. My reaction was quite the opposite. *What happened to your promise? Why didn't you protect my sister?* The answers I got, eventually, were no hero's tale. Russ had stayed on the ranch a while, but his binges on booze forever called. When he returned to St. Helena that September and learned we'd taken Patsy, he split for Portland, end of story.

Watching him soothe her that day, whispering "Shh, Sis, now, now," I decided to leave it alone. Russ was no saint. He had more vices than virtues, but there were times when he tried, like Momma said. After all, he'd planted the seed that sent us to Patsy, and, years before, to that godforsaken barn to find Appoline. When I asked him about the rabbit story, he explained it this way:

"I knew it would get you over there, into that barn, no doubt about it. Somebody needed to find that girl and the way she lived. I never counted on the fire." I wanted to ask him about Patsy then, the way *she* lived, but thought better of it. Russ had his limitations and that's just the way it was.

He and Dad spent the next few days looking for Doug, picking up where my mother left off by calling half the state of Texas. I was sorry when they didn't find him. I will never forget the story of my birth, how my uncle jumped out the window to save me. I still haven't found him, all these years later, but I hope to say thank you one day.

The Sunday of the baptism, the usuals came—Honey and Manny and the blueberry bonnets—and some *un*usuals, Sandy's parents among them, and, for that matter, Sandy, since she hadn't been to church in who-knew-how-many months. Grandma Carsten drove in from Troutdale, still unsure what to think of Patsy. But she was trying, so I predicted mountains of 5-spots in my twin's future.

Georgia Johnson came too, asked by my father to speak, and, oddly enough, all the McEgans, including Butte. I never knew why, exactly. Appoline was slated to sing, so it could have been that, or, more likely, they wanted to see my twin and just how damned identical two girls could be.

Of the ceremony itself, I remember only bits and pieces. Apple sang *Glorious Things of Thee Are Spoken* with the voice of an angel.

"See the streams of living waters, Springing from eternal love…"

And Dad read from The Ritual in The Methodist Hymnal as I held Patsy's hand, all eyes going from me to her, her to me. "Do you truly and earnestly…" the long passage began, and as it finished, Patsy answered, sweet as a bride, "I do."

When it was time for the water, Dad poured from a pitcher. "I baptize you in the name of the Father, and of the Son, and of the Holy Spirit…" I'll never forget his face in that moment. He wore a peace I hadn't seen since Momma.

Georgia spoke, as planned, though I'm not sure if it was before or after the water. I'd never seen her look prettier in her lemon-chiffon dress. She talked about Patsy, her faith, and me, but her thoughts on my mother stood out.

"Hodgkin's disease is no longer deadly," she said. "Just a few years after it took Sharon it was curable. Such a shame. She's here in spirit. Ah know that. Y'all know that. But what Ah wouldn't give for her to be here in the flesh, to see her baby daughters at this baptism, side by side. How she'd love it."

Standing there, next to Patsy, I had to wonder, would she? Because the truth was, my mother had screwed up. Maybe not at first, when she believed the story of my sister's adoption, but certainly in the end, when she knew Patsy was with Astrid and failed to rescue her. I hadn't forgotten my mother's childhood, the abuse she endured. I never would. It was, ultimately, why I forgave her. But she hadn't forgotten either. She'd promised never to let her own children suffer like that, yet she'd broken that promise, no question. And for what? She tried to explain in that final, 22nd letter.

I didn't want to turn your life upside down Grace, not

when you were so young. You didn't know. Thad didn't know. The congregation either. The truth was hard, and some of them were tough enough on me already. I was afraid, and if I admit the truth, selfish. I'd lost your sister, and I didn't want to lose the way you were and the life we had. So I did it this way, letting the truth out slowly so you'd know each other in the end. I hope it was the right decision, Grace. I hope everything turned out fine.

Only for half of us, Momma, only for half.

When Patsy went down, outside the school, it was a nightmare. The grabbing and screaming, the yelling for Sandy to "Get help! Get help!" and the hair I squeezed to stop her head from crashing, the shock of bone against concrete, the grunts and the gurgling and my own panicked cries. We were alone, on the ground, just the two of us, when the light left her eyes—as if leaving my own reflection. Dear sweet Patsy, my sister, my twin. The girl with no mother and hardly a name.

It was only after her death, months later, that I put together the timing. Patsy left us in the final weeks of my junior year, long before I would have received my mother's last letter. If I'd played by her rules, if I'd waited, it would have been too late. More than likely, Patsy would have died on that ranch alone with Astrid, and I... I never would have known her at all.

Like I said, my mother screwed up.

I talked to Sandy about it later, how I'd been driven, with an undying passion, to find the rest of the letters. "What *was* it that made me do it?"

"Curiosity," she said. "What else?"

"But don't you think it was more? I mean I always knew something was missing, all those years. You said so yourself. I saw things. I felt things. And where was she all that time?"

"I don't know, California."

"Exactly. A whole state away. It had to be more, don't you think? Like maybe God was trying to tell me something?"

"You don't really believe that, do you?"

"Why, what do you think?"

"I don't know. Maybe it's a twin thing. Twins are like that, aren't they? They have a sixth sense or something."

"A sixth sense? *A sixth sense?* She was a whole state away, Sandy. How is that more believable than God?"

Sandy shrugged. It's an ongoing conversation between us...

Mirror Image Twins. From a single, fertilized egg. I've learned more about them over the years: reverse asymmetric features; a birth mark on opposite sides; hair whorls swirling in converse directions; and different or even opposite personalities. I laughed when I read that part. Patsy had been sweet, and I was anything but. At night, when we crawled in bed, she used to whisper in my ear that she loved me, words I knew she'd never heard from Astrid. She always said it first and then I'd whisper back, "I love you, too."

Mirror Image Twins. From a single, fertilized egg, when the egg splits late, more than a week after conception. Any later and the twins are conjoined, what's known as Siamese. Longer still and separation becomes impossible, what might have been twins become one. I've grown to realize there's a lot in that concept, like the notion that everybody has a mirror twin who just happened too late. Next time you're looking down, over a pool or a lake or a pond, remember that and see your twin, somebody like you only different, different enough to change you forever.

I learned to ponder these things because of Patsy and to see the world anew. I first noticed this at her baptism, after Dad poured the water and Apple sang her song, when the service was over and everybody clambered to get to Patsy, Hazel and Russ, Grandma and Eloise, Honey and Manny. But Patsy limped down the chancel stairs past them. It was Apple she was after. She'd seen her burn scars, she'd heard her sing with the voice of an angel. She couldn't get to her fast enough.

"Jutht a minute! Jutht a minute!" she kept saying.

My first reaction was to pull her back, the way my old self would have. *Don't talk to her Patsy, she's a dirty McEgan.* Instead, I walked with her and listened as she struck up a conversation. At the first hint of a lull, I said, "Why don't you come to dinner Apple, over at the house? You can sit with Patsy and me, you know, hang out with us. Patsy has a burn too, like yours. Plus, my Grandma cooked this huge pot roast and Georgia made peach pies that smell out of this world."

In that moment, Apple looked at me in her melted skin as if I'd grown a whole new flesh.

And by God I had.

Dear Reader,

Thank you for buying *The God of Sno Cone Blue* and for taking this journey with me.

If you enjoyed the story, spread the word by telling a friend, sharing through social media or by writing a review on Amazon or Goodreads. Word of mouth is how authors survive to write another day! Another option is to suggest this novel to your book club. In the following pages, you'll find Questions and Topics for Discussion to get the conversation going.

Finally, I'd love you to visit my website at marciacoffeyturnquist.com where you can read my articles and find updates on my books. I'm beginning work on a second novel, *Skipping the Light*. Subscribe to my website and you'll be first to know when copies are available.

Again, thank you,
Marcia Coffey Turnquist

About The Author

Marcia Coffey Turnquist, an author and journalist, is currently writing her second novel, *Skipping the Light*. Before venturing into the world of fiction, she spent 12 years as a news broadcaster, working her way back to her hometown of Portland, Oregon and KOIN-TV. Marcia decided to retire from broadcasting to raise the son and daughter who ultimately inspired *The God of Sno Cone Blue*. Her two children are all but grown now, with one off to college and the other not far behind. Marcia lives with her husband Ed and their youngest, plus a terrier named Sport, in the soggy-but-green suburbs of Portland.

Visit her website at marciacoffeyturnquist.com.

Questions and Topics for Discussion

1.   In the opening of the story, Grace talks about her vision of God in the clouds. Have you had any experiences you can't explain and might describe as divinely inspired?

2.   How does Grace's attitude toward religion change from the beginning of the story, after Sharon's death, and, finally, in the end?

3.   Imagine you are Sharon with the same past. Would you have allowed Grace to believe the preacher is her father? Would you have kept her bigger secret?

4.   What do you think of Sharon's decision to write letters to her daughter before she died? Were the letters a more positive influence or negative?

5.   Growing up, did you learn family secrets you wish you never knew? What criteria should a person use to decide whether to tell?

6.   When Georgia comes to pick up Grace, the two embrace and Grace is emotionally overwhelmed. In what ways do Georgia and, later, Hazel Clayton, touch a nerve?

7.   How does Grace's relationship with the preacher change after her mother's death? What are her feelings toward him in the end?

8.   In one scene Sandy mocks Grace's obsession with the letters, and Grace slaps her. But later Grace strives to

mend the relationship, even when she knows Sandy was deceiving her. Why?

9.   Why is Grace so repelled by the McEgans? At what moment do we learn that her opinion of Apple is changing?

10.   Put yourself in Grace's shoes as she reads the last letter from her mother. Would you have made the same decision to go to California?

11.   Besides the fact that Astrid never wanted children, no definitive reason is offered for the pain and abuse she inflicts. Do you think there are always mitigating reasons people are cruel, or are some people simply evil?

12.   How does Grace finally demonstrate her change of heart toward Apple? Why is this so important to the theme of the story?

13.   From the start, Grace and Sandy disagree over the existence of God. Grace sees a flash of light like a halo through the church window, but Sandy doesn't. It seems to be timing, but could it be something more, something profound?

14.   At the end of the novel, Grace and Sandy argue over what drove Grace so relentlessly after the truth. Grace thinks it was God, but Sandy shrugs it off as "a sixth sense or something." An incredulous Grace then asks, "How is that more believable than God?" Flesh out their arguments. Is either more believable than the other?

Acknowledgements

Where to begin? I'll borrow from my TV news days for an analogy: Behind every two-minute story you see are mad dashes to on-scene coverage, video shot by talented photographers, interviews and rebuffs, phone calls and collaboration, writing, editing, updates and rewriting... I could go on. So, you'll understand why I once got a kick out of a viewer's question: "When you're done with your two-minute story, then what do you do?"

Though novel writing is a different beast, there are parallels, including hours of untold assistance from people behind the scenes. In other words, I didn't do this on my own. I'm indebted to the following people who helped this book come to life:

*My husband, Ed, for his unwavering support, and my children, who believed.

*Pete Stone, for his generous and talented work on the cover of this book.

*Virginia Wainright for helping to paint the world my Napa Valley characters inhabit; also her husband Dennis and brother Ray Myers. Fred and Cathy Beringer for wine country and Napa history, along with author Lin Weber, and Diane Smith at the Sonoma Valley Historical Society's Depot Park Museum.

*Dr. Norm Willis, MD, for his expertise in cancer treatment, particularly early protocol for Hodgkin's Disease. Though I hope never to have the occasion, I would trust him in the blink of an eye with my treatment. Besides that, he plays a mean guitar. Dr. Trina Brodsky, MD, for insight into childbirth. And Oregon Burn Center educator Curtis Ryun for background on burn injuries and scars.

*The late Sally Albertson and her beautiful daughters, Kathy Warnaca, Margie Arvidson, and Holly Albertson. While their history as a preacher's family bears no resemblance to this story, I had great fun inserting subtleties from the richness of their lives.

*Many others in the United Methodist community, including The Reverend Dr. Brett Strobel who offered sage advice and helped with research and editing. Plus, he comes in handy when your car won't start. Also, Brett's significant other, living, breathing preacher's wife Melinda Strobel, and The Reverend Bonnie Parr Philipson who read my manuscript and offered thoughtful feedback. The Reverends Tim and Amy Overton-Harris generously recounted memories of church life in the late 1960's and early 70's, along with Bee Hall, and the late Reverend James Airey.

*Amber Henneck Varner, who answered endless questions about horses, and Wendell Styner who schooled me on barns.

*Many friends and relatives who read early manuscripts. Your support kept me sane. Beth Groshans, Jean Haedrich, Tracy Beck, Sean Turnquist, Carol Moses, Elisa Klein (to the pages that gave us our start!), Edie Dorn, Dottie Quinn, Kristine Constans, Kris Butz, Rod Gramer, Susan Sammons, Julie Hicks, Vicki Wentzien, Carol Biamont, Lela Bonzer, Paula Bey, Nicky Stackhouse, Kelli Eickelberg, Meryl Trelease, Beth Brady Potts, Marie Burkhardt, and Dana Louise Jacobs. Also, Clayton and Hazel Coffey (who happen to be my father and mother), Karen Potts, Sally Coffey, and Linda Stone (who happen to be my sisters), and cousins Lin Coffey and Debbie Sauve.

*My writers' group, where of late I've found tremendous support for the art of crafting a story. Special thanks to Diana Kay Lubarsky (my own personal angel), Linda Needham and Lorelle VanFossen (each of you knows why), also Jason Brick, Andrea McKeever, John Copp, Nancy Irland, and Sharon Appleman.

Finally, I am grateful for the ultimate inspiration behind this story. While none can say in His boundless universe the color of God, I wouldn't complain if it be sno cone blue.